T0273012

TO THE
DEATH

To The Death

THAMES RIVER PRESS
An imprint of Wimbledon Publishing Company Limited (WPC)
Another imprint of WPC is Anthem Press (www.anthempress.com)
First published in the United Kingdom in 2014 by
THAMES RIVER PRESS
75–76 Blackfriars Road
London SE1 8HA

www.thamesriverpress.com

A CIP record for this book is available from the British Library.

ISBN 978-1-78308-274-2

This title is also available as an eBook

TO THE DEATH

The History of
*The Jewish Rebellion Against
Rome in the First Century A. D.
and the Murder of Jesus'
Brother, James.*

PETER R. HALL

THAMES RIVER PRESS

Acknowledgments

Many thanks to sisters Katie and Nicola Helps (who really did!) for transcribing the first draft that I had dictated to tape.

Thanks are also due to Laura Stooke of LS Secretarial Ltd who worked on the penultimate draft.

My thanks, too, to my agent Darin Jewell, m.d. of The Inspira Group and my publisher, Mr K Sood, m.d. of Thames River Press.

And last, but not least, to my long-suffering wife, Wendy, who has dealt with endless revisions and produced the final manuscript.

Sources

I would like to express my indebtedness to the following, which have been studied for the purpose of this publication: *The complete works of Flavius Josephus*; translated by W. Whiston, A.M., Professor of Mathematics, Cambridge University, England; published by Thomas Nelson, London, Edinburgh, New York 1855.

The works of Flavius Josephus; Whiston's translation revised by The Rev. A. R. Shilleto, MA, Trinity College, Cambridge University, England; published by George Bell & Sons, London 1889.

Historical Note

This novel is about the Jewish rebellion against the Rome of the Emperor Nero and the death of Jesus' brother James in the First Century AD. It is based on fact. The war was documented by a participant, Flavius Josephus, Jewish intellectual, historian and reluctant army general, sent by the Jewish authorities of Jerusalem to raise and train an army and defend Galilee.

The horrors of the Roman siege of Jerusalem, witnessed at first hand by Josephus, broke his heart. They were among the worst suffering inflicted by man on his own kind in any age. In antiquity the only comparable act of barbarism, inflicted by one people on another, occurred in 1300BC when migrant Jews from Egypt invaded Canaan - a.k.a. Judaea, Palestine and Galilee – to murder the entire population. The Jews' authority for this act of ethnic cleansing? They were following orders; allegedly a direct order from their God.

Deuteronomy, 20:16–18: "But of the cities of the people which the Lord your God gives you as an inheritance, you shall let nothing that breathes remain alive, but you shall utterly destroy them. The Hittite and the Amorite and the Canaanite and the Perrizite and the Hivite and the Jebusite, Just as the Lord your God has commanded you. Lest they teach you to do according to all the abominations which they have done for their gods, and you sin against the Lord your God."

The view that Jesus had brothers and sisters is vehemently denied by the Catholic Church. This denial has got nothing to do with the facts. The denial is based entirely on canon law created by the Catholic Church in AD325.

The brutal murder of Jesus' brother James is fact, and is well documented. *(See Appendix)*

In AD70, Israel lost its war of rebellion against Rome, the occupying military power. The country then became the personal property of the Emperor Vespasian. As a result of this appropriation, no Jew could own land. He could, however, rent it. *The State of Israel ceased to exist.* Ancient Canaan, the spoils of war, had been won and lost by the Jews after a few hundred years of occupation. Jerusalem disappeared off the face of the earth, dismantled by the Romans, stone by stone, down to bedrock.

Josephus' history, *The War of the Jews,* survives to this day. It is a record of one of the bloodiest war in history. The account of the siege of Jerusalem is a harrowing story of unimaginable human suffering, largely inflicted not by the Romans but by *Jew against Jew.*

Finally, a note on Jewish names. Eleazar and Simon are common names that occur repeatedly in Josephus' *War of the Jews.* To assist the general reader, having used either once, I have identified others by using their family name.

There are a number of Eleazars and Simons in Josephus' history. To assist the general reader I have used the family name to differentiate, e.g.:

Name in Josephus' History	Name in To the Death
Eleazar ben Ananias	Eleazar
Menahen ben Jair	Menahem
Eleazar ben Simon	Simon
Simon ben Gioras	Gioras

Eleazar ben Simon became a leading figure in the rebellion, alongside Simon ben Gioras and John of Gischala. In the final weeks of the siege of Jerusalem, Simon was assassinated by John of Gischala, leaving Gioras and John to fight to the end.

1

The man stood in silhouette on one of the high towers of the Temple. Below him was the Court of the Gentiles, its acres of sweeping terraces packed with crowds of people. The outer courts had been taken over with additional animal pens - sheep and cattle to be slaughtered to celebrate the festival of *Passover*.

Drovers and pilgrims stood ankle deep in dung, bartering over the price of an animal for sacrifice. The poor, who wished to make an offering, pushed their way through the mob to the outskirts of the animal pens. Here, traders with huge wicker cages filled with doves, sold birds for a few pennies. This great mass of animals and people swirled and eddied against the rows of columns that supported long covered arcades where merchants had established shops selling more expensive relics and souvenirs. In the shaded colonnades, money changers had also set up their tables alongside the booths occupied by the merchants.

Every foreign Jew, who had come on pilgrimage to visit at least once in his lifetime the Temple of his God, took the opportunity to pay in person the annual sacred tribute of half a shekel. The tribute was paid by every Jew on earth, whether rich or poor, no matter where he lived. This money was sent to the Temple in Jerusalem as atonement for his sins, to be used to defray the expenses of the rites performed for absolution.

As it was unlawful to make this offering in a foreign currency, pilgrims were obliged to exchange their money for Temple coinage. Not only were they charged five percent for this service, they were invariably cheated with inflated exchange rates. What was a man to do? Having saved and scrimped for years to make an often hazardous journey over many months, sometimes years, to reach the house of God, was he to lose this once in a lifetime chance to make his offering personally to his maker? No, he exchanged his savings for the only currency accepted by the Temple priests - that which they had minted themselves and sold at a profit to the money changers.

This was the entrance court to the Temple of the Most High, which stood witness that this was a house of worship for Jews of all nations. It had been reduced by the priests to a foul and stinking farm yard; an abattoir that fed the great altar with sacrificial blood from sun up to sunset every day; incidentally providing meat for the twenty two thousand priests and functionaries, who served the Temple.

The noise was deafening. In a babble of languages and accents, men cursed and shouted to be heard above the bellowing of cattle and bleating flocks of sheep. In the confusion and uproar, tempers were frequently lost and punches thrown. Fortunately no weapons were allowed either within the Temple courts or outer precincts, the exception being those allowed to the Levites, the Temple police, who were responsible for keeping order. Armed with clubs, they would step in when a fight broke out and end it in summary fashion.

It was a patrolling Temple guard who not only spotted the figure on the tower, but also recognised it as the leader of a Jewish sect that acknowledged the dead man Jesus as the Messiah, God's messenger - a sect that would eventually be known as Christians. He immediately ran to his superior and reported what he had seen.

The bored priest who received this information stopped picking his nose and thought with malicious glee of the furore his news would cause. He also recognised the man on the tower as James, one of the dead Jesus' brothers and knew that the present High Priest of all Israel, Ananus, was the son of Hanan, the father-in-law of Ciaphas, who had had Jesus condemned to death. Humming to himself, he sped away to find Ananus.

As he hurried along he speculated as to why James was on the ramparts. A thrill of vicarious excitement swept through him, as with a sudden flash of intuition he realised that James, who had been elected by the Christian Jews as the first bishop of their church, intended to speak to the Jews gathered in the Temple courts.

The High Priest of all Israel, Ananus, was leaving a meeting of senior priests when he received the report of the man on the tower. Muttering his displeasure he hurriedly returned to the meeting.

Knowing the identity of the man on the tower, he knew that a crisis was in the making. Swift, decisive action was needed.

The members of the re-assembled committee discussed the situation. Not knowing why the man was there and what he intended, led to conjecture and confusion. Among them was Eleazar Ben Ananias, Governor of the Temple. This role made him second in command to Ananus. His father, who had served a term as the High Priest of all Israel, was responsible for the Temple's finances and its vast treasury.

Unknown to his fellow priests, Eleazar was a leader in the Zealot party, whose members declared themselves to be Nationalists. Currently they restricted themselves to terrorist attacks on civilians who didn't agree with their political agenda, "Home rule for Israel". As well as killing civilians, they ambushed Roman patrols when the opportunity presented itself. To anybody who would listen, they declared that the Jews should rebel against Rome. As Commander of the Temple police, who were all Levites, Eleazar was prepared to deal with the situation in whatever way Ananus ordered.

Ananus said nothing but sat, thinking furiously. James the Just, as he was known to his followers, represented a serious threat to orthodox Jewry, for he was the acknowledged leader of a new teaching; a teaching that found expression in Judaic Christianity - Judaism in transformation - a new religion which spoke of one God for all mankind. This new teaching saw Judaism as the foundation of Christianity, and in Christianity the ideal Jew. For James the Just, a devout Jew, the Law meant the rule of life as Jesus had taught it, available to all men, gentiles as well as Jews.

To Ananus, an astute and worldly Sadducee, this was a deadly threat. Far too often the High Priest of all Israel was seen to be supportive of Roman law, exercising political power to his own advantage.

As the people suffered under crippling taxes imposed by the Romans, they saw priests living in luxury. The vast quantity of meat offered up daily on the High Altar ensured they lived well. Ananus enjoyed the lifestyle of an emperor, for he controlled the huge inflow of Temple offerings. He also raked in a share of the profits made by the money changers, the merchants and the drovers, who traded in the outer courts.

The house of Ananus, the High Priest reasoned to himself, had a duty to destroy the leader of this new religion. God, he decided, had delivered the brother of the so-called Christ into his hands. Like his brother-in-law Ciaphas, he would distance himself from the actual killing. True he had no Pilate but, he mused, a legal execution by the Jews was possible, for devout Jews were flocking to the Temple in their thousands to celebrate *Passover*. These people were the faithful, the true believers in the God of Abraham and Moses. Let the law of Abraham and Moses he thought, nodding to himself in quiet satisfaction, determine this man's fate.

"Blasphemy!" For the first time he spoke out loud.

The room stilled. Anxious faces turned expectantly towards him.

"This man, out of his own mouth, denies the God of our fathers. He is guilty of the most heinous blasphemy. This whole family is an offence to God. Did not his brother delude the people with tricks and sorcery? Did not" he continued, his voice rising to a shout "this Jesus falsely claim to be the Messiah?" There was another pause. Head bowed, hands clasped in front of him, the High Priest paced the floor. The only sound in the room was his heavy breathing. Every man stood tense and still, watchful, waiting.

The bearded head came up and with it a clenched fist, jewelled rings flashing in the light. "And now his brother rises up like Satan" spittle flew from his lips, his sweating face dark with blood, eyes bulging "to challenge God from the walls of His own house".

The assembled priests, roused by Ananus' impassioned speech, could contain themselves no longer. They screamed and shouted their anger. For a full minute the High Priest could not make himself heard. With satisfaction he viewed the contorted faces, the shaking fists and the eyes wild with outrage.

Raising his hands above his head he waved them to silence. "Brethren, this enemy of God has delivered himself into our hands. Let us go out and question him. He stands in full view of the people. If he truthfully answers the charges put to him, he is guilty. If he fails to answer the charges, his very silence will serve to prove his crime. Either way he will stand condemned out of his own mouth".

Eleazar was ordered to take four priests and ascend the tower James was on. This group left with secret orders. "Under no circumstances is James the Just to leave the tower alive".

A second much larger group of priests was ordered to proceed to the Court of the Gentiles. They were instructed to say or do nothing, until the High Priest himself mounted the top of the Corinthian Gate, from where he would accuse James of blasphemy, a capital crime for which he would either make an adequate defence or die.

The unexpected blast of sound, the distinctive wild skirl of the *shofar*, the ceremonial trumpets made from rams' horns, silenced the crowd. Heads swivelled. Uplifted faces turned on craning necks. Searching eyes swept the Temple's towers and ramparts. Ananus, flanked by his most senior high priests, stood on the top of the Corinthian Gate, trumpeters on either side. He was crowned with the mitre of Aarron and carried a symbol of his high office, the rod the brother of Moses had flung at Pharaoh's feet.

Resplendent in his ceremonial robes he raised his staff to silence the crowd, a silence broken only by the sounds of the domestic animals in their pens. "Brethren, people of the one

God, the God of Israel, His chosen people. Did He not make a covenant with our forefathers, binding us, His chosen people alone, to Him forever?"

A murmur of agreement rose in the still air. The High Priest continued, "The God who delivered us from Pharaoh, leading us to this land. The land He promised to our fathers as He struck off the chains of slavery and led His people out of Egypt. The God who will send us the promised Messiah, a king of kings, to rule over all peoples in righteousness. His chosen people first among all nations, raised up in glory. The God of Moses smote your enemies and delivered up this land to your fathers". The rich baritone continued, lifting their spirits. "Solomon, the son of David, raised this house to the glory of His name, in His holy city". Ananus was a skilled and practiced orator. His words reached every ear and every heart of the multitude gathered below. "Children of the covenant, we alone are His chosen people. He who denies that, denies God".

This final pronouncement was hurled like a challenge from the heights of the Corinthian Gate. It echoed and reverberated round the great court. There was a moment of silence, of stillness and then a great eruption of sound; a roar of approval that brought a small smile of satisfaction to the High Priest's lips. Just being in the Temple precincts was an emotional experience. The unexpected appearance of the High Priest was high drama. The Hebrews were a passionate race and of a volatile nature – as the Romans had found out to their cost. They were deeply moved by Ananus' address; feelings were running high. On religious matters the Hebrews were intractably stubborn, unbendingly obstinate. When pushed on matters of theology, they were capable of foolhardy courage, refusing to give ground on a point of principle, no matter what the cost.

The crowd shifted uneasily. An inexplicable sense of expectation had assailed their collective senses. It was though a tuning fork had been struck, its vibrations resonating endlessly in their minds.

Slowly, majestically, Ananus raised his arm. His fist uncurled and a finger pointed across the open space to the figure standing on the opposite tower. The High Priest spoke directly to the man. "*Just one*, you cry out to the people. You tell them to follow Jesus the Crucified, the false messiah who claimed he was the *Way* and the *Word* of God".

The man on the tower, dressed in a plain white robe, raised his head, the sun darkened face almost lost in the unkempt and wildly curling hair and beard. Brown eyes fixed unblinkingly on Ananus. For a moment there was no response, no movement other than that caused by the breeze which stirred the tangle of coarse, uncut white hair fluttering round his shoulders. James was fully aware of the trap that had just been set for him, as indeed were many in the crowd. A Jew from Armenia, a Pharisee with neither love nor respect for the High Priest said to his brother who had made the pilgrimage with him, "Ananus looks as though he is sucking on a lemon with his arse. This should be interesting".

This sally brought as many appreciative chuckles as it did frowns of censure from the brothers' immediate neighbours. James replied in a level voice, without inflection or special emphasis. "Why do you ask me again about Jesus the son of man? Have I not said on many occasions, that Jesus was the door of the sheepfold, the way to the Father?"

Like a rippling sea every head swung towards the Corinthian. What reply would the High Priest make?

With a gesture that embraced the whole assembly, Ananus replied, "Is not the law, given by God for His chosen people, the Way?"

This was the Law of Moses. The law God had uttered from the inferno of creation. For the sake of which, Jews believed the very world had been created. The law which Jesus himself had said he came not to destroy but to fulfil.

The fanatical descendants of that venerable race, stood with the ghosts of the prophets from their ancient past, waiting for James the Just to reply.

Before he answered, James turned from side to side as though to ensure that every tower, dome and pinnacle of the Holy City was bearing witness. "He who was the Christ, taught the law which God gave to his prophet Abraham - That there is one God for *all* the nations of the earth, Gentile and Jew. That the Way to God is love. To do unto others as you would be done by. For by this hangs the whole of the law".

The crowd gasped for this was the heart of it. Judaism taught that the one God *excluded all except his chosen people.*

If what James had just said was true, the covenant given to Moses was broken. The covenant of Abraham proclaimed *all* men were brothers, under one God.

The High Priest let out a wild shriek and tore his robe, the stitching of which had, in anticipation of this moment, been weakened. In a spray of spittle, one word was hurled across the court. "Blasphemer!"

A great howl rose; a thousand throats producing a hideous animal sound. *Ish –Maveth* - A man of death. All the deadly poison of the religious fanatic was in that sound.

This was the signal to Eleazar and the four priests. They scrambled on to the tower and rushed James, who offered no resistance. They hurled him into the court, the crowd scattering as his body landed with a sickening thud on the stone paving. Unbelievably he wasn't killed outright.

A circle formed around the sprawled body. One leg was twisted unnaturally beneath the torso. An arm had been shattered at the elbow. Blood dripped from chin to breast. The eyes were unfocused, eyelids fluttering wildly. With a deep groan James the Just used his one good arm to pull himself into a kneeling position.

"Stone him".

The command came from the leader of the priests whom Ananus, with earlier orders, had sent to this part of the court. They had also shown a sense of anticipation in bringing with them a plentiful supply of fist sized rocks. The first of these struck the injured James full in the face and knocked out an eye. The ensuing fusillade smashed into his ribs, broke his other arm, tore a large piece of scalp from his head and snapped off most of his front teeth.

The crowd roared their self-righteous anger. Those nearest the front sought missiles of their own. In a brief interlude lasting no more than a few seconds the dying man, swaying on his knees, raised his bowed and bleeding head. In a voice which was surprisingly strong, he called out to his God, "I entreat thee, oh Lord God, forgive them as I forgive them".

One of the police, the son of Rechab, suddenly sprang forward, trying to shield James with his own body. As he did so he cried out "Stop. What are we doing? The righteous one is praying for us".

Startled by this unexpected intervention, arms that had been pulled back ready to hurl another deadly shower of projectiles, paused and the fusillade petered out.

But one of the Temple police, who was also a fuller, stepped out of the crowd. In his hands he carried the tool of his trade – a heavy club. With a savage head butt he knocked the son of Rechab aside. With the mob screaming its encouragement, the skull of James the Just was shattered with a single blow.

2

After the murder of James, Eleazar went to a villa he kept in the lower city. He not only wielded enormous power in Jewish society, he lived in considerable luxury, supported by a generous share of the immense profit skimmed off the Temple's vast revenues.

As a secret nationalist, he controlled one of the many clandestine terrorist groups that were scattered around the country, some of which had hidden agendas that were mostly concerned with gathering wealth and power for themselves. Publicly they professed the common cause, whose manifesto was 'Home rule for Israel'. This and 'Romans out' or 'Roman pigs go home', were scrawled on walls in towns and villages across the country, despite the fact that when caught the perpetrators were crucified.

Among the growing opposition to the Romans was a group of terrorists known as Zealots, who laid claim to be the true champions of the people. Unfortunately, the people had to put up with rival groups of nationalists who were as often at odds with each other, as they were with the Romans.

What they had in common was that they all battened on the people. From Galilee in the north, down through Samaria, Judea and Idumaea in the south, they forced the people to hide weapons, shelter and feed them.

The most feared of these terrorist organisations were the Sicarii, the dagger men, led by a self-styled 'freedom fighter' called Menahem. They got their name from the unusual dagger they carried, which had a thick straight central rib, supporting a wavy double-edged blade coming to a needle point. With these weapons hidden in their clothing, the Sicarii would join a crowd and single out their victims, attacking them with a sudden deadly thrust, then they would disappear from the immediate scene by mingling with the crowd.

While influential Jews were the Sicarii's principle targets, they also assassinated members of rival groups and murdered citizens who refused to support their 'cause' which was financed by theft and extortion.

When Eleazar arrived at his villa he was on edge. The adrenalin rush from the action at the Temple still coursed through his body. The violence of James' murder had left him excited and sexually aroused. He was a man with a large and catholic sexual appetite.

Eleazar kept his wife and children in a town house in Jerusalem's upper city and Amal, his Egyptian mistress, in his villa in the lower city – an arrangement that protected his reputation and kept his wife in ignorance.

Amal had been expensively and carefully trained in Memphis. She had cost Eleazar a fortune but he had never regretted the cost. She knew his moods, his needs. She listened to plots and kept his secrets. She often advised him on a course of action, or counselled caution when he would have been reckless, or boldness when he would have held back. It was Amal who now greeted him on his arrival. She stood quietly while he rinsed his hands in the bowl held by a slave. He looked at her appraisingly from beneath drooping eyelids, eyes still bright from the morning's drama. She smiled and held out her hand, leading him from the entrance hall to a comfortably furnished room where the wine steward and the housekeeper waited deferentially for instructions.

After signalling for wine to be poured, Amal dismissed them with orders to bring the midday meal. Eleazar grinned at her, lowering himself onto a couch, taking a long pull on his wine and rolling his head from side to side to loosen the muscles in his neck. Amal, kneeling behind him, began to massage his neck and shoulders with perfumed oils. Her mother had been a valued Egyptian slave, mistress of the governor of Egypt, Pompeius Planta.

When Amal was old enough to understand, her mother had told her "The blood of Idumaean kings flows in your veins, for I was bedded by Herod Antipas, Tetrarch of Galilee". Amal knew there had never been any question of Antipas ever admitting paternity to any of his many bastard children, particularly a girl born of a slave, but that didn't stop her from dreaming. She knew that being Antipas' bastard made her cousin to Queen Berenice and her brother King Agrippa II, a client king the Romans had appointed to rule Upper Galilee and part of Jordan. He was also given oversight of the Temple with the authority to dismiss and appoint the High Priest of all Israel. In addition, the King was made custodian of the high priests' vestments, without which they could not officiate at religious festivals.

Eleazar grunted with pleasure, closing his eyes and giving himself up to the woman's probing fingers. When Amal judged him to be sufficiently relaxed, she removed his sandals and washed his feet. While she was doing this, slave girls carried in trays of food and set out an array of dishes on low tables. He stretched luxuriously and ran an appreciative hand across the buttocks of one of the serving girls.

Laughing, Amal dismissed them and leaning over Eleazar's half naked figure, began to feed him. "He is dead?" Eleazar, his mouth busy with a breast of chicken nodded. "Will the Romans cause trouble?"

Eleazar frowned while he considered this. He swallowed enough food to make a reply. "Possibly, though the High Priest thinks not".

Amal wiped his beard to which scraps of chicken were clinging. Eleazar was neither a tidy nor a silent eater. "And you?"

Eleazar shrugged and said dismissively, "The Romans have got too much on their hands at the moment to bother about another Jewish prophet". Swallowing the last of the chicken, he took a gulp from his cup, careless of the wine he slopped down his front. "There is unrest", he grated, "throughout the region. Every day the Romans are harried by the nationalists. Meanwhile Rome has an emperor gone mad". He paused to take another mouthful of chicken, smacking his lips appreciatively, before continuing, "Gaul, Germania and the Spaniards, sensing Rome's weakness, are growing increasingly restless".

Amal, who was every bit as ambitious as her master and every bit as intelligent, didn't reply. Eleazar had given her much to think about. Instead she continued to ply him with food, ensuring his wine cup was never empty.

Eventually, relaxed and replete, Eleazar was ready for a different feast, but first he would sleep. Sprawled across the brocaded couch, his head supported by a cushion, he began to doze. When he awoke it was lamplight. The windows were un-shaded and opened. He could see the stars of the night sky. Incense spiralled lazily, its fragrance mingling with the scent of garden flowers carried on the warm air.

Amal held out a wine cup. He drank greedily and struggled to his feet, farting loudly. The smell was appalling, but Amal ignored it. She knew that to Eleazar, she was simply a possession. Possessions don't have feelings or sensibilities. Not that Eleazar ever bothered over much to consider others. It was only in the Temple that he behaved in a circumspect and respectful manner.

Eleazar headed for the bath house that he had had installed – an innovation that he had taken from the Romans. Not that he was concerned with cleanliness; matters of cleanliness were religious. Purity was a thing of the spirit, not the flesh. Such matters involved ritual; they had nothing to do with dirt, grease or sweat. He bathed because he enjoyed the relaxing heat of the perfumed water, followed by the expert attention of a skilled masseur whose probing fingers eased the knots and tensions of the day, stretched cramped muscles and eased aching joints.

He bathed alone. In Eleazar's mind pleasures of the flesh were kept for the torture chamber or the bedroom, where he knew Amal would be waiting for him, with a body that took his breath away every time he saw it naked. Amal had sexual skills that no well-bred woman, Jewish or Roman, had ever heard of, let alone could practice.

When Eleazar entered the bedroom he was naked. She was waiting for him standing by an immense low bed wearing a filmy gown tied at the throat and loosely belted. She knew that Eleazar was as fascinated by the pale apricot of her skin as the firm abundance of her breasts. Amal was so slender he could almost encircle her waist with a double hand span.

He took one of her hands and placed it between his legs. She smiled and drew him to her, her perfumed chestnut hair against his face. She kissed him on the lips, the shoulders and the breast. Roused, he lay with her on the bed. One of his fingers sought her sex, gently stroking. He made no move to mount her, but continued to fondle her. Amal rolled over and straddled him, all the fluids of desire flowing down the golden shadows of her thighs.

She moved slowly, the violin shaped hips rising and falling, with the gentle soughing sound of a wave spending itself against a sandy shore. She felt his body begin to tremble, his mouth gaped redly in his dark beard, gasping for air. She stopped moving. Slowly his meaty fingers, like fiddler crabs, with their tufts of coarse black hair sprouting along their joints, began to patrol her body, seeking the places which pleased her.

As he became charged with desire, blood began to beat in Eleazar's temples; he was breathing hard. Amal raised her legs, hooking them over his shoulders. The kneeling man drove himself into her, to hammer frenziedly against the hill of her rounded buttocks. Amal screamed with pleasure – a wild ululation, a primitive tribal sound from a desert past. She beat her fists in ecstasy against his bowed shoulders, her golden body convulsing with the force of her emotions. Eleazar's body stiffened before he collapsed against her, spent, sobbing for breath. They lay entwined breathing heavily, their lips gently brushing.

The room darkened as the lamps burned low. They drifted off to sleep in a tumble of arms and legs, bodies pressed close, their breath mingling. When they awoke it was dark. Amal couldn't see Eleazar's face, but she knew he was awake.

He was lying on his back, one arm under her body round her shoulders, the other folded loosely, the palm of his hand on his chest. She could feel a tremor as his fingers absentmindedly drummed his breast bone. Amal burrowed into his side and gently nibbled the lobe of an ear, whispering "What are you thinking my love?"

The priest didn't reply at once, but the movement of his fingers stilled. She waited patiently while he thought about replying. He often confided in her, but he wasn't to be hurried. "Rebellion".

The single word, dropped like a pebble down a well, caused her to draw her breath and hold it for a few seconds. The word echoed in her mind. Before she could say anything the man continued, "The whole country is in turmoil. It bubbles with dissatisfaction like a spring of hot mud. The Roman pig is pricked on every side. Troops ambushed, murdered, maimed; weapons and stores stolen. Taxes go uncollected".

"But surely" Amal replied, "Rome will send more troops and crush those who dare challenge its authority?"

Eleazar chuckled, though there was no humour in the sound. "The dog's breath of Babylon", (this was an unflattering reference to Nero) "is an abomination to his own people as well as ours. Along every border of the empire, Rome's enemies see this weakness. They're plucking up the courage to test Rome's strength. Troop reinforcement to Israel will become a low priority".

Amal mulled this over before venturing, "Surely this is nothing more than border skirmishing. It goes on all the time. Not even the Gauls would dare mount a full scale rebellion".

With a grunt Eleazar propped himself up. "Wine woman; you talk too much".

Amal hastily swung her legs off the bed, gathering a robe loosely around her shoulders.

After relighting a lamp she poured some wine, and as she handed Eleazar a cup she persisted, "Who in Judaea would dare a mount an outright rebellion? More importantly, who would follow him?"

She would have continued, but he placed a finger across her lips. "There will never be a better opportunity. Rome is weak. She is also short of money, thanks to that dog's vomit Nero.

The legions are under strength. Many haven't been paid for months. The nations she has conquered and forced to submit are growing increasingly restless. If Judaea rises now, it will be a signal to the others. Rome will be attacked from all sides".

Amal shook her head in bewilderment. While it was true that the numbers of Roman troops garrisoned in Jerusalem and in strategic towns throughout the region were relatively small, they were well armed, well trained, and experienced fighters. They could also call for reinforcements from neighbouring Syria. And who, Amal thought to herself, would join the uprising? Would the High Priest of all Israel accept a field marshal's baton and place himself at the head of an army? "Lord, I fear for you", Amal murmured.

Eleazar eyed her across the rim of his cup. She was sitting on the huge bed cross legged, rouging her nipples. Her posture exposed her sex. He felt himself getting hard again.

"Nationalist groups throughout the country are under orders to step up their skirmishing. The Romans are going to have a guerrilla war on their hands. Working in small groups they will ambush and kill the Romans and those who support them; striking and slipping away. There will be no set piece battles until we are ready for them".

Amal noticed the 'we' but kept her council. "How will", she nearly said *you* but changed it to "*they* deal with this?"

Eleazar's interest in the control and management of rebellious nationalists was waning as he became aware of the size of his erection. "Come here", he growled, sitting with his back propped against the wall, his short thick hairy legs thrust straight out, his now furiously erect member grasped firmly in his left hand.

Amal crawled across the bed to face him and straddled his engorged penis. Sinking on to it Amal sighed with pleasure, as she slowly raised and lowered herself, rising almost to the point of withdrawal before lowering herself to grind fur against fur.

Eleazar's meaty hands clasped her hips to catch the rhythm of that delicious cushioning. "They will be executed as traitors, their possessions confiscated" he suddenly and rather breathlessly blurted out. Amal almost missed a beat at this sudden outburst.

For a moment she was utterly confused, until she remembered her earlier question. She now realised that the nationalists, whatever their political persuasion, had given themselves the authority to murder anybody if it suited their purposes. This would be done in the name of freedom and the cause of 'home rule'.

Hoarse shouts of encouragement from her steed broke through Amal's reverie. With a grin she lowered herself in the saddle and rode hard and fast, her sweating mount bellowing his encouragement.

Sated, Eleazar lay on his back. Amal had withdrawn to the edge of the bed. Like a cat she curled up against a pile of cushions. "Lord, the Sicarii are growing increasingly bold. They will surely bring down the wrath of the Romans".

Eleazar lifted an eyelid and peered at her grating "That cunt Menahem and his scum are planning something big. And it will happen soon". This was a reference to Menahem ben Jair, leader of the Sicarii and grandson of Judas of Galilee, the founder of the Zealot party, of which the Sicarii were a part.

"How soon?"

"Within the next week or so. My spies know that much, but nothing more".

Amal thought for a moment before asking "And you my Lord, what will you do? What will the Romans do?"

"The Romans will retreat to their strongholds and send to Rome for help. In the meantime there will be a civil war." Eleazar wriggled into a more comfortable position. "I will lead those Temple priests who will follow me, to join with my many followers in the city. Together we will overthrow the High Priest of all Israel and take the Temple over".

"But the Romans …?"

"I will not attack Rome. By the time Roman reinforcements arrive, I will be High Priest of all Israel and command the Temple".

Amal almost stopped breathing. Eleazar had announced the removal of Ananus as casually as ordering a lamb to be sacrificed. Keeping her voice neutral she ventured, "King Agrippa will be coming to Jerusalem to meet with his sister

Berenice, who is due to arrive in the city within the next few days. He is a favourite of Caesar and will back the Romans".

"Agrippa is an Idumaean pig guilty of incest", grated Eleazar. "We shall let them find his foul and polluted carcase with the rest of the garbage in the Hinnom valley – killed, of course, by the Romans; perhaps by the procurator himself during one his murderous actions against the people".

Amal poured warm oil onto the priest's fleshy back and began to massage it hard. Eleazar grunted with pleasure. As she worked, Amal thought about what she has just learned. "Rome", she thought to herself "will win in the end. She has to. A successful rebellion would signal her weakness. The empire would be overrun by her subject nations".

She regarded what Eleazar had just told her as madness, but she knew it was unstoppable. Dissent, dissatisfaction, resentment, was everywhere. It was in the very air one breathed. "The gates of war", her mother had once told her "are easy to open but very difficult to close".

How could she survive the coming storm, for she had intuitively decided that even Eleazar could not win? If his own people didn't get him, the Romans would. They wouldn't differentiate between loyal and disloyal Jews.

Berenice! If she could be persuaded that what Eleazar had told her was true, she would be grateful. She might even acknowledge kinship. A plan began to form in Amal's mind. The death of James had angered her, but she hadn't dared show it. His preaching had reached her. In secret and with infinite care, she had gathered information about the fate of the new Jewish sect who called themselves Christians. James had touched her heart when he retold the teaching of his brother Jesus.

With the Jews about to rebel against the Romans it was time, she decided to herself, to change sides.

3

Gessius Florus loathed Palestine. A freedman of Rome who had been fortunate in his marriage to a senator's daughter, Florus had hoped for better things than a posting as procurator to Judaea. The only bright spot on an otherwise gloomy horizon was that his immediate superior, Cestius Gallus, was *Legate* of Syria.

Gallus shared with Florus a contempt for all Jews and everything Jewish. Both men regarded their appointments as an opportunity to become very rich, providing they diligently stripped the Hebrew nation of everything it possessed, and selling as slaves those Jews that had nothing of value. While Florus was systematically looting the country, Gallus didn't just look the other way, he openly supported his procurator, for which he was paid a percentage of every stolen shekel.

To add to their misery the people were harried by bands of outlaws who, taking advantage of Florus' disregard of the people's rights, stole anything that wasn't nailed down. Inevitably nationalist movements began to exploit these unstable conditions. These so called freedom fighters comprised a number of movements and factions, usually at odds with one another, who frequently attacked each other's villages.

The nationalists had competition from minor warlords and the criminal scum that were their followers. These bandits attacked villages stealing anything of value, raping the women and killing every living thing, before burning the place to the ground.

Florus did nothing about the warlords who roamed the country, providing they gave him a cut. As Florus' compliance was cheap at half the price, they were happy to pay him off.

Florus' attitude to the nationalists was different. It had to be. They were busy ambushing and killing Roman soldiers. They also murdered Jews who were Roman citizens of high standing who supported Rome. The procurator regarded the nationalists as a personal enemy as well as the enemy of Rome (they were raising funds through extortion - money which he regarded as being rightfully his and not even paying him tribute). Frustratingly, he found moving against them difficult.

They were an enemy who struck when least expected, and then vanished to merge with the general populace, proving to be an exasperatingly elusive opponent. They did, however, provide him with an excuse for his brutally oppressive treatment of the whole population.

Should a complaint be made to Rome about his behaviour, they would be his cover. He would defend his actions by simply claiming that it was necessary to contain the numerous resistance movements. After all, they constantly attacked his forces. It was his duty to deal ruthlessly with criminal acts of subversion and terror. Weren't his soldiers, officials and Jewish citizens of influence being murdered because they were loyal subjects of the Emperor? Confident that his position was unassailable, Florus set about systematically looting the country.

Squeezed relentlessly from all sides, the Jews were becoming desperate as well as angry. Men who worked from sun-up to sun-down were worse off than slaves. Their families starved as the corn they had grown was bagged and carted away, either by tax collectors, freedom fighters, the so called nationalists, or outlaws.

When a band of outlaws raided a town or village, they were after food and money. If the luckless citizens claimed not to have any, they were tortured, often to death. Men and women were made to dig up the floors of their homes. If no money was found, the disgruntled bandits would frequently beat a man to death, first buggering his children and raping his wife in front of him.

Not even Jerusalem was safe. The Sicarii hunted in broad daylight, stalking their victims in the streets. People were struck down without mercy. Often the victims had refused demands to pay protection money. People were killed, maimed, blinded and turned into helpless cripples if they failed to pay up.

With the country in turmoil, Florus suddenly descended on the Holy City and stole seventeen talents of silver from the Corban, the Temple treasury, on the pretext he was claiming this vast sum for Rome in lieu of unpaid taxes. The high priests were outraged, accusing the Romans of theft.

The city erupted. The people, goaded beyond endurance and whipped to a frenzy by the nationalists, rioted. This created the opportunity Florus had long hoped for. He now had an excuse to legitimately use force against the civilian population of Jerusalem. His orders were to spare no-one. The troops were ordered to kill every Jew they encountered, irrespective of age or sex.

When the soldiers entered the city's Upper Market area, they were met by a large crowd led by nationalists who exhorted the people to resist Florus' men. Ordinary citizens armed with makeshift weapons, clubs, knives, iron bars, found themselves facing well-armed, well trained, seasoned troops who cut them to pieces.

There then followed a running battle, bitterly fought through the city's twisting narrow streets. The Romans advanced in an orderly fashion, shields locked. Their short stabbing swords, designed for close quarter work, chopped and stabbed until the gutters were running with blood.

Behind Florus' relentlessly advancing swordsmen, Roman soldiers skilled in the javelin hurled their shafts over the heads of their comrades. Thrown in unison, spears rained down onto the densely packed Jews with deadly effect. In the grim struggle people shouted, cursed and wept, as they fought to stay alive. Screams of agony pierced the air as weapons found their mark.

Women and children, who had taken refuge in the shops and houses lining these narrow lanes, were forced into the open. Like frightened hares flushed from cover, they ran about in panic, searching for a means of escape, children clinging to their skirts and babies clutched to their breasts. But the press of bodies was so great it was impossible to move in any specific direction. Sick with fear they struggled to stay on their feet and keep their children with them. The Romans remorselessly hacked their way forward. Terrified mothers, finding themselves at the front of the crowd, knelt holding their babies before them and begged for mercy.

They and their children were not just killed. They were butchered. Infants were speared and carried as trophies for a few yards before being contemptuously tossed into the mob. Soldiers wielding swords were carmined from helmet to hip with blood. It ran down their faces and dripped from their chins. They advanced on the terrified Jews struggling ineffectively to escape. Like a blood red hydra of a thousand arms and hands, each armed with a hacking and chopping blade, the Roman forces advanced remorselessly, a monstrous body bristling with spears and lances thrusting, twisting and stabbing in every direction.

When the slaughter burst out of the souk's narrow alleys and tumbled the Jews into a large square, the Hebrews threw down their makeshift weapons and dropped to their knees. Arms raised in surrender, they begged for mercy.

Florus replied by sending in his cavalry. The effect was similar to that of a combine harvester being driven at speed through a wheat field. Heads, arms and legs were sheared from the defenceless people and tossed every which way.

Numb with shock they knelt, staring with unseeing eyes as the Roman cavalry charged them repeatedly. Eventually the Romans were forced to call a halt. The footing for their horses had become dangerous because of the soft going. Like a layer of mud, the plaza's paving slabs were covered ankle deep with blood, faeces and human offal.

When the Roman commander brought the action to an end and declared order restored, he took stock of his losses. The Roman casualties numbered five dead and about one hundred wounded. On the Jewish side five thousand had been killed and a thousand more were wounded, many so seriously they would die later.

4

Jerusalem was full to bursting. Every room in the city that could be let had been taken. In addition to the thousands of Jews that had travelled from all over Palestine to be in the Holy City for Passover, another million pilgrims had arrived from abroad.

To accommodate them a temporary town had been established near the olive groves outside the city wall. As well as huts and tents for people, pens for animals had been constructed. The city authorities, well used to this annual influx, had built latrines, organised the management of rubbish, provided a conduit of fresh water and policed the whole operation, protecting the pilgrims from petty crime and settling the inevitable domestic disputes that arose.

It was this carpet of huts and tents unrolled outside the city walls that Cestius Gallus, appointed by Rome as *Legate* of Syria, had to negotiate before entering the city. The *Legate* decided to visit Jerusalem because Florus had reported unrest, which he had been forced to put down, making an example of the trouble makers. Gallus and his legionaries had passed over a hundred crucifixion sites during the last few miles, their putrefying burdens and attendant clouds of vultures, crows and kites, grim evidence of Florus' response to unrest.

The *Legate* had also noted that in his report, the procurator recorded that if he had any more trouble he would take stern measures. Gallus didn't doubt for a minute that his procurator would keep his word. The thousands of pilgrims pouring into the Holy City had not come with empty wallets. As well as having brought funds to sustain them for a round trip, they had also brought offerings for their God, which they would make at the Temple. The *Legate* knew that Florus would find a way of diverting some of this abundance into his own coffers. Gallus, with an eye to protecting his cut, had made the journey from Syria. He would pretend to listen to the people's complaints. It was important that, insofar as Rome was concerned, he was seen to be diligent in fulfilling the duties of his office. He knew that there was always the possibility that Florus would go too far. Gold had the same effect on him as the scent of blood to a shark.

Among his staff officers Gallus had a young *tribune*, Neopolitanus, to whom he had shown favour because of his connections. He was related on his mother's side to the late Emperor Claudius. So a flattered young officer found himself sitting on a horse next to his commanding officer approaching the Holy City. As Jerusalem came into sight, Neopolitanus was amazed. The descriptions he had been given in Rome hadn't prepared him for the splendour that was coming into view.

It was early morning and the sun flashed in a blinding reflection off the roof of the Temple. Rising a hundred and fifty feet into the air, it seemed to float in the pale blue sky like a pure white cloud, capped with burnished gold. To Neopolitanus the massive building seemed like a mountain covered in snow, its peak crowned with a fiery splendour. Those parts that were not plated with sheets of solid gold were of a brilliant white marble, polished to a mirror finish.

Gallus broke the silence. "A million Jews have gathered to pay homage to their God. What you see before you is His Temple". Before the *tribune* could reply Gallus continued, "Every Jewish pilgrim would consider it a privilege to die defending the dirt of the road you are standing on, so be careful *tribune* when you are in the city, and doubly careful when you are anywhere near the Temple". Neopolitanus assured him he would follow this advice.

"I'm not giving you advice *tribune*", had been the dry rejoinder. "I'm giving you an order. Walk softly, be slow to take offence and watch your manners. Jews are quick to take umbrage, particularly over religious matters which they never give ground on. Ever. No matter what the consequences". Neopolitanus gave his commanding officer earnest assurances that he would be most circumspect in his dealing with the Jews, as he admired the magnificence of the city they were approaching. Gallus said, "Just pray that you never have to assault it, because if you do you will fail. The Jews consider it to be impregnable and I agree with them. When we get to the Antonia fortress, ask the duty officer to explain the city's fortifications to you".

Neopolitanus was surprised to hear a Roman general say that a city couldn't be taken. The invincibility of Rome's military machine had been dinned into him from childhood. Wisely he didn't dispute this with the *Legate*. Instead he saluted smartly and took his leave. The column was now deep into what seemed to be a sea of people. Painfully slowly, displaying the legion's golden eagle, its standards raised and its drums beating, the column made its way through the city gates into Jerusalem.

The road leading to the Antonia also led to the Temple and was packed with people. The pavements were lined with vendors offering a bewildering variety of merchandise. The noise was deafening, with people shouting and arguing; pedlars and merchants calling out the virtues of their particular wares; beggars soliciting alms; herds of penned animals bawling; the rumble of wagon wheels as carts drawn by camels forced their way through. Motes of dust, stirred by countless feet, danced in shafts of sunlight that sliced across the rooftops to penetrate the maze of streets latticed with hard white light and indigo shadows.

As Gallus' *cohorts* approached the Antonia, streams of worshippers were leaving the Temple to cross the bridge into the western half of the city, heading for the souk's markets, swelling the crowds shopping in its narrow shaded streets. The booths lining the souk were piled high with goods brought from every corner of the world – baskets, thimbles, carpets and textiles of every kind and colour. From Arabia – glassware, silver and gold craftworks. From India – spices and precious stones.

From Africa - exotic animals, slaves, gold, ivory and ebony. From Edom - myrrh, aromatic oils, rare woods and precious spices, traded through India by the Parthians, the unconquered tribes Rome feared most.

From China, a land of mystery, its borders closed to foreigners, came silk. Worth ten times its weight in gold, it was only available to a handful of merchants who had survived the journey to Beijing and been accepted as trading partners. Even then they could only deal with one man, appointed by the Chinese Emperor to negotiate the sale of silk, who in turn would only negotiate sales with Rome's designated merchants, be they Jews or Arabs.

At every corner there were vendors selling sweetmeats, water, wine and fruit juices; the sellers clashing finger cymbals to attract attention. In the fish market, stalls were brimming with fresh fish of every description, next to which were barrels of salted and pickled eels. Overhead hung poles supporting bundles of dried fish, stiff as shingles and bleached almost white. Butchers displayed cuts of lamb and goat, the heads of which were impaled on spikes, eyes glaring balefully at prospective customers. Hearts, livers and lungs were displayed on hooks like jewelled necklaces.

The warm air was redolent with a potpourri of scents, spices, incense, vegetables, fruit, flowers, herbs, animal dung, garbage from the markets, sweet smelling oils and perfumes; all mingling with the odours of frying foods and the smells that accompany humans in close contact. A pungent aroma that would intensify as the day got hotter.

To make progress through this seemingly impenetrable mass, Neopolitanus placed a squad of heavy infantry at the head of the cohort who marched in close order, shields held edge to edge along the side of their columns. With trumpets blowing and drums beating out a steady marching cadence, the column moved forward, though not without some cursing and the odd vegetable being hurled in their direction by an irate citizen.

Neopolitanus was not alone in breathing a sigh of relief when they arrived at the Antonia fortress, the headquarters of the occupying troops permanently garrisoned in Jerusalem. A guard of honour had been turned out to meet them. They entered the fortress to a fanfare of trumpets and were greeted by the Antonia's commander, the *Praetorian* Metilius.

After Gallus had inspected the guard of honour, he and Metilius left the business of standing the column down to Neopolitanus and the fortress' duty officer Centurion Crassus Maximus. With the men and their equipment squared away, Neopolitanus asked Crassus if he would brief him about the city and its citizens. "But first", he said, "I must bathe. I stink more than my horse". With a grin Crassus confirmed the stink and said he would be happy to show him the ropes.

In the afternoon, refreshed and glad to be out of their armour, wearing plain linen tunics and leather vests, Neopolitanus and Crassus ventured out of the fortress into the crowded streets, the jostling crowd noisy but amiable. Passover was the most joyous of Jerusalem's festivals; an opportunity to set aside the cares and worries of everyday life and relax. Countless thousands of pilgrims, unable to find accommodation, were squeezed into the homes of friends; sleeping in corners of already crowded rooms, in courtyards and some, in desperation, camping in doorways and tethering the Paschal lamb brought from the country to the nearest post.

Picking their way carefully through the heaving mass, the two Romans made their way along the densely packed streets, stumbling over bedding, pots and pans and bundles of personal belongings, whose mounds indicated possession and occupation of a particular bit of pavement.

"In here". Crassus took Neopolitanus' arm and pulled him into the portico of a pastry shop. "We can get a bite to eat and catch our breath". Neopolitanus grinned and nodded his agreement. The two men found a quiet corner in the cool interior of the shop and after ordering a dish of fried locust en croûte, began to discuss the volatile situation.

Neopolitanus was baffled by Crassus' unwillingness to see the Jewish nationalists' point of view, no matter how misguided it was. "Years ago" said Crassus, "the Jews invited us here. They sent a delegation to Rome and pleaded with us to admit them to the empire, to dig them out of the shit Aristobulus had landed them in".

Through a mouthful of pastry Neopolitanus said, "Then the Roman senate proclaimed Herod King of Judaea. Being an Idumaean, one quarter Jew and three quarters Arab, he was hated by just about everybody. Then of course there was the Jewish tyrant, Herod's son Archelaus, who bled the Jews dry until Augustus banished him to Gaul".

Crassus grinned. "You should go further back than that. Rome made its first treaty with the Jews two hundred years ago. At the Hebrew's request, Rome dispatched military advisors to Judaea and followed this up by sending the troops the Jews asked for to protect them".

Neopolitanus snorted. "The long noses need reminding that Judaea isn't Jewish anyway. They took the country by force of arms from the Canaanites and wiped out the entire indigenous population. They spared nobody; they didn't even take slaves. They claimed their God had ordered them to commit wholesale murder".

"Come now, that's many years ago", countered Crassus, "Seventeen hundred to be precise".

"But" Neopolitanus continued hurriedly before his companion could interrupt "the kettle mustn't call the pot black. Discussions about rights of ownership of particular bits of the world can put us Romans in a difficult position, given the size of our empire".

Crassus shook his head. "The Jews asked for a treaty because it suited them. We agreed because it suited us. We now have, or should have, a friendly state supporting Syria and Egypt. We Romans came here because this country is a crossroads. It is essential to the rule of our empire because we hold Egypt, which everybody wants for its limitless harvest of corn. We also have the Parthians for enemies. Palestine and Syria are the defence buffer between us and our age old foe who", he added sombrely "has never been defeated in battle".

"Well Centurion", replied Neopolitanus, "If a treaty between Roman and Jew is one of mutual self-interest, why do we have endless problems with these people? Why do they not accept the benefits and advantages of the Roman way of life, the protection of Roman armies, Roman law, enjoy Roman culture and the freedom to worship their own Gods?"

Crassus grimaced. "Well we cannot impose our way of life on this stiff necked people. Pompey tried and failed. The Jews are racially prejudiced. We can either accept that and work with it or" he added ominously, "we can wipe the lot out".

"Or" Neapolitanus said "we display the good side of Roman life and hope it will gradually be accepted for its own sake." Wiping crumbs from his lips Neopolitanus stood up. "Come. Show me the defences of the city. The *Legate* recommended the top of the Antonia as a viewing point".

"Agreed", said Crassus, "but I will need time to change. I am due back on duty".

In the early evening, the two men stood on top of the Antonia's highest tower, Crassus in full armour. From the pinnacle on which they stood, the city was laid out like a map. Crassus remained silent to allow Neopolitanus to take in the splendour that was at their feet. It was Neopolitanus who broke the silence. Speaking more to himself than to his companion, he said "Perhaps it is impregnable".

"As you can see" said Crassus "the city, like Rome, is built on a series of hills. Where it differs" he continued "is that unlike Rome, it is protected on three sides by the deep ravines the Jews call Gehenna and Kidron". Neopolitanus stared down into what seemed a bottomless abyss. Crassus continued "You will notice that the valleys are devoid of all vegetation. The sides are bare rock, which is so steep as to be unclimbable".

"That" replied Neopolitanus wryly "is why they build their walls along the edges".

Crassus pointed to one of the hills. "That is the Upper City, known as the Upper Market. The second hill is the Citadel and is covered by the Lower City. The opposite part of the city", he continued pointing to a third hill, "was originally cut off by a wide ravine. During the Hasmonaean period, this was filled in and as you can see it joins the city to the Temple. The Jews call this area the Valley of the Cheese Makers". "But the walls", said Neopolitanus in a hushed voice, "what walls! They seem to rise up from Hades itself and brush the very heavens with their towers and fortresses".

"It's the walls, their fortified towers and massive fortresses, which make this place an invading army's nightmare". Crassus chuckled, but there was no mirth in it. "There are three walls, one behind the other, with over a hundred towers spaced along them and as you have observed, the walls are unassailable because they are on the rims of bottomless ravines".

"How on earth did the Jews get all that masonry of such Herculean sizes to this place?" asked Neopolitanus.

"They didn't", his companion replied. "They dug most of the city out of the ground. Jerusalem stands on limestone the Jews call travertine. When it is in the ground, it is soft and easily worked. However, when it is exposed to air, it becomes very hard, almost impossible to cut. As a result of their excavations the Jews got a bonus. The city stands on cisterns which hold millions of gallons of water. They also have underground caverns containing several years' supply of grain and oil, and every other kind of material necessary to not only sustain life, but supply a defending army with all its needs".

Neopolitanus shook his head in amazement before asking ruefully, "And the fortresses I can see spaced out strategically between the towers?"

Crassus grinned thinly. "At the northern end of the old wall is the Hippicus. It has its own water supply and siege storage vaults, as in indeed do all the towers and fortresses. Above the high base, which is topped by a two story building, is a fortified tower. With turrets and ramparts it stands at one hundred and twenty feet high excluding the base of solid stone, which is fifty feet high. The Phasael fortress further along", Crassus continued, "is even bigger. It is protected by breastworks and bulwarks".

Studying the Phasael, Neopolitanus asked, "What is access like between the different levels?"

"There is a spiral staircase which allows access to each floor. Being a spiral it is easily defended. Each of the fortresses has a similar staircase. Though I must say", Crassus concluded, "the idea of anyone ever succeeding in breaking into any of them is laughable".

Neopolitanus silently digested this information. He was beginning to agree with the *Legate's* earlier remark about the city being impregnable. After a long silence he asked, "And the third fortress in the old wall?"

"That's the Marriam, shorter than the others being eighty two feet high. The building on top of the fortified base is a magnificent palace Herod built in memory of his wife Marriam. The Hippicus was named after a friend and the Phasael after his brother".

"Remarkable monuments", said Neopolitanus.

"He murdered all three", laughed Crassus.

Neopolitanus, no stranger to political murder, made no comment on the savagery. Instead he pointed to the North West. "There, on the corner opposite the Hippicus, what's the very tall octagonal tower?"

"That's the Psephinus Tower; it's a hundred and fifty feet high. From the top you can see the furthest extent of Palestine; sometimes on a really clear day you can even see Arabia".

"Remind me, how many fortresses and towers are there?"

"The third wall has ninety towers, each a hundred yards apart. The middle wall has fourteen and the old wall sixty. The circuit of the walls is four miles. Of course as well as the one hundred and sixty four fortified towers, there are the three fortresses we have spoken about, which are part of the walls".

Overwhelmed, Neopolitanus turned to the Temple which joined the Antonia. "That looks like a city within a city".

Crassus glanced sideways at his companion. "Covering three and a half acres, it is", he replied, "as is the Antonia. But the Temple is best seen close up and not in uniform. Tomorrow I am off duty for a few hours; we can visit it then".

"Delighted", replied Neopolitanus, "but before we go to supper, tell me about the Antonia. From what little I have seen this place is as big as a small town".

"You are right. It is virtually a town, but with fortifications like no town you have ever seen. In general design it is a massive tower with four other towers attached at each corner. Of these, three are seventy five feet high and the fourth – the one we are standing on – is one hundred and five feet high. Where it joins the Temple, stairs lead down to the colonnades giving our soldiers access at all times to the Temple's inner courts".

Crassus pointed. "As you can see, fully armed Roman infantry are stationed along the tops of the walls surrounding the Temple and the colonnades. We always have a show of strength at festivals, to watch for any sign of discontent. The city is dominated by the Temple and the Temple by the Antonia. So the Antonia houses the guards of all three. The Upper City has a stronghold of its own, Herod's palace".

The two men stood gazing at the crowded streets below them. Even at their great height the hum of voices was clearly audible. From time to time the men in the streets would hurl insults at the silent legionaries manning the walls, some of whom were chewing olives and spitting the stones into the crowd. Stoically they ignored the verbal abuse hurled at them.

The two Romans were on the point of leaving the tower when a remark particularly offensive and insulting to Rome was shouted at the silent guards. One of them could stand it no longer. He turned his back on the jeering mob, lifted his short skirt and hauled down his undergarments. Presenting the outraged Jews with his bare arse he blew them a monstrous fart. The Jews howled in fury at this insult and suddenly real trouble flared up.

Crassus groaned, "I must leave you", and sped away pulling his helmet on as he dashed to the stair well. Neopolitanus followed him more slowly. This wasn't his fight, though if called on he and his men would reinforce the garrison troops.

Trumpets were sounding and the Antonia's soldiers were pouring out of their barracks, rapidly forming up on the parade ground. Neopolitanus noted with pride and satisfaction the order with which this was done. Every man in his armour, weapons in hand, standing calmly to attention awaiting their orders.

The fighting in the streets quickly boiled over on to the colonnades and the outer court of the Antonia. A full scale riot was getting under way.

Gallus and Metilius appeared on a balcony overlooking the parade ground in time to see Florus, mounted at the head of a squadron of heavy cavalry, order the gate to be opened. The procurator meant business. The fact that he was grossly outnumbered meant little to him. He knew that the mob outside were virtually unarmed. A few knives, staves and chunks of broken masonry were about to face a well-equipped, heavily armoured killing machine that seriously knew its business.

5

Florus' cavalry cut through the densely packed streets which surrounded the Antonia like wire slicing cheese. Heavy infantry with locked shields and drawn swords followed closely behind. The angry crowds clogging the streets were virtually unarmed. Even so, they fought back with anything to hand, but to little purpose.

Any attempt to flee into less crowded streets was cut off by the cavalry that was now savagely working the edges of the crowd, slicing the tightly packed bodies like a butcher cutting salami.

As the enraged mob surged below the Antonia's walls, members of the Sicarii who had secretly infiltrated it seized the opportunity created by the panic and confusion to assassinate a number of prominent Jewish citizens. The men they murdered were killed for their moderate views, dubbed traitors because they had tried to run a civil administration that recognised Rome's authority. It was easy in the turbulence and confusion to take a blade which had been hidden in a sleeve and slip it between a man's ribs, the victim unable to identify his attacker, his shriek of pain inaudible above the pandemonium created by the roaring mob. His assassin would ease himself away from the scene, to lose himself in the crowd. Over a dozen Jews of high standing, men of authority and power, were murdered by the Sicarii during the riot which lasted half a day.

These murders were nothing compare to the *thirty thousand* Jewish citizens who died that day. Most crushed to death in the narrow streets in which Florus' men had penned them.

36

The Romans suffered no losses but about a hundred men were wounded, two of them seriously. One man had lost an eye and the other had a broken leg.

Florus didn't return to the Antonia. Instead he went to Herod's palace to further the next move in a plan he had conceived during the riot. What he had in mind, was a way of contriving a nationwide revolt. This would forestall any enquires into his own criminal behaviour.

The next day he had a dais erected on the marble veranda overlooking the palace courtyard, where he took his seat. Florus was a tall, heavily built man with reddish hair and pale almost colourless eyes. Dressed in a white toga of finely spun wool he lolled on a golden throne, a goblet of the same metal held loosely in one hand. In the other he held the ivory baton of his *Imperium*, the visible symbol that he was Caesar's legally appointed representative. He was Rome. The power of life and death was in his hands. Only a Roman citizen could appeal his judgement by asking to be sent to Caesar.

In front of the seated prefect, was a low table of marble inlaid with jewels forming an intricate design of flowers and birds - a gift to Herod from an Indian prince.

Florus was attended by a scribe and his staff officers, who stood in a discreet half circle around the seat of judgment.

Ranged along the tops of the palace walls, five hundred hand-picked soldiers armed with javelins stood virtually shoulder to shoulder, while the floor of the courtyard was encircled with a triple row of infantry armed with shields and swords. Several mounted cavalry were positioned strategically, resplendent in dress uniform, crimson capes fastened at the riders' shoulders, draping over their mounts' haunches. Plumed helmets burnished to a parade ground finish, added to the wearers' gravitas. Polished lances decorated with pennants were held at the rest position. This ceremonial cavalry was there as a reminder. The whole wing was standing by ready for action should they be required.

"Sir may the Jews enter?" asked an equerry.

Florus sipped the wine in his goblet and let his eyes travel round the court. Having checked that his men were in place he gave a barely perceived nod. The equerry signalled the men on the gate. The supplicants, who had been waiting in the hot sun for over four hours, could enter.

The first to come in were the chief priests wearing their ceremonial robes. They were led by Ananus. The priests prostrated themselves, before kneeling to address the procurator. Ananus was their spokesman. "Excellency, the whole city is in mourning, on this the eve of our greatest and most joyous celebration. Thousands of its people are dead. The weeping of widows fills the air."

"Who" cut in Florus "do you blame for these deaths? Point them out to me and I will judge them."

"Excellency, thousands of innocents were crushed to death as they fled the rioting" Ananus replied, carefully avoiding Florus' part in the massacre.

"I am sick of Jews rioting. I give you peace. You give me war. War that costs me dearly. Tell me, how do you propose recompensing me for the expense of defending the city from troublemakers who inflame the people, causing them to attack the authorities?"

The assembled deputies gasped at the way things were going and muttered amongst themselves. Ananus chewed his beard and said nothing, but his eyes burned with hatred.

"Answer me priest, when will you pay? I demand restitution for the expenses incurred in putting down Jews who riot against authority, who defy Rome."

Slowly the High Priest stood up. "Excellency, I cannot decide in this matter, therefore let us ask Caesar for a judgement". The silence that followed this was absolute. The High Priest had dared to question the procurator's judgment.

Florus, his face a mask, showed no emotion. He stared long and hard at the High Priest. Finally he burst out laughing, a mirthless bray that revealed to those who knew him the depths of his anger. He waved a hand carelessly to signal the audience was over. "High Priest, the Temple is fined thirteen talents of silver. I will debate with you no more. We shall look elsewhere for compensation. We have, however, noted before these witnesses, your refusal to redress the injury Jewish people have inflicted on Rome".

Slowly, with downcast eyes, the High Priest and his entourage backed away. They left tearing their clothes and loudly lamenting their fate, while Florus gave orders that wagons guarded by several *cohorts* of heavy infantry and two wings of cavalry were to proceed immediately to collect the fortune he had just stolen.

He then returned to the business in hand. Earlier he had ordered that many of Jerusalem's most eminent citizens be arrested. While they were Jews, most were also citizens of Rome, many of Equestrian Rank. They had been held overnight to consider the proposition, that in exchange for their lives they could expiate their *crimes* by signing over their property and wealth to the State.

To help them in their deliberations he had one of them stretched over a slow burning charcoal fire, with orders that the fire was to be kept burning all night and the prisoner turned regularly and basted with oil to ensure an even roast. For many hours the prisoners, who had been kept without food or water, were forced to listen to the tormented man's desperate screams. As dawn approached the screams became a continuous low moan, finally falling silent as the sun rose on a new day. The fragrant smell of roast meat drifting through their cells, reminded the prisoners they had had no food for twenty four hours. Before being assembled for transportation to Herod's palace, they refused in horror the only breakfast offered to them.

These men were legally exempt from the Procurator's judgment. They all had the right to be tried by the Emperor. Florus however, had refused to acknowledge their right to petition Caesar.

As they knelt before Florus, a slave holding a bowl of water, a towel draped over one arm, came and stood slightly behind the Procurator's left shoulder. "Well, having slept on my offer of mercy what is your reply?"

Benjaman Sabinus, who had been elected spokesmen, rose to his feet – an action that caused Florus to frown, but he said nothing. "Excellency we deny the charges brought against us and regret the circumstances which cause you to believe otherwise. As we don't even know what it is we are accused of, we ask as is our right as citizens of Rome, to be sent to Caesar".

"Traitors have no rights" Florus answered coldly standing up. This was a prearranged signal to the slave holding the bowl to come forward. He knelt at the Procurator's feet. Dipping his fingers into it Florus said "I wash my hands of you. We have offered you mercy and you spit in our face. Your treacherous Jewish stubbornness challenges our authority." He picked up the towel without taking his eyes off the kneeling men. "Very well, so be it." Turning away he said to the captain of the guard "Scourge them and then ask them if they have had second thoughts".

The centurion could not help a slight involuntary gasp at these orders. The eyes of the soldiers lining the court and standing guard on the walls, widened in amazement. The staff officers in attendance on the dais sucked in their breaths. They couldn't meet each other's eyes. Florus had just ordered the impossible. Every citizen of Rome was entitled to a fair hearing before Caesar, just as every citizen of Rome was legally exempted from punishments that were considered to be degrading. Scourging and crucifixion were at the top of the list of such punishments.

Florus had ordered the scourging to be inflicted at once. A punishment that entailed the victim being stripped naked and fixed to a tripod, his entire body being lashed with a multi-stranded leather whip that had pieces of metal and shards of bone attached to the tips of the strands.

When the scourging was over, the centurion asked the barely conscious victims to reconsider their refusal to sign away their possessions. When the answer was no, he then produced the victim's death warrant, which had been pre-signed by the Procurator. Death was to be by the slowest, most painful way of dying man had ever devised. Crucifixion.

Of the dozen men Florus had scourged, six refused to sign and died in agony cursing the Procurator from the cross.

Meanwhile, Florus made arrangements for the property and wealth of the other six who had signed, to be transferred to him before sending them and their families into exile – on pain of death never again to set foot in the empire.

6

Florus decided to stay on at the palace. Not only was it an ideal base from which to provoke the civilian population, it was a convenient point from which to manage the wealth and property he had extorted from the men he had scourged.

Among his officers who were closest to him, tied to him as co-conspirator and sharing in the spoils of his crimes was a *Tribune*, Marcus Severus. Marcus was not only second in command to Florus, he was a trusted confidant.

The day after the scourging, the procurator and the *Tribune* were discussing how to sell a piece of valuable property in Rome when Neopolitanus, who was officer of the day, entered the room and after saluting reported "Excellency, Queen Berenice has entered the city and is approaching the palace". Berenice, the daughter of King Agrippa I, would when visiting Jerusalem expect to stay at the Hasmonaean Palace, built by her grandfather Herod the Great.

Florus acknowledged the report and sat thinking. The Queen's authority didn't concern him in the least, but her brother did, for he was King Agrippa II and had been appointed client King by the Romans for Upper Galilee, part of Jordan, and Chalcis. He also had responsibilities in Jerusalem and the use of his grandfather's palace when he visited the city.

But, thought Florus, first things first. "Why had she come to Jerusalem?" Marcus voiced the same question.

Florus answered thoughtfully, "Good question. She and her brother are Jews. I suspect she had come to perform a Nazarite vow".

"I thought", said Marcus, "she had come to celebrate Passover".

"Maybe", said Florus, "but spies tell me that having got away with incest in Caesarea, they have scandalised the good people of Chalcis. I have a feeling the lady has left town to let things cool down".

The burly *Tribune* laughed "Jews stone women for adultery. What's their remedy for diddling with your brother?"

The procurator shrugged. "You may well have the opportunity to see for yourself at first hand, if the news of the lady's proclivity reaches the High Priest. Your original question is the only one that matters to us. Why is she here?"

The procurator received his royal visitor with an outward display of warmth. "Your Highness, forgive me for not calling on you but we had no warning of your arrival. Had we known you intended visiting Jerusalem, for your safety we would have sent an escort to meet you".

Berenice, tall to the point of being statuesque, crossed the room with a sinuous grace and sat down opposite the procurator. As Florus waited for a response, he was struck as much by that feline quality as by her beauty. She had a delicate heart shaped face, its pointed chin giving it an elfin quality. Her widely spaced hazel eyes were tilted slightly, reinforcing the cat like impression. Lips slightly turned up at the corners gave her a mischievous look, which was her natural nature, betrayed by a cheeky smile whose whiteness contrasted with a *café au lait* skin, the creamy texture of which was a perfect foil for the lustrous dense black hair, arranged in the Alexandrian fashion.

She was also dressed in the Alexandrian mode – a style that showed off her figure to perfection, with its firm high breasts, narrow waist, sensually rounded hips and long shapely legs. The fingers and toes of her small finely boned hands and feet were decorated with jewelled rings, the nails painted a brilliant green. Even in repose she had a calm, naturally authoritative manner.

When she replied to Florus it was in a voice that was surprisingly deep and slightly husky.

Every man on hearing it for the first time became instantly aware of its owner. "Excellency, having suffered no personal harm during the recent unrest we are pleased to see you."

She would have continued but Florus interrupted her. "Nevertheless lady, we should have been advised of your proposal to travel. Nationalists are urging the people to rebel against Rome. Towns and villages are being attacked by both sides, often by opportunist bandits. Even", he continued, "in Jerusalem riots are commonplace. My men are hard pressed to keep the peace".

Berenice smiled. "Perhaps my arrival in the city will act as a moderating influence."

Florus, with a wintery smile, extended his hand indicating that she should be seated, at the same time introducing his second in command. "I do hope so lady. In the meantime allow me to present my second in command *Tribune* Marcus Severus, who will be personally responsible for your safety while you are in the city".

Severus saluted and got a short nod in return. "Thank you your Excellency, but I have my own bodyguard. I also travelled with a cohort of infantry and a troop of my own cavalry. With so much trouble on your hands", she concluded dryly, "you will have need of your *tribune*".

"Very well", replied Florus, unperturbed by the refusal. "We will make arrangements for your troops and cavalry to be rested and your personal escorts and slaves escorted to the Marriam. In the meantime, is there anything in particular we can assist you with? We are entirely at your service."

Berenice inclined her head in acknowledgement of this offer. "My brother King Agrippa II has arrived from Rome and is in Alexandria. He comes from Caesar, who has rewarded his faithful service to the empire with the addition of the cities of Tiberias and Taricheae in Galilee and Julias in Perea, with their dependant towns and villages, to his dominion".

Florus was stunned at this reply. Bile burned at the back of his throat, and he coughed to hide his discomfort.

With a slight smile and a lowering of her eyelids, her thick lashes shielding a glint of satisfaction, Berenice continued smoothly "I have come to Jerusalem to perform a Nazarite vow. This requires I be in the Holy City thirty days".

The Procurator shifted in his chair and studded the nails of his left hand. "The city is dangerous lady. Passions are running high. Terrorists commit murder daily. Honest citizens as well as Roman soldiers are assassinated to foster insecurity. In the name of *nationalism* riots are created. Thousands are being killed in disturbances which occur almost daily." The Procurator paused, but getting no response ended abruptly "You would do well to return to your brother while it is still safe to do so".

Berenice looked up and held the procurator's gaze, her face taught with anger at the veiled insult. Getting no reply the Procurator continued smugly "I will provide you with a cohort of heavy infantry and a squadron of cavalry to augment your forces. They will escort you as far as the border with Galilee whence no doubt" he concluded sarcastically "your brother can provide for your safety against the thieving Jewish scum that roams the country, killing and burning in the name of freedom".

A dish of plums stood on the low alabaster table. Berenice selected one and with a tiny jewelled dagger taken from her sleeve, proceeded to peel it. Without looking at the procurator, she replied with studied casualness. "I will return to Chalcis under the protection of King Agrippa, for we agreed I would await his arrival in his palace".

There was a slight emphasis on *his* palace, which caused Florus to tighten his lips. But he remained silent.

"The king arrives directly. However, he has Caesar's business to conduct before we return, so we will remain in the city until this has been concluded and I have completed my vows." Before the procurator could say anything she continued "I have sent messengers to the King at Alexandria to acquaint him of the situation." Again Florus would have interrupted but an upraised hand indicated that she had not finished. "When the King comes, Excellency, it will be at the head of an army".

The Procurator leaped to his feet, his face flushed with anger. "You have no authority to invite a foreign army to enter my province, particularly the Holy City. You will leave at once for your brother's kingdom and advise him to keep his troops at home."

Berenice stood up. "You forget yourself Procurator. I can only assume it is the result of the strain you are under." Florus would have interrupted her but she ground on relentlessly. "My brother the King has duties and responsibilities in this city, both as a Jew and the servant of Caesar. It is not by my authority or your leave, that he will come here, but Caesar's".

Without waiting for a reply Berenice rose and marched out of the room. As she reached the door war she stopped "It is the custom of the King to stay in his own palace when he visits Jerusalem on the Emperor's business. We would be grateful if you would vacate it as soon as possible so that all may be made ready to receive him".

Florus was incandescent with rage but he dared not ignore the demand that he quit the palace. In a filthy temper he moved into the Hippicus fortress, where huge crowds gathered daily, shrieking and lamenting, complaining bitterly about the Procurator's behaviour. For a time he ignored them while he pondered his next move. It was Marcus who persuaded him to act.

The pair was alone in Florus' private apartments sharing a flagon of wine. The *tribune*, voicing his concerns, said "The crowds are becoming bolder in their complaints. Their slanders might reach the ears of Rome. The bastard nationalists egg them on. They take inactivity to mean weakness".

Florus glared at the *Tribune*. "The damned bitch needs spaying".

Marcus was delighted at his master's anger but didn't take the request against Berenice seriously. "I would love to let her feel what a real man's like. A bit different to being diddled by her pansy brother".

"The whole army can fuck her for all I care", Florus grated, "but she mustn't leave this city alive."

Marcus licked his lips. He and his men enjoyed gang rape. The more well-bred the victim, the greater the pleasure in her humiliation. He wasn't, however, reckless. He had survived too many hard and often brutal wars to simply charge in without regard to consequences. "Agrippa is well in with Caesar and his army is a force to be reckoned with".

The Procurator tapped the side of his nose and with a conspiratorial smile said "We shall send him her body with full military honours. I will personally lead the column and express my condolences on her death. Murdered by the mob, who were angered at her presence in the city on account of her love for her brother".

Marcus grinned happy that the blame could so easily be shifted to the Jews.

Florus stood and stretched and said jovially "Get your fat arse in gear and give that fucking mob what for. A few swift, short actions. A few thousand dead will stir things up. Burn some streets down, loot their shops and screw some of their women". Marcus nodded, agreeing enthusiastically.

"If we stick it to them hard, fast and very nastily, the bitch will complain and" said Florus "to do that she will have to leave the palace".

"We can gaff her like a hooked fish", concluded Marcus.

"Wrong", snapped the Procurator. "She will die trampled to death by the mob as you and your men fight to save her".

During the next three days, Marcus harried the citizens of Jerusalem. Craftily he didn't confront the large crowd that gathered in the city's main square, but constantly sprang up where least expected to strike hard and fast. Day and night made no difference to the German. A district or a street would suddenly be surrounded and cordoned off, and trumpets blown as a signal for his men to explode into action. Cavalry and heavy infantry would charge down streets killing everything in their path. Doors were smashed down and before the terrified occupants could flee, they were hacked to pieces. Possessions were scattered in a search for valuables that were hastily snatched up, before a torch was hurled into the building.

Berenice responded to this savagery by repeatedly sending in her own small cavalry troop. Often they arrived too late to do any good and when they weren't, they suffered heavy losses.

At the end of day two of the terror, she had taken ten per cent losses. Her officers grew anxious about their continuing ability to protect her, which was their first duty.

Sick at heart at the butchery she appealed to the High Priest and the city's leading citizens to discuss the situation. Among them was Menahem Ben Judas, a wealthy and influential Galilean, who was also a fanatical nationalist and secret leader of the Sicarii,. Not that they needed any persuasion to come. It was decided they would present themselves to the Procurator as penitents. They would beg mercy for the people, they would appeal to Florus for Caesar's mercy, for a return to normality. To achieve this end, it was agreed amongst themselves that they would accept any reasonable conditions.

The next day, the crowds, subdued and weeping, made their way towards the Hippicus fortress. The senior priests tore their vestments and led the slowly moving mass of people. They rolled like lava across the city. Pouring ash into their hair, the priests begged the people to avoid violence, no matter what the provocation. Ananus personally pleaded with them not to be goaded into some intemperate response.

With his head covered in ashes that smeared his face and fouled his beard, his magnificent ceremonially robes ritually torn, Ananus beseeched the solemn silent crowd that had swollen to thousands. "Do not provoke the Procurator to commit some unpardonable outrage".

He dared not say more, but Berenice did. With her head shaved and smeared with ash, wearing a simple shift of coarse wool and going barefoot as was the custom of those who took a Nazarite vow, she climbed onto a low wall and addressed the crowd. "Brothers and sisters listen to your High Priest, for his advice stands between you and death. Be patient. King Agrippa will soon be with you. Petition him, for he is one of you and loves you".

A low rumble of assent greeted this remark. "He finds favour with Caesar and has Caesar's ear. Be not provoked but let us go to the Procurator in peace". She paused and raised her hand in the direction of Ananus, eyes flushing with passion. "Your High Priest asks for Caesar's mercy for all of us. Let us hope the Procurator will hear our cry and these unhappy disputes are laid to rest".

With Berenice and Ananus leading the way, the principal citizens and city counsellors and the huge crowd surged towards the Hippicus where Florus awaited them.

The cessation of violence annoyed the procurator, who was reaping handsome profits from it. He had hoped that it could be nurtured into a full scale revolt, which would make him even richer, so when Berenice approached the judgement seat he glanced coldly at the barefooted figure who knelt before him. "Excellency the people prostrate themselves before you. They pledge their loyalty to Caesar, to the Empire, and they acknowledge your sovereignty over them, as the Emperor's appointed representative. The people beg to return to your favour. They beg your forgiveness for any unintentional wrong. They humbly ask for your pardon and beg that peace be restored between us".

"Madam, I await your brother so that I can present him with the bill for the outrages your people have committed – though what price I should set for loyal Roman soldiers, who were murdered defending the city against assassins, I don't know." He raised his eyes to stare coldly at the silent crowd. "Ungrateful Jews", he continued, "who spit on Roman peace, who fret and chafe at the Empire's just laws, who reject her gods and murder her soldiers, who kill each other in your lunatic sectarian squabbles, who dare demand peace without any consideration of reparations". He smiled without warmth and continued "Perhaps the officials and priests with you would care to name a figure".

Berenice swallowed hard to contain her anger. Ananus, seeing her discomfiture, approached the dais and dropping to his knees, head bowed, said "Excellency, reparations will be made to assuage any hurt that has been done, but tell us what we must do to find favour in your heart. We are truly sorry that events have conspired to turn your heart against us. Let us prove our loyalty. Tell us what we must do to return to your favour".

With feigned reluctance Florus said "Very well. Tomorrow two *cohorts* arrive from Caesarea. Let the people go out to meet them and welcome them to the city with flowers and greetings. Let the people lead them into the city as friends and protectors, as fellow subjects of Rome. Let them pledge their loyalty to Rome, to the empire, and her soldiers".

In spite of Berenice's protestations, for she was suspicious of the sudden change of heart, the High Priest agreed and said he would organise the reception.

At the back of the crowd Menahem listened to these affirmations of loyalty from the Jews with a satisfaction he didn't bother to conceal. Signalling to a number of his followers who were mingling with the crowd, he whispered instructions. "Call a meeting for tonight".

Marcus, who had been somewhat perplexed by the Procurator's sudden generosity of spirit, was reassured when he received his orders in private. "Take half a dozen men and your best horses. Rendezvous tonight with the commander of the approaching *cohorts*. You'll carry orders that every man is to be instructed not to return the greetings of the Jews. These orders warn them that the Jews are only pretending to offer them a welcome. They are not to allow any Jew to approach them. They will be walking into a Jewish trap, for concealed amongst them are Sicarii. If they are insulted or provoked in any way, they are to defend themselves".

Marcus assured the Procurator, that if any insult was offered to Roman soldiers, the perpetrators would be punished without mercy. With an anticipatory gleam in his eyes, the *tribune* hurried away to pick the men who would ride with him within the hour.

In Jerusalem a handful of men slipped through the dusk to an inn, where in a back room the red headed figure of Menahem

Ben Judas and his most trusted followers were waiting for them. Menahem's red hair signalled a fiery and impetuous nature, prone to act on an impulse without too much regard for the consequences.

Nevertheless, the men who gathered round the table to share a simple meal had been with him a long time, trusting him implicitly. Many were related and shared ties of blood. His second in command, Eleazor Ben Jair, was his nephew.

The low roofed upstairs room ran the whole length of the building. Approached by a narrow staircase, it was guarded by a man sitting on an upturned box nursing a cup of wine. A cord, concealed by the staircase's handrail, ran from the bottom of the stair to the top, passing through a hole drilled into the door, terminating in a tiny bell. The cord at the bottom of the stairs was within six inches of the watcher's hand. It could be used to signal the conspirators, with nobody in the downstairs part of the building being any the wiser. Menahem Ben Judas rose from his chair and the chattering group became silent. "Brethren, the time has come. We attack Masada in ten days' time".

These men had waited a long time for this moment. Many like their leader were Galilean; all of them shared a burning hatred of the Romans. A satisfied murmur rumbled around the room. Menahem continued "We have sworn members of our organisation in key positions in the fortress. They know what they have to do. They are patiently awaiting the order to strike. My nephew Eleazor Ben Jair, will take that order tomorrow morning, when he delivers supplies." The moment was at hand. In the lamp light, eyes gleamed with satisfaction. These were hard men, who had sacrificed a lot to become freedom fighters. Many of them had suffered personally under Roman rule. Not just the imposition of taxes. In the struggle for freedom, they had lost family members, had their homes confiscated, their sons and daughters sold into slavery.

It had taken years of careful planning to infiltrate the civilian population who worked at the fortress. Many were slaves, who actually stayed in the fortress overnight. Other civilians were admitted to the fortress from time to time to deliver supplies. The Sicarii now had enough men inside the fortress who were not only sympathetic to their cause, they had been recruited into their organisation and acknowledged Menahem as their leader.

"With Masada taken, we divide our forces. Eleazor Ben Jair will assume command of the fortress and from there, will attack every town and village within a fifty miles radius". He paused to sip from his goblet. "In Judaea all Roman garrisons are to be destroyed. Where the people fail to support us, their villages will be burnt to the ground; their inhabitants put to death".

This last brought an uneasy shuffling of feet. They were used to assassinating fellow Jews for political purposes. Murder and torture were their everyday stock in trade. But putting whole Jewish communities to the sword?

Menahem pressed on relentlessly. "A Jew who supports Rome is as much your enemy as any Roman. Either can cause your death. Both keep you in poverty. Our fellow Jews are either for us or against us - there is no middle ground. My enemy's enemy is my friend".

Along the length of the table fists pounded the table in agreement. Few doubted that some of them would die in the coming assault, but they were resolved. Freedom or death. They met their leader's eye; clenched fists were raised in salute. A slightly built rabbi, a young man who had spent his entire life as a scholar, asked the question which had formed in others' minds. "What follows Masada?"

"It will take time for the news to reach Rome and for Rome to respond", was the answer. "In the meantime the Roman forces garrisoned throughout Palestine will hole up and keep to their barracks".

Before Menahem could continue another voice was heard, "What about the legions in Syria, and the client Kings in the north who have sworn allegiance to Rome?"

Other excited voices joined in the questioning. Nazarius, a Judean who was a Levite in the Temple, ground out "What about fucking Florus, and that bastard Cestius? Both command many men and they are well armed and", he added viciously, "what about the turncoat Agrippa and his cunt of a sister?"

Menahem laughed at the storm of questioning that had broken out, and banged on the table to bring them to order. "Within Masada is Herod's armoury, a vast collection of weapons. Enough to equip an army of thousands". A thoughtful silence settled on the room. They had forgotten about this priceless cache. "I will arm those citizens of Jerusalem who will swear loyalty to our cause, and attack the city from within. We will lay siege to the Roman garrison the Antonia and kill every Jew who will not fight for his freedom".

Joseph Ben Levi, an older man who had lost his entire family in the recent Roman action, intervened. "Hundreds of thousands of foreign Jews and their families are in the city for Passover. How will we care for them if we start a rebellion within the Holy City?"

"We won't" said Menahem. "Now is the time to sort the wheat from the chaff. Those who will take up a sword and fight for their freedom are martyrs for God. Those who won't are servants of Satan and must die".

At this death sentence on fellow Jews, many of the men looked down at their plates, unsure of whether they should intervene or not. Menahem, knowing better than anybody what was to come, said. "We will take the Holy City and, with Masada, hold it. Our action will cause other nationalist groups to strike. John, the son of Levi of Gischala, will attack in Galilee, though more" he added knowingly "for his own benefit than the cause of Jewish freedom. However, he will kill Romans and we can kill him when it suits us".

"Then there is Eleazar son of Ananias, leader of the Zealots," interrupted Joseph Ben Levi. "He and his followers will fight to control the Temple and ultimately the Holy City, for they know this is where the nation's centre of power and wealth lies".

Menahem nodded in agreement. "Eleazar and his Zealots are a problem. Initially we will offer an alliance. When this has served its purpose the Zealots, along with the Sadduccean priesthood, must die. We will rule the Temple, the City and Israel".

Loud cheers greeted this, but a few cooler heads wondered who precisely would rule and how. Did Menahem see himself as both priest and king?

7

The city's most influential Jews were making their way to the Temple in sombre mood to listen to what their High Priest had to say. They clustered in groups according to their class or profession. Protected by bodyguards, many of the nationalist leaders who were rivals for the people's support mingled with the steadily growing crowd.

A hum of conversation rose as men discussed the recent outbreaks of violence.

While they waited for the High Priest to appear, each man noted the other. Suspicion was everywhere. Nobody trusted the man they didn't know. The nationalists, as well as scanning the crowd in general, took a special note of their rivals, wondering if the time had come for an alliance against the common enemy, Rome.

Pharisees, whose religious doctrine distinguished them from the Sadducees, had swallowed their dislike of the High Priest who was a Sadducee, and turned out in numbers. They loathed the nationalists who stirred up fear and hatred with their sectarian murders. They dreaded a civil war that would pit Jew against Jew.

They had stared into the abyss that was war with Rome and recoiled in horror. Along with wealthy landowners and other citizens of influence, they came to represent the interest of the ordinary citizen as well as their own. War with Rome represented total disaster. Somehow it had to be averted.

There were a few among them who, though being Jews by birth, had little interest in religion. Who had decided, if there was a God, he took no interest in the affairs of men. They reasoned that men were born, lived and died like any other living thing, without rhyme or reason. They believed that 'when you're dead you're done.' These atheists wisely concealed their views and went through the motions. They attended the Temple and brought their children up as Jews. To them being Jewish was an accident of birth.

Such a man was Samuel, who for the first time in his life had penetrated as far as the Temple's inner courts. Samuel, a wealthy landowner who lived in northern Galilee, had come to Jerusalem for the festival of *Passover*. His being in the city coincided with the High Priest making an appeal to prominent and influential Jews, to meet and discuss how law and order could be restored.

Samuel stared in open-mouthed wonder, first at the Corinthian gates themselves. Made of bronze, each door was forty-five feet high and twenty-two and a half feet wide that required teams of Temple priests to perform the opening and closing rituals. On each side of the gates, massive stone pillars supported twin sixty foot high fortified towers.

Samuel strolled through the gates which opened out onto a vast court, where the city's dignitaries where assembling. On the other side of the terrace he could see the walls and gates of the *court of the women* where a large crowd of women had gathered to hear what the High Priest had to say. Among them was Queen Berenice, frustrated at not being allowed to participate in the meeting.

With time in hand, Samuel turned east and made his way to the Sanctuary, to stare dry mouthed at its magnificence. Plated all over with sheets of gold and silver, its fifty feet wide doors soared seventy feet high.

In front of the sanctuary stood the altar, cut from a single block of basalt seventy five feet square, twenty-two and a half feet high, its four square corners jutting out and shaped like horns. Samuel also noticed that the altar was positioned on a gentle slope leading up to it from the south. Priests, who had decreed this, had also laid down the rules for its construction and had supervised the work, for it had been fashioned without the use of iron and once in position, no iron was ever allowed to come into contact with it. Round the sanctuary and the altar ran a thirty six inch high parapet of beautiful rose marble that separated the laity from the priests.

Samuel stood outside this barrier, his fingers resting lightly on the sun warmed stone. Before him was the Holiest building on earth. Thoughtfully he studied the one hundred and five feet high walls that protected it. These were pierced by a single arch that opened into a vast roofless chamber, its walls sheathed in gold. From where he stood, Samuel could see the gates set in the opposite wall which led to the second chamber. Above them were grapevines from which, fashioned in gold, hung bunches of grapes as big as a man.

The Sanctuary itself, the Holy Temple, was situated behind these massive gates and walls. Reached by a flight of fifteen steps, each tread was cut from an individual marble block. Seen from the front, the Sanctuary was the same height and width – a hundred and fifty feet each way. Some of the stones used in its construction were sixty eight feet long, nine feet wide, and eight and a half feet deep. The whole building was overlaid with gold.

In the sun's first light, it was like a second sun, its light so bright it was impossible to look at it directly. Samuel knew from his brother-in-law, who was a priest, that a fabulous Babylonian tapestry hung across the doors of the Sanctuary's second chamber. One hundred feet high, fifty feet wide and richly embroidered, this priceless curtain depicted the whole vista of creation.

Through the gates lay the ground floor of the Sanctuary, a windowless chamber ninety feet high made entirely from white marble. Positioned around the walls of the outer chamber were three fabled lamps of solid gold. World famous as works of art, each lamp had seven arms, branching from a twenty foot tall central column. The seven arms with their perpetually burning lamps symbolised the seven planets.

The innermost chamber measured thirty feet square and was separated by a cloth of gold. This inner sanctum was the Holy of Holies. It contained absolutely nothing. It had held the Ark of the Covenant that had disappeared six hundred years ago when Nebuchadnezzar, King of Babylon, destroyed Jerusalem, burnt the Temple and enslaved the surviving Jews. Re-sanctified, the Holy of Holies had been rededicated to God. Inviolable, unapproachable, this is where the God of Israel resided. On the Day of Atonement the High Priest would take off his splendid robes of office and put on a simple shift of coarse linen, to prostrate himself and in an act of atonement for God's chosen people, offer up prayers of repentance for sins committed, and ask for forgiveness.

With its courts of walls and towers, the vast Temple complex was a city within a city defended by three fortress towers. One of these, the massive Antonia, was attached to it by colonnades and staircases. These staircases led to both of the other two fortresses and the Temple itself. Roman soldiers used these staircases to reach the Temple walls where they were always positioned, fully armed, to watch for any sign of public disorder.

Samuel glanced up. As expected they were there, impassive as statues, the sun glinting off their helmets and weapons, living symbols of oppression. Bile rose in his throat. With a tightening of his lips, he turned away and strode back towards the Corinthian gates.

The commanding sound of the *shofar*, announcing the arrival of the High Priest, reminded him why he was there. Resplendent in his robes of office, Ananus had appeared on the dais. The magnificence of his costume gave the High priest tremendous presence.

The High Priest addressed the crowd. "Brethren, daily the people suffer injustices. In their suffering they grow angry and strike out. Jew is killing Jew. The grieving of the widows and orphans grows louder as husbands are killed for no reason."

The High priest paused, but not a word came from his audience. He continued "The authorities are provoked. Soldiers murdered, bringing the retribution of Rome on our heads. The countryside is ravaged by bandits – anything is permitted to any man, in the name of liberty. Yet every man having lost his liberty lives in perpetual fear".

This time when the High Priest paused a low murmur of agreement ran through his audience. Encouraged he went on "By the authority of our office and the high regard the people have for our wisdom, we must restore law and order and the nation to tranquillity."

"Romans go home" an anonymous voice shouted from the centre of the crowd.

The High Priest raised his hands, his face flushed with anger at this provocative remark, only too aware of the Roman soldiers lining the walls of the colonnades who would report it to their superiors. "It is" he replied, "precisely that kind of seditious and provocative nonsense which is stirring the people up and turning the Romans against us."

"The Procurator is causing most of the trouble". Again it was the anonymous voice. "He presses us too hard". This time there was a sullen rumble of agreement from the crowd.

The High Priest called for quiet, but more and more people began to shout. They hurled abuse at the Procurator Gessius Florus and cursed him.

In the end Ananus had to call on his trumpeters to restore silence. "Be warned" the High Priest grated, "Rome will not tolerate disloyalty. The treatment you have received so far is nothing to that which will come down on your heads if civil disorder continues." Before he could be interrupted he continued hurriedly "We are subjects of Rome not citizens. We are bound by the laws of fealty that that status affords to us." This last was a reminder – a bitter reminder – that as a subject nation they were required to pay tribute to their masters over and above normal taxation. There was also the unspoken reminder that they did not enjoy the same civil rights and privileges as citizens of Rome.

An elderly Pharisee, who was also a magistrate, respected for his piety and loved for his scrupulous fairness when administering the law, pushed to the front of the crowd. "If we are bound by the laws and rules of the Empire's subject peoples, we are still entitled to Roman justice under Roman law". Not sure where this was leading, but sensing battle had been joined by old adversaries, the crowd roared its support before falling silent. What reply would the Sadducean High Priest give?

Concealing his anger Ananus replied, "Roman justice goes hand in hand with loyalty to Caesar. We should all use our powers, our influence, to persuade the people to demonstrate their love for Caesar." Jeers greeted this smooth response.

But the elderly Pharisee hadn't finished. "It is not the people, but the Procurator Gessius Florus who tramples on Rome's laws as he tramples on the people". He had to pause as a deafening shout of agreement greeted this bold statement. The Pharisee continued remorselessly "Let us send our case to Caesar. Let the Emperor judge the rightness of this matter".

Gritting his teeth and inwardly cursing all Pharisees whom he hated from the bottom of his heart, the High priest shrieked "Complaining to Caesar about his Procurator is a dangerous path to take. Does he not have evidence of his troops murdered in cold blood? Are not taxes unpaid? Do not the people of Samaria and Galilee attack each other? We would do well to be careful before we demand of Caesar the removal of his Procurator, whose duty it is to collect those taxes and punish those who take up arms against Rome's authority".

Much grumbling greeted this speech. Many arguments broke out. Suddenly a loud voice rang out. "The people are oppressed, and cruelly abused by a Procurator who has as much regard for them as a butcher for pigs". This shocking statement came from a burly blonde haired man with piercing blue eyes, Benjamon Bar Simon, leader of one of the nationalist factions. It almost silenced the crowd but many found the courage to mutter encouragement.

Meanwhile on the walls, an officer who had been carefully observing the meeting, despatched a soldier to report to the *prefectus* commanding the Antonia that things were warming up and words were flying that, in his view, came close to treason.

Ananus was becoming desperate as he cast around in his mind how he might draw this disastrous meeting to a close, bitterly regretting having called it in the first place.

He was saved by the Pharisee. "King Agrippa will soon be with us. Is he not loved and respected, not only by his own subjects, but by the Jews of this city? Let us put our case before him and ask him for counsel, for not only is the King's wisdom a blessing to the Jews, it is valued by Caesar, who trusts him to rule in his name".

The High Priest, glad to be off the hook, hastily approved this suggestion, adding in a harsh voice "While we wait for the King, do nothing to provoke Roman authority. Use your influence with the people to persuade them to obey Rome's laws".

As the crowd broke up the High Priest, drenched with sweat and nursing a blinding headache, tottered back into the Temple silently cursing the Romans and the Nationalists in equal measure. He must, he decided, speak with the Procurator and his superior Cestius Gallus, the governor of Syria.

Before he could send a messenger to the Antonia begging for an audience with both, who had not yet left for Syria, a second message arrived. The townspeople who had gone out to meet the arriving Roman *cohorts* had been cut to pieces. Survivors were staggering into the city with tales of wholesale slaughter. Thousands of dead and dying Jews, men woman and children, were scattered for miles across the barren plain surrounding the city. They had met the approaching Romans with songs of praise, garlands of flowers and refreshments of fruit and water. When these and their greetings had been ignored and rejected, they had grown angry at the insult, starting to curse the soldiers. This had been the signal agreed with Florus for them to attack the unarmed civilians without mercy. Slumped in his throne, the High Priest started to think about survival. A hundred and twenty years ago the Romans under Pompey had destroyed Jerusalem and the Temple. History, thought the terrified priest, was about to repeat itself.

Amal had also gone to the Temple dressed in the clothes of a peasant. With her face veiled she mingled with the crowds in the court of the women. Horrified at what she had heard, and fearful of what must surely follow, she was on the point of leaving the court when she spotted Berenice. Pushing her way through the crowd she made her way to the Queen's side. In a low voice she said, "Highness, I must speak with you, but we must be discreet."

Berenice was startled by this sudden request, but gave no indication that she had been addressed, other than a quick sideways flick of her eyes to pinpoint who had spoken to her. Without turning her head she replied, "Who are you?"

"I am Amal, a slave owned by the priest Eleazar, governor of the Temple". Berenice noticed that she did not say in Eleazar's household. Without it being said, both women knew that the other was aware of her position as Eleazar's mistress.

"What do you want of me?"

"Nothing, my lady. I am here to warn you of a plot to kill you".

Berenice walked slowly down the court keeping close to the wall. Amal kept pace with her, but walked slightly behind her. Around them eddied the great mob of people. "Who wishes me harm?"

"Eleazar is the secret leader of the Zealots. He is planning to assassinate his father Ananias, the former High Priest of all Israel, then kill the current High Priest of all Israel Ananus, and assume his office. Importantly, he has been waiting for the Sicarii to attack the Romans. He will now make his own strike, but not against the Romans – he is determined to be master of Jerusalem".

"How do you know all of this, and why should any of it threaten my life". Berenice knew the answer to the question, but asked it to test her informant. Inwardly she was in turmoil. This unknown women was claiming that the Jews were about to start a civil war and take on the Romans as well. It was madness.

"Eleazar is no different to any other man in bed. He needs to talk to someone about his hopes, his plans, his ambitions. Mistresses are more discreet than wives; they have to be, they can be removed without any questions being asked".

"But why am I personally threatened," asked Berenice.

"Caesar has favoured your brother the King and enlarged his kingdom. He is known as a loyal supporter of Rome.

The nationalists want him to come over to them in the hope of getting him to change sides. Your death will be blamed on the Romans. Your murder will be laid at Florus' door".

Berenice turned to face Amal, "Why do you tell me all of this? If Eleazar even suspects you of betraying him, your death would not be easy".

"Two reasons. The Romans will win in the end. I want to be on the winning side". Amal became silent.

"And the second reason?" prompted Berenice.

"My mother", murmured Amal, "was a slave at Herod's court. The King bedded my mother but never acknowledged me. We are kinsmen, you and I. My second reason for warning you is the tie of blood".

Berenice mulled this over. "You can never prove such a tie, but your guile in coming to me betrays a certain Herodian quality. How do you know I won't betray you to Eleazar?"

"If it was in your interest to do so you wouldn't hesitate" replied Amal, "but for the moment you will wait to see what happens and then decide what to do about me. In the meantime stay in your palace – keep your guards on their toes and send a message to King Agrippa".

Berenice acknowledged this whispered advice with a barely perceptible nod. She knew what risks Amal had taken in confiding in her. She also knew that, if accurate, the information she had been given could save her life and probably her brother's as well.

"It may become dangerous for you to stay in Eleazar's house. Come to the palace. I will give instructions that you are to be admitted at any time, day or night without question. If what you have told me turns out to be the truth, we will all be struggling to survive. However I guarantee you my protection and that of my brother the King".

"Thank you my Lady", and Amal was gone, lost in the crowds. One thing Berenice had been right about was the power of Herodian blood. Amal had taken her first step towards freedom. As yet she had no plan as to how she could achieve power - only a burning, ruthless ambition that her father would have admired.

8

Menahem Ben Jair, grandson of Judas of Galilee the founder of the Zealot party, nursed the double ambition of ruling Judaea and getting rid of the Romans. The former would have to come first. Attempting either meant putting his life on the line. The Jewish priesthood would not hesitate to eliminate any challenge to their authority - a view the civil authority and the wealthy ruling classes had in common with the occupying Romans.

A consummate politician and a natural leader, Menahem hated the Romans and despised any Jew who co-operated with them. He and his followers had a simple policy. Assassinate any Roman whenever the opportunity presented itself. To carry out these killings, he added a separate wing to the Zealot party - a ruthless group of killers, Sicarii, who carried out the murders Menahem ordered.

The son of a merchant, Menahem's world was that of the caravan; a world of hardship and danger, of journeying through hostile landscapes. He and his kind were handy with a sword and expert with a knife. Trading as far as India and China, away from home for two years and more, they were subject to attack from bandits. Necessity taught them proficiency in close quarter fighting and skill in the use of a variety of weapons.

At twenty six, Menahem had been accompanying his father on such journeys from the age of ten. Slight of build, he had a sinewy strength and desert bred hardiness. Respected for his business acumen, men acknowledged him as a proud, fiercely independent man, who hated the Romans. To the few that knew him well he was a religious fanatic. A fundamentalist who believed he was an instrument of God, charged with the task *of cleansing the Holy land of Israel, of those who were an offence to his God* - pagans who worshipped idols and the gods of earth, fire, and water, who practiced magic and sorcery. Be they Roman, Jew or Arab, they had to die. Years ago he had planned his strategy. He knew that Jewish discontent with the brutally oppressive Roman regime would eventually erupt into rebellion. When it did he would need to be ready - but to do what?

For months he had wrestled with the problem and had got nowhere. In the end he did what his ancestors had done in similar circumstances. He had gone into the desert to fast and pray. There he found the answer; the Roman stronghold of Masada, the symbol of Roman invincibility, the impregnable, totally unassailable, self-sufficient fortress built by Herod the Great. In a flash of inspiration, which he believed to be divine revelation from his God, Menahem knew what he had to do and how. He had to take Masada and arm the Zealots with the arsenal of weapons stored there. When Herod built Masada he had stocked it with enough weapons to equip an army of ten thousand men – insurance against the unforeseen.

When he returned to Jerusalem, he selected twelve of his most loyal followers. Sworn to secrecy, they were given their orders. Over a period of months, posing as cooks and butchers, they were to infiltrate Masada's civilian staff. Sewn into the seams of their clothes were the deadly crystals of poison they planned to use. Inside the fortress they waited for Menahem's orders.

These would come with one of the traders who delivered fresh supplies and news of the outside world. After months of waiting, convinced that God had spoken to him, he called his army of secret supporters to a rendezvous outside Jerusalem.

They came on horse and camel to bivouac in the desert away from prying eyes, their black tents set in a protective laager. Amid the whirl and rasp of summer insects, smoke from their camp fires hung like incense in the evening stillness. Menahem greeted the men individually before leading them in prayer. A sacred droning filling the air, as the evening sky darkened into night.

In the circles of campfire light, Menahem told them his secret. How six months earlier he had infiltrated the Roman garrison at Masada with revolutionary brothers, who, when they received a signal, would open the gates of their enemy.

"The time has come, the time is now. We attack in two days' time". Menahem's announcement caught the gathering by surprise.

The staggering importance of what he had said was so improbable, so impossible, that nobody spoke. The only sound the whispering of a shimmering veil of dust, fluted by the wind through the scattered boulders, suddenly drowned by a throaty roar and the rasp of steel as weapons were snatched from their scabbards. Startled by the noise of the wildly cheering men, horses and camels added their own guttural sounds.

By dawn Menahem and his eight hundred fellow rebels were ready to move. As they rode into the desert to take Masada, the spark of revolution burst into flame. Eleazar as Temple Governor, abolished the daily sacrifices offered for Rome and Caesar himself. Eleazar, Priest, nationalist, zealot, had made his move. He had declared war on Rome. Before the high priesthood and city fathers had time to respond, the Zealots had seized control of the Upper City and the Temple.

Horrified at the rebels' actions, Ananus the High Priest of all Israel, the Chief Priests, Pharisees and Sadducees, and the city's leading citizens and many of the ordinary people, came to plead with the rebels. There followed a day of quarrelling that ended in violence. Stones and other missiles were launched by both sides. Eventually, this long range skirmishing degenerated into a more deadly confrontation. Seizing whatever weapons came to hand – axes, hammers, knives – the two sides fought hand to hand screaming, hacking, tearing and punching indiscriminately.

Horrified at what was happening, the most influential citizens sent messengers to Florus and King Agrippa, begging both to come to the city and put down the revolutionaries before matters got completely out of hand. Florus was delighted with the news, and did nothing. The chaos of civil war would provide perfect cover for him to plunder the country.

King Agrippa had *civil* power in Jerusalem, for he had been given the right by the Romans to appoint the High Priest of Israel. Filled with misgivings, he responded to the appeal for help, despatching two thousand horse archers from Arantas under Darius his cavalry commander, along with Philip the son of Jacimus his senior general.

What followed was seven days of mutual slaughter, the rebels showing reckless courage against the King's horsemen who fought to get possession of the Temple and drive out those who were polluting it.

As Eleazar battled to hold what he had taken and advance on the Upper City, he wondered if the time was right to kill Menahem; a thought that hardened into certainty when, during a lull in the fighting, one of his lieutenants brought him news of the impossible. Masada had fallen. Menahem would be hailed as a national hero when he returned to Jerusalem, bringing with him the weapons and armour looted from the fortress. That would make him more than a threat – he would be a rival. A rival for the ultimate prize. Control of Jerusalem and eventually Judaea.

His assassination had just become a priority.

9

Berenice was in one of the Palace's many gardens when the commander of her personal guard, Nathan - an Idumaean who had been in her brother's service since boyhood - arrived to discuss the murder of the Jews, who had formed a welcoming committee for the reinforcements arriving from Caesarea. Nathan also brought confirmation of the taking of Masada. The murder of its garrison was tantamount to a declaration of war. Roman forces in the region (which meant Cestius Gallus, Governor of Syria) had to enforce Roman authority.

A heavily laden bee hummed an erratic path in front of her face. Absentmindedly she waved it away. Nathan stood silently, giving her time to take in the report he had just delivered.

He felt the warmth of the sun on his armour. The garden was walled and trapped the sun's warmth. He could smell the perfume of a magnolia, its sweet odour mingling with the lighter scent of the carefully tended beds of flowers and shrubs. Shade was provided by the many palms that had been carefully grouped by the garden's Arab designer who, true to his traditions, had incorporated several fountains and softly murmuring streams that filled the garden with the delicate sound of water burbling over stone, splashing gently, its sprays dazzling in the sun. A haven of peace and quiet designed to sooth the spirit and calm the mind.

Berenice sat in an arbour with several of her personal slaves, its latticed shade protection from the sun. Her grim faced commander waited patiently for his orders.

"Rome will exact a reckoning for this day's work that will echo around the world". She spoke as much to herself as the Idumaean, who stood helmet in hand.

"Lady you must look to your own safety. The procurator has already left the city for Caesarea. The *Legate* is making arrangements to return to Syria. They both fear being separated from their main forces".

"Nathan we must strengthen the guard immediately. Treachery and assassination served the nationalists well at Masada – it might be tried again".

The man nodded. "No stranger will be admitted, Lady, for any reason, from this moment on. "And", he continued, "the guard will be doubled and officers will carry out spot checks day and night".

Berenice, nodding her approval, said "The *Legate* may call on us before he leaves. He could even demand I accompany him on the pretext that it is for my own safety. I could," she ended bitterly, "become a hostage".

Nathan frowned but didn't hesitate. "Refuse him admission".

"On what grounds?"

"I will say you are ill Lady and have orders to admit no one other than the King".

"You would refuse entry to the *Legate*? Caesar's representative. You would be risking the charge of treason, punishable by death".

The swarthy face split with a mirthless grin. "If I let Cestius through these gates the odds are there will be treachery and I will die with a knife in my back. If he is refused entry, and is stupid enough to attack, I may fall in battle but I won't go down alone".

Berenice smiled and gently touched the man's arm.

"Go Nathan, instruct your men to admit no one". She paused, suddenly remembering her meeting in the *court of women*. "The exception is the slave Amal. Day or night she *must* be admitted and I am to be told of her arrival. Tell your men to treat her with respect".

Nathan nodded and assured her that he would relay her orders.

Berenice continued "Be assured that when the King arrives he will be told of your loyalty".

The Idumaean touched his forehead with his fingertips and took his leave. He detested the Romans as much as he secretly loved his mistress. As for the Jews of the Holy City, he knew only too well the contempt in which they held all his people – since the time Rome had forced the Jews to accept Herod as their King, who had been born a quarter Jewish and three quarters Idumaean, making him more Arab than Jew.

The feeling was mutual, should they or the Romans come against him he would be ready. As he headed for the guard room, he ran an appreciative eye round the palace's forty five foot high wall. Herod might have been a bastard, he thought, but when it came to building things he wasn't just a genius, he was a military genius.

Two hours later his arrangements were complete. Every man under his command knew what was expected of him. One thing Agrippa had taken from the Romans was the concept of military discipline and duty. The men who fought in the King's army were sworn to the codes of that discipline. Nathan, who had risen through the ranks, was in charge of well-trained disciplined troops who would follow him without question.

When Agrippa arrived ten days later he noted with quiet satisfaction, though with some surprise, the alertness of the men manning the palace walls. He also noted the archers positioned on every tower.

When he and his army swung through the main gate into the outer court to be greeted by Berenice, and Nathan commanding a guard of honour, his practiced eye took in the stacks of war materials readily to hand. He also observed that the opening and the closing of the gate had been covered by cavalry and a triple row of heavily armed infantry. He returned the salute of Nathan and his officers asking dryly "Expecting visitors?"

Stripping off his helmet and gloves he extended a hand to Berenice who dutifully curtsied. "You do well sister to attend our defences, for I have marched through a land on fire these past weeks. But," he continued raising her to her feet and kissing her on both cheeks, "why do you feel so uneasy in the heart of the Holy City?" He waved a hand at the heavily fortified walls. "Are you not protected by Rome? Surely all is lawful and secure here?"

Berenice smiled at the brother she loved above all men. "Now that you are here I am doubly safe. We have much to tell each other, but first refreshment. Nathan will see to your men".

They walked into the castle's sumptuous apartments hand in hand. "I have missed you brother". Her fingers tightened on his.

Agrippa smiled "And I you, sister, we have much to discuss".

While the King bathed, Berenice gave orders for his favourite foods to be prepared. Then attending to her own toilette she thought about the brother she loved and had loved since they were children. From a very early age she had stolen into his bed. With the passage of time innocent embraces had become more passionate.

They expanded their sexual knowledge and over the years added to it by experiment. At sixteen she had been married to Marcus son of Alexander, head magistrate of the Jews in Alexandria. On his early death she was married to her father's brother Herod of Chalcis, who died within a year. She then sought the protection of her brother with whom she lived before marrying her third husband Polemon, King of Cilicia, but she deserted him after six unhappy months and returned to Agrippa who had never married.

They came together like a pair of otters. Tumbling and rolling across the immense bed. Agrippa was tall and slim, hard bodied. He was a professional soldier. Olive skinned with tightly curled black hair, he was clean shaven in the Roman fashion – a practice that scandalised the Jews.

Entwined in total harmony, seeking each other hungrily, Berenice rubbed herself against him, teasing him with her body, agile as a feral cat. Agrippa parted the opening of her sex with his fingers and lowered his head. With lips and teeth he fluttered kisses across her breasts and belly, rasping his tongue across her clitoris, feeling her quiver with pleasure.

Berenice was on fire, her breath was becoming ragged. Their lips met as though they needed to feast on each other. She offered herself to him, opening her sex with slender jewelled fingers. With eyes closed in ecstasy she felt him sheath himself to the hilt. The familiar musk of his body found her nostrils. She sighed with pleasure.

Agrippa's face congested with passion. He buried his head against her shoulder. She could hear his muffled panting like a stallion blowing dust with its nostrils. The power of his thrusts increased. He lifted her almost bodily from the bed. She shivered under the delicious impact of his driving hips. Ripples of pleasure ran over her skin, like water skirling across stone.

She gripped the hard brown body firmly between her legs and cried out, ululating at the delicious sensation that started in her belly and ran down her legs. Swept away on a rising tide of passion, she seized his head, fingers hooking in the coarse black curls. Agrippa's eyes were unfocused, blurred by the violence of his own emotions. Berenice cried out as he lifted her buttocks to penetrate deeper, touching the very bottom of her womb. As she began to slide out of control, he felt the muscles in her legs start to tremble. With her heels drumming against his buttocks he thrust hard against her urgency. As she came she felt him stiffen. Her eyelids fluttered. She cried out, half sob, half scream of pleasure.

As she regained her senses, she felt Agrippa place a kiss in the crook of her neck. Tenderly and without passion he stroked her hair. Berenice floated, eyes closed – drifting, weightless -her breathing slowing, steadying. She burrowed against him "I missed you Lord. Without you my life is incomplete".

"And I you my love, but it would have been dangerous to take you to Rome. The Romans, surprisingly, can be prudish at times, yet they are the most depraved of people".

She nibbled his ear. "During the last few weeks Jerusalem hasn't been particularly safe. The procurator has been killing Jews by the thousand".

At this news Agrippa struggled to sit up. Berenice rolled onto her back, her hazel eyes half closed with the languor of their love making. Agrippa's hands cupped her breasts, rolling her nipples under his thumbs, saying "The whole country is in ferment, the nationalists are everywhere stirring up trouble. The Romans are bottled up in their garrison towns. Neither the *Legate* nor the procurator will have an easy time of it crossing the country".

"But", asked Berenice who was beginning to feel a stirring in her loins under the absent minded fondling of her breasts, "they will be safe once they re-join their main forces?"

Agrippa rolled her unresistingly on to her face. Grasping the cheeks of her firmly rounded buttocks, he squeezed hard. She wriggled among the cushions to get comfortable. Agrippa bit both cheeks gently, before kissing where he had bitten.

"Mutiny is contagious; it has already infected Caesarea. When Gallus gets back there, he won't find a single Jew left in the city. The Greeks have carried out a systematic slaughter of its entire Jewish population. Under the pretext of ethnic cleansing, twenty thousand Jews were murdered within the space of a single day".

Berenice rolled her head to one side to reply. As she did so he pushed a cushion under her hips to lift her enticing rump. "That's on the Syrian border. The *Legate* will surely punish the Greeks".

"He will side with the Greeks. It's the Jews who are causing him problems, and dead Jews are peaceful Jews. In reprisal, the Jewish nationalists have sacked Syrian villages and attacked the neighbouring cities of Philadelphia, Heshbon, Gerasa, Pella and Scythopolis. The whole of Syria is filled with fear and confusion. If," he quickly corrected himself "*when* the *Legate* gets back to his main forces, he might survive".

A probing hand slipped between her thighs, bringing Berenice's interest in the *Legate's* problems to a halt. She gave herself up to the deliciously exploring fingers. Berenice smiled contentedly, settling into the yielding cushions of the bed. Sliding his hands under her body Agrippa stretched himself over her back, slipping himself inside her. She moved her buttocks in time to the rhythmic thrusting. When Berenice suddenly convulsed under him, Agrippa pulled her into a kneeling position, driving into her savagely. She screamed, arching backwards, shaking like a hooked fish. With his arms wrapped round her body Agrippa ran a hand down her belly before plunging his fingers into the wet matt furred between her legs, caressing her where his shaft entered her body. She rose in his embrace slippery with sweat. She could feel his teeth at the nape of her neck; she could feel his hands smoothing the inside of her thighs running with juices. Her orgasm flung her head back. She let out a howl of sheer animal pleasure. He held her close, still hard inside her. As she trembled back from the brink, he slid out of her and turned her on her back, hooking her legs over his shoulders and spreading to receive him. The glove of her soft flesh, holding him fast, began to pulse rhythmically.

She crossed her ankles round his neck, her breath rasping. Blindly she reached for him, moaning his name. He matched the rhythm of their bodies. Suddenly she clenched her fists and beat against his chest. He seized her round the waist, back bowed, carried away on a tide of his own. The blood beat in his temples, he could smell her, warm and musky. He groaned with pleasure, his head beginning to swim. Berenice's head thrashed from side to side. Agrippa could feel his sister's orgasm shaking her body. Fingers dug into his back, her eyes rolled back into her head, she keened deep in her throat — a wild, savage sound. He felt the scouring shock of his own release as they fell together, their sweat soaked bodies sliding against each other. Exhausted, they slept in a tumble of arms and legs, entwined as they used to be as children.

It was raining when Amal arrived at the main gate. As she separated herself from the crowds scurrying to find shelter, her approach to the main gate was noted by the guards posted along the walls.

"Visitor main gate". The shouted warning brought a senior officer to the battlements. The officer on duty in the gatehouse tower gave orders to the bowmen in the turrets each side of the gate, to notch their arrows.

If anything more than the lych gate needed to be opened, heavy infantry and more archers would be summoned to fortified positions within the courtyard. The main gates could only be opened in Nathan's presence and even then only on his personal command. Standing orders decreed any other attempt to open them was to be regarded as treachery, the perpetrators to be cut down without any questioning.

The officer guard opened the spy hole on the lych gate. He said nothing, simply staring stonily at the hooded figure.

"I am Amal. Queen Berenice will see me". Amal did her best to keep her voice steady, but her legs were trembling, as much with excitement as fear.

The soldier slammed the spy hole closed and signalled for the small door to be opened for the few seconds it took for Amal to slip inside. By which time Nathan's second-in-command had arrived in the courtyard. He nodded to the duty officer and said to Amal "Come with me". She was led to an anteroom, where a woman and Nathan stood waiting to receive her.

Nathan addressed her in a neutral voice. "I am the commander of the Queen's personal guard. This is Drucilla, the Queen's maid. She will provide you with a change of clothing and some refreshments. In the meantime I will tell the Queen you are here".

Amal smiled. "Thank you sir but my clothes are fine. The shower was a light one".

Nathan smiled bleakly. "Drucilla will assist you to change your clothes. Those are her orders".

Amal reddened slightly. She was to be searched for weapons, poison, anything that could be construed as a threat. "Of course commander, I understand – I wasn't thinking. Forgive me".

Nathan inclined his head and left the room. He was uncertain of this women's status. She was a slave and therefore not entitled to any courtesy, yet she was to have immediate access to the Queen.

He relayed Amal's arrival to a slave of the bed chamber. This was in spite of her being with the King. Berenice's instructions had been explicit. She was to be told of Amal's arrival immediately.

Kneeling outside the door, the slave scratched at a panel. For a moment or two there was no answer, then Berenice appeared. "My lady the Lord Nathan sends his apologies for disturbing you, but a woman who calls herself Amal is in the palace".

"Thank the commander and tell Drucilla to provide Amal with whatever she needs. I will be with her directly".

"What is it, my love?" Agrippa had woken up.

"Amal has sought sanctuary my brother. It's started".

Agrippa was out of bed reaching for his gown almost before Berenice had finished speaking. "Have her brought to my chamber immediately".

Berenice recalled the slave, "Inform Amal the King will see her". Nathan personally escorted a startled Amal to the royal suite where she prostrated herself before Agrippa, who indicated she should rise and invited her to sit.

"You have done us a great service. My sister and I are in your debt". Agrippa smiled as he spoke, attempting to put Amal at ease.

She dipped her head. God she is beautiful thought Agrippa, his face inscrutable, but his sister had sensed the interest and smiled inwardly.

Berenice asked the critical question "What has happened that caused you to leave Eleazar's house?"

"Menahem, son of Judas, a Galilean is leader of the Sicarii. He has reached an agreement with Eleazar".

Agrippa leaned forward in his chair unable to contain himself. "What agreement?"

"Menahem has taken Masada".

"But", interrupted Agrippa with a harsh laugh, "that's impossible. Masada is impregnable".

"Not if you have men on the inside".

"You mean Menahem infiltrated men into the fortress to mingle with the soldiers garrisoned there?"

"Not the soldiers, but the slaves and workers who provide the fortress' day to day services, those who do the fetching and carrying, the cooking and cleaning. Many of them are Sicarii. Masada has fallen". Agrippa stifled a groan.

"The plan", Amal continued, "is to hold the fortress as a rallying point for the rest of the nationalist movement".

Agrippa was silenced. He stared unseeing at the women before him, his mind in turmoil.

"You said he had an agreement with Eleazar", Berenice interjected softly.

"Eleazar has persuaded the priests of the Temple to accept no gift, sacrifice or offering from foreigners".

Agrippa leapt to his feet. "What? Is the man mad? Such an action is tantamount to declaring war on Rome".

"They have abolished the sacrifices offered for Rome and Caesar himself", she continued relentlessly.

"But", spluttered Agrippa, "what of the high priests? What of the Ananus, High Priest of all Israel? Damn it, surely he isn't in on this madness?"

"No, those chief priests loyal to Ananus are utterly against what Eleazar has done, but they are helpless. Eleazar is not only backed by the rank and file Temple priests and the Temple servants, he is also backed by a large secret army of freedom fighters. He is commander of the Zealots".

"We must leave this city, but first we must warn the Roman authorities" said Agrippa turning to his sister. "Summon Nathan. I want two hundred of his best men, armed and mounted to go to the Antonia".

She nodded her understanding, and spoke briefly to one of her personal slaves, who had been standing quietly to one side.

"While we are waiting for Nathan, Lord, we should consider what service we can render to Amal, who has risked much to bring us this news".

"Of course." Agrippa smiled thinly at Berenice and turned to Amal. "I understand you claim kinship with our family which may or may not be true. There is no way of knowing, but anything is possible given Herod's appetite for women. However, let us set aside the improbable and consider the possible. That which is within my gift is yours for the asking".

Amal bowed her head and said, "I will not press my paternity, for I cannot prove it your majesty. But I can prove my loyalty to the house of Herod. I ask for my freedom and a place within Queen Berenice's household".

"Your freedom is granted. As for your place within my sister's court," he continued "that's not for me to say, but if she turns you down be assured of a place in mine".

Berenice burst out laughing "I will gladly find you a place in my household. I have need of somebody with brains and diplomatic skills.

"Find Drucilla and tell her I will instruct her later about your position. Also your first task is to dictate your manumission to my scribe. The King will sign it later".

Amal backed out of the room her heart singing. As she left she almost bumped into Nathan. The army commander nodded briefly to her, before stepping forward to salute the King.

T he *tribune* Metilius, the commanding officer of the Antonia fortress, felt sick when he received the news of the attack on Masada. Nathan, who had brought the news, waited with the Antonia's staff officers who had been summoned by Metilius.

The garrison commander knew what he had to do, but how best to accomplish it? "Gentlemen, we need to act. Belated though it may be, we have to send a relief column to Masada. There is always the possibility that the Jews' treachery didn't work as well as expected. Then we arrest Menahem and as many of his followers as possible. If we can make an example of them, his supporters will think twice about what they do next. We must pull in Eleazar as well as the High Priest and the chief priests for questioning. That includes the principal citizens of this accursed city.

"Also, we must make contact with the procurator who has returned to Caesarea, and we must get word to the *Legate*, Cestius Gallus, who is somewhere in Galilee on his way to Syria. And finally – Rome - how do we get word to Rome? The nearest friendly port is, of course, Caesarea".

Nathan cleared his throat, "Sir may I make a suggestion?" Metilius nodded. He wasn't about to turn anything down.

"King Agrippa has arrived with a considerable force. In addition there is Queen Berenice's personal guard and the palace guards. The King's loyalty to Caesar is unquestioned. He also has a large army in his own kingdom. The King can get your message to procurator Gessius Florus in Caesarea and, if Cestius Gallus is in Syria, reach him also. Equally as important, as the King marches northwards, messengers can be sent to every Roman garrison to warn them that the country is in rebellion. We can either retreat to Antioch and prepare to withstand a siege, or take to the field in support of those Jews in Jerusalem, who remain loyal to Rome".

There was a murmur of general approval at this plan. Metilius thanked his gods that not only was Agrippa in the city, but he had a substantial army at his back.

"Agreed. Return to the King with a request that he carries news of this…" Metilius was almost lost for words and spluttered, "this insurrection. I will have a report prepared for the Emperor within the hour. I will also prepare reports for the procurator and the *Legate*, acquainting them of the situation".

Nathan bowed in acknowledgement.

Nobody else ventured anything more. "Right let's get moving. Nathan is to report to Agrippa once the reports have been written. In the meantime, Crassus' two *cohorts* to be dispatched to force march to Masada".

"Orders for Masada sir?" Metilius grimaced. "Officer in charge to send a report of what he finds, before doing anything. He can then proceed at his own discretion. I want no heroics. If Masada is in the hands of the rebels, he is not to attempt any kind of engagement but to return immediately".

Crassus saluted and the meeting broke up. Only Nathan remained behind while Metilius dictated furiously to his scribes.

In spite of the heat the Centurion Marius and his legionaries force marched into the harsh desert wilderness of Judaea. Fortified by Herod the Great the isolated rocky height of Masada rises, seventeen hundred feet above the west coast line of the Dead Sea. Its half mile length is inaccessible, except by two inland tracks along which men can pass only in single file.

The first of these is a three and a half mile long path called the Snake, because of its constant twists and turns and its exceptional narrowness. It is broken as it rounds projecting cliffs and often turns back on itself. Walking along this path is like walking a tightrope. To slip is to die, for on either side are immensely deep canyons. The summit is a plateau measuring three quarters of a mile round. This is enclosed by a limestone wall twenty feet high and ten feet wide, along which are erected thirty seven towers each seventy five feet high. From these one can pass through a ring of chambers cut into the inside of the wall.

As Marius' sweating men approached the citadel, they became aware of the circling vultures. Hundreds of them sailed in lazy circles, before swooping down to the rocks at the base of the sheer cliff on which Masada stood. They were feasting on the corpses of the Roman soldiers who had garrisoned the fortress. Later, when Marius' men collected the dead to bury them, it became apparent that many had been flung alive from the cliff tops. Even worse, many were horribly mutilated having first been tortured.

As Marius and his men toiled they were subjected to taunts from the Sicarii, who lined the walls of the fortress, but Marius stuck grimly to his task. When he had finished he ordered a cross to be constructed from the camp materials he had brought with him. His last act before he retreated was to plant this in the middle of The Snake. A reminder of what the rebels could expect if they were ever taken alive.

11

When Eleazar discovered Amal had gone missing he was beside himself with rage. In the end he suspected she had been kidnapped by his enemies. But which ones? While the Zealots were a powerful nationalist group, they weren't the only one. There were a number of Zealot groups, each loyal to its own leader. But now wasn't the time to concern himself about a woman. The taking of Masada meant he had to make a move or be out of the game.

Without explanation he had bundled his family out of their house in the fashionable part of the Upper City and moved them to a property in the Lower City, ordering them on pain of death to stay indoors.

His next move was to mobilise his followers and put them on the streets as a citizen army, which the populace could either join or risk being accused of favouring the enemy. Thousands of Zealots answered the call to arms, pouring into the crowded streets. Under the orders of men appointed as his officers, they headed for the Temple chanting "Death to the Romans" and, ominously, "Death to the chief priests who have betrayed us".

As mobs of armed men charged through the streets, citizens were knocked aside and the contents of shopkeepers' stalls sent flying in all directions. Shouts and curses filled the air.

Picking up reinforcements on the way, the Zealots' forces swept through the Jerusalem like water from a breached dam. Tens of thousands of men surged irresistibly through the warren of streets latticing the Lower City, the noise of their coming a continuous rumble that grew in volume with every passing minute. From the tops of both the Temple and the Antonia, it seemed as if the whole of the Lower City had somehow attained a life of its own.

The High Priest and the chief priests stared in disbelief at the river of people advancing relentlessly towards the Temple. The Roman soldiers on the walls, with more experience in such matters, retreated into the Antonia fortress at a dead run slamming the gates shut.

As trumpeters sounded the alarm, hundreds of soldiers inside the fortress quickly took up their stations on its walls. Metilius hurriedly pulled on his armour, shouting for his officers to attend him.

Slower to react, the High Priest Ananus nevertheless quickly realised that his own position was untenable. He had twenty thousand Levites, Temple policemen, available to defend the Temple and, of course, the people. The hundreds of thousands of pilgrims inside or camped just outside the city, would spring to the Temple's defence without question. But they had to be mobilised.

In the meantime the Temple was a trap. Bottled up, they could not appeal to the faithful for help. The High Priest turned to one of the priests who had joined him on the Temple walls. "We must flee to the Upper City. There we can appeal to the pilgrims and the peace loving responsible citizens of the Holy City". The clutch of priests surrounding Ananus stared mesmerised at the advancing wall of nationalists. An unpleasant sound filled the air. Ananus frowned. It was like the bellowing of stampeding cattle. It was, he suddenly realised, coming from the densely packed mob advancing remorselessly towards the Temple.

Rapidly he dispensed orders. There was no time to take anything. "Surely", he reasoned "the advancing mobs are Jews. They will stop short of violating the very house of God".

"Then" asked Zacharius one of the chief priests, "why do we need to flee? They are all Jews; they will respect our office. Surely we are safer here then if we run".

"Whoever they are", snapped the High Priest, "they are the enemies of Rome. If we stay and collaborate with them, we are as guilty of treason as they are. The Romans will be as merciless with us as with them".

"Now go, summon the Temple guards, send messages to the authorities in the Upper City, send messages to Agrippa, but do it speedily and when your duties are complete, make your way to the Upper City".

As the chief priests ran to carry out the High Priest's instructions, the priest Zacharias asked "What of the Roman garrison? Surely they will defend the city. Will they not send messages to the procurator in Caesarea, and to the *Legate* who is on his way to Antioch?"

The High Priest shrugged. "You can see the Romans are manning the walls of the Antonia. For the moment they are spectators. In less than an hour they will be completely surrounded by half a million Jews whose passions, already inflamed, will kill anything or anybody that stands in their way, including", he added grimly "us."

"The Temple governor; I haven't seen him all day. I hope he is safe". Zacharius' voice was filled with concern.

"Go" said the High Priest abruptly, the thought of the whereabouts of the Temple governor had also suddenly occurred to him – and with that thought a sudden suspicion. Recently Eleazor had been absent from many Temple duties. He had been seen in the company of known Zealots. When Ananus had casually questioned him, he had been evasive.

Staring across the rooftops the High Priest had a sudden premonition. He closed his eyes, his faced screwed up as though in pain. He groaned deeply. Eleazar was one of them. He knew it with absolute certainty. And he was coming to kill him. The same ruthless burning ambition that had taken him to the post of the High Priest was present in Eleazar. Ananus prayed and, for the first time in years, it was more than just ritual.

The High Priest raised his arms aloft, tears coursing down his cheeks. "Hear me O God of Israel. Let me be your instrument of vengeance, for I will destroy him without mercy". With a final glance of pure hatred at the advancing mob, Ananus left the walls. He knew that only chaos lay ahead. If the Jews were to survive as a nation, the Romans must be made to see that it was the nationalists who were the rebels, not only against Rome but in starting a civil war against their own people.

What followed was a week-long bloodbath. Eleazar and his followers over-ran the Temple but were careful not to violate it. To do so would have caused the thousands of civilians who had taken up arms and joined their ranks to have turned on them, for they were religious men who revered the Temple. Their quarrel was with Rome and any Jew who supported it.

Day after day, Eleazar's men fought to enter the Upper City, which was defended bravely.

Ananus' makeshift pilgrim army had answered the call to arms, manning the barricades hastily thrown up, blocking the streets leading into the Upper City. More of the faithful were stationed on every rooftop. Using crowbars they prised stone blocks free, hurling them with devastating effect onto the heads of their attackers who were packed tightly between the high walls of the buildings approaching the Temple.

King Agrippa sent two thousand troops, supported by cavalry, with Darius in command. This encouraged Ananus to send out sorties in company strength which fought hand to hand with the nationalists, with neither side gaining an advantage.

On the eighth day of the battle, Menahem sent a message to Eleazar. He was outside the city with twenty thousand supporters, many of them well armed from the contents of Herod's armoury at Masada. In addition he had gathered up a citizen army of another ninety thousand men and armed them with whatever came to hand. He was offering to enter the city and form an alliance with Eleazar's Zealots. Eleazar, confident that he could retain control, agreed to this and together they launched an all-out attack. Pouring men into the Upper City from all directions in overwhelming numbers, Eleazar and Menahem eventually fought their way onto the rooftops.

Ananus and Agrippa's men were now severely outnumbered. Also, their men were tired, having no fresh reserves to call upon. Slowly but inevitably they began to retreat, contesting every building, every metre of street. This hand to hand combat was savage. Men hacked at each other as though demented. The streets were literally running with blood. Dead and dying men, horribly mutilated from axe and sword, lay in the streets. Others lay slaughtered in doorways. The dead and dying piled against the street walls, the pavements carpeted with bodies. As the frustration of Roman oppression found release, Jew killed Jew with mindless ferocity.

Gradually, by sheer weight of numbers, the defenders of the Upper City were driven out. Darius' horsemen, unable to find room to manoeuvre in the increasingly choked streets, suffered terrible losses, as the Jews attacked the horses' legs with iron bars, bringing them and their riders down to be quickly slaughtered.

Carrying containers of oil, a band of Sicarii selected by Menahem, broke into the records' office and proceeded to burn it. He wanted this done to destroy the money lenders' contracts, thus making it impossible for them to recover their debts. This popular move was designed by Menahem to enlist an army of impoverished debtors to his cause.

The Upper City was Jerusalem's most fashionable residential area. Here were located the houses of the city's richest and most influential citizens. All the chief priests and members of the Sanhedrin lived there, as did the city's councillors, judges and wealthy merchants.

As the insurgents crowded into the Upper City, they were reinforced with thousands of ordinary citizens who were fighting alongside them. Many saw an opportunity to become rich. Looting became widespread. Soon the streets were filled with men staggering out of houses laden down with stolen goods.

Terrified merchants, who had locked themselves in their homes, were tortured to reveal hidden stores of gold and precious stones. Murder became commonplace. For a time the entire fighting force was completely out of control. Wives and daughters were violated in front of their husbands and fathers. Make-shift carts were piled high as the new owners attempted to get away with their prizes, only to be attacked by their comrades!

With the insurgents' attention diverted, many of the leading citizens and chief priests escaped into the city's sewers. A chief priest, Ananias, and a handful of senior priests, judges and city councillors, escaped with the aid of Agrippa's forces back to the Upper palace.

With the gates of Agrippa's palace safely closed behind them, the survivors collapsed exhausted. Even though he was on the point of exhaustion, Ananias demanded an immediate audience with the king. Dirty and dishevelled, his normally beautifully coifed beard an unkempt brush, he knelt trembling with shock in front of Agrippa, who out of pity helped him to his feet and conducted him to a chair.

Before Ananias could speak Agrippa said "Wine" and handed the Priest a goblet with his own hand. Gratefully Ananias drank deeply his bloodshot eyes blinking unfocused over the vessel's rim.

Ananias spoke first, his voice bitter. "My own son has betrayed me, betrayed his people, and betrayed his God".

Agrippa said gently. "God is above betrayal. We must all answer for our own actions to Him. Leave Eleazar to God and consider the people. God's chosen people. What will become of them?"

Ananias stared into space, his dirt streaked face haggard with the strain of what had transpired. "He foretold this". It was barely a whisper. Agrippa remained silent. "And his brother Jesus – could he have been right?" The High Priest bowed his head, he was a broken man.

"Jesus the one they call the Christ?" Agrippa asked, incredulous that the high priest could even entertain such a thought.

Ananias pulled on his wine and held the cup out for a refill. He smiled though there was no mirth in it. "I have seen dozens of men who claim to be the Messiah. We are still waiting. This Jesus was no different, but his prophecy of the destruction of the Holy City will bolster his image".

"But the man is dead; he is of no consequence. His brother James might have threatened the teaching of the Temple but he is gone too. It is over".

"Maybe, but there is another brother, Simon, and he has a child, a baby named Joshua".

Agrippa stared thoughtfully at Ananias. The man should have been concerned with the civil war that had engulfed his people and not the relatives of some obscure carpenter's son his predecessor had crucified. The King, determined to take control of the situation, said "The nationalists have stopped fighting to celebrate their gains. We must take advantage of this lull to escape the city".

Ananias ignored this, saying more to himself than to Agrippa "Why do the people listen to these false Messiahs? They see what happens to them. We crucified Jesus. We crushed James. Could we have done these things to the true Messiah? No. God would have intervened to save His chosen one".

Agrippa shifted uneasily in his chair. "True" he mused, "the one they call Jesus is dead, but strangely his followers grew in numbers every day. Paul..." The word popped out of him without thinking.

"What about Paul?" grated Ananias.

"He came before me and Berenice for questioning before he was sent to Herod, who sent him to Caesar".

"You should have killed him when you had the chance".

"Nero did that, so his blood is not on my hands".

"What about this Simon, the other brother?"

Agrippa stood up and paced the room. "An unusual man, he owns the largest shipping fleet in the world. He has the contract to provide Rome with grain from Egypt".

"A Jew", Ananias was incredulous, "has such wealth, such power?"

"A Jew, yes, but also a citizen of Rome and married to the granddaughter of Augustus".

"Is this Simon a Christian or a Jew?"

"A Jew I think. What does it matter? Our immediate concern is to manage a safe retreat from this place, to my kingdom".

"I must stay", said Ananias. "My duty is to the Temple".

"You will die. Eleazar must be planning to take over the office of High Priest of all Israel".

Ananias groaned and tore at his beard. "The Romans will surely destroy my people, so what does it matter whether I continue to live for a few more days".

"You can mediate with Rome on behalf of your people. Expose the nationalists, make them carry the blame. Offer up the life of your son Eleazar in payment for his crimes. Better still, kill him if you get the chance. Rome would accept such a gesture as clear proof of your loyalty".

For the first time hope flickered in the High Priest's breast. Nobody knew what lay ahead. God might yet deliver the traitorous Eleazar into his hands. "I will send his head to Caesar in a jar of honey".

Agrippa nodded. "Come, you must rest and I have much to plan. I need to see my captains".

12

A grim faced Agrippa sat with his senior officers. In front of them a detailed map of the Holy City had been unrolled onto a large table. Next to it a second map displayed the countryside of Upper Judaea and Lower Galilee. Berenice sat at her brother's side, much to the discomfiture of a scandalised Ananias, Who would never have discussed anything of importance with a woman.

Philip, son of Jacimus, Agrippa's senior general gestured with a pointer. "Your Majesty, the nationalists are in control of both the Lower and most of the Upper City. Their next target must be the Antonia fortress – then they will sweep through the rest of the city".

Agrippa studied the map carefully. "At the moment we have two rebel groups in alliance against the authorities – which means Rome. While a great many of the lower classes have rallied to their side, they are scum, untrained and have little military value".

Philip, who had risen through the ranks, was a man of very few words. He discussed military matters with his King as an equal and frequently forgot to mind his language.

At a nod from Agrippa he offered his advice. "Scum they may be, but there are countless thousands of them. They can come at us and the Romans faster than we or they can kill them. That bastard Menahem is a rabble-rouser. He is inciting the faithful to a Holy war. We have got to get the fuck out of here in double quick time".

Ananias, who had had no intention of saying anything, cleared his throat. "Among this so called scum are pilgrims, Jews of good family; pious, God fearing, hardworking people. A great many of them are camped outside the city. They are not tainted by this madness. They will listen to the King. He can rally them to our side".

Philip raised an eyebrow but said nothing. It was worth thinking about, for it was true. Nearly a million pilgrim Jews were camped outside the city. They would rise as one man in defence of the Temple. It mattered not one jot that they were unarmed and untrained. Their sheer weight of numbers would be irresistible. Philip acknowledged Ananias' suggestion with a wintery smile. The King's general knew only too well how unstable such a vast crowd could be. How easily it could be roused into a religious frenzy. How easily it could turn on those who thought they controlled it.

Berenice spoke his thoughts. "Once the pilgrims get word of what is happening here they will go berserk. They will listen to no one".

"And" finished Agrippa "they will die in their tens of thousands. Menahem has the forces in Masada to attack them from the rear should he choose to, but he won't. He will want to use these people against the citizens of Jerusalem and the Romans in the Antonia".

Ananias was sweating with anxiety. The talk of leaving, of the city falling to the nationalists, terrified him. He would be penniless. His house had been burnt down. He had been betrayed by his son. He had no idea if his wife was still alive. "We must try to establish contact with the procurator to warn him of what's happened. He has Roman troops at his command. He must return to the city and liberate it".

The general replied "Yes we must contact Gessius Florus to get a report sent to Rome. However, his forces are insufficient to mount a counter-attack. The Syrian legions are a different matter. Cestius Gallus could launch a successful counter-attack - it depends on what is happening in the rest of the country. In any event we must get a message to him".

Berenice interrupted. "From Caesarea to Antioch is not a problem, but a lone messenger trying to make his was through Galilee wouldn't stand a chance. That's prime bandit country".

"I agreed with the Queen your Majesty". Philip had never been slow to acknowledge Berenice's shrewd mind. He knew Agrippa valued her advice. Her incestuous relationship with the King her brother didn't bother him. His sexual preferences were boys, preferably Greek, for their beauty and training. He supported Berenice saying "While Menahem's lot are busy filling their purses we should leave the city, appeal to the pilgrims to form a citizen army and restore the rule of law. Meanwhile, we make our way to Caesarea avoiding Masada and the fanatics who have taken it over".

Agrippa clapped a hand on Philip's shoulder. "Right as always old friend. Here we are bottled up like rats. Eventually Menahem's dogs will find us and kill us".

Ananias rung his hands. "Majesty", his voice trembled, "the Temple. We cannot leave the Temple - God will never forgive us", he ended pompously.

"The Temple governor, your son, will answer to God for what happens to the Temple and His Holy City", snapped Berenice.

"Lady, Eleazar is a viper. I have disowned him. I have prayed that he will be punished with everlasting fire for his criminality, for his blasphemy". Ananias bit his lip. Unable to contain himself, he had acknowledged Berenice's presence by answering her.

The Queen turned to him, her voice ice cold. "James the Just was condemned to death for blasphemy. His brother Jesus also died at the hands of your family".

Ananias stepped back as though he had been struck.

Agrippa said nothing. There was a light in his sister's eye; he recognised the signs. She was angry. Why? He hadn't a clue. Philip was also baffled. This sudden twist in the discussion was beyond his comprehension so he stayed silent.

"Highness", stuttered Ananias "James committed the greatest of blasphemies. He claimed his brother Jesus had brought a new covenant to God's chosen people.

"Not true", Berenice snapped, her face flushed with anger. "I have read the transcript of that trial many times. Your kind had him killed because he threatened their grip on the people. . He told men that he had not come to change the law but to fulfil it". She slammed her fist onto the table. "Jesus told men", she continued, "that they should pray directly to God; that they needed no priest to mediate between them and God. That God didn't require blood sacrifices. The priesthood, even the Temple, were made redundant. The Covenant God gave Abraham was with *all peoples and nations*, not just Jews".

Agrippa was amazed. He had never guessed that his sister had such strong feelings over the issue of Jesus.

Angry at the exchange between his sister and Ananias, he said coldly "Leave us. We need to consult with our officers".

Mortified at having allowed herself to incur her brother's anger, Berenice murmured "Yes my Lord" and backed out of the room.

Agrippa turned back to the maps. "Philip, send men to the pilgrim camps on the northern side of the city. Buy camels, clothing and trade goods. We will disguise one hundred of our men as merchants to send them across the dessert to Caesarea".

Philip nodded "Yes my Lord, I will lead them myself".

"No", replied the King. "It is too dangerous. The caravan will be attacked by bandits. Terrorist groups are roaming the countryside. Their chances of getting through are slim. I need you to lead the main body of our force which, because of its size, may escape attack, but will be slower. The bogus caravan will travel light and fast. Make certain you buy only the best beasts and pick good men, who will be well armed".

"Yes my Lord – and when do they leave?"

"Get the Caravan equipped and on its way within twenty four hours. Don't argue about costs. Spend whatever it takes to buy the best animals available. We will follow within forty eight hours. But be prepared to move at a moment's notice. We may not have the luxury of choice. Much depends on Menahem's next move".

"And Eleazar's". This bitter comment was from Ananias. "The zealots are not natural allies of the Sicarii. Sooner rather than later there will be a falling out. Only one of them will survive".

"God help the people", murmured Philip. "A faction fight within the city will be a bloody affair. The people will be caught in the middle, many will die".

Before either the King or the High Priest could reply an officer entered the room and saluted. "Sir, a man is at the gate asking for our protection. He claims to be Hezekiah, brother of the High Priest".

Ananias clapped his hands and said "Hezekiah. I thought he was dead. Your Majesty, I beg you admit him, for if this man is truly my brother, I will rejoice for he is dear to me".

Agrippa thought for a moment and then said "We will go to the walls. If the High Priest identifies this man as his brother we will admit him".

The dishevelled figure who was eventually admitted told of his escape from the nationalists; a nightmare journey, neck deep in liquid filth through the city sewers. Many were still down there hiding, too terrified to come out, having nowhere to go, while above ground the rebel forces, completely out of control, were attacking the city's population.

Civilians were being butchered wholesale, their possessions stolen. The families of wealthy citizens were being subjected to the most brutal tortures. "Nothing", Hezekiah concluded bitterly, "the Romans had ever inflicted on those condemned to death in the arena was worse than what the Jews were doing to each other".

"You have much to talk about with your brother", Agrippa said sympathetically. "I will leave you. In the meantime quarters will be prepared for you. You have our protection for as long as you need it".

Hezekiah prostrated himself before the King, uttering his heartfelt thanks. The events of the last few days had been hideous. Their memory would trouble his sleep for the rest of his days. Left alone the two men embraced. Ananias spoke first. "The sacred scrolls. We must get the sacred scrolls. They are the key to controlling the office of the High Priest of all Israel in the future".

Hezekiah sighed at his brother's ambitions. Ananias had survived attempted assassinations, a critical populace, intrigue within the priesthood, plotting within the Sanhedrin. But, Hezekiah thought, he is right. If this family was to return to the office of High Priest of all Israel, it must have something to bargain with. The nation was in turmoil. The Temple itself stood at the eye of the storm. The future was unreadable. The sacred scrolls were forever. When the killing stopped and the survivors raise their heads from the dust, they would surely follow the keeper of the sacred scrolls.

"How can we secure them?" asked Hezekiah wearily. "The nationalists are everywhere. Menahem has taken the Temple and controls it. No services are held." He paused and swallowed, tears rolled down his face. In a voice breaking with emotion he continued "The everlasting fire has gone out. The altar is cold. No sacrifices are made. Its ashes blow in the wind. Surely God has forsaken us". He concluded sadly, "What is happening to us now is a just punishment. The Lord has turned his face from us". Weeping, he ended "Perhaps James the Just was right".

"Never", screamed Ananias, who leapt forward and seized Hezekiah by the beard. "To deny the covenant of Moses is blasphemy. Be careful brother, for I will not hesitate to denounce you".

Hezekiah pulled himself free and angrily pushed Ananias away. "And Paul of Tarsus? Will you send messages to Caesar denouncing him because he spread a new covenant, one that is made between the one God and all mankind?"

Ananias hurled himself across the room and grappled with Hezekiah. A slave posted at the door, hearing the commotion, ran to report it not daring to interfere. A somewhat bemused Darius who had retired to his quarters was brought to separate the struggling men. "If you have differences to settle, may I suggest you do so outside. May I also suggest that swords are more efficient than fists and are certainly more dignified?"

Both men, badly out of condition, were gasping for breath. They ignored Darius. Ananias glared at Hezekiah. "I want to know one thing before I disown you. Are you faithful to the God of your fathers? That we are His chosen people? That His covenant is with the Jews and the Jews alone?"

There was a long silence before Hezekiah finally answered sombrely. "I don't know. I have prayed to God for an answer, but have received none. I only know we, His people, have sinned. What is happening to His Holy City, to His Temple, is a judgement on us. I will help you to save the scrolls. After that I intend going into the desert to be alone with God to ask for forgiveness".

Darius turned Ananias and said gruffly "Will you accept this?" Ananias nodded briefly and stormed out of the room.

Darius said to Hezekiah not unkindly "Enough for today. Take a bath, get some rest. There are enough enemies and to spare outside these walls. You don't need any inside!"

It was still dark when Ananias and Hezekiah, dressed in the nondescript clothes of ordinary citizens, slipped out of the Palace. Agrippa had been against their leaving but couldn't argue against an attempt, no matter how foolhardy, to retrieve the sacred scrolls.

In a window high above the street a Sicarii, one of a team posted to watch the palace twenty four hours a day, spotted the two men as they eased themselves through a side door leading into the street. "Two men have sneaked out of the palace".

His companion, a small thin man with a broken nose said "Right. I will report to Judah" – Judah being the leader of the group using the building as an observation post.

Ananias and Hezekiah had reached the steps leading to the court of the Gentiles when they were suddenly surrounded. A band of Sicarii had been lying in wait for them. Resistance was as useless as their protestations. Their hands were tied behind their backs without a word being spoken and they were marched unceremoniously through the dark streets.

The light of the new day was seeping steadily across the rooftops as they arrived at a particularly fine house in the Upper City. Ananias noted bitterly that it was not too far away from his own property that had been burnt and looted.

The brothers were frogmarched through the villa's splendid main hall and bundled into a small windowless room. Sitting on the bare stone floor, they contemplated their fate, Hezekiah being the first to speak. "You realise we have fallen into the hands of the Sicarii?" Further conversation was cut short by the return of their captors, led by a bad tempered man with a hare lip carrying a club. Without a word being spoken they were pushed and prodded along a series of corridors, ending up outside the double doors of the main chamber. Hare lip dragged the door open while his companions shoved them through. With sinking hearts the two men realised that the well-armed men in the room were there as bodyguards to Menahem who, hunched over a parchment, ignored the two priests, continuing to speak quietly to the men closest to him.

Ananias whispered to Hezekiah, "It is just possible they will do a deal".

Hezekiah replied "I agree. Their brand of nationalism is centred on self-interest".

Menahem looked up, nodded, and the brothers were prodded forward. Menahem didn't speak; instead he studied his two captives with intense interest.

Ananias licked his lips. He found the pale eyes disturbing. Hezekiah couldn't read them. He was beginning to be afraid.

Menahem smiled but there was no warmth in it. "Well well, Ananias and his arse licking brother. Couldn't keep away from the old place hey? Well you're just in time - in time for a Coronation. Maybe we should let you perform it before we kill you".

Ananias couldn't believe his ears. Coronation? Whose he thought? Menahem, guessing what was passing through the bewildered priest's mind, said "Mine you old fart. *Mine*. It's about time the Jews had a king to rule them, instead of having to touch their forelocks to the fucking Romans and then crawl on their knees to you".

Ananias glared at the Sicarii war lord and turned his gaze onto the other men, silent but interested parties to the unfolding drama. "Repent whilst there is still time. In abusing me you abuse God. All of you", he bellowed, "are out of your minds. Not only have you declared war on Rome, you have declared war on your God. The first will surely kill you. The second will deny you His presence for all eternity".

Menahem stood up laughing putting a hand on the shoulder next to him. "He hasn't lost his touch has he, the old wind bag. Always good with words, but refuses to exercise that silver tongue for his new King. What about his brother then? Perhaps he would like the job he spurns. Maybe we should make him the High Priest of all Israel". This last drew a few ribald comments. Menahem walked slowly across the room, his eyes fixed on Ananias. "You are too quick, priest, to dismiss my claim to the throne of David and are not in a position to threaten me. When you are dead another will not only crown me, he will proclaim me to the people Defender of the Faith, appointed by God to deliver his chosen people from slavery, while you will be remembered as a collaborator, the betrayer of the chosen people who delivered them to their enemies the Romans".

"I serve God", shouted Ananias. "Even now it's not too late to lay down your arms. I will intercede this very day to the commander of the Antonia and plead your case. This act of repentance will restore you to the favour of your God, who forgives the truly repentant sinner".

Menahem spun on his heel to face the high priest. "The Zealots are scheduled to launch an all-out attack on the Antonia at sun rise, which I guess is just about now. Why don't we take you and your brother up to the roof and find you both a comfortable seat from where you can watch Eleazar lead the attack".

Ananias dropped to his knees, head bowed, howling with rage, while Hezekiah hurled abuse at the laughing Menahem, who signalled to one of the men and whispered in to his ear. The man nodded and turned to his companion. "Bring them to the roof, then fetch timber and organise a carpenter and his tools".

The brothers were dragged, angry and protesting, to the roof. The man to whom Menahem had whispered instructions, was a goat herder turned full time rebel. "Hold them fast", he grunted. In his hands he held a pair of shears used for clipping wool from the backs of his former charges. "The chief", he leered, "doesn't want either of you beauties to miss anything – not by so much as a blink of an eye". He nodded to the men holding Ananias, who flung him to the ground. One of them imprisoned the priest's head between his knees, while with great delicacy the goatherd clipped Ananias' eyelids away.

On seeing what had befallen his helpless brother, Hezekiah had screwed his eyes tight shut, but the goatherd knew his trade. A leather thong was fastened over Hezekiah's head and around his jaws. An assistant then firmly pinched the victim's nose and held it. After a minute or two, his face purple, heels drumming on the ground, the suffocating Hezekiah's eye lids fluttered. The goatherd caught each one in turn on a metal pin. Then, after indicating to the man holding the victim's nose to release him, he cut both eyelids away.

While this was being done the carpenter had arrived with his tools. Other men carried baulks of timber and some poles. "Strip them". Within seconds both men were naked. Within minutes the carpenter had roughly dressed and pointed two of the poles. These were fixed securely to the roof parapet looking towards the Antonia. The sun had not yet risen, but there was light enough to make out the troops patrolling the walls.

First Ananias then Hezekiah, arms bound to a cross bar, were hoisted into the air, where they were manoeuvred to sit on the pointed stakes. Ropes tied to the cross bar were secured to the parapet. They were unable to move, not even to throw themselves off the posts on which on they had been sat, for the posts had a three inch diameter and had been roughly pointed. Thus penetration wasn't too deep. Over the next few days it would slowly become deeper as Menahem ordered weights to be fixed to the suffering men's legs. The final torment would be the flaying of their bodies to attract insects.

When the two men begged for water, their guards gave them as much as they wanted to prolong their suffering. When eventually they begged for death they jeered at them. Before he went blind, Ananias saw Eleazar and the Zealots attacking the fortress of the Antonia from three sides. Day and night battle was waged, the Zealots throwing endless reserves of men against its walls. Hundreds of scaling ladders and assault towers, using a design copied from the Romans, were used in these attacks. The Zealots and their citizen army died in their thousands. The Antonia was truly impregnable but its defenders needed to sleep. Their enemy, already several hundred times their superior in numbers, could rest their men without halting the attack.

On the sixth day of the battle, the sun blackened, eyeless, fly-blown corpses of Ananias and Hezekiah stared blindly at the besieged fortress, their crow pecked faces ravaged by birds and insects. On the twentieth day the bloody battle paused when the Romans hoisted a flag of truce.

Metilius, its commander, wanted parlay. In return for safe conduct for him and his men to Caesarea, he would surrender the Antonia. However, he and his men were to retain their standards and their weapons. They were to be allowed to march out of the Antonia under escort with a solemn and binding oath of free passage. Menahem rejected the terms and tendered his own.

Their lives would be spared. Under oath, they would be given the right of free passage to Caesarea and would be provided with a well-armed escort to protect them. But they would not be allowed to retain their weapons. They would be allowed to retain their eagle and their standards, but they must not be displayed during the march to Caesarea.

While Metilius was discussing these terms with his senior officers, Menahem was discussing with Eleazar the best place to conceal enough men to attack the Romans once they had laid down their weapons. Neither of the two nationalists had forgotten how the Romans had slaughtered the unarmed Jewish citizens who had gone out to welcome the arriving *cohorts* from Syria. The Jews who assembled for the ambush of the Antonia's soldiers had lost fathers, brothers, cousins, mothers, sisters, sweethearts, children, to Roman treachery.

There was also the fact that the Roman legionaries manning the Antonia were not in fact Roman nationals, but Syrians who had volunteered to join the Roman army. It had been Arab Syrian conscripts who had betrayed them and massacred the Jews sent to welcome them.

They needed no reminding of the law of Abraham and Moses - eye for eye, tooth for tooth, hand for hand and foot for foot.

13

Metilius, wrapped in his cloak, stood on the Antonia's walls and stared into space. His senior officers who had accompanied him remained silent. Even in the poor light the reality of the last few days' carnage was painfully obvious.

"Gentlemen, we have to consider our position and determine what to do about it". None of Metilius' officers volunteered an opinion; their position was hopeless and every man knew it.

"We are not just surrounded, we are drowning in a sea of Jews", Metilius continued. "There are so many of them, if they choose to they can not only mount a continuous round the clock assault, they can do so from a dozen different points. Even this impregnable fortress must eventually fall under that kind of pressure. I fear it will be sooner rather than later".

In the half-light the cloak wrapped figures, had avoided each other's eyes. Would Nero come to their aid? Would he be as loyal to them, as they had been to him? To think not was dangerous; to say so was treason.

There had been a general clearing of throats but nobody spoke. Instead, they had stared out across a city they hated, at a people they despised.

"We can at least die well", said Crassus. As Metilius' adjutant he was the youngest officer present.

"Dying is easy to say, but a bloody sight harder in the doing", answered Metilius bitterly.

"Would you have us surrender," snapped Crassus, "and spend the rest of our lives as slaves?"

Before anybody could reply, Metilius cut in "I have asked for terms". A gasp went up, but the Roman commander wasn't to be put off. "If we stay here we will die and in dying make no significant contribution to the final outcome. We will die for nothing. If we negotiate terms we will live to fight another day. We will return with Caesar's legions and take our revenge".

The gleam of light from the rising sun gilded the men's sombre faces. Gaticus, his second-in-command, voiced the thoughts they all held. "Caesar may find fault in our surrender. We don't know if either the procurator or the *Legate* will attempt an assault on the city".

"Festus will stay in Caesarea with his gold" snapped Metilius. "As for Cestius, he will wait in Antioch for reinforcements before he leaves the safety of his Syrian base. No, if we are to be saved, we must save ourselves".

Crassus couldn't stand the shame of what his commanding officer was proposing. To give up a well found fortified position, without a fight, was an act of extreme cowardice. If they survived every man would be tainted with it until the day he died.

"Sir, even if the Jews grant us terms, we will have to face our peers in Rome. The Antonia's strength is legendary; to give it up without a fight will brand us as cowards".

"Cowardice", Metilius screamed, his eyes bulging. "You dare accuse your commanding officer of cowardice?"

"No Sir", stammered Crassus, "I am simply saying what we do may be misconstrued by others. Possibly with malice if they were to profit by it".

But Metilius wouldn't be mollified. Glaring at the young centurion he roared "You are under arrest. The charge is treason". A murmur of consternation arose, but nobody dared to intervene. "Gaticus, take his sword. This officer is confined to his quarters until his court martial".

Metilius chewed his bottom lip. He couldn't meet the eyes of his officers. "Dismissed gentlemen. We shall reconvene when the so-called nationalists reply. In the meantime go about your duties and make sure this place is as unassailable as we believe it to be".

When Eleazar learnt that Metilius wanted to negotiate the terms offered, he was with his most trusted men, priests who had backed him against his father.

The man who was the go-between was a Greek, a scribe employed by the garrison commander. "Where", asked Eleazar, "would such a meeting take place?"

"The fortress", answered the Greek "in a chamber at street level. It opens next to the Court of the Gentiles. This allows both sides to have a discussion without either having to enter the other's territory".

Eleazar pursed his lips. "We will need to exchange hostages."

The Greek bridled, "You have the word of a Roman *Tribune*".

"You forget Greek", Eleazar spat, "we are used to having the word of the festering hyena Cestius Florus, appointed by Rome to shaft us as hard and as often as possible while telling us it won't happen again – until the next time".

The Greek bowed his head. "Very well Sir I will see what we can do".

"I don't give a fuck what you do. Tell those turds in the tower, there will be an exchange of hostages at midday tomorrow followed by an immediate parlay – or not at all".

The Greek shrugged. "Very well sir, I will give the commander your answer". The Greek turned to go.

"Wait" said Eleazar. "What happens to you in all of this? The Romans send you out to save their skins. What of you – are you the dog that licks the fingers of its master?"

"I am a slave", the Greek said softly, "in the service of a Roman *Tribune* in the middle of a civil war. If I were a dog I would be free to choose sides, or not as the case may be".

Eleazar heaved himself off the bench and strode across the room to stand within inches of the scribe, staring him closely in the face. "What value do you place on freedom Greek?"

The scribe remained silent, his face devoid of emotion. Getting no reply Eleazar continued, "As a go-between in this matter you can influence the outcome. Metilius must be shitting himself to have asked for safe passage". Eleazar paused.

"He will ask your opinion on how you found us. Your opinion will influence how he behaves". The Greek held Eleazar's gaze. "You could be free".

The Greek laughed dryly. "A free man. Without a country, without family, without friends, without money, without a home. A beggar standing in the middle of a bloody war, where Jews are not only killing Romans, they are killing each other".

"Wrong" said Eleazar. "You could be a free man, with the position of scribe to the Zealots' revolutionary council. When we have swept the Roman lice from our land, you would have a place in the city's foreign administration".

The Greek remained silent for a moment, thinking. He had been deeply shocked at the Roman commander's decision to ask for terms. If terms were agreed what would happen to him? Would Metilius march out of Jerusalem with his slaves and household servants? Where was he planning to go? Would he abandon his slaves and servants and simply march his legionaries away, leaving the garrison's civilians to fend for themselves?

"I accept your offer", the scribe replied stiffly.

"Good man, you have made the right decision. Come, take some wine with us before you go. Let us part as comrades". As he spoke Eleazar drew the Greek to the table, one of the Zealots poured out a cup of wine and handed it to him. Eleazar grabbed his own goblet and raised it. "The toast, gentlemen, is freedom". Wine cups were swept aloft and bumped together with a cheer.

When he reported back to Metilius he was careful to keep his voice neutral of expression, but long skilled in the use of language he was careful to choose positive phrases. When the question finally came, as he knew it would, he was ready. "Scribe, what kind of man is this terrorist leader?"

"He is the son of a high priest Excellency, a man of learning. A man who is used to politics, to making decisions. He will listen carefully to whatever you propose. He will respond rationally".

Metilius was astounded to learn Eleazar was the leader of the Zealots. He knew the man well. He also knew about Amal and wondered what had happened to her during the fighting.

Suddenly he thought of Ananias. "He has turned on his own father." The scribe was stunned to hear this - it had simply escaped his memory.

He remained silent. The Roman commander didn't regard his scribe as a confidante. If he asked his scribe questions from time to time it was often rhetorical, simply a matter of clearing his mind. "Where is Menahem in all of this?" He turned to the Greek. "Was he at the meeting?"

"No sir. From what I overheard, he has gone to Masada to collect more weapons from the fortress' armoury." The scribe knew the value of this piece of intelligence. He also knew the impact it would have on Roman morale. The armoury at Masada was enough to arm ten thousand men. The Greek had chosen his moment well.

That did it for Metilius. The idea of an even better armed citizens' army to support the nationalists terrified him. "Arrange a meeting for tomorrow", he snapped and left the room.

The scribe smiled to himself as he opened his writing case. The Roman garrison commander had panicked, making a rushed decision without consulting his officers.

The dream the Greek kept in the deepest, most secret crevices of his heart, stirred. He felt its movement. It took him a moment or two to recognise it. It was hope.

The meeting was marked by extreme suspicion on both sides, though Eleazar was at pains to appear calm and reasonable. After an hour of discussion, Eleazar made his final offer to the Romans. "You will leave the Antonia with your personal possessions. You will also be allowed supplies and baggage animals for your march to the port of Caesarea. You will come under the protection there of the procurator. He will provide you with a ship to Rome or you can join your forces with his and re-enter the battle".

"Weapons. We demand that we be allowed to retain our weapons and standards". Metilius was sweating; the stress of the negotiation had given him a headache. At his previous attempts to persuade the Jews that his men be allowed to retain their weapons, he had failed. "Without weapons, we will never make it to Caesarea. If we are to die we will at least die fighting and have", he ended savagely, "the pleasure of taking a great many of you with us to Hades".

Eleazar shook his head. "No weapons. We will provide you with an armed escort".

Metilius pressed his fingers against his aching temples. The officers who had joined him in the discussion had been persuaded to agree to surrender, but at least half of them would not yield on the question of weapons.

Eleazar watched the Roman carefully. How close was he to giving in? None of the Roman officers said anything. Metilius badly needed advice, but couldn't bring himself to ask for it in case the deal collapsed. Absentmindedly he pinched the bridge of his nose. As he did so his eyes met those of his scribe. In that split second the Greek took a chance. Without taking his eyes off the Roman commander, he gave a barely discernible nod.

The Roman officers missed it; so did the Zealots but Eleazar didn't. He lowered his eyes to conceal his satisfaction.

"Agreed".

An imperceptible sigh greeted the single word.

Eleazar rose. "Excellency, you have made a wise decision. You have saved your men from a futile and useless death. 'Until tomorrow, then. I will personally ensure that your departure from the city is without incident. Your escort will be sufficient to ensure your safe passage to Caesaea".

Metilius breathed a sigh of relief. "It's going to be alright", he told himself.

"Excellency might I suggest your scribe returns to the city with us. We need to draw up a document confirming our agreement. We are not familiar with how such a treaty should be best worded, bearing in mind that Caesar himself will be the recipient".

Metilius blinked in surprise at this offer. Eleazar stood smiling, perfectly at ease, the picture of magnanimity.

Metilius nodded. "A good idea; take him with you. He is an excellent administrator.

The Greek, totally amazed at this turn of events, bowed and said "By your leave Excellency, I will collect my writing materials and go with", momentarily he was at a loss as how to address Eleazar and then he remembered Eleazar was a priest, "with the priest", he murmured.

Agrippa, with his sister and Amal, left Jerusalem before dawn. The King insisted on being at the head of the column. Berenice rode at his side. For safety's sake Agrippa placed his baggage animals in the centre of the train. Without undue hast, with his standards and banners displayed, the King made a measured progress out of the city to take the road to Caesarea.

In the half-light they approached the vast temporary settlement. Camp fires burned everywhere as the waking pilgrims rose to go about their business. Recognising the King's standards they saluted his passing, for he was held in high regard by the ordinary people. Many of them recognising Berenice who, like them, had come to Jerusalem as a pilgrim, saluted her and were reward by a courteous wave or an inclination of the head.

Agrippa's steward, Ilderim, had ensured that the King and his sister had a plentiful supply of coins which they dispensed generously to those who begged for alms.

Delays were inevitable, for among the vast multitude encamped for miles outside the city, Jews of importance and substance had established what were veritable small villages to accommodate their families, servants and guards. When such men became aware of the King's passing they rushed to greet him, begging him to honour their house by stopping for refreshment.

To avoid causing offence Agrippa would dismount and embrace the man, begging him to understand that he had urgent business in Caesarea. Berenice would graciously ask the pilgrim for a goblet of water, which a servant would be dispatched to bring. Thus the social niceties were observed. By mid-morning they had cleared the last of the encampments and were moving swiftly along the road to Caesaraea.

At nightfall they made camp in a wide stony valley, far enough away from the nearest hill for it to be used to ambush them.

Agrippa had spent years observing Roman military methods and had incorporated them into his own army. Before any man was allowed to take his ease, a trench was dug around the camp. The King's tent was then placed at the centre of a tented village whose streets radiated out from the centre. Sentries were posted and officers patrolled the perimeter. Outside every tent was a stand holding the men's weapons. Every man knew exactly where to go and what to do if an alarm was sounded.

As was his practice when campaigning in the field, the King invited his generals and senior officers to dine with him.

Berenice was not invited to join them, and dined in her own tent with Amal for company. The two women had grown to like each other although Amal, conscious of their difference in rank, was careful never to treat the Queen as an equal, in spite of being invited to do so on several occasions.

The floor of the tent in which the two women were sitting was covered in fine silk and wool carpets from Persia. Oil lamps on stands placed around the interior cast a soft warm light.

Heaped cushions and chests to hold clothing and personal possessions were the only furniture. Trays of food and drink were placed on the low tables. A young girl sitting crossed legged in the corner played a harp. Smiling, Berenice said, "the King likes you".

Amal dipped her head, "I am pleased my Lady, for his Majesty has done me much honour. I will be in his debt forever".

Berenice chuckled, leaning against a mound of multi coloured cushions. She said, "You miss my point, no doubt deliberately. When I say the King *likes* you, I mean as a woman as well as a person. And", Berenice continued, watching her from beneath dark lashes, "that's most interesting – because he hasn't looked at another woman for years".

Amal stiffened. "God", she thought, "what do I do now? Acknowledge that which everybody ignores, that the King is sleeping with his sister, then assure her that I am no threat, or simply tell her that I'm not interested?"

"My Lady", said Amal, "the King has been kind to me. I am in his debt as I am in yours".

Berenice leaned forward locking her hands round her knees, her head tilted to one side as she appraised Amal. "You are beautiful and clever. You claim a blood tie. The Jews of Galilee and Judaea have declared war on Rome and their challenge will not go unanswered. Sides will have to be taken".

Amal's head snapped up and she stared into Berenice's eyes. "I am yours and the King's to command my Lady. What significance can your hand-maiden have in such momentous events?"

Berenice reached across and took Amal's hand in hers, gently turning it so that it lay palm up. She studied it intently. "It matters a great deal, if it is your destiny to achieve greatness".

"And what else do you see my Lady? Greatness is not happiness. Am I to be happy?"

Berenice considered for a moment before saying, "Is not happiness a condition of the heart, not a state of mind? The answer to your question is concealed from me, though not your pain. Yes you will know pain, but you will also know joy. But happiness is another matter. Are any of us truly happy?"

"James the Just was". Amal was as startled as Berenice at her own reply. She had spoken the words without thinking. No thought of James was in her mind.

"Why do you say that?" asked Berenice.

Amal sighed. "I saw him on his knees, his body broken. He was dying, but it was in his eyes, in his voice as he prayed for those killing him".

Berenice who had unconsciously held her breath at the mention of James' name asked, "You were there?"

"Yes". The two women sat in silence. Outside a desert fox screamed, an unearthly blood curdling sound. Amal said softly "He prayed for those who were destroying him. To a God he claimed was the God of *all* mankind. The God his brother Jesus proclaimed had declared a new covenant for all men, not just the Jews, which is why the High Priest condemned him to death. Ciaphas refused to believe that God's covenant was with all mankind. If he had, he and the High Priesthood were finished. The Temple was finished. Ananus was faced with the same situation as Ciaphas; James the Just – Jesus' brother – had to die.

Berenice moved closer to Amal, her face inches away from hers. "Do you believe him?"

"Who, James or Jesus?" she parried, eyes narrowing, suspicious of the question. This woman, this Queen, was a Jewess. True she was a Hasmonaean and did not observe the strict practices of the orthodox, but she was still a Jew though her private life condemned her utterly for incest was punishable by death. It was a heinous crime - any trial would be a formality. Her station in life would not protect her if ever a charge was brought.

Berenice persisted. "Do you believe that Jesus was God's prophet?"

Amal's answer was softly spoken. "He claimed that he came to uphold the law not to destroy it. He claimed that through him God was announcing that His covenant was with the *whole* of mankind – with every man, woman and child on earth. This is the covenant God gave to Abraham. This is God's law and it is unchangeable. It is forever. This was the message that God had entrusted Jesus to deliver to mankind".

Tight lipped Berenice reached into the folds of her gown. She withdrew a slender golden chain. On the end of it was a golden fish. "Do you know what this symbolises?" she asked quietly, "What I risk in letting you see it?"

Amal took the fish in her fingers. "Yes my Lady, I know what you risk and you must know what I risk when I say yes. Yes I do believe that Jesus was God's messenger and believe his brother James was also".

Berenice hugged Amal to her, tears in her eyes. "Now they are gone, both murdered. How will we ever atone for what we have done? God will surely punish us for killing those he sent to deliver us".

Amal shook her head. "Jesus preached love - love is forgiveness. It has no measure. No beginning. No end. God is love. We only have to ask and it is given unconditionally, without terms, forever, to everybody, all men, including Jews, who are guilty of the sin of pride, pride in believing that God would shut all of mankind out from His love except the Jews".

Berenice kissed Amal tenderly. "We are sisters in Christ, as well as blood. Whatever the future holds, we will face it together".

"The King", Amal asked huskily. "Will he not be angry at this; may he not accuse us both of blasphemy?"

Berenice smiled. "The King is a righteous man, but he is not a Sadducee. He greatly admired James the Just. As a pious man, he was angry at his murder but it happened before he could intervene. However, he has sworn his allegiance to Caesar. On oath he has pledged to defend Roman interests, and will do so to the death".

"Against the Jews of Palestine?"

"Against anybody", was the grim rejoinder, "who challenges Rome's authority. He will argue that upholding Roman law is upholding the civil law. The Romans have never interfered with how we Jews worship. The King will defend his sworn word with his life", she ended firmly.

Amal frowned slightly as she concentrated. "And", she asked, "the Christians? Rome is mercilessly attacking Christians. They are being killed daily in their thousands in Rome's arenas; their property is confiscated and they are sold into slavery".

"Nero is using them as scapegoats", said Berenice, "to divert the mob's attention from his own madness".

"If the Christians in Palestine", Berenice continued, "attack Rome's interest, the King will put them down without mercy. In his eyes they will be traitors. However," she continued dryly, "the few Christians that exist in this tormented country keep their heads down. They have had enough to worry about trying to stay alive.

"The war of the Jews" she ended grimly, "will be fought to the death. The Romans have to make an example of the Jewish rebellion to retain their credibility throughout the Empire – and the Jews have nowhere to go. All they can do", she ended sadly, "is die".

14

The route from the Antonia to the city's main gate had been cleared by Eleazar's Zealots. When Metilius and his men marched out of the Antonia, it was into streets eerily silent. Every building along the route was blind, windows shuttered, doors locked. Not a single street trader plied his wares. Apart from a few scavenging dogs competing with weary crows among the rubbish, the Roman column had the streets to themselves.

The disciplined ranks marched through the oppressive silence, the only sound the tramp of their hobnailed sandals, the creaking wheels of their supply wagons and the jingle of the horses' harness.

Before leaving the fortress, Metilius had addressed his men. "Soldiers of Rome, it is our sworn duty to defend the empire against its enemies. To be prepared to die in the service of the Emperor". The fortress' commander had paused to ensure the import of his next words reached every man. "We are surrounded by tens of thousands of armed nationalists. Tens of thousands more Jews who have come to the city as pilgrims, are outside the walls, aching to die for their invisible God.

"Across the entire country rebels have sacked villages, even entering Syria in their impudent confidence. The cities of Sebaste and Escalon have been burnt to the ground. The cities of Anthedom and Ghasa are destroyed, their citizens slaughtered". Metilius paused to mop his brow, the silence solid, every eye from the silent ranks fixed on him.

"Philadelphi," Metilius continued, "Heshbon, Gazara, Pella and Scythopolis, are now in the insurgents' hands. Their Roman garrisons", he ended ominously, "have been wiped out".

Virtually all Metilius' legionaries were made up of Syrian Arabs who had volunteered for the army. They also brought with them an inherited antipathy for all Jews. They listened to their commander in silence.

Swallowing hard he continued, "The Greek port of Caesarea is the headquarters of the procurator and the Fifteenth Legion. From there messages can be sent to Caesar requesting reinforcements. In the meantime we can join with the Fifteenth Legion and wait with them for Cestius Gallus and his Syrian legions, for he will surely march on Jerusalem to punish the rebels".

What Metilius had no way of knowing was that as even as he addressed his troops, the Greek population in Caesarea had seized the opportunity to *cleanse* the city of its Jews.

Florus, who was in the city, learning that the Greek authorities had voted on a policy of "ethnic cleansing", had shrugged his shoulders, negotiated his usual cut and looked the other way.

Metilius continued, "When we leave the Antonia we will meet our escort, which will guarantee our safety to Caesarea. It is at this point we will lay down our arms." As a groan greeted these words, the Commander looked sharply at his centurions, who simply stared stonily into space.

"Those are the conditions of the solemn treaty we have agreed. We have a choice. Staying here to die like rats in a trap or accept the Jews' terms of a safe conduct to Caesarea, from where", he concluded, "we live to fight on, to return with Caesar's legions.

When they had marched out of the Antonia, more than a few secretly doubted they would ever see Caesarea. At the city gates Eleazar was waiting to receive them. With him, drawn up into orderly ranks, was the heavily armed escort that was to accompany them. Outside the fortress a breeze scented with juniper could be felt. Herds of black goats being driven out to pasture passed by, their owners wide-eyed at the sight of mounted soldiers.

As Metilius and his senior officers conferred with Eleazar and his subordinates, the column stood at ease. A donkey brayed somewhere. Sparrows flickered across the stones lying at their feet, the early morning air pellucid as crystal under a pale blue sky.

Eleazar spoke directly to Metilius, indicating with a sweep of his hand an area of flat ground. "Please ask your men to stack their weapons. While they are doing that your officers can discuss with mine how they will perform their escort duties, the arrangements for camping at night and the route we will take".

Metilius inclined his head in acknowledgment and turning in his saddle gave the order to disarm.

As the Roman soldiers filed passed and stacked their weapons, Eleazar discussed the route with the Romans. There was little dissent. The Romans had built the road on which they were to travel. They knew every inch of the terrain between Jerusalem and Caesarea. Bereft of their arms the Romans felt naked, viewing the heavily armed escort that virtually surrounded them, with a feeling of foreboding.

The day, however, passed peacefully enough. The military routines governing the march, the taking of rest periods, agreeing plans for the first night's encampment, had passed without incident. In the late afternoon, emerging from a ravine, the Roman column made its way onto open ground patched with clumps of thistles. This was a point where several wadis met and the scouring of winter rain had created a small hill.

The escort, which had been out of sight for several hours, suddenly reappeared. Ominously it had been reinforced. The Romans suddenly found themselves surrounded by thousands of heavily armed men. On the low hill a group of horsemen silently watched them. Metilius gave the order for his men to form a square which out of habit they did, but as more than one man observed, "Without weapons, what's the point?"

Metilius could just make out the figure of Eleazar among the group of horsemen. He was on the point of calling out when a blast from a ram's horn sounded. This was the signal for the silent ring of men and horses to suddenly open, revealing companies of archers. A second blast was the signal to fire. The air turned black with arrows. The defenceless Romans didn't even have their shields for protection. They called out in anger, cursing the Jews, damning Eleazar. But to no avail. Four times the archers fired before the ram's horn sounded again, then the encircling Jews charged in, swords and axes swinging.

In less than an hour they had massacred the entire Roman column. Unbelievably they took Metilius alive. Disgracefully he had begged for his life, even offering to convert to Judaism and be circumcised. When Eleazar, who had roared with laughter at this, had recovered, he agreed. Then he and his men laughed and jeered as Metilius had to suffer the painful indignity of the operation, carried out by a nationalist using a none-too-clean knife and who, on Eleazar's orders, also slit Metilius' tongue.

Returning to Jerusalem the victorious rebels passed a dirt poor village, a conglomeration of tumbledown mud brick houses divided by a few rutted streets. The village elder was given the Roman Commander as a present and, when Eleazar's men marched on, he dragged the *praefectus* into an almost pitch black room. Here a patient ox plodded endlessly round, milling the village's corn. Unable to utter an intelligible sound, the wildly gabbling Roman was stripped naked and fixed by his wrists to a pole in company with the shackled ox.

Before closing the door on his new acquisition, the village elder ran an appreciative hand over Metilius' buttocks. His new owner determined to ensure the Roman would be as well looked after as his beast. "Even better," he mused, for as well as pleasuring himself, there would be those in the village who would pay for the novelty of pale flesh.

15

When Eleazar returned to Jerusalem he found the city centre packed with thousands of Sicarii. Every street leading to the Temple was lined with Menahem's followers. Deeply suspicious, the leader of the Zealots ordered the gates of the Antonia fortress, which he had taken over, to be shut. After posting a double guard, he and his closest confederates made their way to the fortress' walls which looked out over the Temple. What they witnessed took their breath away.

A coronation was in progress. Menahem, dressed in cloth of gold and accompanied by hundreds of his followers, was walking slowly down the central aisle of the inner court where a number of priests were gathered around a golden throne positioned under a canopy of royal purple. An incredulous Eleazar hissed to his companions "The bastard's being crowned".

"But that's impossible", replied Absolom, one of his lieutenants. "He is not of the house of David".

"Neither was the Idumaean pig Herod", interjected Judah, another of his companions, "yet he ruled for twenty years".

"Go into the city", grated Eleazar. "Find as many of the city's father as you can. Tell them what's going on. Tell them, if they storm the Temple to put an end to this blasphemy, we will support them".

"The people will never attack the Temple" muttered Absolom.

"Yes they will, if blasphemy is being committed and the house of God profaned. It can only be cleansed by the blood of the transgressor. Now go and rouse the people".

Eleazar returned to the Antonia, ordering his subordinates to get the Zealots ready to attack down the staircases that led directly to the Temple. "Let's make good use of what the fucking Romans left us" he shouted. "Place a chain of men between me and the Antonia staircases. On my signal, attack – which will be when I wave this scarf". Eleazar unwound a gold and white scarf from his throat and tucked it into his sleeve.

Eyes slit with hatred, Eleazar crouched in his hiding place above the Temple court, watching as Menahem took his place on the throne. The smell of incense reached his nostrils. To the sound of trumpets, high priests in their vestments of purple and gold unrolled the sacred scrolls. As the reading commenced, hundreds of Sicarii who had gathered to witness Menahem's triumph, prostrated themselves. A golden crown lying on a purple cushion, edged with cords and tassels braided from gold and silver thread, was brought in solemn procession.

Bile rose in Eleazar's throat. His normally dark face flushed with blood, his whole being filled with hatred. Tearing his eyes away from the scene below, he gave the prearranged signal which rippled down the line of hidden Zealots.

Absolom, who had readied his forces, nodded to a trumpeter who blasted out the signal.

Archers who had crept along the Temple balconies stood up, arrows notched. They volleyed flight after flight into the Temple court. As this murderous hail fell on the unsuspecting Sicarii, hundreds of heavily armed men poured across the Temple steps, to attack the gates leading to the inner court. As these gates were breached, the archers received a signal to stop firing.

As Eleazar's soldiers burst into the court they were reinforced immediately with hundreds of citizens armed with stolen Roman weapons. Eleazar, knowing the value of the Roman short sword - the *gladius* - had made certain every one of his followers had one. They also carried the light round shield favoured by Arab cavalry. Outnumbered and caught unawares, the Sicarii were overrun. Few of them even had weapons for they had respected the Temple law.

They were cut to pieces. Eleazar's orders had been specific. No prisoners, nobody to be spared – except Menahem who was to be taken alive.

The great swirling mass of attacked and attackers pulsed like some enormous jellyfish with an energy of its own. Eleazar found it difficult to pick out individual figures. He was about to leave his vantage point, when a flash of gold made him concentrate on a knot of figures that had broken away from the main group. Eleazar hissed with rage. It was Menahem, surrounded by his personal bodyguards, who was fighting to reach one of the exits. Eleazar screamed orders but could not make himself heard about the roar that filled the court.

Helpless to stop it, Eleazar watched Menahem edge nearer and nearer to an exit. With a curse of his own the Zealot leader ran towards the staircase. It would take him back into the Antonia. Pausing only to snatch up a sword, he shouted at the officer left in command of the fortress, "A hundred men to me now". Without waiting for confirmation he sprinted for the entrance to the Temple.

It says much for the Zealots' training, which owed much to Rome, that the officer who had received Eleazar's order had fifty men under a competent officer at Eleazar's heels within seconds, and was busy organising a second fifty before the first had cleared the door.

As he burst out of the Temple, Eleazar hurtled down the steps in time to see several stallholders at the end of the road picking their goods out of the gutter. They were also cursing and shouting, fists raised in anger.

Without a second's hesitation Eleazar ordered his men to continue the pursuit. He would wait for the rest of the attack force. Impatiently he started commandeering horses. "Get him", he roared, "but alive. Succeed and you can name your own reward". He grabbed the captain of his men by the throat "Fail and I will have you flayed and staked".

The young officer led his men in frantic pursuit, upsetting for a second time the merchandise of the street vendors. More of Eleazar's men arrived. "Horses!" he snapped. "I want them fast, no arguments. Kill anybody who argues; anybody. Now go".

The captain nodded and turned his men away.

Menahem and a dozen of his closest companions, the remains of his personal bodyguard, had escaped the city through the gate close to the Hinnom valley. The track they were on cut through dense scrub. Turning and twisting, the path snaked around the base of the city wall. Massive boulders and huge outcrops of rock flanked both sides of the narrow path, creating a tunnel effect. Loose scree, slipping underfoot, slowed the fleeing men down.

Menahem knew that his only hope was to reach Masada. His plan was to secure horses from the pilgrims camped on the plain. As he and his men scrambled along the floor of the ravine, they stopped from time to time to listen for sounds of pursuit, but so far none had come.

A young boy, who often grazed the family's skinny black goats along the canyon rim, was perched in the shadow of a rock. He watched the fleeing men with interest. They were taking more chances than was safe on the rough ground. Whoever is after them, he mused, is feared.

He watched for a few more minutes before scrambling to his feet. He was thin as a rake, his sinuous body deeply tanned and uncut dark brown hair secured with a leather thong tied round his forehead. His only clothing was a tattered woollen smock belted at the waist ending at his knees. At his waist was a pouch that held a dozen or so carefully selected round pebbles – ammunition for the sling shot looped through his belt and his only other possession, a cheap wooden handled knife, kept in a homemade leather sheath on his belt.

Barefoot and as nimble as one of his own goats, he flitted over the tumble of boulders and rocky outcrops, making his way to the gate leading back into the city. Here he looked around for a vantage point. Scrambling onto a low roof of one of the many buildings that butted the wall, he settled down to wait.

Benjamin Bar Levi and a dozen young men burst into the main street at a dead run. Panting heavily, sweat streaming down

120

their faces, they shouldered their way through the crowded street to the gate. "Two minutes", he snapped to his winded men, who took advantage of the rest to gulp water from a public fountain.

Benjamin's gaze scoured the street with its many intersections. Automatically his eyes ran along the windows and rooftops. The boy was watching him, perched like a thrush, black eyes bright with interest. Benjamin spotted him. "Did you see men run this way?"

The boy tipped his head, a slight smile curling his lips. "I have to watch my goats; my family rely on me to eat".

"Which way did they go?" Benjamin was positive that the boy knew.

"My family is poor; my herding a few goats will not change that".

Benjamin's eyes narrowed, there was more to this boy than most, but he was in a hurry. He reached into the pouch in his belt and took out some coins. "Payment now for information. Later, you come and see me. Decide if you want to join us".

Without a second's hesitation the boy leapt off the roof, a naked brown foot landing as light as a feather on a veranda. With the skill of an acrobat the boy bent and grabbed the balustrade and dropped into the street. "Come", and he was gone through the gate and clambering over the rocks. Slightly dry mouthed, for he was not good with heights, Benjamin and his men followed.

Squatting on top of an outcrop, the boy pointed to the barely discernible path. "They went that way. They will come out in an old wadi almost opposite the eastern gate. From there they will make their way to the pilgrim camp. They can hide there, a few fish among many". Bar Levi sucked his teeth.

"Or get horses and flee", his second-in-command said.

"But to where? Menahem would surely not give up - he still has hundreds of loyal followers".

"Masada!" Of course, that's where Menahem was heading for. Bar Levi turned to his men. "Back. We must catch up with Eleazar. They are heading for Masada".

The boy watched them go. The coins firmly clenched in his fist would feed his family for weeks and, he thought joyously, his sister would have to look after the goats. He had been promised man's work. The Zealots would give him a sword.

Mounted on sturdy horses, Eleazar led his men northwards, travelling along a ridge running parallel with the slightly higher skyline to avoid detection. They had travelled through the hills, climbing all the time, to try and get a view of the men they were pursuing. As evening approached they looked across the arid wasteland of upper Judaea. Suddenly beautiful, the hills turned a deep violet in the last of the day's light. Eleazar eased himself in the saddle. The harsh cry of a raven caused him to look up. The summits of the mountains furthest away were reefed in a shawl of scarlet cloud. In the gulf between them, the Dead Sea lay like a sheet of beaten silver.

Gambling that Menahem was heading for Masada, Eleazar and his men had taken the route across the high country, hoping to intercept his quarry and trap him with a well concealed ambush. The rebel leader knew that they would have to stop soon. His men and, more importantly his horses, were desperately tired.

He called to his most trusted lieutenant "We will stop soon, look for a spring". Absolom lifted a hand to acknowledge the order, knowing he would be lucky to find water. Little grew in the parched pebbly dirt that passed for soil. Apart from a scattering of thorny scrub, the rocky ridges were gangrened over with grey thistles that only wild mountain goats would eat. A few stunted shrubs offered little to the horses and mules, but it was better than nothing. On the skyline a few cacti were clumped defiantly.

Eleazar raised an arm. "Dismount. We will camp here". He had chosen a high spot from which their fire could be seen. If Menahem saw it, he would assume it belonged to a shepherd. It was doubtful he would associate it with pursuit. More importantly, Eleazar had sent scouts ahead. Riding with two spare horses they would not only see the fire, they would know it was his.

With night fast approaching, Eleazar ordered his men to the tasks of making a night camp. Already the sun had gone, the sky lit by its afterglow. As the day tremulously faded, a huge red disc of a moon floated round the shoulder of the mountain, its soft light bathing the whole plateau. With the sun gone, a blast of icy air swept down from the high plain of Moab, shivering the tiny spring Absolom had found, bubbling clear and cold through the snail starred stones.

The tired men quickly chopped a few branches from the desiccated shrubs, and started a fire. Sparks swirled upward into the dark sky. The horses and pack animals were hobbled and turned loose to find what sparse grazing was to be had. After a simple meal the rebels, wrapped in woollen cloaks against the night's bitter cold, huddled round the fire, discussing their chances of intercepting Menahem.

They were up in the dark, kicking the embers into life for something hot before they took up the chase. As they stood yawning the scouts returned, prudently calling out a warning of their approach. Covered in dust, their horses' heads drooping with exhaustion, necks slathered with dried sweat, the weary scouts slid out of their saddles, easing aching backs. They had travelled overnight across dangerous ground and had been glad of the full moon.

Eleazar embraced them. "Come my brothers, warm yourselves, take some food".

Isaac, who had led the scouting party, stretched his shoulders. He appreciated the courtesy of a welcome taking precedent over his report. As a cup was thrust into his hand he had one quick swig before speaking. "They have traded horses gone lame, for camels from the Bedouin". He paused to clear his throat, spitting a gobbet of phlegm into the glowing embers, where it hissed furiously. "They are not using the track which is a direct route, but swinging in an arc across country. I anticipate they will re-join the road where it becomes a pass, skirting the cliffs on which the fortress stands".

Eleazar shot out a hand and gripped his officer painfully hard on his shoulder. "We have them". His voice was low but vibrant with triumph. "You have done well my brothers. Rest here for a few days and then return to Jerusalem". Isaac protested. He and his men wanted to join in the fight, but Eleazar shook his head. "If you won't admit to exhaustion your horses will. They would drop under you before we reached our objective and" he continued ominously, "we have no spare mounts. No. Rest up here and make your way back to the city. We won't forget the work you have done this day, nor the reward you and your men are entitled to".

Two days later Eleazar and his men had reached their objective - the massive rocky heights that towered seventeen hundred feet above the western coastline of the Dead Sea, on which Herod the Great had built his fortress.

Within sight of the safety of Masada's unassailable position, Menahem found himself suddenly surrounded. His assailants, who had lain in wait for him behind the protection of a low hill, suddenly appeared. An ominous frieze of dark figures poured like bitumen across his path. In desperation Menahem turned to flee, but to no avail. Men hidden in a fold in the ground galloped into view, lining up across the road behind him. For several minutes nobody moved, nobody spoke. The only sound came from the beasts - a gentle clearing of nostrils tickled by dust, the chink of harness and the stamping of an impatient nervous foot.

Menahem's supporters felt a sudden chill. The dark host encircling them not only outnumbered them twice over, they were mounted on horses. Quicker to turn than camels they could prove decisive in a battle. Unspoken, fear ran like quicksilver through the ranks of Menahem's followers. They could see safety tantalisingly close.

One man suddenly panicked, lashing his camel into a furious gallop. The rest followed - bolting in every direction, unreasoning fear urging the fleeing mob to desperate speed. The deserting Sicarii had one collective idea. In the dusty confusion they might slip through their enemy's ranks, which many of them did. Confused and disorientated by the swirling dust. Menahem's mount was knocked off balance and he was unseated. His startled mount, snarling and spitting, raced off into the cloud of dust its departing companions had raised.

Throughout the day they tortured him by applying red hot irons to his feet. As evening approached, a man took a pair of shears with heavy blades. These were used to cut away the thick horny growth of the feet of sheep and goats. They were now employed to snip off Menahem's fingers and toes, joint by joint. Each crunch of the heavy blades biting through bone as easily and as crisply as a carrot, was accompanied by shrieks of agony.

The next day, men who were butchers by trade carefully removed most of his skin. When they had finished, they spread-eagled and staked him well clear of any shade. Before leaving, Eleazar poured a jar of honey over his weeping flesh as an added attraction to the cloud of insects already gathering above the moaning Menahem, who begged for death.

16

grippa's horses and camels moved northwards. As they climbed out of the Samarian hills, they could see banks of green on different levels. They passed flocks of sheep and goats, interspersed by female camels moving with stately dignity in comparison to their leggy young, who skittered uncertainly after their mothers. Small herds of cattle, marked on their rumps with tribal signs of identification, raised their heads as the long column of mounted men passed between them. The camels' plate-like feet moved silently over the sand, the only sound the creak of saddles, the tinkle of metal on metal and the slosh of the water skins.

In the distance they could see Jericho, drowned among its palms. Beyond the hill they were crossing, a swirl of golden cliffs caught the sun.

Riding with Agrippa at the head of the column, Berenice admired the wild flowers that grew among the sparse grasses. "A beautiful land" said Agrippa.

"Yes my Lord, but its beauty is like that of a woman, it attracts many suitors".

The King smiled but didn't reply.

Towards the end of the day, as they reached the outskirts of Caesarea, Agrippa had expected to be met outside the city gates. Custom required the city fathers to welcome him with the traditional offering of bread and salt.

With his general Philip, Agrippa studied the city walls which lay about half a mile away. The gates were open, the normal daily traffic could be seen coming and going. "The traffic is light my Lord, there should be much more movement".

Agrippa pursed his lips. Berenice, who had dropped back to ride with Amal, spurred her horse forward. "Philip is right my brother – and where are the city fathers?" She pointed "And the guards on the walls? We are in full view but they have simply ignored us. Something is wrong".

The King cursed softly. He had expected to be able to enter Caesarea without delay. He turned to Philip. "Send Nathan and a dozen men to ride into the city. Hopefully the Roman procurator is in residence. Nathan is to find out what he can and return. I will expect him back by mid-afternoon at the latest". Philip saluted and hurried away to organise the party he would send to reconnoitre the city.

Berenice nudged her horse closer to her brother's. "If the procurator is in the city my Lord, he will be holed up in the palace". The palace she was referring to had been built on a massive rock that stood at the centre of the superb harbour, built by their kinsman Herod the Great, for Caesarea was the principal port by which products entered and left Palestine. Luxury goods from the east were exported to Rome from this port, which had no equal in the region.

Philip approached Agrippa and saluted. "Majesty, I recommend we build a secure camp. Not here, of course, but four miles back there was a small oasis with fresh water".

Agrippa fingered his beard absentmindedly while he thought about his general's advice. He grimaced. More time would be lost. He knew what Philip's idea of a secure camp would be. After all, the King himself had introduced the concept, which was part of the standard Roman military manual. A secure camp meant one that was capable of withstanding a serious assault.

"It's odd", he mused, "that nobody has come out to greet us".

"All the more reason to stay away". It was Berenice who interrupted his thoughts. "The Greeks are tricky bastards". Agrippa smiled bleakly at this disparaging remark. Hasmonean dislike of Hellenism went back a long way.

Philip was grateful for Berenice's interjection. "Sire?"

"Very well, we will wait here while you check out the oasis as a suitably defensive position".

"Sire, that has already been done as a contingency. I ordered it when we passed it by". Agrippa nodded. He would have been surprised if Philip had not already considered that option.

Before sunset Agrippa's men had built a substantial camp. Constructed along Roman lines, it was surrounded by a ditch ten feet wide and four feet deep, topped with a six feet high wooden palisade.

Copied from the Roman model, Agrippa's army included a pioneer corps of engineers who had their own draught animals and baggage train. The prepared timber for the camp's perimeter was designed to be portable. Along with the army's artillery, a variety of catapults that hurled specialist ammunition – stones, fire pots, lumps of iron - there were giant bows that required three men to operate them. When fired, a nine foot iron tipped javelin was released with devastating effect against close order infantry or cavalry.

Agrippa's tent, together with that of Berenice and his officers, was placed at the centre of the camp, as were their stores and supplies. From this hub, streets had been marked out and each company of men allocated a space. Horse lines had been established and parties sent out to forage for firewood. Latrines had been dug. Sentries were posted. Officers detailed to do the rounds had been warned to keep their men alert.

When he was in the field, Agrippa's pavilion served as headquarters and personal accommodation. It was here with his officers that he received Nathan and one of his scouts returning from the city. That Berenice, attended by Amal, was invited to the meeting was unusual, but Agrippa's men were used to Berenice's presence and that her brother treated her as an equal. Often the King would turn to her for an opinion, for he valued her advice.

Nathan and his scout prostrated themselves and assumed a kneeling position. "Make your report".

Nathan touched his fingers to his forehead. When he spoke, he addressed Philip. He would not speak to the King directly unless Agrippa addressed him directly. "Sir, the Greeks have risen against the Jews who live in the city. The city fathers agreed a policy of cleansing the city of its Jews. Orders were given to the city police and the Jewish quarter sealed".

Berenice and Amal exchanged glances, but didn't say anything. "What about the procurator, is he in the city? Did he intervene?"

"Yes sir, he sent a message to the Greeks asking if they needed any help". A startled Agrippa drew his breath in sharply.

"And the city fathers?" the King asked.

Nathan turned his head to face his King. "Lord, they asked the procurator to assist in surrounding the Jewish quarter, to ensure none could escape".

"What happened?"

"Lord, the Greeks outnumbered the Jews ten to one. Caesarea," he continued "is as you know, Majesty, a Greek city. They killed twenty thousand Jews within the space of an hour. They spared no one".

"And Florus sanctioned this?"

Berenice could contain herself no longer. "This man is supposed to represent Roman law – to ensure the safety of its citizens, not collaborate in their murder".

"Survivors?" the King continued.

"A few hundred, Majesty. The procurator rounded them up and sorted through them. The slave transports in the harbour had been commissioned by him". Nobody had to ask what happened to those unfortunate prisoners who didn't pass muster at the sorting stage.

Agrippa stood up and began to pace angrily. He knew only too well that what had happened in Caesarea would reverberate round the region. "We must turn away from this place and the lunatic who rules it. We will, however, stay long enough to send a message to Rome. Caesar must be told of the mad dog who rules in his name".

Agrippa had been right about the knock-on effects of the Jewish massacre at Caesarea.

As he and his column made its way to Antioch, they passed through a land on fire. Jews, wild with anger, left their villages and attacked their gentile neighbours. Time and again on his march to Antioch Agrippa was attacked, but his well-trained men successfully beat off the marauding bands.

In the following weeks the King's army marched past more and more cities that had become embroiled in the civil war.

The Syrians had also started killing Jews, not only through hatred, but to avert their own peril. The border with Syria was filled with confusion. Every city was divided into two camps, the survival of one depending on the destruction of the other. The days were spent in bloodshed, the nights in fear. The Syrians, having rid themselves of their Jews, remained suspicious of Jewish sympathisers. Syrians, overcome by avarice, looted the property of their victims with impunity. The dead lay unburied. Worse was to come, as the unreasoning monsters of racial hatred and religious intolerance, slipped their chains.

The Syrians of Scythopolis had turned on their Jewish citizens, slaughtering thirteen thousands of them; an act which caused all the cities in the region to take up arms against their Jewish colonies. In Escalon two and a half thousand were put to death and in Ptolemais two thousand were slaughtered in a morning. At Tyre even larger numbers were killed and at Hippus and Gadra the same thing happened.

Emboldened, the rebels seized a fortress called Cypros overlooking Jericho. After exterminating the Roman garrison they razed the defences to the ground. Soon afterwards, the Jews at Machaerus persuaded the Roman garrison to leave the fort and hand it over to them in return for a safe passage. The Romans, afraid it would be taken away by force, agreed to withdraw under a truce. Accepting the guarantees provided, they handed over the stronghold, which was promptly occupied and garrisoned by the Jews who had always lived outside its gates.

17

Antioch, the queen of the east, was the third largest city in the world, second only to Rome and Alexandria and the official residence of Rome's imperial *Legate* of Syria, Cestius Gallus. A Greek city of five hundred thousand inhabitants, it had been endowed and enlarged by the Romans when they conquered Syria. From this metropolis the Romans controlled the trade routes to the Levant and beyond. It was in this city that St Paul took the momentous decision to baptise gentiles; they were the first to be called Christians.

This was the city Cestius Gallus ruled, in all but name, as a king. The court of the Roman *Legate* was every bit as splendid as that of the emperor in Rome, attracting to its glittering circle a multitude of rapacious and self-serving officials.

Surprisingly, Cestius tolerated a large Jewish community because they were more than useful to him; they were indispensable. The fabled wealth of the Levant was brought to the city by Jewish merchants and hence to Rome, whose citizens had an insatiable appetite for luxury goods and were dazzled by the unusual and eye-wateringly expensive jewels and silks from India and China.

More importantly, the world's banking system had been set up by Jews and run by them. It had major branches in Antioch, Alexandria and Caesarea, all linked not just to Rome but anywhere in the Roman world and the Levant. Money that needed transferring between cities need only be deposited in one. Payment in another city did not require the physical transfer of coin. A slip of paper carrying the seal, signature, and secret code of a Jewish banker, was all that was required, making money available anywhere in the Roman Empire.

It was in this city, the first in the world to have street lighting, that Cestius Gallus learned of the uprising in Jerusalem and the annihilation of its Roman Garrison. The shock of what was deemed impossible had made him feel physically sick. When he had learned of the taking of Masada, he was.

Gallus knew he had to respond, and quickly, to the situation in Jerusalem. Delay would encourage the rebellious Jews and cause the deepest suspicion in Rome. Two reports were hurriedly despatched – the first to the Emperor, and the second to Gessius Florus in Caesarea. The first acquainted Nero of the facts, the blame spread evenly between the Jewish ruling classes and the Procurator of Judaea, Gessius Florus. It stated that Gallus, at the head of the forces available to him, was marching on Jerusalem with the intent of punishing the rebels. It concluded that he was outnumbered fifty to one and would appreciate any support the Emperor cared to send. The letter to Florus ordered him to assemble all his forces and to wait for Gallus to arrive in Caesarea. In the meantime Florus was to hold himself ready to explain how and why two calamitous events had occurred within his area of responsibility.

He then summoned his banker for an urgent meeting. When Moses ben Jacob arrived, Gallus was in the garden, sitting in the shade and studying his accounts. After greeting Moses, Gallus said "There is serious trouble in Judaea – some sort of uprising in Jerusalem. The civil authorities are being challenged by rebel factions. The city – indeed the whole country – is on the verge of civil war".

Moses was so shocked by this bald statement that he was rendered speechless, although he was very much aware of the fact that rural Jews were balanced on the knife edge of poverty. Roman taxes had pushed Jewish farmers to the point where they were one bad harvest from starvation.

A grim faced Gallus continued "There is more than one faction involved in the insurrection. Rebels have taken Masada and its garrison has been murdered – don't ask me how! And", he went on remorselessly, "the Antonia is now in the hands of criminal scum who call themselves zealots".

Finally, Moses found his voice. "What", he croaked, "of the Procurator, Gessius Florus?"

Gallus grimaced and shrugged. "Florus has much to answer for, not just to me but to the Emperor. He and he alone is responsible for maintaining law and order in Judaea". The banker noted that the *Legate* had distanced himself from his subordinate, but said nothing.

Gallus flicked nervously at the document in front of him before continuing "I am blameless, of course, but will have to clean up the mess. Who knows what the final outcome of this madness will be". Before Moses could comment he continued, "Close my accounts in Antioch and transfer the funds to Gaul".

A deeply disturbed Moses, his face expressionless, asked, "What of your land holdings here?"

"Put them on the market but don't hold a fire sale. There will be buyers here in Antioch as well as Rome".

Moses cleared his throat. "Is there", he asked diffidently, "anything else I can assist your Excellency with?"

For a moment he thought the sweating Gallus wasn't going to reply, but he handed him a parchment. "This is a list of my most valuable artworks. I am making arrangements for them to be crated. You", he paused before asking, "can arrange secure storage?" Without waiting for a reply he continued, "Find buyers for them, but slowly. They are priceless. Realising their worth will take time".

Moses accepted the scroll without comment. He was fully aware of Gallus' valuable collection of bronzes and marble statues. Some, of immense antiquity, were of so fine a workmanship as to be beyond price.

"You will excuse me Excellency. You have given me much to attend to".

As Moses rose to take his leave Gallus pursed his lips and nodded, saying, "Yes I have, and I value your discretion. You may double your usual commission".

Moses bowed his thanks before hurrying away.

Gallus, who had four legions under his command, chose the Twelfth, adding six thousand men drawn from the other three. As they marched from Antioch they picked up five thousand archers, five thousand cavalry and six thousand infantry from client Arab kings who had sworn allegiance to Rome.

Eventually Gallus arrived in Galilee with thirty thousand men under his command. King Agrippa, with a sizable portion of his army, also joined Gallus (whom he privately detested) ostensibly as an advisor. His real purpose was to act as a mediator between the two sides, if he ever got the chance.

The two forces, his and Agrippa's, met outside Joppa. Gallus divided his forces and attacked the city on two sides. The inhabitants had no time to escape; neither did they have any military experience. Having few weapons they put up little resistance, seeking to hide or flee from the killing machine that had suddenly descended upon them. The Legionaries and their mercenary allies rampaged through the town slaughtering the defenceless population of eight and a half thousand souls. After stealing everything that had the remotest value, the Romans celebrated their victory by setting fire to the town.

Standing in the town's smouldering ruins, a tight lipped Agrippa learned from Gallus how the unrest had spread to Alexandria in Egypt. Later, alone with Berenice, he recounted what had taken place. "There was a minor disturbance between Greek and Jew at a meeting the Greeks were holding among themselves. Three Jews who were secretly at that meeting were discovered, accused of being spies and burnt alive".

"Without trial?" Berenice was outraged.

"Since when", replied Agrippa bitterly, "did Greeks allow Jews civil liberties?" After a brief pause he continued, "The Jewish community rushed out and threatened to torch the amphitheatre where the Greeks were meeting".

"And the Governor?" asked Berenice. "What was he doing? Sitting on his hands as usual?"

Agrippa sighed. His sister had always been headstrong. "After the usual bull-frogging in the council chamber, the governor ordered the city fathers, the most respected men in the community, to go to the Jews and appeal to them not to provoke the Romans garrisoned in the city".

"Hmmm. And then?"

"The Jews marched on the Governor's villa shouting abuse and hurling rubbish at his guards".

There was a long silence. Berenice hardly dared to ask, "Tiberius punished them?"

"He had ordered the two legions at his disposal to be on battle-ready standby, along with two thousand infantry recently returned from duty in Libya and en route for Rome".

"Oh no".

"He ordered them to attack – not simply drive them away – break a few heads – scare them shitless – but a full scale attack".

Berenice stood up. She suddenly felt sick. She wrapped her arms around her body to stop herself shivering. "It's out of control". She spoke more to herself than her brother. "It's like a forest fire jumping across open ground to start more and more fires".

"And it will get worse". Agrippa said softly.

Berenice leaned against her brother, holding him fiercely. She was only too aware of Egypt's importance to the Empire. Without her corn Rome would literally starve, relying on the corn ships which arrived daily from Alexandria to feed the capital. For anybody to threaten Rome was to invite the full force of Roman retribution.

Numbed with shock, a grey faced Berenice clung to her brother. "Home," she whispered, "we must go home. The nationalists are mad dogs. In the name of God, brother kills brother. The Romans", she ended bitterly, "will thank their gods that they face a divided enemy, who will do much of their work for them".

With the stink of the unburied dead in his nostrils Agrippa faced Gallus. "I will not" he said coldly to the *Legate*, "march on Jerusalem without a direct order from the Emperor".

Gallus couldn't believe what he was hearing. "I order you", he grated, "to join with me and put down this rebellion, or be branded a traitor".

The King stared at the angry Roman for a moment. When he replied it was in a firm voice. "I was appointed by the Emperor. I report directly to him. I have no jurisdiction outside of my own kingdom. You", he ended, "have no jurisdiction over me".

"The Emperor will hear of this treachery!" Gallus shrieked.

"Yes", replied Agrippa. "He will hear of what happened and more much more. It will be in my report to Rome".

Gallus' advance was brutal. On reaching the Greek city of Caesarea, a chastened Florus was ordered to leave most of his men behind to ensure the city's safety. "You", said Gallus spitefully, "will be at the head of the first assault on Jerusalem's walls".

Gallus continued his advance along the coast arriving eventually at Lydda. The town was virtually deserted, its citizens having gone to Jerusalem to celebrate the feast of Tabernacles. Sixty or so people remaining, mostly elderly, were casually put to the sword and the town burnt. Gallus' forces were now on the main road to Jerusalem, which winds through the hills at Beth-Horon.

In Jerusalem the rebels, seeing Gallus so close to the city, charged out in a surprise attack. In a sortie that went in their favour, five hundred Roman legionaries and one hundred and fifty cavalry were killed. Simon ben Gioras took the opportunity to attack the rear of the column. Cutting out a number of baggage animals, he dashed back to the safety of the city, cheered by the Jews lining the walls.

A chastened Gallus' next move was to choose a site on which to build a series of forts for the protection of his forces. This was done with usual Roman thoroughness. In a very short space of time, five substantial forts had been constructed, their outer defences encircled with deep ditches and strengthened with the addition of wooden walls and watch towers. With these in place the Roman engineers positioned artillery in a strategic arc to protect the whole encampment and started building roads. With thirty thousand men plus animals needing to be fed and watered on a daily basis, supply lines were established and protected.

Gallus was in no hurry to attack. Instead he relied on the rival factions within the city to do his job for him. He spent the next seven weeks sending out well armed foraging parties to seize all the grain in the neighbouring villages, whose able-bodied inhabitants he ordered to be chained and driven back to serve as slave labour. The old and the young were killed out of hand.

True to his word, Gallus ordered the Judaean Procurator to lead the first assault. This was against the neglected and unrepaired third wall. To the *Legate's* surprise the Jews fell back in apparent disarray. The jubilant Romans stormed it and the second wall; again they met with little resistance. Scarcely able to credit their luck, the Roman forces had the whole of the new town at their mercy and promptly set fire to it, the timber market providing extra fuel. With the new town well alight, the Romans advanced as far as the Upper Palace. If Florus, who was leading the way and knew the city well, had made a determined push against the main city wall, Jerusalem would have been theirs. Instead, he advised Gallus to hold his position and was supported in this by the *Legate's* senior officers. What the wavering *Legate* didn't know was that Florus didn't want Jerusalem to be taken. An early and successful victory would vindicate the *Legate* and damn him. He would be on the first boat back to Rome, to answer to Nero for the loss of Masada and the Antonia garrison; to say nothing of the general uprising against Rome.

Florus, knew success at Jerusalem would not go well for him. Somehow he had to turn the situation to his advantage, which meant things had to go badly, particularly for the *Legate* - a man who was a ditherer and had had little experience in military matters. He was a politician. The son of a *consul* he too was a *consul*, who lacked the wealth needed to buy real political power, and whose prime reason for accepting the Governorship of Syria and the overseeing of Judaea, was the opportunity to extort the fortune he lacked.

Knowing that Gallus' officers were as corrupt as he was, Florus had secretly bribed the *Legate's* second in command,

Tyranius Priscus, and those officers most senior and closest to the *Legate*. They had been paid to ensure any assault on Jerusalem would fail, resulting in an early withdrawal while they awaited reinforcements from Rome. Above all, this would buy Florus the time he needed, in order to arrange for Gallus to have a fatal accident or be killed in the withdrawal.

Consequently, inexplicably to the legion's soldiers, their commander did nothing for two months. Gallus then ordered that the Antonia was to be assaulted. A picked band of legionaries was ordered to undermine the wall, opening up the chance to attack the Temple. It was at this point that a number of priests offered to open the city gates if Gallus would spare the city. Before he could decide whether or not to accept the offer, the would-be collaborators were found out. The furious nationalists threw the traitors off the walls and bombarded their broken bodies with rocks.

All of this happened in early November. Winter, which promised to be early, was approaching fast and the highlands of Judaea would be scoured by freezing ice-filled winds. An army camped in the open for any length of time would find just staying alive a full-time job.

So, with the city his for the taking, the *Legate*, gulled by his own officers, decided to withdraw and wait for reinforcements from Rome - a decision that presented him with an immediate problem.

During the weeks he had dithered, the Jews had been busy. Every building in the narrow streets surrounding the new city had been evacuated. Tons of masonry had been added to the stone prised loose with iron bars from their roofs. Under the cover of darkness men supplied with food and water had taken cover on the flat rooftops, hiding in the mounds of stone that would become ammunition. At pinch points in the streets and alleys that spread like a web around the Roman position they collapsed walls, blocking the road to any would-be advancing infantry.

Unaware of these preparations, Gallus knew that pulling out of the city and re-joining his main forces would not go unchallenged. He needed time to achieve this and time to put distance between his forces and the Jews. A few officers who had not pocketed Florus' gold argued against retreat. Threatened with a court martial for insubordination, they had fallen silent, at which point Gallus played them a particularly dirty trick. He ordered them to hand-pick six hundred of their steadiest men and take up a defensive position on the roofs of the buildings not occupied by the Jews. They were ordered to cover Gallus' retreat by delaying the Jews for twelve hours. They were to do this by spreading themselves thinly and calling out to each other as though on sentry duty. Under no circumstances were they to leave their posts in an attempt to re-join the main force, until twelve hours had elapsed.

It says much for Roman training and discipline that the doomed men obeyed their orders and held their positions, fighting to the last man before being overwhelmed and killed.

Meanwhile, Gallus' forces retreated through the mountains with the Jews in vengeful pursuit. The *Legate*, hell bent on speed at all costs, disregarded the first and last rule of mountain warfare against an enemy that knows the terrain. He failed to take command of the high ground. Before the Romans had even got as far as Beth-Horon, they had taken a mauling. The Roman column, compressed between the valley walls, was attacked from above. First they were showered with javelins and arrows. Then they experienced avalanches of loose scree and stones, released by tripping trigged boulders.

With their way blocked, the Romans were forced to turn back and seek a new route, only to be hit by Jewish cavalry galloping out of the narrow side gullies and concentrating on the Romans' baggage train and siege weapons. When Gallus' cavalry tried to relieve the pressure, the Jews focused on injuring and killing their enemy's horses - a much easier target than armoured riders. Repeatedly the Jews attacked hard and fast, hit and run, never directly engaging with an enemy that was the best in the world in set piece confrontations.

Nightfall had brought some respite to the battered Romans, who finally sought refuge in Beth-Horon. When Gallus gathered his officers together and asked the whereabouts of the Procurator, he was told he was dead, mashed to pulp by one of the boulders bouncing wildly down a mountain slope.

At dawn, a haggard Gallus woke to the realisation that the worst was yet to come. Every hill was lined with the enemy - waiting, ready, totally silent.

Forced to continue, the Romans marched and were harried all the way. By the time they reached Antiparis six thousand had died – the equivalent of a complete legion. They also counted the loss of the Twelfth Legion's eagle - an unspeakable disgrace. At this point Gallus abandoned his baggage and his siege train of artillery, which the warlord Simon ben Gioras and his followers delivered to the authorities in Jerusalem. Gioras had hoped that this would buy him a position of authority in the city, but was rejected by the ruling council who did not want a warlord in their midst when they attempted to negotiate with the Romans.

When Gallus eventually made it as far as Caesarea and the safety of the legions stationed there, he was a broken man. His campaign had turned into calamity. The rebels now controlled the whole of Jerusalem. They held the strongholds of Machaerus in southern Peraea, Masada and a large part of Judaea. At this point, some of the city's leading citizens left Jerusalem and headed for Jordan.

Learning of the *Legate's* defeat the citizens of Damascus, a predominantly Greek city with a long standing grudge against its Jewish minority, decided to get rid of them. They achieved this by rounding them up and holding them in the city's gymnasium, from which they released them in batches to cut their throats at leisure.

18

To celebrate his thirtieth birthday, the Emperor decided to tour Greece. He would liberate Hellus (which meant it would be exempt from tribute). This tour of Greece would celebrate the world's first *artistic* games at which, of course, Nero would win all the significant first prizes. It was in Greece that Nero came under the influence of a Satanist and magician; a Greek named Karkinos.

Under the magus' influence, an already seriously flawed character slipped into madness. He came to believe that his role in life was to become an artist of the highest aesthetic and spiritual standing. As a living deity his destiny and duty was to demonstrate by example. People were told to abandon accepted morality and copy his example. Nero, utterly without morals, announced anything was allowed; that the moral laws of society were an invention and were to be discarded.

In the Grecian artistic games, the senators and their wives were *invited* to participate in competitions embracing music, poetry and chariot racing – three categories based on the Greek festivals of antiquity. What was not part of Greek antiquity were elderly Roman matriarchs being forced to lose their dignity, capering in an unseemly manner on the stage, whilst their equally elderly husbands, powerful and respected senators, found themselves in clumsy combat in the gladiatorial arena.

Not to be outdone, Nero himself pranced about on the stage in the feminine roles; a particular practice that scandalised a senate heartily sick of its ruler. More than a few minds were secretly scheming as to how they might rid themselves of the monster who had the power of life and death over them, who offended their sensibilities and insulted all the virtues and morality that embodied what it was to be Roman. They had put up with Nero's scandalous incestuous relationship with his mother, but refused to support him when he scandalised the whole of Roman society, by marrying a freedman called Doryphorus in a ceremony complete with dowry and bridal veil. The couple celebrated their marriage by indulging in one of Nero's favourite pastimes of dressing up in the skins of tigers and disembowelling men and women tied to stakes. This revolting behaviour reached its peak at a banquet turned orgy, given in Nero's honour by Tigellinus. The entertainment took place on a raft, moored on a lake owned by Marcus Agrippa. The raft had been towed by gilded barges rowed by degenerates and unfortunates; the disfigured and malformed.

On the quays, brothels had been stocked with high ranking courtesans who had to vie for trade with lower ranking prostitutes, male and female, who solicited competitively, indicating by lewd posturing and gesturing their unnatural and bizarre sexual services. That which caused the most offence had been the panders offering children of all ages for their use. The sexually inexperienced youngsters stared about in bewilderment and incomprehension – and eventually terror as their role became apparent.

Like all dictators, Nero worried about possible rivals. He began to imagine enemies everywhere as his behaviour massively alienated the senatorial class. Increasing paranoia deepened his suspicions. Prominent senators were charged with imaginary crimes and executed if they refused to commit suicide. Nero wasn't the first emperor to employ a system called *bonadamnatorum*. Condemning men to death and confiscating their estates and all their worldly possessions; the dependents of his victims left penniless and banished from the empire on pain of death if they ever returned. In sixty five, Nero had ordered the Empire's best general, Corbulo, to return from the east and then ordered him to kill himself. Tragically, in the following year, Nero recalled the commanders of the legions in

Lower and Upper Germany, the talented Scribonius brothers, Rufus and Proculus, ordering them to commit suicide or face execution. This brought about the demise of Rome's three outstanding generals, whose loyalty to Rome and the Emperor was unswerving.

As a further safeguard against a putsch in his absence from the capital, the entire senate and their families had been *invited* to join him in Greece. Among these was the fifty eight year old retired general Flavius Vespasian, who had played a part in Claudius' invasion of Britain where he had captured the Isle of Wight and later Maiden Castle, for which he was awarded the insignia of a Triumph. Made a *consul* in fifty one, he retired two years' later to the country. This took him away from court and particularly Nero's mother Agrippina, who had taken a dislike to him. With good reason, Vespasian feared the daughter of Germanicus Caesar and sister of Caligula. When Claudius died in fifty four it was from being poisoned by Agrippina, who was his second wife.

Ferociously ambitious and determined to be Empress she contrived to get Nero, her son by her first husband Domitius Ahenobarbus, accepted as heir to the purple in place of Britannicus, Claudius' own son by his former wife Messalina.

Within a year of Nero's succession Britannicus was dead, having fallen victim to a poisoned dish of mushrooms served to him by Agrippina. She was consolidating her hold on the Empire by sleeping with her son Nero and having herself declared Augusta – an act which eventually prompted Nero to have her assassinated.

Called out of retirement, Vespasian became governor of the province of Africa which he successfully administered for two years. While he was in Africa his wife died, leaving him with the responsibility of two sons. The eldest, Titus, a serving officer in the army; the youngest aged thirteen, Domitian, was a strange youth, with a liking for pain – other people's - particularly when he was the cause.

Returning from Africa, Vespasian was surprised and chagrined to be invited to join the Court in Greece. The general, who was indifferent to the arts, particularly singing and music, could not find a credible excuse to turn down the royal invitation. It was during an excruciatingly boring poetry reading by Nero – one of his own of course – that a courier arrived from Judaea; a senior *tribune* sent by Cestius Gallus from Antioch. The crash of his hobnailed sandals on the marbled floor announced his presence, interrupting the senators, court nobles and their wives, who were gathered in an admiring circle round Nero as he proclaimed one of his excruciatingly bad poems.

Flanked on each side by Nero's personal bodyguard, the *tribune* saluted and dropped to one knee. Nero, incredulous at the interruption, stared at him in silence. The entire court held its breath. The *tribune* cleared his throat. "My Lord Caesar, I bring greetings from your most loyal subject Cestius Gallus, *Legate* of Syria and Judaea". The soldier paused before continuing. "The *Legate* sends you a report of the grave circumstances that have arisen in Judaea". At this the *tribune* offered the scroll he had brought.

Sensing that whatever was written on the proffered report was something he didn't want to know, the Emperor refused to take it. Instead he caught Vespasian's eye and, with a barely perceptible nod, indicated he was to accept the unwelcome news. Vespasian dismissed the courier and waited. He made no attempt to give the message to the Emperor, though he knew without being told that it contained dire news – as indeed did Nero, who had flung himself into a chair frowning heavily, lips compressed in anger.

After what seemed an age, he held out his hand with a deep sigh and breaking the seal unrolled the report. Its contents brought him to his feet with a roar. "Rebellion". The word was literally spat out, saliva splattering those nearest to him. "The filthy, ungrateful Jews have rebelled".

The gasp from the assembled courtiers was lost in the tirade unleashed by the Emperor. Pounding up and down on the dais, sweat streaming down his face, he castigated his absent *Legate* and the rebellious Jews in equal measure. In the middle of his rant, Nero stopped as suddenly as he had started, remembering he had murdered Rome's best generals. Who could he send to Judaea; somebody who would do the job, and would not have dreams of Empire? That man, he suddenly realised, was standing next to him; a capable soldier from an ordinary family with no political background – a safe pair of hands.

So in February, the fifty-seven-year old Vespasian was appointed to the rank of *Legatus*. His orders were to avenge Rome for the loss of a legion and its eagle, to punish the Jews for insulting the Emperor by ceasing to offer the daily sacrifice for Rome and for the Emperor, to set an example to the world of Rome's power and be a lesson to those who thought to challenge it. His orders were that Israel was to cease to exist, Jerusalem to be razed to the ground and the Jewish people annihilated.

With him would go the man who would replace Gallus – Gaius Licinius Mucianus who, like Vespasian, was 'old school', a statesman and a soldier.

Vespasian, glad to take his leave of a court he detested and an Emperor he held in contempt, set out for Antioch via the Hellespont and Turkey. Here he took command of two legions, the Fifth Macedonica and the famous Tenth Fretensis, and marched to Ptolemais. From there he made his way to Acre and was met by King Agrippa who pledged his loyalty. Together they marched to Sepphoris, already garrisoned by Roman troops. This would be Vespasian's headquarters for the coming campaign.

First he would gather all his forces and only when they were under his command would he move. Throughout his military life Vespasian had stuck to a policy of attacking each target with maximum force, eliminating the enemy to ensure there would be no survivors to trouble him later. Having settled at Sepphoris his first task was to send orders to his son Titus and an old friend, Tiberius Julius Alexander, who had served as a staff officer under the senior general Gnaeus Domititius Corbulo during the campaigns against the Parthians in sixty two. He was an experienced soldier who, under Claudius, had been appointed procurator of Judaea in 46–48.

Meanwhile, Judaea was an opportunity for Vespasian, who saw the war as a chance to get away from Nero. It would be Tiberius who would advise Vespasian to adopt the strategy of allowing the Jews of Jerusalem to destroy themselves. He also pinpointed the three rival leaders and their followers – Eleazar ben Simon, leader of the zealots; the private army of John of Gischala; and Simon Ben Gioras, who was supported by men from Idumaea, the southern part of Judaea that the Romans did not control. All three, Tiberius pointed out, had different agendas. John strove for political freedom. Simon on the other hand stood at the head of a Messianic movement. Eleazar was a nationalist who wanted the Romans out of Judaea, with himself in power as ruler of Jerusalem.

19

The six hundred recruits wore cloaks as protection against the elements. Those who had belongings had them strapped in a bundle carried on their shoulders. It was a dark night, with dampness in the air that signalled rain was on the way. The newly arrived trainees, anxious to get into the warmth of the barracks that surrounded the parade ground, envied the legionaries who had been their escorts and who had been dismissed to its warmth and a hot meal.

The ragged lines of volunteers shivered in the icy rain that had started to fall. The vast recruit training camp, located in the country north of Rome, was ideally suited to its purpose. Here the would-be legionaries would eventually take part in field exercises that simulated combat in every kind of terrain and in conditions and circumstances dictated by their tutors.

Gaius Iovis the duty centurion, immaculately turned out, was flanked by a dozen NCOs and the *optio*, the junior officer responsible for the administrative tasks associated with the men under the centurion's command; punishment records, administering the men's pay, savings, equipment, sentry rotas, organising weapons inspections, feed for the section's mules, ration collection and barrack inspections - all of which had to be carried out and recorded accurately, much of it on a daily basis. This required the *optio* to be literate, good with numbers, have organisational skills and a firm grasp of logistics. He performed these duties as an addition to being a soldier, and was not excused any of the day-to-day duties of a legionary. The rank and his performance were pre-requisites to promotion to centurion.

Gaius Iovis was as indifferent to the weather as he was to his new charges' discomfort. "The men who brought you here" he bellowed "are soldiers of Rome; the best in the world. You signed up to join them and my job is to make sure you are fit to do so. Those of you who work hard in the next six months will leave here as legionaries. Those that fail – if they survive - could end up in the Empire's mines or chained to a galley oar." With that ominous promise the shivering men were finally dismissed to barracks.

The drill instructors arrived before dawn, canes swinging, iron shod sandals booting the startled bleary eyed recruits out of their warm cots. They were herded into the dark street and driven like cattle to the stores, where they were stripped of their civilian identities.

Stark naked, the shivering men lined up at the long counters, where the quarter master's assistants handed out their new clothes and equipment - tunics, jerkins, woollen breeches, heavy cloaks, mess tin and, most importantly, a pair of heavy sandals soled with iron studs. As no attention had been given to sizing, men hurriedly swapped various garments they had been issued with. Eventually standard issue tunics were dragged over standard issue rough wool breeches. Sandals were laced and heavy leather jerkins pulled over heads and buckled fast at the sides.

Centurian Gaius arrived with a blast of cold air from the door he kicked open and a roar that silenced the room. "OUTSIDE - NOW!"

With the drill instructors mercilessly hammering them with their canes, the hapless recruits staggered into the cold dawn, to be driven onto the parade ground where they spent a long and painful day learning the basics - to move and to stop on command, to march in step and to turn left, right and about. They had to stand to attention and to memorise their position in the rank allotted to them. They ended their first day marching to the armourer's stores, to receive a mail shirt, a helmet and a dagger. Barely having time to try out their new possessions, the armourer's assistants issued training javelins, large rectangular shields made of cane and wooden swords weighted with lead. These weapons were greeted with incredulity by the new recruits. They were the object of much ribald comment until Gaius put in an appearance.

The weeks that followed were filled with endless drilling. The dawn trumpet called the recruits to assembly dressed and equipped for inspection, followed by a breakfast of barley porridge and watered wine. Then back to the parade ground to learn the complicated parade drills.

Gaius and his teams of drill instructors stalked their ranks. Every mistake was punished with a savage blow from the thick canes they carried and a volley of curses. Painfully they learned to stop and turn, to wheel and to march in step with perfect precision. Then they learned the battlefield drills, unique to Rome's legions; their complex formation changes, open order to close, line to square and back to line. They learned how to form the tortoise formation and the wedge. Without breaking step they learned the difficult but vital manoeuvre performed within the square, whereby men in the middle and the back move forward and the men at the front move back out of the front line, thus presenting the enemy with a rested adversary. In a battle that could rage all day, this manoeuvre was of incalculable value to the Romans.

During a close engagement, visibility could become a problem as they and the opposing armies stirred up great clouds of dust. Noise was another element which, combined with poor visibility, caused confusion, making communication difficult. Commanders used standards as rallying points, but moving their forces tactically as a battle developed was difficult. Using voice commands was ineffectual. To overcome this, the Romans had designed a trumpet, the *cornicon*, with a particularly penetrating note. They also developed signals to manoeuvre their forces across the battlefield. So important were these trumpeters that they never entered the thick of battle, staying close to the overall commander and protected by his bodyguard, ready to sound out his orders which would ring across the battlefield.

Instantly recognising these signals was so important, that Gaius simulated the noise and dust of battle by turning out the cavalry to mill around his trainees, churning up dust. The noise was supplied by a military band!

The recruits, blinded by dust, bumped and barged by the cavalry's horses and deafened by the enthusiastic band, were forced repeatedly to respond to the blare of the *cornicons* and carry out a series of complicated battlefield manoeuvres.

From a wooden tower Gaius appraised their performance. Nothing less than perfect was acceptable. "They are" he observed drily to one of his aids "only playing – nobody has any weapons!" Importantly, burdened with the weight of their equipment, they had built up the muscle and the endurance to do this for hours on end. This was just as well for, six weeks into their basic training Gaius started to lead them out of the camp four times a week on punishing route marches which started after three long hours on morning parade. At the day's end they trudged back to base in the dark. Disgruntled and bone weary, they would wait to be dismissed by the *old man* who had been with them all day. Even the toughest among them grudgingly acknowledged Centurion Gaius' fitness and wondered if they would ever match it.

It was at about this time that Gaius and his drill instructors started to talk to the recruits. At first the men found this somewhat unnerving, having been subjected almost exclusively to curses and invective screamed at them for the last two months. They had also become accustomed to being struck hard, without warning, for the slightest failure or slowness to respond instantly to an order. Anybody foolish enough to indicate, by lifting so much as an eyebrow, that any of this was unwarranted, could double around the parade ground ten times carrying a fifty pound log above his head, or spend a week filling in full latrines and digging new ones. Offences warranting more serious punishment escalated rapidly – stoppage of pay, double guard duty, flogging, and as a last resort, execution.

During brief rest periods Gaius and his drill instructors began to educate their charges, explaining how the Roman army functioned; getting the men to understand why it was so successful; what their part in it would be and, very importantly, other than their pay what they could expect to get out of it. Which was a pension after twenty five years' service, free land and slaves to work it if they were prepared to colonise the most recent of Rome's conquests. Plus, if you were not a Roman citizen, you were granted citizenship.

At this point in their training, the recruits were introduced to camp construction, which took place outside the walls of the fortress. Under the ever present drill instructors and Gaius' watchful eye, their first task was to observe. A circular arena had been marked out with coloured pegs. Outside the marked arena a cohort of regular troops from the barracks was standing easy. With them were several wagons, their contents sheeted over. The mules that hauled them had been hobbled and turned loose to browse.

"From now on at the end of the day you build a camp, which is a defensive position. As we are in not hostile territory, this requires a considerably less complicated structure – which means less work!" What had really registered with the troops was not the amount of work necessary to achieve the task that lay ahead of them. It was what they would be required to do it at the end of every day, including those days they had forced marched thirty miles!

While Gaius had been addressing the recruits, the regular troops had unloaded a quantity of picks and shovels. After each man had been issued one of each, they were ordered to take up a position within the outer circle marked by white pegs. Gaius ordered them to start digging. Each man was allocated a section of circle six feet in length and six feet wide, which he was required to excavate to a depth of four feet. "The spoil of which", Gaius growled, "is to be piled up on the inner side of the ditch and stamped down". Even though they were toughened by months of exercising, marching, and weapons training, the recruits found the digging hard going.

After two hours hard graft, the trench was completed to the centurion's satisfaction and a thirty minute break called. During the time they had been digging the regular troops had unloaded the supply wagons. The result was a vast quantity of stores stacked in piles, each marked with a different coloured pennant.

"Right, on your feet, listen and learn - or you can fill that bloody trench in and dig another". Gaius' words brought the weary recruits to their feet with alacrity. "You now have to construct the camp – your camp – which may well be the thing that ensures your survival.

"You will be split up into teams. Each team will be assisted by three regular troops. You will obey them in all things or answer to me. Teams will be allotted different tasks. These will take place in an ordered sequence. First, the commander's tent will be set up in the centre of the camp on the spot marked. All of the commander's equipment will be placed inside it. Second, all the animals and wagons and stores will also be placed in the centre. Latrines will be dug, a cookhouse established and the hospital wagon made ready.

"Next, the officers' tents will be placed in an inner ring around the centre. Fourthly, streets have been marked out radiating from the hub of the commander's tent. Along these streets you pitch your tents in the allocated spaces. Outside each tent you will set up a tripod and every man will place his weapons on it ready to hand. Fifthly, every man will know exactly where he is to go if an alarm is sounded.

"Finally, the *optio* will establish a sentry roster and set the password for the day. Sentries will be posted immediately. When the camp has been established to my satisfaction, and only then, will work cease and you will be free to take your ease".

This last brought an ironical cheer from the recruits, who were beginning to have a grudging respect for the man who could march them into the ground, outfight any two of them and never show any sign of fatigue. Meanwhile, an NCO was preparing another phase of their training, the building and working of artillery, plus the setting up and use of ladders and towers to scale obstacles and rams to batter down walls. More sophisticated machines and methods were the province of the legion's engineering core and the legion's architects who designed war machines.

All of this weaponry was capable of construction at field level and was prefabricated for easy transportation. Gaius' men would eventually become expert in the use of a wide variety of these weapons. There were machines called *tormenta* that catapulted a variety of materials at defenders on the walls. Incendiaries and rocks could be hurled in large quantities with devastating effect. Used in conjunction with the *tormenta* were the *ballistae,* powered by two horizontal arms which were stressed with tightly wound ropes of horse hair. The arms were drawn to the rear with a lever to provide the torsion power to hurl a large stone with tremendous force. Often the *ballistae* was hauled up into a tower and protected by snipers armed with slings or bows.

Similar to the *ballistae* was the *onogar.* Because of its size the *onogar,* which had a frame of solid timber, was used at ground level. A type of catapult, it hurled huge stones, often covered with pitch and set alight before being flung over the walls to destroy buildings.

A weapon used very effectively against defenders manning city walls was the *Scorpio,* a crossbow like device that fired heavy, metre long arrows with great accuracy and tremendous force.

While the defenders were under attack, battering rams were brought up to hammer the walls. Each was a huge beam, similar in size to the main mast of a large ship. One end of it was capped with iron shaped like a ram's head. This was suspended from a second beam with cables around its middle, which in turn was supported at both ends by posts fixed into the ground. Drawn back by a team of men, it was then swung with all their power, so that its head hit the wall. This was done repeatedly, day and night, with teams of men ensuring its force never waned. When operating the ram, the whole structure and its operators were encased in a mobile shelter called a tortoise – the *testudo* - from which the ram would swing out of the shelter, similar to a tortoise's head appearing from its shell. The frame of the *testudo* was covered with uncured hides which rendered it fireproof.

Roman infantry, who were to assault the walls as well as having ladders, used siege towers. These came in a variety of sizes and designs, often with different devices attached to them such as artillery, drawbridges and rams. Towers were between fifty and seventy five feet high and often sheeted with metal plate to protect them from fire. Occasionally they would be fitted with leather hosepipes into which water could be pumped.

Walls could also be attacked by mining. Sometimes tunnels would be dug in secret under the walls as a means of entering the city. Alternatively, caves would be dug under the walls' foundations and underpinned with wood. Inflammable materials were then packed in and fired; all of which was designed to cause their collapse.

Building and maintaining this array of weapons, was an army of *auxiliary* specialists who were attached to every legion. Highly skilled engineers, they would go ahead of the advancing army, building a road on which the legions advanced.

Late into the night Gaius sat with the *optio*, drawing up the recruits' training schedules that would cover every aspect of the transportation, assembly and use of this devastatingly effective weaponry.

What the Centurion Gaius didn't know was that he and the *optio*, along with his recruits, would soon see active service in Judaea – to fight a war that would last seven bloody years and change the course of history.

20

Ananus had been ill for days. Nothing the physicians dosed him with could alleviate his diarrhoea. His frequent trips to the latrine had been replaced by a hastily constructed commode. Bowel movements were a scalding pain in his gut. "It is", he gasped to his doctor, "like a piece of kinked wire being pulled out of my arse every time I shit – which is every few minutes".

In spite of the shivering and the sweating that accompanied his condition, the High Priest was forced to stay on duty. In the wake of the mayhem that had descended on the Holy City, a power struggle was taking place. Even in his present incapacity, exercising the power of his office as High Priest of all Israel was paramount. Ananus knew that he had to establish some form of government before Eleazar succeeded in having him murdered.

For the moment he was relatively safe in his private quarters deep within the Temple complex. With him, other than his doctor and several Temple police who were there as a bodyguard, was one of the city's senior prefects, Joseph ben Gorion. "Call an immediate meeting of the Sanhedrin and the city elders". The stricken Priest paused to expel a gaseous blast that added to the already malodorous stink that pervaded the room. "The agenda for the meeting is to determine a new government to replace the defeated Roman authority. If we don't establish the rule of law, this city will descend into chaos within the week".

It said much for the power of his office that, sick or not, within the hour the seventy members of the Sanhedrin had been assembled, along with the rich and influential and the city's councillors.

They met in the great chamber normally reserved for meetings of the Sanhedrin. Ananus was carried in on his reeking commode. By his side in constant attendance was the chief physician, who by now had wisely acquired several assistants. In the event of a tragedy, the blame could not just be shared but shifted.

Bolstered by a little warmed wine, a haggard Ananus passed the agenda he had scribbled to ben Gioron to read out. In a sombre voice he read, "Let us set aside the wisdom or not of rebelling against Rome. What is done is done and will not easily be undone. If Israel is to survive, if we who hold the land of Israel are to survive, we must not just face the armies Rome will send against us, we have to defeat them. Or parlay a peace. To do this we need not just an army; we need a well-trained, well equipped, well led army. We have none of these things yet.

"We need a central government here in Jerusalem to uphold the law, to administer justice, to run the country and", there was a pause, "to determine a strategy to wage war, which is not the same thing as deciding the tactics for an individual battle. This army that we raise will have to be fed. That means providing a hundred thousand meals three times a day, every day and a hundred thousand gallons of water every day. Not here in the city, but in the field, in the desert, in the mountains, in the heat, in the cold and the wet. You will need the same again for the pack animals. I could go on with what you will need if you are to avoid dying, let alone winning – but the point I hope is made.

"Before you leave this meeting you have the responsibility of doing at least three things.

Firstly, appoint a supreme commander and deputy to run the government and the country.

Secondly, you must immediately organise the repair of those city walls which are incomplete.

Thirdly, you must divide the country into regions; I suggest six. This has been done in the past and was successful. Then you must appoint men to govern them. Men who can rise, train and lead a peasant army; these must be generals to match those that Rome will send against you. Finally, the civil war raging in the city must stop. If it doesn't, it will do the job for the Romans. All they will need to do is pacify the countryside and wait for Jew to kill Jew in the Holy City – which is what is currently happening".

There was a long silence following this announcement. Before it could be broken, the stricken Ananus was born away.

The Jews in the great hall, after having a collective sigh, already traumatised by the horror of what was happening in the streets, would have gladly gone home there and then but Ananus had anticipated this. The Temple police, armed with clubs, informed them that the doors of the hall would be locked and only reopened when they had reached decisions on who would be the supreme commander, who would be his deputy and who would be the governors of the designated regions. In the meantime refreshments would be served.

It took the remainder of the day and the best part of the night, but come dawn the weary councillors and the Sanhedrin reached a consensus, sending Ananus a list of who would do what. In doing so they gave him the wooden spoon. He was made supreme commander with Joseph Ben Gorion as his deputy. Their first task was to provide Temple funds and raise twenty thousand men to be employed repairing and strengthening the wall against the inevitable siege.

Foundries were ordered to operate day and night turning out weapons – swords, daggers, axes, javelins, arrows and bows. Other craftsmen were organised to produce armour, helmets and shields. To bolster morale, Ananus ordered that the city would strike its own silver coins, dated year one.

The country was divided into six administrative districts and their governors despatched.

Idumaea – Eleazar son of Ananias.

Jericho – Joseph ben Simon.

Peraea – Manasses.

Thamna, Lydda, Joppa – John the Essene.

Gophna Aqraba – The central region. John son of Ananias.

Galilee – Josephus ben Matthias.

The promotion of Eleazar, son of Ananias, to the governorship of Idumaea, was intended to remove him from Jerusalem and weaken the Zealot party. It was a ploy that worked better than Ananas could ever have hoped for. Having left for Idumaea, Eleazar simply disappeared, never to be seen again. It was assumed that he and his party had been caught in a sandstorm and buried alive – a not uncommon occurrence when crossing the region's vast deserts.

His misfortune was another's gain. His place in the Zealot leadership was taken by another Eleazar; Eleazar ben Simon, who had fought against the forces of Cestius Gallus at Beth Horon.

Despite opposition from the High Priest Ananus, Eleazar ben Simon had established himself in Jerusalem where he attracted Galilean Zealots seeking refuge in the capital.

He was very much helped in his bid for power by the enormous wealth he had acquired during the battle with Gallus. Simon had had the good fortune to capture the Roman *Legate's* war chest intact.

Josephus was born in the first year of Caligula's reign. His father Matthias was a Priest and his mother, of Royal Blood, was descended from the Hasmonaeans. Josephus was precociously intelligent. So much so, that by the age of fourteen he was being consulted by the church elders on points of Jewish law.

Josephus was about thirty when he set about the organisation of his district with energy and skill. His first act was to conciliate the local people by allowing them to manage their own affairs. In every town, a council of seventy and a bench of seven were appointed. His next task would be the raising of an army and the fortification of the towns in his region, Galilee.

21

They trudged in grim silence across the deserted battlefield, littered with the remains of unburied Jewish and Roman dead – shattered skulls, broken vertebrae and cages of shipwrecked ribs, black with dried blood. Everywhere was the obscenity of the scavenging jackals, pulling and tearing, and the ungainly waddle of the vultures which shrieked and squabbled, quarrelling over an abundance of titbits.

Josephus, at the head of his newly formed army, knew this sight would either harden their resolve or fill them with fear. With dusk gentling the hills, they needed to camp, but the thought of sleeping in this charnel house was unbearable. As he turned to speak to one of his lieutenants, he spotted a severed hand amid the debris. It was still firmly clutching the sword that its owner, a Roman soldier, had been carrying. With a grimace he said to one of the men at his side, "Send a mounted scout ahead to find a campsite for the night clear of this abattoir".

The man nodded and lurched away to pass on the order. He was John, son of Judah, a hunchback who sometimes allowed people to touch his hump for luck in return for a coin. He had attached himself to Josephus' army for companionship as much as anything, his affliction denying him the company of normal people.

In desperate haste, Josephus had organised the defence of the principal towns in Galilee. Thanks to his efforts and the funds he had brought from Jerusalem, the walls of the towns of Taricheae, Tiberius and Mount Tabor had been rebuilt. They had also managed to strengthen the larger villages in upper and lower Galilee and along the border into Jordan. It had angered Josephus that the people of Sepphoris, the capital of Galilee, had rejected his help. They said, "We will see to our own defences at our own expense". Knowing that the citizens of Sepphoris were pro-Roman, he left them to it.

Josephus, with his experience of Rome and first-hand knowledge of how formidable Rome's well trained legions were, had no illusions as to how effective his best efforts would be. At best they would slow the enemy down. Nonetheless, Josephus did not spare himself in knocking his army of peasant farmers into shape. In three months he had sixty thousand infantry that, though untried, knew their business.

More promising was the forty thousand cavalry he had put together. Natural riders on either camels or horses, it was simply a matter of training them to obey orders; to act on command with purpose and grasp basic cavalry tactics. At least ten thousand of these men were either proficient with a bow or capable of teaching others. In the end, Josephus ended up with forty thousand cavalry, twenty thousand armed with sword and lance, and twenty thousand archers armed with sword and bow.

As news of Josephus' achievement spread he was acknowledged as the most important and most powerful man in Galilee. Local bullies and would-be bandits, who were no better than gangsters, soon learnt that this Pharisee priest turned soldier was a firm believer in the law of the prophets. His justice was biblical and summary. Inevitably his success and imperviousness to bribery brought him enemies; mostly small fry they could be ignored. Larger fish were eventually dealt with. There was one exception – a war lord and racketeer of long standing, with a reputation for brutality that did not stop short of murder. John of Gischala commanded a private army. His principal trade was extortion in the form of a protection racket.

The caravans and traders that passed through the town of Safed, in the wild country north of the town of Gischala, were forced to pay John and his enforcers for their protection against the perils of the journey ahead. Or be attacked by Gischala's thugs who, when they were not protecting the caravans, terrorised the local hill villages.

A major source of John's income came from an olive oil monopoly he had established.

Throughout Galilee his men had visited olive oil producers and told them that they and they alone, would buy their oil. They also fixed the price they would pay. Those that refused were warned that they would no longer receive the *protection* of John. At first nothing happened. Then the unfortunate farmer was subjected to a reign of terror. One day he might find a dead dog in his well. A week later a barn would burn down. If he still said no, his donkeys and other livestock would disappear. Then he would be kidnapped, taken into the desert and beaten, left to crawl back to his farm. A final ultimatum would be a threat to kill his wife and his children. Having suffered at the hands of these gangsters he never doubted that this would happen – so he capitulated. If he didn't, he would wake up one morning to find the head of his wife in a bucket outside his door.

John also tried to undermine Josephus' authority, by putting it about that the young Jewish general was preparing to hand the country over to the Romans. He used the charge of traitor and the accusation of collaboration, to demand Josephus' death. Knowing that Josephus had enemies in the Sanhedrin who were jealous of his success in Galilee, John denounced him to the authorities in Jerusalem, having first paved the way with a substantial bribe.

In response, a commission of three Pharisees and three Sadducees with an armed bodyguard set out for Galilee. Josephus' father, however, had written to his son from Jerusalem, warning him of the plot against him. Josephus responded by sending men into the countryside to rally the peasants and pay his dues to the local headman. The commission found itself interviewing peasants who declared their respect, admiration and thanks to Josephus for his protection and care.

When the commission tried to speak to Josephus, he sent them a letter of apology. He couldn't attend the meeting; he was busy fighting Placidus, a lieutenant of Cestius Gallus, who was in charge of a local garrison. He also sent messengers, Galileans, to Jerusalem to report this true state of affairs to the Sanhedrin and their loyalty to Josephus. The commission was immediately recalled, giving Josephus, at the head of his army, the opportunity to march on Tiberius which immediately opened its gates to him, the city elders pledging their loyalty to the Jewish cause.

Meanwhile, during the winter of 66/67, the whole country was as turbulent as Galilee. In Jerusalem, Ananus had ordered that work to defend the city was to be given an overriding priority. The walls had been repaired and artillery captured from Cestius Gallus had been positioned. Vast stores of swords, axes and spear heads had been forged and every able bodied man was under military training.

Taking advantage of the lack of policing in the countryside from anybody's militia, be it Roman or Jewish, Simon ben Gioras put on the mantle of a warlord and ran riot, burning towns and villages, torturing and killing the inhabitants for their possessions. In response Ananus sent troops to put him down, forcing him to retreat to Massada from where he promptly preyed on Idumaea, forcing its rulers to protect the villages by garrisoning them.

22

Titus, Vespasian's eldest son, in spite of being short and thick set, was extremely fit and an excellent horseman. Fluent in Greek and Latin, he had served in the army in Britain and Germany. A student of philosophy and law, he had made a good marriage to the daughter of a retired commander of the *Praetorian* Guard. Unfortunately she had died in childbirth, and Titus' second marriage ended in divorce. Fortune, however, smiled on him and he was made a *quaestor*, an appointment to public office, helping to supervise the treasury and financial affairs of the state and its armies.

When Vespasian ordered him to come to Judaea, he was able to do so because he had relatives who would stand hostage for him in Rome – Titus' younger brother, the thirteen years old Domitian, and his uncle, Vespasian's brother Flavius Sabinus, who was the prefect of Rome. On receiving his father's orders, Titus left Italy and travelled to Alexandria where he assumed command of the Fifteenth Legion Appollinaris, and made his way to Ptolemais, a Greek city and port in Galilee, to meet his father. Their combined forces of three legions totalling eighteen thousand men were quadrupled in size by reinforcements provided by the client Kings in the regions; this support being one of the terms laid down by Rome when they were appointed.

Vespasian, with over sixty thousand men under his command, was ready to plan his campaign. At fifty seven years of age he was a distinguished veteran. He had also served in Thrace, Crete and Cyrenaica. An able administrator he had been raised to the rank of *consul* and awarded the governorship of North Africa.

Acknowledged as a man of integrity and character, who dispensed justice honestly and with great humanity, he returned home not noticeably wealthier than when he went. Reluctant to become part of Nero's court, he had only done so when to refuse would have caused, one could say, fatal offence.

His reputation in the army was that of a successful but unimaginative commander, reluctant to take a chance, only willing to move when he had carefully considered his options and worked out a thought-through strategy. His men, appreciative of the care he took of their lives, were ferociously loyal. They also shared his somewhat earthy sense of humour and marvelled at his ability to recall individual names and incidents from previous battles. He had the invaluable gift of being able to walk down a line of soldiers, stopping suddenly to drop a hand on a man's shoulder, address him by name and recall some detail of a battle they had both been in.

A story that was legend in the legions was that of a raw recruit, a youngster barely eighteen years old, facing the full force of twenty thousand painted Britons screaming for blood. Obviously nervous, he was spotted by Vespasian as he rode down the line. The General had reached down and clapped him on the shoulder saying, "All you have to do son is two things. Keep a tight arsehole and look after the old bugger on your right. The even older one on your left will look after you".

The roar of laughter that this brought steadied not just the rookie, but the whole line. With shields locked and swords drawn, the trumpets had sounded above the screams of the attacking Britons who had charged fearlessly in overwhelming numbers, to be received by a wall of iron that moved relentlessly forward, swords flashing as it marched to war.

Settled in a comfortable chair, Vespasian unrolled the scroll he had received earlier in the day. Military intelligence was prized by Vespasian, who spent time and money gathering it. Taking a sip from the goblet next to his elbow, he commenced reading.

There is, he read, *Upper and Lower Galilee, bordered by Syria and Phoenicia. To the west lies Ptolemais and Mount Carmel. Galilee's southern border is created by Samaritus and Scythopolis as far as the tributaries of the Jordan River; the start of the kingdom of King Agrippa. Beyond Galilee's northern frontier lies Tyre. Lower Galilee runs from Tiberius to Ptolemais on the coast, which extends to the great plain. Encircled by powerful foreign neighbour, the two Galilees, in spite of having been frequently attacked, have never been fully conquered. Galileans are renowned as warriors, and the land they defend so fiercely has rich soil and an abundance of water. As a result of these twin blessings, they produce an abundance of every kind of crop. All types of trees are easily grown, including olives and grapevines. Lush grasslands provide grazing for large herds of cows that support its substantial diary industries and the region has grown wealthy by the selling of its agricultural surpluses. The capital of Galilee is Sepphoris, more Greek than Jew, and as a consequence very pro-Roman. This would make an excellent HQ for the Galilee campaign. Its Roman garrison is commanded by the tribune Placidus.*

Vespasian, satisfied with what he had read, had begun to plan his campaign. His first act would be to strengthen the garrison at Sepphoris with one thousand cavalry and six thousand infantry. Eventually, this combined force would successfully overrun their immediate neighbours and in doing so inflict severe losses on Josephus' supporters.

In the coming months, Vespasian would wage a war of fire and sword from one end of Galilee to the other. Fire and sword spared nothing and nobody. Any town or village that failed to surrender immediately was destroyed, its population killed or enslaved and the town burnt to the ground.

A year after arriving in Judaea, Vespasian was sitting on his horse at the edge of the desert contemplating his next move. The raw smell of hot dust was in the air. The air was so dry that mucus in the nose dried to a crust. Vespasian cleared his throat and spat. He was eager to begin. Behind him his army was arranged in conventional order. The foreign auxiliaries, mostly Arab, formed the rear guard, a mixture of mounted and foot archers. Their orders were to defend against an enemy suddenly attacking from ambush. They were also responsible for reconnoitring woods and ravines, dried up river beds – anywhere the enemy could conceal itself.

After the auxiliaries came a mounted body of heavily armed and armoured Roman legionaries, followed by ten men from every *century*, carrying the tools necessary to mark out the site chosen for the evening's camp. In close attendance marched the pioneer corps, who would build the road ahead, grading rough surfaces and felling obstructive trees. These were followed by the personal baggage of Vespasian and his senior officers, guarded by a picked cavalry contingent, behind which rode Vespasian himself, closely supported by a bodyguard of soldiers armed with javelins.

Next came the cavalry. This was followed by a mule train that transported the battering rams and artillery. Behind them came the generals, the prefects of the *cohorts* and the *tribune*s. Protecting the leadership was a massive bodyguard of elite soldiers. Finally came the legions' standards surrounding the eagle, which was an effigy cast in pure gold and mounted on a pole. The King of Birds, symbol of the Empire – sacred emblem of Rome - to be defended to the death.

It was followed by the trumpeters and the whole army marching six men abreast, shoulder to shoulder, with centurions who maintained the formation. The servants of each legion followed. They had the task of looking after the baggage carried by the mules. Bringing up the rear were the mercenaries and, finally, a protective rear-guard of heavy infantry and a double troop of cavalry.

Unsurprisingly, Vespasian's arrival in Galilee was without incident. Only a fool would have challenged the might of his army. That first evening and the following days were occupied by the building of a substantial fort. It also gave the Romans an opportunity for a show of force. The legions marched and counter marched in perfect formation. The archers darkened the sky with a veritable blizzard of arrows and the infantry demonstrated its ability to put twenty thousand javelins into a targeted area with a single throw. Meanwhile the cavalry thundered over the plain casting lances of their own, before unsheathing their cavalry swords, the *spatha*, a straight double edged blade a meter long with a specially rounded tip.

The latter was to prevent the accidental stabbing your own foot or thigh and being flung off your horse. The double edged blade enabled the rider to swing and chop on either side of his mount simply by swinging his arm from side to side.

Orchestrating these different forces through their complex manoeuvres, conveying vital information – military orders - to every man on the field of battle, was achieved by the use of trumpets, the *cornicons*. A Roman commander, observing the way a battle was developing, needed to respond by not just moving his troops about the field, but doing it selectively if his troop deployments were to be effective amid the tremendous noise that any battle created and the inevitable clouds of dust that filled the air. As thousands of men and animals often milled about in a relatively small space, the human voice could go unheard. Signal flags were often obscured or only partially glimpsed. But the piercing blast of the *cornicons* reached every ear, different orders conveyed in the prescribed sequencing of notes blaring out. The disciplined squares turned as one, reformed, reshaped, changed direction. Tired fighters at the front stepped sideways and backwards. Fresh men took their place – a manoeuvre of inestimable value in a battle that could last all day. This manoeuvre also allowed precious water to be supplied to fighters struggling in hot, dusty conditions.

Vespasian knew there would be hidden watchers. This show of force was designed to give them second thoughts. To make them ask the question, did they really want to face this enemy on the field of battle?

Among those secretly watching eyes, had been some of Josephus' men. They had journeyed from Josephus' camp pitched not far from Sepphoris. When they reported back, Josephus lost half of his force to desertion. Disappointed and angry, Josephus knew that he no longer had enough men to challenge the enemy.

Worse still, he knew from the mutterings in the camp that many of his troops would ask for terms if they got the chance.

23

In Jerusalem John's men spread the word that, in a bid to stay in power, Ananus had sent emissaries to Rome to parlay for peace; a deal that would keep the High Priest of all Israel and the city's ruling class in power. As John plotted to take control of Jerusalem, he accused Ananus of betraying the people. He then turned his attention to the rank and file of the priesthood, persuading many that Ananus had betrayed them. John also wrote to the Idumaeans, claiming that Ananus was a traitor who, in a bid to stay in office, was secretly negotiating to hand over the country and the Holy City to the Romans.

John's men we so persuasive in spreading the lie of Ananus' treachery, they even convinced Simon ben Gioras. Even so, John was skating on thin ice. Appealing to the Idumaeans was a risky business.

John's recruiting of Gioras to ask the Idumaeans for assistance was a masterpiece of duplicity. Gioras' envoys to the Idumaeans would claim that the forces of evil, in the form of Ananus and the priests loyal to him, had formed an alliance with the city's ruling classes. To save their own skins and cling onto power, they were prepared to surrender the Holy City to the Romans.

The Idumaeans, in spite of a blood relationship uniting them to the Jews, had a history of resentment. Southern Judaea had been settled by the Edomites, an Arab people, who had taken over all of southern Palestine making Hebron their capital. When the Israelites had won back all of these gains they allowed them to remain in the country on the condition that they converted to Judaism.

Gioras, ever distrustful of John, had reasoned that if he agreed to manage the negotiations to the Idumaeans, he could turn it to his advantage. In the event of relationships becoming strained at some point in the future, he would be remembered by the Idumaeans as the person who had promoted their interests. Knowing the nature of the Idumaeans, Gioras was confident they would agree. As a race they were fiery by nature; resentful of discipline but susceptible to flattery; ready to take up arms at the merest suggestion of offence.

The two envoys were chosen for their political skills. Both were fluent and persuasive speakers. The Idumaeans, who had been monitoring the war, were deeply angered by what was taking place in Jerusalem. They were a receptive audience and voted overwhelmingly to give their support to the rebels.

Meanwhile Ananus, unaware that envoys had been sent to what he regarded as an old enemy, was horrified when he learned that the Idumaeans had decided to side with the Zealots. With the Idumaeans on their way, he barely had time to close and bar the city entrances and post extra men on the wall, when their army of twenty five thousand horse and foot arrived at Jerusalem's gates.

The High Priest was desperate to try and defuse the situation. Fearing that he, personally, might not go down too well as an advocate for peace, he decided his deputy would make the appeal. So taking his stand on a tower facing the Idumaeans, Jeshua made his plea.

"God's Holy City is being fought over like a bone by dogs who have gathered the support of bandits and criminals. Godless scum, who have ravaged the whole country before entering the Holy City. Even as I speak, they carouse drunkenly in the sanctuary. If you had been invited by the city fathers to join us against an outside enemy, you would be welcome. What reason, what cause has brought you here? If it was the lie that we were going to sell God's City to the Romans, it is the peddler of this filthy treason, offensive in the sight of God that you should seek out. You are free to enter the city of God, though not by force, to see for yourselves that what I tell you is the truth. So called nationalists have entered the very heart of the nation – The Temple – which they have made their headquarters for their operations against us. Lay down your arms. Come into the city by right of kinship to serve as judges in this matter. But know that while you bear arms, these gates will remain shut."

Jeshua's speech failed to persuade the Idumaean rank and file, who were angry at not being freely admitted. Simon, son of Cathla, one of their leaders, managed to silence the angry shouting of his men and addressed the priest. "You are willing to admit the Romans and deny your kin entry. We have of course" he said sarcastically "come to attack our own people, we who have answered the call to help you stay free. We Idumaeans will defend the house of God. We, the men you are excluding from our ancestral rights! We Idumaeans will defend the Temple and the city and fight for our common cause, resisting the enemy from without and the traitors within. We shall stay here as soldiers of God."

This speech was wildly cheered by the Idumaeans, not that they were in any way appeased, boiling with anger at their reception and exclusion from the capital, bewildered that the zealots who had called them in had not come to their aid. They could not go home. The disgrace of doing nothing was unthinkable, so they settled down as best they could in a makeshift camp outside the city gates. During the night, a massive thunderstorm struck the city and the camp. Lightning flashed continuously and thunderclaps bursting repeatedly made speech impossible. Both the Idumaeans and the people in the city saw this as a portent of disaster, an omen that heralded a terrible catastrophe.

So the Idumaeans sheltered beneath their shields, waiting stoically for the storm to end, while the zealots met to discuss how they might help them. Eventually, under the cover of the storm, they forced the locks of the city gates and admitted the Idumaeans, whose first thoughts were to join forces with the zealots.

Once inside, their combined forces attacked Ananus' citizen army. In a nightmare scene, the two sides came together in the fractured dark. In desperate hand to hand combat, the war cries of the Idumaeans were echoed by the zealots. The thunderous noise, coming from all sides, was amplified by the raging storm. No-one was spared and any who begged for mercy by reminding the Idumaeans of ties of blood, were killed. Crushed by the shields of the advancing combined forces, Ananus' men were cut down by a vengeful enemy bent on their absolute destruction.

When dawn broke, a watery sun illuminated the outer court of the Temple, revealing its walls, pillars and floor running with the blood of the nine thousand who had perished in the battle.

After the briefest of respites, the Idumaeans turned on the city, looting and killing indiscriminately.

Ananus and his deputy Jeshua, unwilling to flee the Temple, died on their knees, calling on God to avenge them.

With the priests of Israel floating face down in blood, the Idumaeans and the zealots seemed to lose all reason. They fell on the population like wolves. Ordinary citizens were rounded up and murdered out of hand in frenzied attacks that were indifferent to age or gender. The wealthy of the city, along with its councillors and men of noble birth, were singled out for execution. Ten thousand of the city's best men died in this manner. Their bodies, refused to their families for burial, were left to putrefy in the streets.

Eventually the killing madness lifted. Men weary with the effort of wielding swords, stopped in mid stroke. Like sleepers awakening from a deep sleep, they looked at their hands and arms black with blood, their bodies blooded to the chin. In a daze they came together, suddenly aware of what they had done and were ashamed.

Later, one of the zealot leaders, Benjamin, came to the Idumaeans to ask for a meeting. "I am deeply sorry" he said, "for the part I have played in these events, as are many of my brothers. I think" he continued after a pause, "I think in the heat of the moment, we went too far. You answered our call for help in good faith, for which you have our thanks. But what" he continued soberly "has happened here was not what was intended and for which we must answer to God."

There was a murmur of agreement from the Idumaeans. Eventually their Chief, Simon of Cathla, spoke "The allegation of treason was not proved. We acted in haste and are guilty of many excesses that were jointly committed. We came in good faith to help you in your hour of need. We leave you filled with sorrow at your lack of respect and evil behaviour."

In the Roman camp, deserters brought before Titus gave him detailed information of these internal divisions. Such news was welcomed, Titus' comment to his men being "While the Jews kill each other with such ferocity, they do our job for us. We would be foolish to distract them."

When his men begged him to march on the city, he answered "To do so would only give them cause to reunite." Titus preferred to let the civil war run its course, saying "The gods, even the Jewish God, is handing the Jews over to us without our having to lift a finger. They must" he concluded with a grin "have managed to displease both, so calamitous is their situation." Titus was also grateful for the Jews fighting each other, because as they grew weaker he grew stronger, able at last to rest his legions which had been fighting in Judaea for four years, only being taken out of the line when the opportunity presented itself.

From the news the deserters brought him Titus knew the Jews were not using this time to continue manufacturing weapons, reinforce their defences and train the refugees. Instead they were being weakened by dissention and the civil war they were waging. Just as keen as the Romans were to capture deserters alive, the warring factions wanted them dead, so escape had been made difficult. Every exit was guarded and anybody attempting to leave the city was summarily executed. The exceptions were the lucky and the wealthy. The latter could buy their way over the walls. The poor died. Hedges of dead bodies lined the main roads. Many who would have fled the city stayed knowing they would die. They stayed in the hope of a burial in Jerusalem.

Amid the horrors of the city, pity itself died. Paralysed with fear, the starving citizens envied the dead. They were at peace.

Even in death, there were priests and men of learning who reminded any who would listen of the ancient prophecy *"If the people turn against each other and pollute the Temple, it will be destroyed and God's Holy City will be conquered in war."*

The Zealots, disbelieving the truth of this, refused to change their course, believing that in the end they would triumph.

John was prepared to die, trying to fulfil his ambition of being the sole ruler of the nation. To further these ends he gradually built up a separate army, recruiting the cruellest, most vicious and brutal criminals who would fight and kill for money. Everything he did was aimed at securing sole sovereignty. Many gave way to him through fear. Some were genuine followers for he was skilled at persuading people to his cause and generous with the money he had stolen. However, many of his followers left him, as the alliance with the zealots began to break up. Many hated the idea of a King, so they opposed him. The one thing the rebels had in common, irrespective of their allegiances, was that every man chose to face the war with all its miseries, rather than give up his liberty.

The city was now at the mercy of three momentous calamities – war, tyranny and fundamentalism. Now a fourth calamity was coming, in the form of Gioras, who had holed up in Masada.

As lawlessness spread, every local headman turned minor warlord began plundering the neighbourhood with impunity, before disappearing with his supporters into the desert bad lands. In fact, every corner of Judaea was going the same way as the capital, as Jew killed Jew, murdering blood relations without a second thought.

24

The Arab mercenaries were facing west, their faces lit by the sunset. The image of the mountain and the dying light falling on its flanks was reflected in their eyes. They waited quietly, patiently; night ambushes were not a thing to rush. Outside the walls of Gabara, a few gaunt, mange stained camels settled in the dust. A boy leading some scurvy donkeys hurried to a gate before it was slammed shut for the night, the evening air redolent with the indistinguishable smells that accompany humans in tight quarters. Soon it would be owl light.

They squatted on their haunches, waiting, watching. Sharp faced men, lean and hard, who fought for money. Their sullen eyes betrayed their meanness of character, their hard jaws their lack of pity. At the last moment they would enter the town, their task to murder the guards of the western gate and open it to Vespasian's army. Their reward – anything they could steal.

Clad in black from head to toe with only their eyes uncovered, they flitted silently as shadows to a chosen spot of the town's defensive wall. At a hand signal from their leader, a rope attached to a muffled grappling iron had them on top of the wall in minutes. Invisible in the shadows they waited for the patrolling guards who, peering outwards, died silently from a blade thrust from behind.

Minutes later, Vespasian's men stepped over the dead guards and crept into the town. The gate through which they had gained entrance was not the main gate, but a minor portal used principally by garbage carts.

Vespasian's soldiers, surprised to find the walls virtually without sentries and the main gate guarded by old men, had it open in seconds and a hundred archers through it in a heartbeat.

In minutes, Vespasian's army had marched into town. In hours they had sacked it. The able bodied males were taken as slaves; the rest of the population were put to the sword. After ransacking the town for anything of value, which included its food stores, it was burnt.

Meanwhile Josephus, who had journeyed to Tiberius, found himself unwelcome. When they suggested he would betray them to Rome to save his own skin, he decided to write to the authorities in Jerusalem. His letter would be an objective analysis of the situation. If they agreed with him, then the logical thing to do would be to sue for terms. If that was the case, he would be prepared to act as the nation's advocate. If they were set on continuing to fight the Romans, they must send him trained recruits.

Vespasian, sensing the tide was with him, was now keen to attack the city of Jotapata, for his intelligence had informed him that a large number of the enemy had taken refuge there. They had done so because the town was a natural fortress that Josephus had reinforced with new walls and towers.

He immediately despatched a legion to force-march ahead of his main army. With them went a substantial number of specialist engineers and road builders, charged with turning a tortuous stony mountain track into a road. Meanwhile Josephus, who had left Tiberius a week earlier, slipped into Jotapata just in time to lift the spirits of the despondent Jews. When Vespasian learned of this from a deserter, he was delighted. Without hesitation he ordered Placidus to take a thousand horsemen to put a ring around the town a mouse couldn't get through. This was done with the express purpose of preventing Josephus escaping.

The next day, Vespasian and the entire army arrived after force marching until dusk, taking his army to the high ground north of the town, three quarters of a mile from its walls, to ensure the Jews would see just how big an enemy they would be up against. His aim was to dampen the spirits of those inside.

Vespasian, satisfied that his ploy had worked, rested his troops who were weary after twelve hours of marching; although he did place a double line of archers around the town, with a third ring of cavalry, to deter any attempt at leaving. With no hope of escape, and determined not to surrender, the Jews did not give way to despair. On the contrary they vowed to sell their lives dearly. The next morning the Jews formed up outside the city walls in a direct challenge to the Roman forces.

Vespasian responded by deploying his archers, slingers and long range artillery, ordering them to keep up a steady barrage. Using this as cover, he then ordered heavy infantry to assault the wall at its weakest point. Josephus, seeing the danger, ordered the whole Jewish garrison to storm the advancing Roman infantry, driving them back from the wall in hand to hand fighting. With neither side willing to give ground, they both suffered heavy losses. The Jews with nothing to lose and the Romans filled with pride were locked in mortal combat, hacking and stabbing at each other in a kind of madness that lasted the whole day.

At nightfall the combatants staggered apart bearing their wounded away. They left behind a battlefield muddy with blood and carpeted with body parts. The fallen, heaped in grotesque mounds, bore silent witness to the animal courage displayed by both sides.

The next day, with the stars paling in the east, both sides readied themselves to resume hostilities. The Jews, seeing the forces ranged against them, prepared to march out and do battle. Shivering in the cold air, men coughed to clear their lungs before strapping on their armour. They met like pit-bulls, mad with the scent of blood, both sides determined to carry the day.

In a desperate attempt to gain the advantage, more and more men were committed to the madness in front of Jotapata's walls, but to no avail. Neither side would give an inch. The combatants stood on the bodies of the fallen to get at each other. Neither would respond to the orders of their commanders to disengage. Throughout the day Roman and Jew fought each other breast to breast, eye to eye, in a primordial frenzy. Only darkness once again forced the adversaries apart.

For five more days the two sides engaged one another, the Jews' determination and fighting spirit never wavering. The Romans, their pride hurt, knew that their honour was at stake. For them there was no possible outcome other than death or victory, though the difficulty of taking the town was becoming more and more apparent.

Jotapata is perched on the edge of a cliff, a precipice of sheer rock protected on three sides by deep ravines. Josephus had taken advantage of this when he built the town's walls. A circle of natural rock curtains shielded the town so effectively as to become part of its fortifications.

Vespasian, knowing he had to come up with a new strategy, had called a meeting of his senior officers where it was decided that they would build platforms against the most approachable section of wall. Ten thousand soldiers were ordered into the countryside to collect materials. The hills were scalped of trees, and mountains of stones were collected and hauled back to the site.

A second force of legionaries was ordered to make large mobile shields from timber and animal hides. These would be used to protect their fellow soldiers from the missiles being hurled at them from the tops of the walls. The Romans then organised a third working party of some five thousand men to dig vast quantities of earth, and transport this in panniers on the backs of mules to the waiting builders.

In response, the Jews hurled huge lumps of stone onto the enemy's shelters in an attempt to disrupt the building work. To protect his men, Vespasian organised a ring of artillery. By using every piece available to him, he was able to assemble two hundred engines to bombard the Jews on the wall. These were used to mount a synchronised attack of devastating power. Catapults fired lances two metres in length. Arab archers volleyed flights of arrows that turned the sky black. Stone throwers of various kinds hurled a mixed freight into the air. Stones, weighing a hundredweight or more were launched, along with fire brands and nets full of smaller missiles.

Under this onslaught the Jews were driven not only from the wall, but the section of town immediately inside it. To help clear the streets and squares immediately behind the wall, the Romans hurled javelins high into the air, to plummet down in a rain of random killing.

The Jews, beaten back from the top of the wall, sallied forth in company strength, smashing the shields that protected the working parties and putting them to the sword. Then, without drawing breath, they charged the main platform the Romans were building and set fire to its uprights and shields.

Vespasian countered this by strengthening the earthworks and bringing up additional numbers of troops, to help the men toiling to build other platforms. The Jews, seeing these rising higher and higher, soon to be level with their battlements, began to lose heart.

Josephus, ever inventive, ordered the town's stonemasons to raise the wall higher. When they refused, on the grounds that the constant barrage of missiles made it impossible, he ordered his men to erect posts along the walls and fix wet ox hides to them, so that stones hurled against them would be turned away, the wet hides giving without splitting when struck. Other types of missiles would either glance off or be stopped. Firebrands would simply fizzle out against the wet leather.

With this protection, the builders toiled day and night to raise the wall by thirty feet. They also built towers along it and finished the whole project with a strong wooden platform. The Romans, who fancied themselves already in the town, were despondent. Vespasian, exasperated by this stratagem, was even more irritated when the Jews resumed night sorties against him. He was mildly alarmed when they had the nerve to engage him in company strength during the day.

Josephus now brought every tactic and ploy of guerrilla warfare into play. Groups of picked men were sent out at night to sabotage anything they came upon. If it was moveable and of use, it was stolen; if it wasn't, it was wrecked or burnt. All the various constructions the Romans were in the middle of building - assault ladders, ramps, towers – were fired.

Vespasian, deciding enough was enough, recalled his men from the battlefield and set about blockading the town. Jotapata under siege would either starve or surrender.

Inside Jotapata, the town's granaries were full, but they lacked sufficient water. There being no spring within the walls, the townsfolk depended on winter rain to fill their cisterns. It was now late summer and water was short. Josephus, who had rationed it from the outset, was forced to extend this rationing to the townspeople, who resented this being imposed. From the high ground overlooking the wall, the Romans could watch the Jews forming lines to receive their water rations, so they made this area a target for their javelin throwers, causing many injuries and deaths.

An anxious Vespasian, meanwhile, could only hope that the town's tanks would run dry sooner rather than later. Meanwhile, he had forty thousand men to feed and water, plus almost as many animals – every day.

Josephus, very much aware of Vespasian's circumstances, was determined to undermine his enemy's resolve. He ordered his men to drape the walls and battlements in Roman view with sheets and pour water onto them, so that the whole wall ran and dripped with this precious fluid. The result was uproar in the Roman ranks, when they saw so huge a quantity being thrown away as a joke by men whom they thought had scarcely anything to drink. Vespasian himself was shaken, for he had pinned all of his hopes on capturing the town through the effect of his siege.

In Jotapata Josephus called a meeting of the town's leading citizens. He and they faced up to the fact that the town could not hold out forever. Josephus made the point that his own survival was important to the Jewish state, and he would need to organise his escape sooner rather than later. The people begged him to stay. Josephus countered this by saying that if he escaped, he could raise an army in Galilee and come to their aid. By staying with them, the Romans would attack the town more fiercely to ensure his capture.

If, on the other hand he slipped away, this would reduce the pressure on the town. This argument was rejected out of hand.

The people begged him on their knees to stay, so he agreed, but only on the condition that they accepted his terms. "You have accepted", he declared gravely, "that there is no hope, not just of escape, but of survival. Not just that you will die, so will your mothers, your wives, your children". In the absolute silence this brought, he continued, "If you had a future, you would be remembered for your courage. But nobody will live to tell of your bravery". He paused to turn from side to side, seeking the eyes of his men and the ordinary citizens who had taken up arms. "If you must fight, fight as men with no future. Take vengeance now on the Roman who will kill your family when you fall in battle."

The next day Josephus led an attack in force that got as far as the Roman camp, where they set fire to its breast works. Over the next two days they repeated these sorties. Uncaring of their losses, they hurled themselves at their enemy like berserkers. The only way of stopping them was to kill them.

Vespasian, angry at losing seasoned Roman infantry, responded by making the Arab archers and stone throwers face these sudden attacks. Attacks which came at odd times – dawn, late evening, the middle of the night. He did, however, support the auxiliaries with his artillery, which he kept in continuous action. It was this that eventually forced the Jews to back off, but outside the range of the missiles being hurled at them they attacked the Romans relentlessly. They came forward without a thought for their own lives, their only thought and most fervent desire was to kill before they themselves were killed.

As the days dragged by, these sorties continued. Vespasian began to feel that it was he who was under siege. In desperation, he urged the towers and platforms that had survived be moved closer to the walls. He also ordered the ram to be brought up. This massive baulk of timber is capped by a great lump of metal shaped like a ram's head. No wall can withstand a prolonged battering from this juggernaut. Put in motion, it pounds away day and night, making sleep impossible for the defenders, as vibrations from its impact travelled through their beds, rattling the vessels on their shelves and shivering the liquid in their chamber pots.

The Romans now pushed forward. Their catapults and other artillery that had been edged forward started a supporting bombardment. Archers and slingers also came to the fore to keep up a constant shower of missiles aimed at the top of the wall.

Consequently, the Jews could not man the ramparts. This enabled the Romans to move the ram to a new position. Under the protection of overlapping shields, roofed by ox hides, the Romans attacked an old section of the wall. Under its battering, Josephus saw that it would give way if he didn't act. Under his orders, sacks of chaff were lowered by ropes to the spot where the head of the ram was striking the wall. This tactic worked instantly; the ram was rendered ineffectual. The Romans hit back by attaching reaping hooks to poles, and cutting the ropes the sacks were suspended from. Immediately the ram was once again set in motion and the wall began to crack.

Josephus, who had anticipated this event, had prepared bundles of wood soaked in oil. These were then dipped in bitumen, resin, pitch and brimstone. Setting these brands alight they charged out and set fire to the Romans' hurdles, their scaling ladders and as much of their artillery as they could before being cut down. Frozen by the Jews' unbelievable courage, the Romans panicked. When they did gather their wits about them, things were well alight and beyond salvage.

At night, under Vespasian's personal supervision, the ram was set up again. It was at this juncture an event occurred that could have changed the course of the war. Vespasian was wounded. He took an arrow in the foot. Though the wound was relatively minor, it caused consternation in the Roman ranks. Suddenly things had gone from bad to worse. The news ran through the army like quicksilver. Titus arrived at the spot fearing for his father's life.

Vespasian, very much aware of the psychological impact of the incident, called for a horse. Snapping off the arrow, he mounted the animal and rode slowly through his lines, exchanging words of encouragements with his men.

Titus ordered the attack on the wall to be redoubled. Every available piece of artillery was to be brought forward and set to work without pause day and night.

Josephus's forces were now taking terrible losses from the constant fusillade, in spite of which they held on to the ramparts. They set up a barrage of their own against those attacking the wall. They rained fire and stones on those operating the ram, but with no effect. Meanwhile they were constantly hit by missiles.

Within the town, the screams of the women and children echoed the shrieks of men dying in agony from their wounds; the sound of dead bodies flung from the ramparts an ominous, constant thudding. The ground that circled the walls was puddled with blood. Soon it would be possible to climb to the battlements on the corpses heaped against the base. The noise was terrifying, magnified by the rocky walls of the surrounding mountains. In the early morning, before dawn had broken, the wall yielded. The Jews filled these breaches with warriors, who held back the enemy with shields and swords.

Next day at first light, Vespasian called up his army for the final assault. His first task was to try and draw the defenders away from the breaches. To do this he selected some of his best heavy infantry, positioning them against the gaps in the wall. Protected by full armour and armed with long spears, they were waiting for wooden gangways made by the pioneer corps to be put into position. These were necessary for the Romans to force an entry, enabling the infantry to charge through the breaches in the wall. Behind the armoured spearman, Vespasian had drawn up the cream of his infantry. The remaining cavalry were positioned across the entire slope. Their job was to intercept anyone who attempted to escape when the town was captured. Still further back he placed Arab archers to pick off anything that slipped past the cavalry.

Other soldiers carried ladders ready to position them against the undamaged sections of wall. This might, Vespasian thought, draw some Jews away from the breaches while the rest, facing the concentrated fire of his archers and slingers, might break.

Josephus, realising what Vespasian intended, positioned older men with the exhausted and wounded on the undamaged sections of wall. Here, he reasoned, the fighting would be less fierce. Where the wall had been broken through, he positioned the best warriors, each group led by four officers; it was here he placed himself so that he would be in the midst of the fiercest fighting.

He also ordered his men to bend double under their shields the instant they heard the deadly hissing of the incoming volleys of arrows that would precede the legions' advance. Finally he warned them that the greatest moment of danger, would be when the gangways fell into place. They must, he said, forestall the enemy who expected to charge across these unimpeded *by being first*. They must jump forward onto these gangways and sell themselves dearly, for this was where the fighting would be the hardest. He said grimly, "You are already dead, be waiting in heaven for your wives and children who will soon join you. Whilst you still live, let every man fight to the death for them. Remember, take vengeance for what is to come", were Josephus' final words to his men.

In unison, the trumpets of all the legions sounded followed by a savage battle cry that burst from twenty thousand throats. This was the cue for clouds of arrows from every side to fill the sky. Remembering Josephus' instructions, his men shielded their bodies from the incoming shafts. When the gangways dropped into position, the Jews charged over them before the astonished Romans could take a forward step. They engaged the enemy without fear in a desperately magnificent display of prowess and fighting spirit. No Jewish warrior broke off his struggle with an opponent until one or the other was dead.

But eventually the Jews were worn down by the non-stop battle, unable to replace their men as they died. On the other hand, the Romans' exhausted units were relieved by fresh troops. As soon as one Roman unit was beaten back, another came forward. Standing shoulder to shoulder the Romans urged each other on. Their long shields locked, they formed an impenetrable wall which, with the line pushing as one man, forced the Jews up the slope.

The Jews were seconds away from utter disaster when Josephus signalled the men on the wall. They were ready with containers of boiling oil. The Jews poured the bubbling liquid from every side onto the packed Romans. Scalded and burnt, screaming in pain, the Romans broke their ranks. In agony, they twisted and rolled down the slope away from the wall. Trapped in their armour they couldn't escape the torment. Burning oil swiftly ran under their armour, seeking out every crevice, coating their bodies from head to foot, their flesh consumed as though by fire. Imprisoned in their armour, the legionaries could not escape the searing fluid. Leaping into the air like hooked fish, bodies and limbs contorted in torment, they fell back from the wall, easy targets for the Jews' spears and arrows. The Romans who had not suffered the boiling oil pressed forward. Screaming with rage in their eagerness to get at their enemies, they threw caution to the wind, straight into the trap Josephus had prepared for them. As they stormed forward onto the gangways, Josephus and his men retreated. Arriving at the gangways the Romans simply lost their footing. It was impossible to stand upright. Many fell head-long to be finished off by Jewish spears. Some Romans fell on their backs and, unable to get up, were severely injured by the flailing hobnailed sandals of their companions.

This situation had been brought about because the Jews had poured boiled fenugreek over the gangway's planks, rendering them twice as slippery as ice. Seeing his men being badly mauled, but not understanding why, Vespasian ordered his trumpeters to sound the recall. He then ordered the huge platforms to be raised. On them he had built prefabricated towers, each fully sixty feet high. These were encased in metal on all four sides, so they were too heavy to overturn and virtually fireproof. They were manned by archers, spearman, light artillery and slingers. The Romans, protected by the towers' metal cladding, begin to fire arrows and other missiles through slits in the metal panels at the defenders on the top of the wall.

In their exposed position the Jews, unable to defend themselves from these missiles, were unable to fight back. Their enemy was not only concealed, he was beyond their reach, the tops of the towers being outside the range of their spears.

Forced to abandon the wall, they joined the combatants at ground level, determined to keep the enemy outside the city. For another day Jotapata held out, but at a terrible cost. Jewish dead were piling up against the walls at an alarming rate.

On the forty seventh day of the siege, the Roman platforms reared over the wall and by a remarkable coincidence they captured a Jewish deserter who bought his life by betraying to Vespasian the circumstances in the city. He informed Vespasian of how weak the remaining men were, through a shortage of rations and water. Very importantly he reported that, because of their losses, the remaining men were totally exhausted. Through constant fighting with no respite, they were close to being unable to withstand another assault. This coward then suggested that a night attack at a particular point on the wall would succeed in entry being gained and the gates opened.

With his father's permission Titus decided to make such an attempt, accompanied by a *tribune* and a picked squad from the Fifteenth Legion, who had volunteered to test the traitor's information. At the midnight hour Titus and his men scaled the wall. With only the moon to light their way, they successfully disposed of the sentries on the gate, which they opened to the *tribune*s Sextus Calvarius and Placidus. With their men they swiftly secured the opened gates to the Tenth and the Fifteenth legions who marched silently into the city, sweeping through the sleeping centre. The heroic defenders, lost in an exhausted sleep, were unaware that the town had fallen.

When the town did begin to wake, it was to a dense fog that had rolled in off the mountain and enveloped the town. Under its cover the Roman forces moved silently to take possession of the town's key positions. The Jews did not know the town had been taken until the killing began.

The Romans, with their memories fresh with the struggle to win Jotapata and the reversals and losses they had suffered, applied the rule of fire and sword. They trapped the people in the narrow streets and drove them like beasts brought to the abattoir. Bumped and jostled in the steeply sloping lanes, they slipped and stumbled as they attempted to flee from the killing machine sweeping down from the citadel like a tidal wave.

An exhausted squad of Jewish soldiers, who had taken refuge in a cave, committed an act of treachery against the Romans that was in part responsible for the ensuing massacre. A group of Roman soldiers led by Antonias had discovered the Jews and demanded their surrender. Having shouted their acceptance, one of the Jews asked Antonias to give him his hand to seal the agreement and assist him in climbing out of the cave. The centurion, trusting the Jew, gave him his hand and helped the man to the surface. The Jew then suddenly lunged and stabbed the centurion, severing an artery and killing him. The Roman response was to go berserk. Nobody was spared, male or female, young or old. Over the next few days they hunted those who had taken refuge in the sewers and other hiding places, including a network of caves on the town's southern outskirts. In all fifty thousand Jews were killed.

To make sure this city never rose up again against him and to serve as a warning to others, Vespasian ordered Jotapata to be torn down and burnt. He then ordered a detailed search to be made for Josephus' body, which meant sorting through mounds of corpses. He also ordered that the cave system on the edge of the town be investigated. The Roman general knew that it was very unlikely that Josephus had escaped, so tight was the net he had spread. The Jew was either dead or in hiding. Either way, he informed his officers, he would have Josephus' body before he left Jotapata.

25

Nursing a lump the size of an egg on the side of his head, his vision blurred as the result of a blow received in the fury of the fighting on the wall, a haggard and exhausted Josephus retreated into the crush of screaming, panic stricken Jews fleeing the advancing Romans. The mob, in its desperation to escape, had to clamber over the putrefying unburied dead who had lain for weeks where they had fallen. Josephus would never forget the bluebottles and their offspring, the heaving mounds of maggots feeding on the bloated bodies.

Swept along by the fleeing mob, he felt a tug at his elbow and swivelled his head. It was one of his officers, Jacob. "Come with me - some of the men have found a place to hide". Josephus, his head throbbing and his peripheral vision worsening, nodded and grasped Jacob's arm. Because of the press of people it took them an hour to reach the waste ground at the far end of the city's slums; a piece of ground that was a mass of giant boulders, great slabs of stone tilting in every direction, the result of natural movement of the earth in past millennia. This desolation was home to a bunch of idiot beggars when they were not on the street soliciting alms.

Terrified of what was happening they were huddled among the boulders. Alive with vermin, they squinted at the world with rheumy eyes wild with fear. Plastered with dirt, sucking on ropes of snot, they cowered and gibbered at the appearance of Josephus and his companion. "Ignore them and follow me", Jacob gasped, scrambling between the abraded slabs of stone. Reeling with exhaustion, wondering if he could keep going much longer,

Josephus struggled after his companion. Just when he thought he could go no further, Jacob stopped. They were standing in a fissure of rock that reared twenty feet above their heads. At its base was a concealed hole, overgrown with weeds and dead grass.

Jacob crouched and called. Several minutes elapsed before he got a cautious reply. Almost fainting with relief, he gave a password that resulted in the appearance of a ladder. Gratefully the two men scrambled down into the darkness, to be met by a man holding a tiny oil lamp. After removing the ladder he led them down a short tunnel into a large cave.

To his amazement, Josephus stared at the group of people who had taken refuge there. Half of them were his own men, the rest town councillors and their families and a few of the town's leading businessmen.

Later Josephus would learn that, in anticipation of the disaster that had overtaken them, the cave had been stocked with food, water and other essentials that would last several weeks. For the first few days Josephus rested, thankful that his vision, no doubt aided by the cave's darkness, gradually returned. Tiny oil lamps were only being used for essential purposes and to dispel the absolute blackness of their subterranean home.

When he had recovered, Josephus and a couple of his men left the cave to search for an escape route and to note the position of the Roman soldiers. They did this without knowing that the Romans were in fact searching for him. By an unfortunate coincidence, a woman who had taken shelter in the cave decided she also would go out at night. In this case it was to search for her missing children. Lacking the guile and experience of Josephus and his men, she inevitably fell into the hands of the Romans. With a sword at her throat, the Roman sentry demanded to know where she had been hiding. Joined by a centurion who snarled at her "answer him bitch" she knew she was seconds away from death.

She gathered her courage, saying "If you want the man you are seeking, take me to your commander".

With a quick intake of breath, the centurion said "Tie her". Back at the guardhouse the senior centurion on duty viewed the captive coldly, but he wasn't about to start taking chances on such an important matter.

He reported in person to his opposite number on Vespasian's staff. Minutes later he was standing to attention before his commanding officer and his son. "At ease", Vespasian said. "What do you think?"

"Don't know Sir, worth a listen. Thought I should report before questioning her".

Vespasian nodded saying "Bring her in".

"Search her first" interjected Titus.

The duty officer Gaius Iovis replied "Sir", saluted and left to collect his prisoner, slightly miffed that he had been unnecessarily told to search her.

Twenty minutes later a discomfited and outraged Jewish matron who had been strip searched, was led in front of Vespasian. Without preamble Vespasian asked bluntly, "You know where the Jewish general Josephus is hiding?"

There was a moment's silence while the woman, Rachel, gathered her composure. "Yes", she snapped.

The flat of a sword from the guard at her back dropped her to her knees "Yes, General, sir", he shouted. Vespasian frowned but said nothing.

"Yes General" she said shakily, the fragility of her position suddenly coming home to her.

"Well", said Vespasian, "it's simple. You lead us to him and you go free with a reward and free passage for you and your family out of Jotapata". He paused before adding matter-of-factly, "Or die. Which is it to be?"

Screwing up her courage and doing her best to keep the shake out of her voice, Rachel replied "My husband is dead General, I need help to find my children".

Vespasian nodded. "If they are to be found, I will find your children. Now go with my officers and show them where the man I seek hides". Given the importance of the task in hand and the prize at stake, Vespasian immediately despatched two *tribunes*, Paulinus and Gallicanus with orders that Josephus, if found, was to be offered safe conduct if he would surrender.

Led by Rachel, the first thing the *tribune*s did was to secure the area with a thousand picked legionaries.

This done, they approached the entrance to the cave and called out to its occupants. Josephus, sick at heart at his discovery was suspicious that once in Vespasian's hands he would be humiliated and then executed, refused the offer. While this was taking place Titus remembered that a *tribune* serving in the Fifteenth Legion knew Josephus, having served in Jerusalem with King Agrippa II.

Nicanor was sent for and, after being briefed by Titus personally, was sent to negotiate with Josephus. Once at the cave Nicanor assured Josephus, "Vespasian admires you as a brother general", adding, "If Vespasian was laying a trap he would not have sent a friend. Such an action would have besmirched Vespasian's honour and", he concluded huffily, "he himself would never be part of so dishonourable an affair. The deceiving of anybody is bad enough, but a friend is totally unacceptable".

In spite of the assurance Josephus hesitated and asked for time to think. The other *tribune*s present, Paulinus and Gallicanus, angry at the way things were going, were all for smoking Josephus and the other refugees out. Nicanor refused to do this on the ground that Josephus might be injured. "Vespasian has expressly ordered Josephus be captured alive and unharmed. "If" he warned, "you over-ride me I will withdraw and report back to the commander-in-chief".

In the end common sense prevailed. Nicanor was allowed to continue talking to Josephus. As Nicanor renewed his appeals, Josephus recalled a recent dream, in which he believed God had forewarned him of the catastrophe that would engulf the Jews in their war with the Romans and the future of the man who would conquer his people.

An expert of the prophecies in Holy Scripture, Josephus firmly believed that what he had experienced in his dream was in fact the word of God. Standing in the gloom at the bottom of the shaft leading to the outside world, he knelt to pray. "Lord, we your people have sinned and the Romans, your instrument of punishment, bear down hard. You have chosen me as your servant to know the future of my people. I place myself in my enemy's hands to do thy bidding not mine".

His fellow companions in the cave hearing these words had crowded round him. Their spokesman, voicing the thoughts of all, said angrily, "The laws of the Jews ordained by God Himself gave our race the courage not to fear death. We demand you stay loyal to Him and His people, and do not betray them by an act of treachery. Are you such a coward that you prefer to live as a slave, then die in freedom's cause? Even if the Romans keep their word and you are pardoned could you, in the memory of all those you demanded lay down their lives for freedom, stoop to accept it?"

The silence that followed this declaration was palpable. Josephus, his face drawn by fatigue and emotion, swayed on his feet. Suddenly swords were drawn, blades glinting in the lamp light. Josephus replied, "Why, my friends are you so eager to die? No, not just to die but to commit suicide, for I know you have discussed this among yourselves before I joined you". Getting no reply he continued, "You claim it is noble to die for freedom. I agree, but on the battlefield, not by your own hand. From God we receive the gift of life. His to give and His to take back when He, not man, decides. I shall not go over to the Romans to betray everything I am. If I did so I would be lower than those who desert to the enemy, for their desertion is in exchange for life. I go to do God's will even unto death".

Those among his audience who remained unconvinced continued to point their swords at his throat. Josephus, putting his trust in what he regarded as divine revelation, said, "Let us put ourselves in fate's hands. Let us draw lots. Whoever draws lot number one is killed by number two and so on. Only the last man will commit suicide and in doing so, in so noble a cause, will surely win God's mercy".

After some consultation the group agreed, and Josephus drew lots with the others. Then each person in turn offered his throat to the other. The only variation was for the few women and children. Their fathers, husbands and brothers despatched them first, before offering their throat to a companion. One by one the bodies fell silently, no man flinching or turning away from what he saw as duty. Soon the air reeked with the smell of blood.

At the end Josephus was left with one other man. Josephus, who had spoken so fervently against suicide, couldn't bring himself to kill not just a fellow Jew, but a warrior who had stood with him on the wall and fought the enemy to the bitter end. So Josephus laid down his sword and, after agreeing with Nicanor that the offer of amnesty would cover them both, he surrendered to the Romans.

The jubilant *tribune*s, headed by Nicanor, marched their prize to Vespasian knowing they would be well rewarded.

In his tent the Roman General, with his son Titus, contemplated their prisoner. Titus, impressed by the calm demeanour of the prisoner, reflected on the vicissitudes of fortune and the lack of any certainty in life's course. Later he was to successfully argue with his father to spare Josephus from being sent to Nero, which would almost certainly have seen him end up dying in the arena.

So Vespasian ordered that Josephus be held in custody and be well treated, for he had a use for him. A task that would require Josephus to appear in public, looking well cared for and not as some enemy prisoner suffering under the victor's heel.

Before being taken away, Josephus asked to speak to Vespasian in private. Intrigued, Vespasian ordered everyone except his son Titus to withdraw. "Understandably sir" said Josephus, "you regard me as just another captive, albeit an important one; but still just a prisoner. I come, however, as a messenger sent by God himself. I know the law both civil and military. My death by the Emperor Nero's hand or yours is inevitable. How long will Nero, and those destined to succeed him, remain on the throne before your turn comes? You, my Lord Vespasian, will be Caesar and Emperor".

Assuming that Josephus' speech had been made to save his skin, Vespasian signalled to the guards he was to be taken away. Later, however, questioning other prisoners he discovered

Josephus' reputation of second sight had been proven on many occasions, even in childhood.

At the outset of the siege of Jotapata for example, he had predicted it would fall on the forty eighth day of its siege and that he would be taken prisoner.

So although Vespasian kept Josephus under lock and key, it was with many privileges. Titus, who had taken a liking to their prisoner, also treated him with kindness and respect.

26

In the early morning, Titus the *tribune*s and senior centurions had gathered in Vespasian's campaign tent for a briefing. Maps and documents were spread across trestle tables dotted with wooden blocks to mark positions of interest. A large map hung on a frame was the focal point. Vespasian, joined by Titus, motioned for the officers to find a seat while Mucianus, who was to conduct the meeting, moved about the tent greeting men by name.

With everybody seated Vespasian raised his hand for silence and without preamble opened the briefing. "Replacements for our fallen comrades and those seriously injured will be with us within the next two weeks. Our immediate task is to bury our dead. This will be done starting today and completed over the next few days. It will be done with all ceremony and with full military honours. To avoid disease, the enemy dead are to be collected and dumped in a deep ravine. With the town cleared we need to consider the state of our men. We have over five hundred seriously wounded and the same again hurt badly enough to be declared unfit for duty. Those who are fit are in need of a breather."

Vespasian paused to sip from a glass before continuing, "It is my intention to kill two birds with one stone. The town will be demolished - this will take time. Our wounded need time to recover, at least until they are fit enough to travel in the hospital wagons. Your victories in this campaign do not go unheard in Rome. The taking of Jotapata and the capture of the enemy's general are of great importance and will shorten the war. When news of this reaches Rome, your names will be honoured. The Emperor himself will speak of you with pride".

A low murmur of satisfaction rippled around the tent and Vespasian waited patiently before continuing. "We shall probably be camped here for six weeks; then we march. Our final objective is Jerusalem, but in getting there we have to continue with our policy of pacification. The country has to be cleared of our enemies; the Emperor's orders were very clear. He wants the Jewish problem solved once and for all".

Vespasian paused to sip from a beaker, continuing "The next phase of our campaign will take us south towards our ultimate objective, Jerusalem. Our enemy will resist us every inch of the way. They know only too well the price of rebellion. Knowing your enemy is vital to achieving success on the battlefield. Good military intelligence is worth an extra legion. We are fortunate in this campaign to have King Agrippa and his men as our allies. The King and his men fight loyally by our side; they share our wounds, our losses. I am proud to call them brothers in arms".

A loud cheer of approval greeted these remarks and a grave faced Agrippa rose from his chair and bowed to Vespasian and the gathering. When the noise subsided Vespasian continued. "As you know, General Mucianus has served in this region for many years and is an expert on it and its people. I will hand you over to him, to take us through what lies ahead. Before doing so, can I say it is very important that what you learn today is passed on to the men who serve under you. Legionaries fight better if they think their officers know what they're doing". This last remark, delivered with a grin, brought an answering burst of laughter.

Mucianus nodded to Vespasian and took his place in front of the map. "Majesty, General, Gentlemen. Knowing your enemy saves lives – yours in particular. The enemy in this case is rebellious Jews. It is of course much more complicated than that, and we need to understand those complications if we are to succeed".

Mucianus picked up a pointer and tapped the map. "By the way," he said "interrupt at any time with questions. This area north of Judaea has a large gentile population. It prospers in a quarrelsome bunch of provinces where Jews, Greeks and a patchwork of squabbling near eastern nationalities live in a permanent state of tribal distrust." Glancing at his attentive audience he continued, "When we Romans came to Judaea, we made it the strongest military power between the Roman provinces of Egypt and Syria. It was also a buffer between the Empire and the Mesopotamian Parthian threat to Rome's total control of the Eastern Mediterranean. Also, this area is bandit country. Various opportunist warlords operate in the area, relying on our being too busy with the uprising to deal with them. Before we move from here we will clear the surrounding countryside of any potential trouble".

"Sir?" the questioner was a grizzled veteran, probably serving his time out. Mucianus nodded acknowledgement. The veteran centurion said, "Sir, the countryside the locals refer to as upper Galilee is rich and fertile, well watered and will grow just about anything. When we have won the war will you be settling any of it?"

Mucianus burst out laughing, the vested interest so obvious that his companions shared in his mirth. But when the laughter died down, they waited expectantly for the answer to what was a serious question. Roman soldiers coming to the end of their contracted twenty five years of service were frequently settled as pioneers in recently conquered territories. The arrangement suited both sides. Rome established an outpost of trained soldiers in case of future trouble, at no cost. The retiring legionaries acquired a free farm and slaves to work it.

"Live long enough to claim it, fight well, and you and your comrades will have land and slaves to work it". Mucianus' reply brought a rousing cheer. The next question was more sober in content.

"Sir, why have the Jews rebelled against Rome? We allow them freedom to worship their God and manage their own affairs".

"Good question *tribune*", replied Mucianus. "Deserves a simple straightforward answer, but it won't get one". This brought a ripple of laughter. Mucianus continued, "A lot of Judaean power rests with the priesthood, which means the Temple in Jerusalem. A devout Jew accepts no authority or master other than his God. However, the civil authorities who administer the city and the country acknowledge the necessity and duty of co-operating with Rome. They and the High Priest of all Israel balance civic duty with duty to Rome and Roman laws, with duty to their God. They keep them separate and maintain the peace. In fact, many high ranking councillors, Jews of power and influence in Jerusalem, are Roman citizens".

This brought a rumble of comment which died away as Mucianus continued, "In Jerusalem you have the misguided – Jews who for theological reasons promote rebellion. You also have the opportunists, who see a chance during a time of turbulence to seize power and become rich. Finally, there are the politicians who see a chance to peddle their brand of nationalism and take control of the country. These diverse groups are clearly rivals and are our unwitting allies. Already they are at each other's throats. In the name of their God they have started a civil war in the city and are taking no prisoners". This last drew a gasp from its audience and caused even Vespasian to raise an eyebrow.

Scarcely had this amazing piece of information been absorbed when another hand shot up. "Silence", called Mucianus. "The centurion at the back. Your question soldier".

"Where do we go from here sir?"

Mucianus grinned, "To glory son". This brought an ironical cheer. "We march to Ptolemais, which is of great importance to us and loyal to Rome. A Greek city that was once the most important harbour serving Galilee and to this day is of strategic importance. In Ptolemais we will gather our strength and march to Jerusalem. There we will plant the eagles of Rome to do battle with the enemy".

A week later they arrived in Ptolemais without incident and were received by the city fathers, bearing the traditional offerings of bread and salt. The city gates stood open and the civilian population welcomed them with garlands of flowers and warm applause. After discussing the disposition of his forces with Mucianus, Vespasian sent two of his legions to Caesarea for the winter. The Fifteenth he sent to Scythopolis, to avoid straining Caesarea's resources.

Meanwhile in Rome, Nero, who was busy working on his latest musical composition, reluctantly agreed to receive Tigellinus the Commander of the *Praetorian* Guard.

A grey faced Tigellinus and three of the *praetorian's* most senior officers were knelt on one knee, heads bent, in front of the seated Emperor. To his left, in a cloud of her own courtiers, the heavily pregnant Poppaea froze like a cheetah into a hunting stillness.

"Insurrection?" Caesar whispered the word, eyes wide with disbelief.

"Insurrection?" This time it was bellowed as the white mountain moved. Nero rose to his feet, shaking with rage. Incoherent with anger, saliva flew from his lips as he glared at the unfortunate messenger.

An ashen faced Tigellinus continued with his report. "Galba with the Sixth, the Ninth and the Eleventh Legions who have declared him Caesar, is marching on Rome".

"Crush him. You have the *Praetorian*". The outraged and terrified Nero was shambling up and down the room, his head swinging from side to side. Had he ever seen one, Tigellinus would have been reminded of a polar bear. The little red eyes suddenly fixed on the luckless *Praetorian* commander. "We can count on the *Praetorian*?"

"To the death".

"It may come to that sooner than you think", snapped Nero viciously. "Why is Galba doing this to me?" The bottom lip trembled and a fat tear ran down the white cheeks. Nero shivered uncontrollably. Unconsciously he lifted the hem of his toga and put it in his mouth, sucking on it noisily.

"Vespasian". Nero's arm shot out and he clutched his guard commander's arm. "Recall Vespasian and his legions".

Tigellinus swallowed and tried to answer, but failed – the words simply wouldn't come out. One of his officers came to his aid though even his voice faltered. "Vespasian's troops are either at sea or are three months away, Divinity. In any event if we recall them Judaea is lost and that will encourage others. The Empire could be overwhelmed".

Nero screamed at this news. He tugged at the neck of his tunic, ripping it along the seam. Foam collected at the corners of his mouth. "You", he pointed a shaking finger at Tigellinus, "are supposed to protect me, to lay down your life for me".

"Majesty, the *Praetorian* are loyal, I swear it".

Nero charged across the room to stand inches from the quaking guard commander. "Where is the army? Rome has fourteen legions to defend her".

"They stand aside, Divinity, to see which way the gods will declare".

"Stand aside - gods?" Nero was apoplectic. "I am a god, how dare they not worship me. Why would they desert me?"

Tigellinus could find no answer to this.

"Karkinos". Nero's voice rose in triumph. "Send for the magus - through him we will summon legions from Hades, soldiers who are immortal. Galba and every man who fights under him will be crucified. Go!"

Shaking with reaction, the *Praetorian* officers and their commander backed out of the room. Left alone but for a silent Poppaea, whom he had either forgotten or was ignoring, the gross white figure lumbered up and down the room. Poppaea lay impassively on her side, a jewelled hand resting possessively on the mound of her belly.

"Perhaps," she said softly, "now is the time to declare our unborn son your heir".

The sweating Emperor froze in mid stride, the button eyes focusing short-sightedly on the reclining Poppaea. Without warning his foot lashed out. She screamed in agony as the toe of the heavy sandal buried itself in her belly. Grunting with the effort, Nero savagely booted her again. At last he had found something on which to vent his anger and frustration.

"If", he panted between kicks, "your bastard", - kick - "wants" - kick - "to wear" - kick - "the purple, he had better put in an appearance".

In helpless horror, the Augusta's servants watched as blood suddenly coursed down the legs of the semi-conscious Empress. At the sight of blood, Nero beamed at the broken figure rolling at his feet, moaning in agony. Before leaving the chamber, he turned the twitching Poppaea over with his toe and jumped on her from a small stool.

27

Simon ben Gioras, a charismatic hothead with a silver tongue, attracted the disaffected to his side in ever growing numbers. Ananus, unable to control him, had turned him and his followers out of Jerusalem, in the hope that a spell of rough living in the desert would moderate his rabidly anti-Roman views.

He had been wrong. Gioras swiftly realised that the hard life of a desert nomad had little appeal to either him or his followers, so he had continued to use Masada as a base.

When the news of Ananus' death reached Masada, he knew this was the time to make a move. He and his followers left for the hill country, sending scouts to the outlying villages and small towns. The message they carried to the downtrodden and dispossessed was simple. Follow Gioras and become rich. If you were a slave you would instantly be free. Why work in the fields all day for a master who took everything you produced? Gioras would put a sword in your hand; help you to take back that which was rightfully yours.

Unsurprisingly, he quickly attracted recruits. Men sick of working like the donkeys they drove for subsistence wages.

With what was soon a substantial force, he swept through the villages in the hill country picking up more recruits. His growing reputation as a warlord and an evangelist became feared in the towns and by their authorities, as respectable citizens began to support him. His next move was to establish a secure base in eastern Judaea.

In the border area of Idumaea lies the Pharan Valley, sheltered by limestone cliffs where the dominant sound to reach one's ears is the bleating of goats, the sound of servitude. These cliffs and their many caves provided him with a ready-made citadel; accommodation for what was now an army, storage for his loot and the vast quantities of grain he had seized.

The authorities in Jerusalem, worried that Gioras intended to attack the city, decided on a pre-emptive strike. They assembled an army and marched out of Jerusalem full of confidence. Gioras had no choice but to meet them head on. In the ensuing conflict he inflicted heavy casualties, forcing the remnants of the citizen army to retreat back to Jerusalem.

They left a victorious Gioras to return to his base in the Pharan valley, where having regrouped he mounted an attack on the town of Hebron, seizing its new corn harvest and a surprising amount of money from its unresisting inhabitants.

When news of this reached Jerusalem it was the cause of much sorrow and anger. The Jews of the Holy City held the little town in special reverence, it being the oldest town in the region. At two thousand, three hundred years old it was older even than Memphis in Egypt.

It was also a sacred site of immense importance to both Jew and Arab, who acknowledged Abraham as a common ancestor, who had settled there after migrating to Hebron from Mesopotamia when his descendants moved to Egypt. Cut from single blocks of limestone, the sarcophagi of the father of nations and his wife Sarah were housed in a cave on the edge of town; a place of pilgrimage for Jews and Arabs.

From Hebron, Gioras with his whole army, now fifty thousand in number of which fifteen thousand were heavy infantry, swept across Idumaea. Meeting with little resistance, he determined to build a reputation as a great general, a man to be feared as much as respected. Aping the Romans, Gioras put the land to fire and sword.

The Zealots in Jerusalem, afraid to face Gioras' forces in open battle, started a hit and run campaign against him. The barren hill country was ideal for laying ambushes. Its stony heights and steeply sloping canyon walls of bare rock were its only passes. Even these had to be negotiated with care. As a constant reminder of their instability, shards of razor sharp scree constantly dribbled down their unstable flanks. In this fissured wasteland, such a trap resulted in the capture of Gioras' wife and her servants. Delighted with their prize, the zealots raced back to the city, convinced that Gioras would immediately surrender to ensure his wife's safe return. The result was the very opposite of what they had hoped for. Incandescent with rage, Gioras camped outside the city walls. Anybody who ventured outside, for whatever purpose, irrespective of age or sex, was taken prisoner and tortured to death.

At night, many were burnt alive in cages hung on poles outside the city gates, their agonised shrieks shattering the night air, making sleep impossible. Others had their hands chopped off, and endured the agony of having the bleeding stumps cauterized with a red hot iron. These unfortunates were then allowed to return to the city, with their severed limbs in baskets strapped to the backs of mules. They also carried a message, a warning that worse was to come if Gioras didn't get his wife back. These threats terrified the citizens and the zealots equally, so they returned his wife.

Meanwhile, Vespasian launched a campaign to subdue those parts of Judaea that had not surrendered. Cerealis, commanding the Fifth Legion, swept through upper Idumaea, smashing through the town of Caphera, razing it to the ground. He then assaulted the town of Capharin, which promptly opened its gates. Without pause, Cerealis pointed his legion towards Hebron which kept its gates closed, but with little effect. Within days Cerealis had forced an entry and put the entire population to death, before burning the town to the ground.

This marked the subjugation of the entire region. Only the great Herodian fortresses remained defiant – Herodium, Masada and Machaerus – marooned to be dealt with at a later date. Now the Roman eagle was poised to swoop on Jerusalem.

In Jerusalem hundreds of Idumaeans who had joined John's forces rebelled. Taken by surprise, many of John's zealots were cut down. The rest fled, taking refuge in an old royal palace once owned by the Adiabenian royal family.

Hard on their heels, the chasing Idumaeans followed them in before the gates could be shut. From there the retreat continued as a bloody running battle into the Temple, where John had set up his military HQ as well as his living quarters. Seeing John besieged, the citizen army spread througout the city rallied to his side. The citizen army's leaders, who were the remaining chief priests, held a council and voted to admit Gioras into the city.

Gioras, convinced that he was destined to be King of the Jews, chosen by God to be the nation's salvation, agreed to be their ruler. He entered the city hailed as deliverer and protector, resulting in John of Gischala and his supporters becoming trapped in the Temple.

Supported by the citizen army led by the priests, Gioras attacked the Temple. John, making a stand on the colonnades and battlements, beat off these early assaults but not without heavy losses. One advantage John did have was that of looking down on his enemies, which enabled his archers to fire down on Gioras' forces with deadly effect.

The dead and the dying were strewn everywhere. Corpses of priests and laymen were piled one upon another. The blood of men and sacrificed beasts pooled into lakes in the sacred courts. In the meantime, increasing numbers of heavy missiles smashed against the altar and sanctuary, debris falling on the priests and worshippers who, in spite of everything, were still paying homage to God. Destitute, homeless people had had no option but to flee to Jerusalem for sanctuary. Satisfied that he had added to the city's considerable burden of refugees, Gioras again camped outside the walls, killing anybody who ventured outside.

The weeping citizens declared they feared Gioras outside more than the Romans – and that the zealots inside were more terrifying than either. Of these the Galileans were the worst. It was they who supported John of Gischala and he rewarded them by giving them licence to loot the city. The houses of the prosperous were sacked and their owners killed after being tortured to reveal any hidden wealth. Their wives and children were raped for sport, before being allowed to die.

The factions fighting for control of the city were now divided into three. Simon and his zealots, who had captured the Temple treasury; John of Gischala and his supporters, who were being directly targeted by the zealots; Gioras and his Messianic army, who was determined to emerge as the outright sole winner.

The entire city was a sectarian battle ground. Between them, the citizens were being ripped apart as though by hyenas. The old prayed for the Romans to come and save them. Loyal peace loving citizens, terrified and utterly dismayed, knew they had no say in the tragedy being played out. With their lives engulfed in catastrophe, they could not even flee. In their grief and fear, they were bottled up inside by the warring parties and outside by the Romans.

Large flocks of vultures gathered over the city, riding the thermals, ominous smuts of black spiralling in a cobalt sky.

28

Vespasian had returned to Caesarea to assemble his forces and prepare to march on Jerusalem itself, when a messenger arrived from Rome. The man, who had arrived by ship, was a senator, Silvius Emidius, who worked closely with Vespasian's brother Sabinus in the civil administration of the capital. Whatever news the senator had brought, it would be of great importance. That the messenger was not a military man, suggested it was of a political nature.

Vespasian received the senator with the usual exchange of pleasantries. He ordered refreshments and, when they were both seated, opened the conversation. "You have, I suspect, important news for me".

Emidius, who was sweating slightly with anxiety, drew a deep breath to steady himself. "General, I have to tell you that the Emperor Nero is dead".

Vespasian, though shocked by the news, remained impassive. "How?" was his only response.

Emidius pursed his lips and said "Suicide. But" he continued hurriedly, "after the senate, by an overwhelming majority, declared him to be an enemy of the state and issued his death warrant".

The silence following this declaration was prolonged. Deeply shocked, Vespasian's mind was in turmoil. The senator said nothing. A career diplomat, he knew when to keep quiet. "Who rules now?" Vespasian finally asked.

The senator cleared his throat. "Galba", he said shortly.

Vespasian considered this without speaking. Galba was from a noble family and was extremely wealthy. He had earned a reputation in the provinces of Gaul, Germania, Africa and Iberia.

On Nero's death, supported by Nymphidius the *Praetorian* Prefect, he had assumed the title of Caesar and marched straight to Rome. Vespasian finally spoke. "Of course I will immediately swear my allegiance to the new Emperor. I will also send my son Titus to pay homage to the new Emperor, to request his instructions with regard to the Jewish rebellion".

The senator nodded and murmured his approval. Vespasian, his mind clearing, rose and paced the room. "I will summon my Generals and inform them of the Emperor's death, and Galba's succession. I will also inform our allies, particularly King Agrippa. Tomorrow the whole army will be assembled and we will swear allegiance to the new Emperor. I hope you will be our guest at the ceremony".

Emidius, aware that his presence as a witness to this hugely important ceremony would serve Vespasian well, said "I would be honoured, *Legate*, to join you and will include this in my report to the senate and the Emperor".

Vespasian smiled absently, before saying "While you are in Caesarea, this villa is at your disposal. I will return to my camp just outside the city. Arrangements will be made for the ceremony to take place in two days' time. Now if you will excuse me". Emidius, satisfied with the outcome of what he had feared could have been a difficult meeting, stood and bowed as Vespasian took his leave. What was to transpire following this meeting was a string of events, unprecedented in the Empire's history.

Having broken the news to his senior officers and King Agrippa, Vespasian suspended all military operations, including his proposed march on Jerusalem. Titus was ordered to Rome to pay homage to the new Emperor and get his orders for the war they were waging. With the same objective, Agrippa set off for Rome with Titus.

Never one to miss a strategic opportunity, the fifty eight year old Vespasian took advantage of Agrippa's absence to entertain Queen Berenice – an unexpected romantic interlude in the widowed general's life, who afterwards reflected that his extravagant gift of pearls had been a sound investment. However, like all good things in life, such things come to an end. Titus returned early. While he had been making his way to Rome, Galba – after a reign of only three months – was assassinated and Otho seized the throne. Agrippa, however, decided to complete the journey, but an uneasy Titus turned back and returned to Caesarea.

In Caesarea, Vespasian's officers had started to meet in informal groups to discuss the state of the Empire, and particularly their own circumstances. What, they had asked themselves, could they expect in the future?

They decided among themselves that if it came to a civil war, they would be best served if their commander Vespasian made a bid for the throne. We are, they argued, five legions and have the support of Syrian and Arab auxiliaries. We have experienced officers who have never lost a war. We have allies in Italy. Vespasian's brother Sabinus is Prefect of Rome and both have friends in the senate. Also Vespasian's other son, Domition, is now eighteen and has supporters among Rome's influential families. These will be joined by men of wealth and power who will support Vespasian, because it is in their interests to do so. If Vespasian doesn't claim the throne, we who are fighting and dying for Rome, will be set aside.

On their behalf Mucianus, who agreed with them, formally requested Vespasian to accept Sovereignty, with the legionaries loudly demanding that he should command them against any that opposed him.

But Vespasian hesitated. He had privately given thought to what his men were now articulating. The key to success was, however, out of his control, and he knew it. Without the support of the city of Alexandria he would not be master of Egypt, the most important province in the Empire because it supplied Rome with a third of its annual corn consumption. Vespasian had calculated that if he controlled Egypt, he could make life difficult to the point of impossible for whoever ruled Rome.

He also needed the support of the two legions garrisoned in Alexandria, which controlled Egypt.

He knew that if he had these two things in place, he could use Egypt as a shield.

With Judaea and Galilee conquered, Vespasian had relieved Tiberius Alexander of his duties as second in command, returning him to Egypt to resume his governing of the province. Titus was promoted to command all forces, reporting directly to his father. Vespasian decided that he would declare his intentions to Tiberius and ask him for his support.

Before receiving Vespasian's letter, Tiberius Alexander had unsurprisingly carefully considered his own position. As governor of Rome's most important province, he literally lived like a King and, providing he kept the grain ships moving, he was far enough away from Rome to be untroubled by political intrigue. Like Vespasian, he was an old soldier and regarded civil war as unthinkable. The Empire would fall and along with it his tenure of office. Rome needed a stable government fast. That meant a reliable man at the top – a position he wasn't remotely interested in for himself. Vespasian, he decided, fitted the bill and had the backing of his men.

After consulting with his officers and, very importantly, recommending backing Vespasian, he assembled the legions and the city's dignitaries. After reading Vespasian's letter to them, he invited the soldiers and the civilians alike to swear allegiance to Vespasian.

Security in uncertain times carried the day. Support for Vespasian was overwhelming, so in July 69 the populace and the legions of Alexandria swore allegiance to Vespasian. In doing so they made him Emperor in waiting. Tiberius then set about preparing to receive Vespasian. His first task was to send messengers to every province, declaring Vespasian Emperor of the East. Cities throughout the region celebrated the news and offered sacrifices on Vespasian's behalf. The Moesian and Pannonia legions, with a view to the future, promptly swore allegiance to Vespasian who had left Caesarea for Beirut to meet the deputations from Syria and other provinces who came to offer their congratulations.

Vespasian then sent Mucianus to Italy in command of a powerful army. Mucianus, unwilling to risk his forces in a sea crossing in winter, marched his army overland. This was in the autumn of 69. In the meantime Antonius Primus, commander of the Third Legion garrisoned in Moesia who had declared for Vespasian, was confronted by General Ceacina Alienus who had been ordered to punish his defection. The two armies met at Cremona. Before they could engage in battle, Alienus changed sides after persuading his men that to do otherwise would put them on the losing side. Alienus, however, hadn't persuaded all of his men that switching sides was a good move. During the night his senior officers arrested him and tied him up, with the intention of taking him to Rome and charging him with treason.

Primus, not best pleased at this change of heart, met Alienus' forces which, without a commanding general, retreated towards Cremona. Fearing they would enter the city and become safe from anything but a prolonged siege, Primus led his cavalry in a headlong charge to out-flank and surround them. He then brought up his army and using his archers massacred Alienus' thirty thousand men, at a cost to Primus of four thousand casualties. After sending a report of his victory and his intentions to Vespasian, Primus looted the town before resuming his march on Rome.

Eventually the legions of Primus and Mucianus joined up and declared they were taking possession of Rome on behalf of Vespasian. They then called a meeting of the senate and put forward a motion that Vespasian's youngest son, Domitian, should be head of state until his father arrived. The ordinary citizens cheered this proposal and a weary senate ratified the motion and appointed Vespasian emperor.

Arriving in Alexandria, Vespasian was met with this amazing news and was soon receiving ambassadors from all over the world, who had come to congratulate their new sovereign and swear their countries' continued allegiance.

With the whole Empire secure and the supremacy of Rome re-established, Vespasian turned his attention to the final stages of his Judaean campaign. He was, however, eager to leave for Rome as soon as winter ended. With this in mind, he poured all his energy into putting things in order in Alexandria.

He sent Titus the pick of his army and made him commanding general of all forces in Judaea with Mucianus to be his second in command. His orders were that Jerusalem was to be levelled. Rebel Jews who survived the war were to be shipped abroad and sold into slavery. Large tracts of land were to be awarded to their Arab allies, with choice portions of good land made available to legionaries due for retirement, who were willing to settle in the region. The handful of remaining Jews would not be allowed to own land. If they wished to farm, it would be as tenants. In fact "all land in Judaea/Palestine would become the personal property of the Emperor".

With his sovereignty secure, Vespasian turned his thoughts to Judaea and his son. A letter, he decided, was long overdue.

29

Titus was enjoying a breakfast of cold cuts when a box of mail arrived. The document that caught his eye and was fished out first, bore his father's seal. Gesturing to his steward to replenish his goblet, he broke the crimson wax with the tip of his dagger and settled back to read what would turn out to be the most momentous letter he would ever receive in his life.

Hail Flavius Titus Vespasianous
From your father Flavius Vespasianous Augustus
My dear Son

News of your preparations for the final assault on Jerusalem is most welcome, and we look forward to your complete victory. The events of the last year in Rome have been the most significant in the history of the Empire. An account of which we desire to be accurately recorded in the history of the Empire, particularly those events which are interwoven with the war of Jews, which we have waged for five long years at great cost.

The vacuum caused by Nero's death caused in a power struggle that could have resulted in a devastating civil war. A war that may well have brought the empire to an end. With the throne empty and no natural successor, Servius Galba declared himself emperor. Within three months he was dead – assassinated by Salvius Otho who committed suicide when challenged by Aulus Vitellius.

When Primus and Mucianus' legions entered the city he tried to hide on a building site dressed as a common workman. Discovered, he was taken to the very spot in the *forum* where Galba had been assassinated. Declared an enemy of the people, he was executed.

Fortunately our prisoner, the Jewish scholar Josephus, is writing an eye witness account of the war and will be able to record these events. When it and the war are finally concluded, it is my intention to place a copy in every library in the Empire.

From your earlier reports I know you have come to value Josephus' assistance and have noted your recommendations with regard to a reward for his loyalty. You may, of course, furnish him with anything that is within your gift as Caesar of our forces in Judaea. You may also confer on him, in my name Roman citizenship and a gift of land in Judaea. In addition, when he comes to Rome he will have a pension and our old house in Rome to live in.

The senate has agreed that, when you have won the final victory, we will share a Triumph together. Nothing in this world will give me more pleasure and pride.

I salute you
Your father
Vespasianous Agustus.
Rome

After ordering three legions to their quarters in Caesarea and Scythopolis, Titus rode up to the strong hold of Gischala with a thousand picked horsemen. He was tired of bloodshed and knew from his spies that the majority of Gischala's population, peasant farmers, only wanted to live in peace. But John had no intention of being captured by the Romans. He treacherously pretended to be ready to agree terms but said that, as it was the Sabbath, he would need to postpone the formalities until the morrow. Titus, as a sign of his own good faith, withdrew to Cadesh Napthaly.

When night fell, John, surrounded by a mob of unarmed men, women and children, whom he later abandoned, made off in the direction of Jerusalem. As a consequence, six thousands of John's wretched dupes were slaughtered and the women and children brought back, whereupon a weary Gischala opened its gates to Titus. The whole of Galilee was now at peace – a peace bought by the death of hundreds of thousands of ordinary Jews who had no say in the politics of revolution.

As soon as he arrived in Jerusalem, John strutted about declaring himself to be a patriot. Older people, who had heard it all before, knew him for what he was - an unscrupulous, calculating egoist who had already been defeated by the Romans. But the city's impressionable and disaffected youth, fired by the dream of home rule, flocked to his support. The Holy City was soon severely divided, its population split by implacable factions, its streets divided by sectarianism into 'no go' areas.

Things were made worse by the demands of a long standing tradition that the city gates must stand open to any child of Israel who wished to enter. Outlaws, bandits, war lords, anarchists, terrorists and nationalists from all over the country converged on this sanctuary. In the confusion of the infighting there were no sentries posted on the walls. The opportunists and carpet baggers found it easy to infiltrate the pilgrims fleeing to the city for protection.

To strengthen their position the rebels decided they wanted to replace the Temple priests with their own men. They decided to activate a most obscure pontifical law, that of *Eniahan,* which allowed them to carry out a travesty of an ancient custom, which was to cast lots as to who should be High Priest of all Israel. The lot fell to a village stonemason, Anius Ben Samuel. He was carted off to the city, dressed in the sacred vestments and taught by rote the sacerdotal functions - of which of course he knew nothing.

The group which had carried out this blasphemous act were of course Simon's zealots, who then installed themselves in the Temple.

30

Between Simon and John, a "stand-off" had developed. Simon controlled the Upper and Lower City and the Great Wall. John controlled the Temple and the surrounding area as far as the Kidron Valley. Between them stretched a wasteland of burnt out buildings, testimony to the savagery of the civil war. A truce between the two was agreed and even though mutual suspicions lingered, they joined forces. John and Simon's first combined sortie was a disaster. They had barely cleared the city gates, before turning on each other. They were like rabid dogs, snapping at anything and everything in a mindless frenzy. Within a week of its ceasefire the war within a war was resumed. "It was as if" Josephus observed "the Jews suffer less at Roman hands, than they do at their own".

As the agony of the Holy city continued, the despairing citizens began to believe that God had turned his face from them in punishment for their sins. Many were plunged into a deep depression and simply stayed in their homes, faces turned to the wall, devoid of expression, unable or unwilling to speak. Having polluted the sanctuary, desecrated the Holy of Holies and rendered unclean the High Altar, its sacred flame never to be relit, the rebels continued to fight each other. The victims of the return to war and murder lay unburied in the streets, their putrefaction bringing more death from disease.

Such were the circumstances Titus found on his arrival at Jerusalem. With his legions busy building their fortifications, the young general decided to take a closer look at the city he had heard so much about. With no sign of anybody outside the city walls, Titus ordered a cohort of cavalry to accompany him on a tentative reconnoitre.

As they cantered forward he scanned the wall. From a distance no point of weakness could be seen. As they approached the edge of the valley, protecting what was the first of three walls built one behind the other, he discounted any attempt to enter its bottomless depths. After being out for a couple of hours Titus noticed that at a point in the fortifications, the ramparts were lower and did not connect to the inner second wall. Instead they were interrupted by a small building. He learned later that this was a temple to a high priest. Surprisingly, this important junction in the walls' defences was unguarded. Titus then looked hard at the Antonia fortress. He decided that a possible route into the city might be through the less well protected new city and the allegedly un-take-able Antonia Fortress.

After Titus had ridden out to survey the city, Josephus had asked to be allowed to approach the walls in an effort to establish contact with the rebels. His efforts, even under a flag of truce, were met with a shower of missiles, resulting in one of his accompanying party, the centurion Nicanor, taking an arrow in his arm.

When Titus returned, he issued orders that the new city's suburbs were to be torched. At the same time he ordered the construction of mobile attack platforms to begin. To accomplish this, a vast quantity of timber was needed. Every tree – except the olive – in the area was felled.

The proposed platforms were in fact massive mobile towers. Between seventy five and one hundred feet high, they had several stories each designated to accommodate a wide assortment of artillery, plus assault troops supported by archers and javelin throwers. These machines and their men were protected from enemy fire with sheets of toughened ox hide or metal plates.

Inside the city, the rebel leaders had a dilemma. John's men were eager to take on the Romans and had to be held back. John's concern wasn't the Romans, it was Simon he had come to fear. Simon, confident that he had John contained and being positioned nearer to the Romans, decided to go on the offensive. The artillery Cestius had abandoned and had been captured by the Jews, he mounted along the wall nearest to the Romans. Under its covering fire, he and his men charged out of the city to attack the Romans with a direct frontal assault.

The Romans weren't exactly caught unawares, but they were certainly surprised. Many soldiers working high on the platforms' scaffolding would have been killed by the Jewish artillery, but for the shields and ox hide screens that had been fixed in anticipation of such an eventuality. On the ground, the legionaries engaged as builders threw down their tools and seized weapons placed ready to hand and formed up in their ranks. After fierce hand to hand fighting, resulting in casualties on both sides, Simon's men executed an orderly withdrawal and returned to the city.

Titus then decided that what he regarded as a "cheeky" attack needed a response, so he ordered a hundred and eighty of his most powerful stone throwers into action. These monsters could hurl a rock weighing a hundredweight four hundred yards. Having brought these heavyweights into a forward position, Titus ordered them to commence firing continuously day and night, with instructions to randomly alter the timing, range and trajectory of their bombardment.

In spite of this, the Jews fought doggedly to stop the Romans completing their platforms, using the time they gained to plan what they would do to counter them, knowing that eventually they would be completed.

Simon and John at last realised that they faced a common enemy and that their only hope of survival was to join forces in a common cause.

When the Romans started to pound the wall with their rams both men, surrounded by their officers, had run to the wall wild eyed in fear. They had yelled to each other that they had to unite. The shouting and screaming of the terrified people filled the air. Crowding the streets, they surged towards the Temple, praying and cursing. To calm them down, Simon announced that they should come into the Temple and from there to the wall.

John, even though he was suspicious of Simon, gave his permission and opened the Temple doors. Differences set aside they united under a joint command.

Their first action was to carry hundreds of firebrands to the top of the wall and fling them against the half-finished towers. At the same time, other men concentrated on continuously bombarding the Romans manning the rams. In the confusion created by these attacks, Jewish volunteers sprinted out of the city and attacked the Romans operating the stone throwing artillery. Against this sudden and determined attack, Titus was forced to defend his war machines by bringing up a troop of cavalry supported by several *cohorts* of archers.

In an effort to protect the teams operating the rams from the deluge falling from above, he ordered that a protective roof be constructed. In all of this chaos it was the newly deployed Arab archers who were the most effective, laying down a continuous covering fire. But the wall did not yield. In fact it showed no signs of doing so. The Jews, keeping to the city walls, continued to watch the Romans who had returned to their various tasks around their camps. No sooner had order and calm been restored, than the Jews launched another assault.

A thousand strong, armed with swords, each man also carrying a torch, burst out of the city. Like wolves attacking a stag, they flew across the open ground. Within minutes the partially constructed platforms were blazing. With scarcely a pause, they charged the artillery, flinging fiercely burning torches onto them. The Roman front line infantry that answered the call to arms was routed by advancing Jews.

Amid the burning artillery a furious battle developed. The Romans were desperate to save their war machines. The Jews, equally determined to destroy them, were joined by more and more Jews charging out of the city to join the battle. Roman trumpeters urgently sounded the call for reinforcements. Mucianus, who had been at one of the other camps, arrived on a lathered horse to take command, its *tribune* having been mortally wounded. The Roman legionaries, who had a reputation for bravery and success, rallied to their new general in order to face an enemy that was beginning to get the upper hand.

With burning timber crashing round them and thousands of screaming Jewish warriors flinging themselves against their line, the Tenth Legion surpassed even its reputation for courage under fire. Mucianus, knowing that the scales were tipping against him and that he was now hopelessly outnumbered, was unable to retreat. The Jews having cut him off from the main camp forced the veteran general decided to make a stand. The trumpeters blared his orders and six thousand legionaries responded as one man. The legion started to manoeuvre, revolving and tightening; always facing the enemy, it presented a wall of shields. Within minutes the entire Roman force had formed a square of interlocking shields bristling with long spears, their butts driven into the dry stony earth.

Over the tops of this barricade twelve thousand eyes, shaded by the iron of their owners' helmets, viewed the Jews implacably. A challenge the rebels accepted with relish, throwing themselves fearlessly against their enemy, hurling spears as they ran forward sword in hand.

This compacted mass of struggling men was suddenly split when at last Titus, at the head of his entire cavalry resources, arrived on the scene.

They charged the swirling mass of men at full gallop. At virtually point blank range they hurled javelins into the densely packed body of Jews who, because of the deafening noise of the battle, had not heard them coming. Three times the circling riders plunged their javelins into their enemy, before drawing their long cavalry swords, sweeping in to harvest an enemy caught between two fires. Now it was the turn of the Jews to seek a way back. Under constant attack from Titus' cavalry who herded them like sheep, they fought their way to the safety of the city, bitter in defeat, knowing how close they had come to a famous victory. The battered Romans, shaken by the engagement, were forced to acknowledge their opponent with grudging respect.

A few days later, when they started to repair their artillery and to rebuild the platforms, they did so under the protection of two legions in full armour. As the days passed, the frustrated Jews could only watch as the monstrous towers were completed. Then, under the covering fire of Syrian and Arab archers, they were inexorably inched into position. Up to this point the Jews had stood up to everything the Romans had thrown at them. Courageously they had successfully taken the fight to them, but from the outset the introduction of the towers caused them great problems. The highest stories overlooked the wall, and the Romans on them were out of range of the Jewish spear throwers. This enabled the Romans, firing downwards, to hit the rebels with a veritable blizzard of stones, arrows and javelins that swept the Jews from that section of the wall where the rams were beginning to take effect.

The biggest of the rams, nicknamed Satan by the Jews, eventually opened up a vertical fissure that was widening with every blow. The Jewish defenders, exhausted by constant fighting and little sleep, decided that as there were two more walls further back they would retreat. Instead of defending the gap opened up by the ram, they gave way to the Roman infantry, who plunged through the opening and fought their way to the gates that the rebels had abandoned. With the gates captured, the way was clear for Titus' forces to storm into the northern suburbs that Cestius had destroyed.

Titus quickly consolidated his gain, establishing his army between the two walls as far as the Kidron Valley. With his archers manning the walls they had taken, the engineers set about turning the recaptured artillery round to face the second wall to which the Jews had retreated. Titus, calling up reserves, was then able to relieve the troops who had made the breakthrough and send out soldiers to probe the enemy's strength who, having fallen back, set up a determined defence of the second wall.

With John's men fighting from the Antonia and the northern colonnade of the temple, Simon's brigade occupied the approach near the tomb of John the High Priest. Importantly, he was defending the ground as far as the gate through which water was taken into the Hippicus Tower. The Jews, having retreated to the second wall, now counter attacked, mounting a series of sorties to fight the Romans at close quarters. This hand to hand combat in the confined area between the two walls was brutal and bloody, with neither side able to get the upper hand. The Jews, fiercely attacking in strength throughout the day, left nothing untried in an attempt to defeat their enemy. Only nightfall brought a halt to their efforts. Then, at first light, the battle restarted.

During the night Titus had replaced his front line troops with fresh fighters; a distinct advantage over the Jews who did not have his depth of reserves. Having done so, he now went on the offensive, pushing relentlessly against a tiring opponent. In the coming nights his artillery targeted the Jews with firebombs. As these flaming missiles burst against the walls or landed on the ground immediately behind where the Jews were trying to rest, they had the desired effect. The Jewish defenders got no sleep. Four days later the exhausted Jews abandoned the second wall and Titus entered the area known as the New City.

In an effort to bring the fighting to an end, Titus gave orders that prisoners were not to be killed and the troops were not to pillage the houses. Under a flag of truce he offered to meet the rebel army outside the city to discuss terms. Either way the Temple, the city and its civilians would suffer no further harm. The citizens who longed for peace wanted to accept this offer, but the rebels refused it. Threatening the civilians with execution, they resumed the fight. The renewed conflict took the Romans into a warren of narrow streets that the Jews knew intimately. This knowledge enabled them to outflank the Romans. Fearing they would be trapped, the Romans tried to withdraw but were held up. The Jews, fighting like mad men, relentlessly attacked their enemy from every side, coming at them in sudden rushes from side alleys and then attacking them head on in desperate hand to hand fighting.

As the Roman legionaries started to die in increasing numbers, the Jews escalated the pressure – but not without a price. Their reckless courage cost them lives in equal measure.

Forced back to the second wall, the Romans were trapped. They had not widened the earlier breaches, and with the Jews virtually locked against them, they dared not turn to scramble through these narrow gaps.

Titus saved the day, bringing up archers that he placed on the rooftops and at the ends of the street. Here he made a stand with one of the centurians, Gaius Iovis, who once again proved himself. Together they held the line with Titus directing volleys of arrows against the rebels; a constant barrage that pinned the Jews down. Under this covering fire, the last of the legionaries finally got clear.

The rebels' success at driving the Romans out of the city convinced them that when the Romans mounted another attack they would defeat them again.

The Roman counter attack, when it came, was with overwhelming force that was met bravely by the Jews, who resisted the Romans for three bloody days that saw thousands die on both sides. On the fourth day, Titus threw everything he had at the enemy and crushed the last vestiges of resistance.

To regain control of the second wall, he set about demolishing it at the northern end. To ensure he wouldn't be pushed back again, he garrisoned the towers on the portion of the wall that he allowed to stand. Titus knew, however, that taking the third wall was going to be exceptionally difficult. After he had thought about it, he offered the rebels a ceasefire, so that they could discuss amongst themselves terms of surrender.

Mucianus suggested to Titus that this temporary cessation of hostilities could be turned to their advantage. It was an opportunity, he said, to display the full might and power of Rome in a peaceful way. At the same time, what he had in mind would provide an enormous morale booster to the army. With the plan explained, Titus roared with laughter and clapped him on the shoulder telling him to get on with it.

Mucianus gave orders that there would be a full inspection of the army by its commanding general, to include the awarding of citations and battle honours, immediately followed by a pay parade. All of this was to take place in full view of the enemy.

A week later, Jewish spectators would be packed the full length of the old wall and the north side of the Temple. People would crowd rooftops. Every window would hold watching eyes. Every vantage point in the city would be packed with spectators to witness a sight that would take several days to unfold.

First the Pioneer Corps built a reviewing platform, shaded with a giant awning. In the middle of this was placed a golden throne flanked by two silver thrones, whose appearance was as much as a surprise to Titus as it was to the Jews. As Mucianus observed later "Don't ask sir. The engineers have their ways and means." They then levelled the ground for two miles in every direction to parade ground standards. At discreet intervals latrines were dug and screened. Stables were established. Prefabricated buildings were brought on site to hold stores of food and provide temporary shelter. Water was piped in. Each side of the reviewing platform was flanked by the pavilions of the heads of the supporting auxiliaries. Chief among these was that of King Agrippa and Queen Berenice, who flew her own standard.

To discourage any interference with these preparations, two hundred pieces of artillery were positioned ready for instant use. These were supported by an Arab force of two thousand *auxiliary* horse archers who kept up a constant patrol of the whole area. An elite wing of Roman cavalry, decked out in all its finery, made its presence known with showy charges, swords flashing in the sunlight. When all was ready, column by column, thirty thousand legionaries in full battle armour marched out; five legions, each with its own eagle and battle standards, drums beating. The crimson capes of its mounted officers, flowing across the haunches of their mounts, passed in front of Titus flanked by Mucianus and King Agrippa.

It took two hours for this glittering spectacle of gleaming armour and weapons to pass before Titus who, with his second-in- command Mucianus and King Agrippa, scorning the seats provided, stood to take the salute. It was a sight that awed the citizens of Jerusalem and caused the rebels to tighten their lips. Over the next four days, in accordance with custom, tables were set up and chests of gold and silver coins were brought out. In turn the men came forward and in full view of the watching Jews, each man had the money due to him counted – his to take away or have banked for him by the *Optios* who supervised the proceedings.

On day five, as the rebels had not responded to his offer of peace, Titus began building more platforms, planning to invade the Upper City by assaulting the Antonia. Josephus, who had received word that the rebels had imprisoned his parents and his brother, was determined to make one last appeal to them. Raised up on a partially completed platform he proclaimed "If you do not accept the peace the Romans offer you, you will die. Not because you turn your back on Caesar, but on God. Yes God. We, the children of Abraham, God's chosen people, have only one purpose in life – to honour and obey His Holy Law. *To do unto others, as you would be done by, for thereby hangs the whole of the law.* What have you done? Not to the Romans but your fellow Jews. There is no crime so vile it has been left undone. You are ruled over by the scum of nations; blasphemers who have spilt the blood of the innocent on the sacred altar, who have fouled this hallowed spot beyond redemption, beyond salvation. This Holy place, respected by the Romans out of regard for our customs and laws, you have turned into a place unfit for the keeping of pigs. It is not the Romans you should fear but the God of your fathers who even now, you wretched depraved people, will not abandon you.

Lay down your weapons and ask God not the Romans for mercy.

For the Almighty has left this place for ever.

Was this not foretold?

You were warned, but would not listen.

Deaf to the prophets He sent you.

The prophecy of the destruction of the Holy City and His Temple was foretold before your grandfathers were born.

And now the time has come, when the living will envy the dead and only the truly repentant will find salvation".

A moment of silence followed this appeal. It was if a judgement was in the balance. Finally, it was broken by an atavistic howl and the sibilant hiss of stones showering down. Knocked to the ground, Josephus was saved by the cohort standing by, who rushed to shelter him with their shields.

31

With tears running down his cheeks, Josephus ended his appeal. Unmoved, the rebels hurled jeers and catcalls at the despondent figure trudging slowly back to the Roman lines. Those citizens who had managed to find a place on the wall were horrified at the outcome. As they spread the news of what they regarded as a disastrous outcome, panic set in. With no hope of a peace settlement, more people were determined to flee the city and throw themselves on the mercy of the Romans. Property was sold for what it would fetch. The most treasured of valuable possessions went the same way. The only currency that held its value was gold coin.

The hundreds of criminal gangs operating in the city muscled in wherever they could, to take advantage of this desperate situation. The lucky ones who were allowed to leave the city, having paid the rebels a substantial bribe, were not allowed to take anything with them. To foil them, they swallowed gold coins with every member of the family helping to cheat the robbers, planning their recovery once they were safely out of the city.

When these refugees reached the Roman lines, Titus ordered that after questioning they were to be allowed to go where they wished. A few, daunted by the prospect of trekking in to the desert with no possessions, except those which could be recovered from their bowels, returned to Jerusalem.

As the months stretched into years, people began to lose their reason as the famine grew worse. Criminal gangs roamed the city in search of food, breaking into houses and ransacking them.

The terrified occupants, too weak to resist, were tortured to reveal what they did not have. The lengths these gangs would go to in forcing people to give them food beggared belief. Victims were judged by their appearance. If they were fat, obviously they had access to secret stores of food. If they were wasted, they were not worth bothering with. Those who still had gold exchanged it for a single measure of corn. That valued each grain as being worth its weight of that precious metal. Having traded in secret, they ate in secret. In fear of discovery, no table was laid. Partially baked bread was grabbed from the oven and hastily gobbled, in fear of it being snatched from their mouths.

The rebels who had commandeered the city's remaining stores of food, refused to share them with the general population, arguing that they needed them to keep their soldiers fighting fit.

The armed gangsters roaming the city stayed well clear of the rebels. These depraved savages would stop at nothing to satisfy their needs. They killed the old for a crust. No mercy was shown to the young. Infants were casually swung against a wall, heads cracked like egg shells on unyielding stone. Worse still, this barbarous tribe harboured psychopaths who killed and maimed to satisfy nameless appetites. Monsters any normal society would either have put down or kept chained. Rape and murder were commonplace.

These outcasts lived on a staple diet of rats – huge beasts as big as cats, fat and sleek from feeding on the thousands of corpses rotting in the streets.

As the ordinary citizens suffered at the hands of criminal scum, men of wealth were rounded up by Simon and John to face trumped up charges of treason. Paid informers denounced them, claiming they were planning to flee the city.

Taken to cellars, these men usually disclosed where they had hidden their wealth. If the sight and sounds of their loved ones having the instruments of torture applied didn't do the trick, they themselves were subjected to them. Having secured what they wanted from these unfortunates, the rebels killed them and their families, and flung their bodies into the street. Like hyenas, they ripped the carcass of the Holy City to pieces.

No city in the past or in the future would be visited by such bestiality. No generation would give birth to such evil. The depraved behaviour of the Jewish rebel leaders meant they would stand at the bar of history, revealed to the world as the worst of humanity – fundamentalists, fanatics, terrorists and ruthless warlords who destroyed the Holy City, the Temple and the Nation of Israel.

Meanwhile the Romans had nearly completed building their platforms, though they had done so at a cost. Many legionaries died from missiles fired by the Jews. While this was going on, increasing numbers of starving Jews were creeping into the ravines in search of anything edible. Fearing that arsonists might be mingling with the civilians, Titus ordered them to be rounded up. One such encounter would live forever in the memory of the Roman patrol that was out that night. They discovered a group of Jews huddled in the darkness around a smoking fire, cooking a meal.

Crouched like primeval savages they slashed at a roasting joint with their daggers. As they wolfed down the bloody haunch, the scout who had found them stifled a cry of revulsion on seeing what he thought was a goat ended not in a cloven hoof but in a human foot. Its toenails glistening with fat in the firelight. Having been discovered, the cornered Jews tried to fight their way clear but were easily subdued and captured. Taken back to the Roman camp, Titus ordered that they were to be crucified in full view of their countrymen lining the wall.

This tragedy was played out daily, with an average of five hundred men per day being captured. The Roman soldiers, bitter at a war that had gone on for six long years, extracted a grim revenge on these men. They nailed up their prisoners live, in every conceivable attitude – upside down, horizontally and diagonally. This macabre spectacle quickly numbered thousands, attracting flocks of birds of prey. It was a grisly addition to the theatre of death that the citizens were forced to watch, as the rebels drove them to the walls with whips. Even children were forced to witness what happened to "deserters".

Meanwhile, Titus went from platform to platform, demonstrating that he would soon be ready for the final attack. After twenty days of continuous labour, all four of the huge platforms were ready. The Fifth Legion positioned theirs opposite the Antonia. Another, built by the Twelfth, was positioned in support fifty feet along the wall on the left hand side. On the right hand side, the Tenth placed a tower near the Almond pool. The Fifteenth moved their tower to attack the wall near the High Priest's monument.

John, however, had not been idle. As well as his own men, hundreds of citizens had been drafted in as miners. Day and night they had dug deep to get under the wall; then they had cut a horizontal shaft. These galleries were carefully supported by wooden props for John's mine took him directly under the Fifth and Twelfth legions' platforms. These were then enlarged into caverns that he packed with barrels of bitumen and timber faggots coated with tar. Both sides were ready at the same time. The Romans eased their towers into their final positions and the Jews set torches to their underground bonfires. The Jews' final touches were to run leather hoses down the tunnels to the seat of the fire. Using bellows, they pumped air to the heart of the fires they had set. The resulting conflagration burned through the supporting props in minutes, culminating in the barrels of bitumen exploding.

With the ground collapsing beneath them, the platforms the Romans had laboured so hard and so long to make, disappeared, falling in chaos into the bowels of the furnace raging beneath them. There was no escape for the legionaries manning them, who fell into the flaming craters to be burned alive. A horrified Titus watched helplessly, as clouds of black smoke billowed out of the gigantic pits that had swallowed up his men. A dense cloud of dust and debris was hurled skywards, as more and more barrels exploded. This was followed, by sheets of flame shooting heavenwards as the platforms added to the fuel the Jews had packed underground. Within an hour, Jewish ingenuity had destroyed months of work by their adversary. The shocked Romans fell back in despair. They had been certain that victory would be theirs. This reversal plunged them into depression. Morale hit rock bottom.

The following day Gioras struck while the enemy was in a state of shock. The Romans, in anticipation of the platforms' success, had moved their battering rams close to the wall and were ready to put them to use. These were the rebels' targets, but first they launched a diversionary attack against the remaining platforms, drawing the Roman forces away from the rams. Three volunteers then ran out of the city armed with firebrands and swords.

Throughout the war, neither side produced three braver men. Attacking the legionaries manning the rams, they set fire to them. Standing fast while the flames took hold, they fought off the enraged Romans. With such an example of courage, the rebels charged out of the city to engage the enemy. In minutes, the two sides were locked in the most desperate hand to hand fighting.

To add to the confusion, the Jews were setting fire to anything that would burn. With the remaining platforms well alight and the rams engulfed in flames, the rebel forces which now numbered several thousand launched a direct frontal attack, driving the Romans back to their camp. Here, the retreating Romans, shamed by Jewish courage, halted their headlong flight and made a stand.

At this point of crisis in the battle, Titus arrived from the shambles of the Antonia.

Outraged, he cursed the men who, after capturing the enemy's walls, were in danger of losing what they had won. He stood down a badly wounded centurion, and with grim determination took command of his men. Leading from the front, he tried to outflank the Jews. Their leaders, however, alert to this new danger, signalled with blasts on rams' horns to wheel and counter this manoeuvre. Without let-up the battle raged on, dust filling the air, the noise deafening, confusion spreading. The Jews held, desperate in the knowledge that victory was their only option. The Romans, shamed by retreat and knowing that Titus himself was in the front line, fought like men possessed. It was simple. Like their opponents, death before dishonour was the unspoken common creed. With their objectives achieved - the platforms destroyed, the rams disabled, and the Roman army given a very bloody nose – the rams' horns sounded for a withdrawal. The rebels wisely decided to return to the city, having secured a famous victory.

With their platforms destroyed the dejected Romans, their morale at rock bottom, trudged back to their camp. Thousands of Jews who had poured out of the city in support of the rebels returned triumphantly, singing hymns of praise to their God. Many of the defeated Romans started to believe that by using the traditional methods of war, they would never take the city. Not unaware of the misgivings and doubts sweeping through his army, Titus called for a council of war.

With his most senior officers assembled Titus said, "Gentlemen, we have suffered a setback. We must now decide how we can reverse it. Make no mistake, next time we take to the field we will be victorious or dead. There is no question of a Roman retreat from this province and there is no question of Caesar needing to send further reinforcements. As officers, we are responsible for deciding how the army fights. We create the strategy that will decide how the war is fought. We decide the tactics that will be used to achieve that strategy. Doing these things and doing them well, is what it means to have the honour of being an officer in the Roman army. Right now things are tough. Our soldiers are dragging their feet and hanging their heads. I am amazed and alarmed to discover that apparently we are commanding legions without any backbone".

Mucianus would have interrupted, but Titus waved him down. "What happened today," he continued, "came close to a rout. A collapse in the face of a determined enemy who, with inferior weapons, inferior numbers and inferior officers and inferior tactics, forced Roman soldiers to break and run. While I am in command, while I live, that will never happen again. If an officer orders a retreat, then it will be an orderly fighting withdrawal, a military decision which any officer can make and be responsible for. Troops deciding for themselves to pull back, are guilty of cowardice and mutiny. They have no place in Rome's legions. For the remainder of this campaign,

Syrian archers will be positioned behind our infantry. Any man who cuts and runs will be executed and left unburied, his name struck from the legion's records as though he had never existed".

"Now we have a war to fight. One that is a long way from won. Its outcome may seem to some of you to be in doubt. If this is the case you should leave the field and return to Rome. We need to think as our enemies think. They will have said their goodbyes to those they love the most. With courage, they face us with only one thought. Tomorrow the enemy will come, sword in hand. Read your enemy's intention in his eyes. *I will fight you to the death*. This is the moment of reckoning; the moment that decides life or death with honour. So what do we do gentlemen? Our troops look to us for direction, they await our bidding".

Mucianus, a veteran of many crises, was a soldier with a long and successful career. His voice was steady and his demeanour calm. "There are several options open to us. I am certain that as this council deliberates, they will be put forward for discussion. For my part, I reflect on the fact that thus far we have only brought up a fraction of the forces available to us. This in itself is of no particular significance. However, knowing what we now know, I recommend we discuss the merits of an all-out assault, using all our forces en masse. How and when we do this we need to discuss separately, because these are tactical matters. This meeting is about strategy. I recommend to you an all-out assault as a strategic move".

Sextus Cerealis spoke next. "Any strategy carries risk - that is the nature of war. So I won't speculate on what the outcome, good or bad, could result in from an all-out attack. Whatever our next move is, the question of *how*, is critical. We cannot afford to lose men at the same rate as the enemy if for no other reason than we cannot expect Rome to send us reinforcements. A new Emperor will want to husband his military strength, knowing that inevitably he will be tested. Somewhere in the Empire, somebody will decide this is a good time to challenge the new man".

As a murmur of agreement met this statement, Cerealis continued "Whatever we do, eventually we will need more platforms. They are the only way we can realistically hope to get troops in numbers inside the city. Yes, I know timber is non-existent and will have to be brought by ship and then overland. Yes, I know it takes time to build the bloody things. But we have no choice. Whatever we decide, keep at the front of your minds three things.

One, the defences of this city are the best in the world. Two, our enemy is determined and prepared to die fighting. Three, very importantly, our enemy believes he can win. Why? He believes that by forcing us to fight for every building, we will take unacceptable losses. He believes that by dragging the war out, eventually we will give up and go home".

A rumble of conversation ran around the tent, dying to give way to Aeternius Fronto. "It is good that we analyse our situation and face the facts of circumstance squarely. We may end up making the best of a bad job, but at least we won't have rushed in like fools. We won't have caused the unnecessary deaths of our men – who, let me remind you, are getting fewer as this war grinds on. It is four years since we arrived in this place. We have lost two thousand Roman legionaries and three thousand auxiliaries, and at any one time we have another thousand men recovering from their wounds. Whatever we decide, we must consider these losses. We must consider how long we have been here and, very importantly, how much longer can we be expected to stay. Finally, there is a factor not yet spoken of that is of paramount importance. It is the political implication of what we decide. This, in my view, should guide us to our decisions. Yes, I know you will claim to be just simple soldiers and know nothing of politics; a wise course for a soldier to steer, but absolute bullshit".

A roar of laughter greeted this, relieving the sombre mood of the gathering. As it died away Fronto continued, "Not so very long ago, you made the most significant political decision of your lives. One that will change the course of the Empire's history and for which each and every one of you can and will be held personally responsible for". The silence that greeted this was profound. Titus, eyes narrowed, face inscrutable, waited as they all did for what was coming next. "You declared Flavius Vespasianus Caesar, for which I salute you".

A great roar burst round the tent. When order was finally restored, Titus rose to speak. "No general anywhere could take more pride in you and our legionaries than I do. No general has such officers of good sense, of such excellent experience, to guide him in considering what his course should be. I believe that it is your words of wisdom that will not only win this war for Rome; it will do so with the greatest honour. When it comes, the triumph you will share in Rome with Caesar will be remembered forever". This was the signal for thunderous applause and the stamping of iron shod sandals.

"Let me", said Titus after a pause "summarise what you have drawn out as the key facts. To explain in the light of these, what our strategy to win this war will be. Firstly, we have this most extraordinary situation of Jew killing Jew inside the city. Even as they attack us, they attack each other. Secondly, the city is packed to bursting with pilgrims and refugees. Four hundred thousand extra mouths to feed and they have no food. The rebel factions have taken control of what food remains after a disastrous fire swept through their warehouses. Nearly a million people are starving to death. Disease and famine are doing our job for us. At least five hundred criminal gangs, ranging in numbers from ten to a hundred, are plundering the city. They roam the streets day and night killing anything that moves. Cannibalism has been reported. The High Priest of all Israel is dead. The Holy of Holies is polluted and defiled. The everlasting Eternal Flame on the High altar has gone out.

"No longer are sacrifices and prayers offered each day to their God. The streets are choked with two hundred thousand putrefying corpses. Every day, hundreds of Jewish civilians risk death to flee the horror that Jerusalem has become. They run to us begging for mercy. They flee in terror from the crazed fundamentalists, who insist on fighting to the death.

Platforms are necessary, but at best they are an aid to securing a foothold. To build them it has been said we have to import timber. Yet we must not allow the siege to be so prolonged that, like the Greeks at Troy, we give up and sail home – which means that, among other things, we must halt supplies being smuggled into the city.

"So we will construct a wall of earth, a great embankment with a twenty foot deep moat at its base. Fortifications will be positioned along its length. To this end timber will be obtained at any price and brought in by ship and then finally overland. This wall will wrap itself around Jerusalem, halting only when it comes to the bottomless ravines, on which its walls are built.

When it is completed, the wall will be four and a half miles long with fifteen forts to defend it".

To the watching Jews' amazement, forty thousand legionaries and sixty thousand enslaved Jews captured during the Galilean campaign, completed this task within a month; an astonishing feat of engineering in such a short time.

The building of this *circumvallation* caused Jews unable to leave the city to lose all hope. With the days slipping by, the famine became more intense. Bodies piled on bodies, a rotting putrescence bringing cholera and other diseases to strike down the weakened population. Men, gaunt as ghosts, haunted the city's plazas, eventually keeling over never to move again. The living, too weak to bury their kinsfolk, turned their faces to the wall and prayed to join them. In the people's misery, no weeping or supplication was heard. Hunger stole all emotion. Dry eyed and slack jawed, those who died slowest watched in envy those who succumbed before them. As it had been prophesied *the living envied the dead*.

A deep silence enveloped the city. It was as if God had died. In these final moments of despair and pain, evil visited the civilian population of Jerusalem in the guise of their fellow men. Criminals broke into their houses and stripped the living and the dead of anything of value. As the stench of the dead and dying citizens became unbearable, Gioras and John ordered that they be buried. Because of the numbers, this proved to be impossible so, in return for a meal, those still able bodied threw the corpses from the walls into the bottomless ravines.

Taking a turn on watch, Titus was sickened to see these ravines mounded with rotting corpses, stinking and foul smelling. These piles of putrefying bodies were never still or quiet. They undulated as the countless thousands of rats fed on them.

Titus now started to make more platforms, though the scarcity of timber hampered progress. Concentrating on the Antonia, he was eventually able to raise these by an additional four levels. The rebels, watching this operation, decided to cull the remaining citizens. This forced the most desperate to lower themselves down the wall on ropes in a bid to reach the Roman lines. Most were killed by Titus' Arab archers.

In the camp of the Syrian auxiliaries, one of the deserters was observed picking gold coins out of his excrement. As news ran round the camp that the Jews were "shitting gold", their fate was sealed. The Syrian Arabs disembowelled the fugitives and rummaged through their bowel, jesting, "We can at least grease our swords on Jewish guts". In a single night a thousand prisoners were disembowelled.

Meanwhile in Jerusalem, a city councillor, was made responsible for dealing with the city's unburied dead. Overwhelmed by this impossible task, he deserted to the Romans. He told Titus, "Four hundred thousand bodies of the poor have been thrown out of the gates. For others the numbers are unknown. When it became impossible to bury this vast number, some were collected up and packed into the biggest houses. We then nailed the doors shut". What the official didn't say was that the poorest people had begun raking the sewers and old dung hills. In desperation they were eating the refuse they found there – a practice that brought its own relief as what they ate killed them.

The man, overcome by emotion, had to pause for a moment. Titus waited patiently as he struggled to compose himself. With a sigh the Jew continued, "The rebels have imprisoned Josephus' family. All are held in solitary confinement".

"Have they been tortured?"

"Not yet, though they are given very little food. If they don't die of starvation, I am sure they will be used as bargaining counters".

"How many are held?"

"His father, mother and brother. At first it was believed they had managed to escape the city, but it was not to be".

Titus thought for a moment before saying, "I will grant you your life in return for your silence over the matter of Josephus' family. If he learns of their imprisonment he may break down. If he does, I will have no-one to act as a go-between. This is as important to the civilians in Jerusalem as it is to me, for I am anxious that the killing stops". So the two men parted. Titus had come to hate Judaea; the place seemed at best indifferent to human presence. At the end of yet another day's brutal fighting, he sought out the company of Josephus whom he had taken to addressing as Doctor Josephus. This, he felt, acknowledged his prisoner as a scholar and played down his military persona.

The Roman had come to admire Josephus' wisdom and intelligence. To the Jewish scholar's surprise, Titus was a far more sympathetic interlocutor than he had suspected. Consequently, during the three years they were thrown together in Judaea, the two men formed a lasting friendship, so when Titus joined him that evening to sit at the campfire, he was somewhat taken aback when the young Caesar asked him a most unexpected question. "What is it to be a Jew? Is it an accident of birth, or the teaching of your parents and your priests that persuades a child to believe what his father believes?"

Josephus laughed dryly before replying. "Both – though the former is necessary to the latter. However, Jews are now having to consider a new teaching, one that challenges traditional thinking".

"In what way?" asked Titus.

Josephus grimaced and shrugged. "A new prophet named Jesus claimed that God does not need blood sacrifices, nor does He need a Temple. Most interestingly of all, Jesus told men to pray to God – who is their father – directly. *No priests are required*".

A stunned Titus said "How do you feel about that?"

Josephus smiled thinly. "The Essenes would agree with him. As for me, I can see his point. But I wonder if the common man doesn't need the focal point of ritual to find his way to

God. Maybe the furore caused by these so-called Christians and their Christ are like stirred mud clouding bright water. Leave them alone and eventually they will settle into the sediment of history. I believe the answer", Josephus continued, "probably lies in two things. Firstly, in holy men who down the centuries claim God has revealed Himself to them. To prescribe how men should live and how men should behave to each other. To explain what the relationship between mankind and God should be. These holy men, the prophets, had unique powers given to them by God. These powers allowed them to perform wonders as proof that God was working through them".

"And the second?"

"The second lies in logic. The gift of reasoning the Greeks have brought to humanity. You Romans are the military masters of the world, but the Greeks reign supreme intellectually."

Titus shook his head ruefully, acknowledging with a grin his companion's reasoning. "I accept the point you make, but where in philosophy will I find the God of the Jews?"

"By examining Greek thought on the origins of not just existence, but *why* there is anything at all. And" continued Josephus, "*who* was the creator? And most importantly, *how was it created*?" Titus would have interrupted but Josephus, holding up a hand, continued "There are brilliant speculations to all of these questions. In some cases, so-called proofs are offered, but for every question answered, not just two new ones are revealed but a dozen. That, of course, is the nature of philosophy".

A surprised Titus asked, "This is accepted by Judaism, by the Temple priests?"

Josephus replied dryly "Virtually every word would be regarded as blasphemy. If I were to air such thoughts within the Temple precincts I would be put on trial".

"Rome has many gods", said Titus, more to himself than to Josephus, who said, "Why don't we set aside the question of gods and look at what philosophy has to offer us on the question of creation".

Titus brightened at this suggestion. "*Zeus*, that's a good idea, but let me re-charge our cups, for I think better with a good wine to lubricate my mind". With that he refilled both their glasses. "Where do we start?"

It never occurred to the Roman that he had just served a man who was, in all but name, his slave. Josephus nodded and said "Let us start with nothing". Titus lifted an eyebrow but remained silent. "Nothing", continued Josephus "came before something; in fact, everything in creation, the sun, the moon and the stars. Before earth, mankind, animals, plants, Aristotle's atoms – before any form of life. No matter who, or what, or how they were made, *before* they were made there was nothing! And", he concluded, "it is, of course, absolutely impossible to get something from nothing".

Titus remained silent, frowning in concentration. Josephus waited patiently. The Roman, a trained lawyer, could find no fault in the statement. He was also surprised. The clarity of logic was undeniable; the profoundness of the thinking at the very heart of man's search for the answer to the most important question of all 'Who or what created not just man but everything?'

Titus sipped his wine, turning this over in his mind, in no hurry to make what might prove to be an ill-judged opinion.

Josephus, pleased that his pupil had accepted the concept of creation as being necessary to existence, said smoothly "Let us leave God out of the discussion. Instead, let us refer to him as the Creator".

"Agreed" beamed Titus "but I must go. One last question. Who made the Creator?"

Josephus had to smile at his guest's perception.

"The Creator", the Jew answered, "is *unmade*. He is *without substance*, existing as nothing within nothingness. All powerful. Unknowable. That we humans have the ability to *vaguely comprehend* his existence; that we know of Him – is His gift to humanity".

"This belief you accept on trust, as a matter of faith?"

"Yes. But remember this belief is founded on revelation. The one God - ineffable, unknowable, all powerful, the first cause, creator of everything – revealed himself to man through his prophets. We Jews believe we are a people chosen to be the living proof of that revelation; to be as a light to the world".

Titus studied the wine in his glass, his mind in turmoil. With a smile he rose to leave. "Next time, you can tell me *why*".

With a smile, Josephus asked the question, "Why, what?"

The Roman said softly, "Why should there be anything instead of nothing?"

Josephus slapped his leg in delight, grinning hugely. "Make certain you have plenty of time and bring some decent wine with you. The question of *why*, like *how*, is beyond human reason and comprehension. Nevertheless, the giants of Greek philosophy have speculated on both. Before we next meet arm yourself with their wisdom, for in our debate we will venture into the realm of the supernatural and the divine; many would say unknowable.

"Agreed", said Titus. "I look forward to our debate, for which I will prepare by consulting Aristotle, the father of the inductive method, for he teaches us to observe and verify facts in order to discover the laws that control them". With a smile and a lift of the hand in farewell, he was gone, leaving a surprised Josephus who had not expected the young Roman to evince such erudition.

32

Under a cloudless Judaean sky, a sweating Titus sipped from his water bottle and considered his objective. He knew that the key to the city was the Antonia, and that taking it would be difficult. To have any chance, he had to bring up the rams and put them to work. Knowing this would be fiercely resisted, he ordered that one hundred ballistas be brought forward, with a vast quantity of ammunition. His intention was to set up a constant fusillade of stone balls against the men manning the section of wall he intended to attack with the rams.

In spite of this, when the attack started the rebels, shielding themselves as best they could, began dropping blocks of stone on the rams. Fortunately for the legionaries operating them, they were partially protected by a mobile covered tunnel that deflected most of the chunks of stone dropped from the wall. As the engagement gathered momentum, both sides began launching fire arrows which on the Romans side caused Titus to order shields of wet ox hide to be deployed.

When night fell both sides stood down and rested. Just before dawn, an area where John had dug his tunnel to try and get underneath the wall suddenly collapsed, the noise of which brought the Romans to full alert. Sentries, not knowing what it was, sounded the general alarm while the Romans cautiously advanced on what was apparently a breach in the wall they had been ineffectually battering. They were, however, disappointed. John had anticipated this might happen and built a second wall behind it.

Two days later, a Syrian *tribune* in charge of the advanced camp guarding the platforms, decided to take action on his own initiative. He picked twenty of his toughest soldiers and ordered the standard bearer of the Fifth Legion to join them, plus a trumpeter. Fully armed, with all metal fitments bound with strips of cloth to avoid accidental noise, they crawled through the ruins surrounding the Antonia. Using a muffled scaling ladder, they climbed the wall and garrotted the first sentries they encountered. Then, with his soldiers ready to charge, he ordered the trumpeter to sound the advance. With the trumpet braying non-stop, the twenty legionaries, roaring their battle cry, charged along the wall swords at the ready. The other Jewish guards, many of whom had been dozing, were either pitched headlong over the parapet or stabbed. The screams of the dying guards and the roaring of the berserking Romans, coupled with the manic blaring of the trumpet, panicked the remaining sentries who fled convinced the enemy had climbed the walls in numbers

When Titus heard the trumpet, he flung himself out of his tent and without a second's hesitation, ordered the call to arms to be sounded. As the trumpet blasted, men poured out of their tents, grabbing the weapons stacked on a tripod immediately outside before running to a designated place. Within three minutes, six thousand fully armed men stood in their ranks awaiting their orders. In the adjacent camps, which had responded in the same way, another twenty four thousand legionaries were ready to march. Ordering a thousand elite troops and twenty officers to join him, Titus left the camp at the trot heading straight for the point where the wall had collapsed.

Equally startled and confused, the rebels ran to the Temple. While the Romans poured into the tunnel John had dug to undermine the Roman platforms. John and Simon, realising that they were on the edge of disaster, rushed with their followers to meet this threat, knowing that if the Romans gained entry to the sanctuary it would be the beginning of the end. The two sides met at the entrance to the Outer Court, clashing in a struggle, where neither side could win the advantage. The Romans pushed forward relentlessly in an attempt to capture the Temple; the Jews desperately trying to drive them back to the Antonia.

Archers and spearmen were of no use to either party. Locked together in hand to hand combat, the carnage on both sides was appalling. As men fell, dead or dying, they were trampled underfoot. The Romans, used to this kind of close quarter work, stamped in unison on the fallen. Their iron shod sandals and powerful leg muscles, developed by constant marching, crushed ribs and snapped arms and legs as they stamped down. In the increasing confusion of battle, with no room to manoeuvre, there was no question of retreat. On both sides, the men at the front were relentlessly pushed forward by the men at the back.

With the seething mass of screaming men hacking at each other in mindless fury, something had to give and it was the Romans. Under the desperate suicidal pressure of the Jews, the Roman line began to buckle. Heavily outnumbered, Titus' men had fought non-stop for nine hours and desperately needed reinforcements, which had not arrived. The legions had not followed Titus, having received no orders to do so. In spite of their own exhaustion, the Jews, who were at full strength having committed their reserves, pushed forward relentlessly. Inch by inch, the Jews forced the Romans back to the Antonia, where at last Titus' men received reinforcements and the Jewish advance was halted. Vitally, Titus was able to start pulling exhausted troops out of the front line, and replace them with fresh men. With his position secured and reinforcements arriving, Titus ordered Josephus to address the Jews. He was to make John the same offer as before. If John was determined to fight it out, let him leave the city and meet the Romans in a place of his choice. It was in no-one's interest that the city be destroyed. To continue polluting the Holy City, Titus argued, was an offence against the God of the Jews.

Josephus mounted the wall at a point where he could not only be seen and heard by the combatants, but also by the civilians who were huddled in the ruins. He delivered Titus' offer in Aramaic, using all his skill as a trained orator in an effort to persuade the rebels to lay down their arms. The people listened in silence but John screamed abuse at him. Josephus' answer was damming. "You lay the fault of your sins on the Romans. Have they not always observed our religious laws? They now offer to assist you, in restoring the daily sacrifices you no longer make to God.

"It is the Romans, whom you call enemy, that demand you atone for your crimes against God. Even now, John, it is not too late to repent. It is you, a Jew, born in the very centre of Judaism that the Romans ask to save the heart of our nation. Remember Jehoiachin, King of the Jews who, before the Babylonians captured the city, exchanged his own freedom to save the Temple. His sacrifice is remembered eternally, immortal to all generations. With this example before you, I beg you, for the sake of God's chosen people, to choose peace. The Romans have given their word, sworn by their gods, to pardon you and your men.

"That you revile me is of no concern, but remember who I am. I am a Jew of noble birth. I am trying to bring peace; I am trying to spare men who have earned God's anger. Who amongst you does not remember the prophecy, the written word of our Holy oracles, passed down through the centuries, pronounced against this city that is now being fulfilled? Is it not prophesied that the day will come when Jew will kill Jew? When the living will envy the dead?

"That Jews will pollute the House of God

Are not the city and the Temple filled with corpses?

Who killed them? Not the Romans.

Who allowed the sacred ever-lasting fire to go out? Not the Romans.

"Rather, they have been sent by an avenging God to purge this place with fire and sword.

Like Sodom and Gomorrah, this seat of corruption will be no more".

Unable to continue, a distraught Josephus, who was weeping uncontrollably started to turn away. Pausing, he gathered himself for a final pronouncement. "Even now, you undeserving sinners, God will listen to you. His forgiveness, His love, is unconditional. It is forever. Ask for His forgiveness and it will be yours. Ask for His mercy and you will receive it. Return to the God of your fathers and save yourselves. Lay down your weapons and submit not to the Romans but to the will of God". With these parting words, Josephus left the wall, tears streaming down his face. The rebels, jeering and screaming in anger, hurled stones after the disconsolate figure.

The citizens who had witnessed this event were badly shaken. They were convinced that they were as good as dead and the City lost. With the rebels lining the wall, a large group of these desperate people burst out of the city through a carelessly guarded postern gate, and dashed towards the Roman lines.

Skidding to a halt when faced with a wall of Roman shields, they turned to face the city. Weeping they begged John's men to open the gates to the Romans, and accept the offered peace. This appeal brought a violent reaction from the rebels who, after cursing them for cowards, gave orders for spear throwers to attack the remaining civilians who packed the Temple courts. Catapults and stone throwers were swivelled from their outward facing positions, to add to the carnage. Within minutes the Temple courts were heaped with bodies. The rebels then poured into the sacred precincts, swords in hands, to finish off the wounded.

A furious Titus shouted, "I call on the gods of my fathers to witness that I am not compelling you to desecrate the Temple. If you change the battleground, I will protect the Sanctuary, for we Romans have always respected your right to worship your God in the manner you choose, and in accordance with your Holy Laws". As Josephus translated this promise, John spat over the wall and turned his back contemptuously on the Roman commander.

A grim faced Titus, unable to bring up his entire army, ordered Mucianus to pick the best twenty five soldiers from every *century*. With a hand-picked centurion in charge of every newly formed *century* and a *tribune* in charge of every thousand, this task force was placed under the command of one of Titus' best generals, Sextus Cerealis, a decorated soldier of proven ability.

His orders were to attack the guard post at dawn. Titus declared he would lead the first wave, an announcement that caused consternation in his high command. It was the threat by Mucianus and Cerealis of instant resignation that persuaded him to step aside. Their argument was that he was needed in the Antonia, from which he could observe the coming battle and direct operations.

In the darkest hour before dawn, Cerealis ordered scouts to creep out, hoping to find the enemy's sentries asleep, but was disappointed. As the alarm was raised, the rest of the rebel guard swarmed out to repel the attackers. With the sentries battling to hold the Romans, the alerted rebels started to arrive in numbers to support their comrades. Spurred on by a mixture of anger and fear, the Jews hurled themselves at the Romans. With shields locked, the Romans charged forward in tightly knit squads. Knowing that in the darkness and confusion of fighting in a restricted area the risk of disorientation was very real, Cerealis had had the foresight to issue a password to his men. The Jews, unable to break the Roman line, pulled back as much as they could and launched a series of darting raids, hoping in this way to find a weakness. In fact, these haphazard tactics resulted in many Jews being injured in the dark by their own comrades, who were slashing wildly in their confused state at anything that moved. Came the dawn and the two sides drew apart, but continued to hurl missiles at each other. Eventually the battle stagnated, neither side able to advance or retreat.

From the top of the Antonia Titus, observing and directing his forces, now set in motion his strategy to take the city. For months he had been strengthening the numbers of the pioneer corps which now stood at twenty thousand men. The officer engineers who commanded them had also been reinforced, by experts drawn from Tiberius' Egyptian legions.

Weeks in advance, Titus had warned them that they should plan where and how his main force would enter the Holy

City. He now gave the order for that work to begin. Under the protection of a wing of cavalry and a large contingent of *auxiliary* archers, they had built a wide road from their main camp, aimed straight at the heart of the city. Entry would be through the wall over the tunnel John had dug. Cerealis' men had used this opening to launch their attack, and had established a firm foothold.

To gain access to the Temple area, the engineers began to tear down part of the Antonia itself. The Jews, who were doggedly holding on, fought even harder when they saw part of the Antonia crumbling before their eyes. In desperation they torched the western colonnade, where it joined the Antonia, and demolished another large section with crowbars.

The Romans began to position their four platforms. One opposite the north-west corner of the Temple's inner court, one between the two gates, a third stationed opposite the western colonnade of the outer court and the fourth deployed against the wall near the tomb of a former High Priest.

The Roman engineers then set fire to the colonnades, to open up a route for the road they had built. With the burning colonnades shooting flames a hundred feet into the air, the Jews decided to tear down the staircases that joined the rapidly diminishing Antonia to the Temple, around which the battle raged without let-up. In fact, the rebels never ceased in their fight to continuously inflict casualties on their enemy. Finally, in desperation, they filled the roof space of the remaining western colonnade with flammable material, packing the area between the joists and the ceiling with bundles of wood coated in tar, and hauling up kegs of bitumen before retreating.

As the battle raged around the colonnades John, who had been waiting for an opportunity to get rid of Simon, struck. In the confusion Simon, momentarily isolated from his bodyguard, had a blade slipped between his ribs. Unnoticed, his body slipped to the floor to be trampled by the milling crowd.

The death of Simon led the way for Gioras to form an uneasy alliance with John of Gischala.

Meanwhile, legionaries, unaware of the trap set in the western colonnades, chased after the retreating Jews. When it was packed with legionaries, they set it alight at both ends, bowmen firing volley after volley of fire arrows to ensure a quick result.

Surrounded by roaring flames, with no escape some legionaries jumped down, rather than burn to death. A few survived, suffering terrible injuries. Others committed suicide, preferring a quick death from a blade to the horror of burning alive.

The next day the Romans assembled in the ruins, swearing to avenge the blackened lumps, no longer recognisable as their comrades, which crusted the stone flags.

33

For a week, the powerful battering rams had been pounding the wall incessantly, to no avail. Against stone blocks thirty feet long, ten feet high and ten feet deep, bonded so perfectly it was impossible to get a leaf between the joints, they made no impression.

Frustrated, the legionaries decided an attempt to scale the wall would be made using assault ladders; an attempt that was violently repulsed. Using poles the Jews pushed the ladders backwards, toppling them and the men on them onto their companions below. A variation of this was to push the tops of the ladders sideways, with much the same affect, luckless legionaries falling to their death or suffering serious injury. So Titus decided to call off the use of assault ladders. Instead, he set fire to the huge gates.

The Jews, who had anticipated that eventuality, knew they would be forced to retreat and now did so in an orderly manner, abandoning the outer court of the Temple to make a stand in the inner courts.

Not prepared to lose more men in what had become a war of attrition, Titus summoned his senior generals. These were the *tribunes* Sextus Cerealis, Larcius Lepidus who had replaced Trajan, Titus Phrygius, Aeternius Fronto, Marcus Julianus (Gessius Florus' successor as procurator of Judaea) and his second-in-command General Gaius Licinius Mucianus.

He invited opinions as to how the sanctuary should be regarded and how it should be treated, the latter being a question of a political nature. The overall reaction was non-committal, the strongest reaction was that it should be razed to the ground, otherwise it would always be a rallying point for Jews not just in the region, but worldwide. More moderate voices had argued that it was an architectural wonder and should be spared. Also, attempting to destroy it could prove costly. The Jews could be relied on to defend it to the last man.

Titus could see both points of view. He agreed that it would be fiercely defended, so he thanked his generals, telling them he would think about what they had said and adjourned the meeting. Not in a hurry to come to a decision, he gave orders that the army was to be given time off to recuperate. Those kept at their posts against surprise attacks were to be frequently rotated.

The Jews, however, were in good heart having rested for a day, launched a series of probing attacks against the Roman forces holding the outer court of the Temple. The alert Romans held their position, but being light in numbers they were vulnerable. Sensing an opportunity, the Jews sent in extra men and pressed home their attack.

Titus, who was watching from a high point in the Antonia, knew that his outnumbered men could not hold out indefinitely. Without hesitation he ordered a cavalry troop to intervene, though the circumstances were not best suited for horses. The Jews, however, pulled back under this extra pressure, but whenever the Romans showed any signs of relaxing they resumed the offensive, attacking ferociously. A centurion in charge of the ground troops quickly realised he had to take the offensive. With cavalry support, he gave the order to advance. This sustained and determined effort pushed the Jews back to the inner court, where they formed a defensive line of their own.

When fire suddenly broke out, it caused consternation in the Jewish ranks. Later, they were to claim it was a Roman fire arrow that was the cause. This, however, was not possible, as the Romans had not brought up any archers. With the sanctuary in view and the Jews in some disarray because of the fire, the legionaries renewed their attack on the inner court. As they began to get a foothold, one of the Roman soldiers, in contradiction to standing orders, picked up a piece of burning timber and hurled it through a window of one of the many ante- rooms built round the sanctuary. As the Jews saw a sudden burst of flame in the sacred building, they let out anguished screams. In panic, they stopped fighting. The Romans, not certain of what was happening but quick to take advantage of this change of circumstance, pressed home their attack.

Titus, who was resting, was brought the news by a runner. Horrified, he ran to the building with thoughts of extinguishing the blaze. His staff officers, bewildered by this sudden turn of events and caught unaware by their commander in chief's reckless dash to the front line, could do little else but scramble to keep up with him. They were, however, followed by a large body of legionaries, called to arms by an alert *tribune*.

Very quickly the whole of the Temple mount descended into chaos. A huge number of extra Roman troops charging into the fray were without proper orders and short of officers, while the Jews were desperately trying to do two things at once – fight the fire and contain the enemy. With all the shouting and screaming from both sides, the confusion worsened. Titus, red in the face, couldn't make himself heard above the din, and his over excited legionaries were slipping out of control.

The two sides, Roman and Jew, jammed together fought each other savagely. They were like two pit bulls that had taken hold of each other; neither would let the other go unless the other was dead. To slip was to die, trampled on by either side. Many stumbled into the still glowing fires of the colonnades and were burnt alive. As the great mass of combatants neared the sanctuary, the legionaries pretended not to hear Titus' commands. Instead, many of them picked up more burning torches and hurled them into the many chambers attached to the main building. Hundreds of civilians, seeing smoke billowing from the Temple, had run uncaring of their safety to the scene. The rebels, struggling to try and contain the Romans who had gone on the rampage, could do nothing to assist them.

The sudden arrival of hundreds of screaming, arm waving, hysterical citizens triggered an unreasoning rage in the Romans.

They went berserk. Flight was impossible. The civilians were slaughtered wherever they ran. The armed rebels, who tried to maintain resistance, were swept aside and crushed. The legions' battle cry, a thunderous bellow, sounded over and over as they surged forward.

As the slaughter gathered momentum, the heaps of dead bodies around the altar grew higher. A river of blood poured down the sanctuary steps. With the legionaries, like the fire, out of control, Titus entered the Temple as the flames consumed the attached chambers. Realising there might be time to save the main building, he ordered the centurion Liberalius, who was captain of the spearmen in his bodyguard, to lay about him with a javelin shaft in an effort to bring some of the rioting troops to order. Titus was desperate to organise men into firefighting teams. But Liberalius' efforts were ineffective. His comrades were bent on killing the enemy and looting a building they believed to be bursting with treasure – a view that was reinforced by the fact that the dome on its roof was covered in the precious metal.

When Titus ran to assist Liberalius, some of his men took the opportunity to set fire to the Temple doors. With the sanctuary itself now on fire, Titus had to make a quick decision. Of all the treasures adorning its magnificent interior, in the few minutes remaining to him, what should he save? In this moment of crisis, his legal training came to the fore. He ordered his bodyguard to spread their cloaks and fill them with that which was irreplaceable and the most fragile – the written word. Before they were driven out of the building by the fire, they had salvaged the scrolls of the Torah, the sacred writing of the Law. These scrolls contained the early history of the Jews from the creation of the world to the death of Moses. They also covered a large number of laws governing daily life, including food laws and festivals. With the flames running up the walls, Titus and his bodyguard left the sanctuary, clutching not the solid gold vessels and goblets used in services, but armfuls of parchment rolls.

As smoke poured out of the doors, Titus had a few minutes to reflect on the building that, from its inception by King

Solomon to the present day, had for over a thousand years been a place of uninterrupted worship by the Jews to their God.

As the flames roared through the Temple, the anguished screams of the faithful, ordinary Jewish citizens could be heard. With the whole of the Temple complex engulfed in fire, it seemed because of its elevated position as if the whole of Jerusalem was ablaze. The shattering noise that accompanied the conflagration simply added to the horror. A din that grew in volume as the converging Roman legions, roaring their war cry, surrounded the crowd of civilians who were now mingled with the rebels, the whole packed in a tight mass throughout the Temple courts. The screams and shouts from the blazing hill were answered by the crowds, struggling in the corpse choked streets; a primeval sound that echoed from the surrounding mountains.

Yet more horrific than this tumult, was the vision that filled the eye. The Temple, appeared to be dissolving, as from its foundations flames engulfed its walls. Smoke poured from every aperture to form a gigantic plume, swelling to form a menacing black hammerhead in the cloudless sky.

Charging across its terraces carpeted with the dead, the legionaries clambered over the mounded corpses as they pursued their enemy.

Amid the carnage John rallied his men. With death staring them in the face the rebels, with a desperate effort, pushed the Romans back and with a final shove, broke free of the outer court into the ruin of the Upper City, where Gioras and his followers had managed to flee.

The remnants of the civilian population, who still had the strength and the will to do so, took refuge in the remains of the outer colonnades. A refuge that was short lived as the Romans, angered by the burning of the sanctuary, decided to use fire as a weapon, setting ablaze all the remaining buildings in the Temple complex. This included the remaining colonnade where six thousand civilians had sought refuge. This was torched from end to end by packing timber underneath it before setting it alight. There were no survivors. A few, like rabbits in a wheat field flushed by the reapers, were cut down by Roman swords.

With the rebels fleeing in all directions, the Romans held a victory celebration. In the midst of the flames, they brought their standards and eagles to the Temple area and erected an altar where, roaring their battle cry, they saluted Titus as imperator.

With their forces beaten, Gioras and John could not escape the city because of the earth wall, the circumvallation Titus had built. With nowhere to go they asked Titus for parley. Surprisingly, in spite of being rebuffed on so many previous occasions, he agreed, taking up a position above the Gymnasium, where he could be seen and heard. From this position his archers could cover the bridge that linked the Temple with the Upper City. With an assassination in mind, Mucianus ordered two thousand picked legionaries to cover the approach to the bridge, with orders to kill anybody who set foot on it.

With the rebel leaders contained, Titus surveyed the dense crowds that had gathered to witness the confrontation. Surrounded by the remnants of their forces and curious civilians, John and Gioras came forward. The Roman soldiers were equally curious as to how Titus would receive their appeal.

With Josephus at his side as his interpreter, Titus spoke first. "You are responsible for the utter ruin of your nation. Without any regard for Roman military might, with self-interest and arrogance, you destroyed your people and your city. You polluted and then brought down the Temple and its Holy Sanctuary. This you have done out of vanity and self-interest, and for this you will answer to your God.

"Your grandfathers took this land from the Canaanites by force of arms. It became the Jews' as the spoils of war, to do with as *you* pleased. We took it from you in war. It became ours to do with as *we* pleased. You killed the Canaanites. We allowed you to live. We placed over you rulers of your own race. We upheld the Laws of your fathers. We gave you absolute control of your internal affairs. Paramount to this, we permitted you to raise taxes for your God. We allowed you to collect a Temple tax, throughout the empire and send this money to the Temple in Jerusalem. And what happened? You declared war on us! Like a mad dog, you bit the hand that fed you.

"When you desecrated your Holy places, I appealed to you to stop, offering you the opportunity to fight elsewhere. All my overtures were treated with contempt. You set fire to the Holy Temple that Jews all over the world reverence. Frankly, you disgust me, but to save further bloodshed, I will make you one last offer. Throw down your weapons and I will spare your lives".

Silence followed Titus' speech; the only sound was that of burning buildings. Finally John spoke. "If called upon, all Jews regard themselves as soldiers of God, who will fight the battle He chooses for us. You, our enemy, are in His hands, as we are ourselves. He will dispose of us all, according to His will. We cannot surrender, because we swore on oath not to do so. However, we ask to be allowed to leave this place forever. We ask for free passage through the circumvallation, and to be allowed to go into the desert with our wives and children".

Titus, out of patience, refused this demand, saying "You must now be prepared to fight to the last man".

With a nod of acknowledgment, John turned away and with Gioras disappeared into the crowds.

A furious Titus called his senior generals together, and ordered them to give the army permission to sack the city.

The next day, the soldiers set fire to the Council offices and the area known as the Ophel. With dozens of fires set, the resulting blaze swept through the narrow streets, consuming the houses packed with the bodies of those who had died of starvation. The legions then charged through the rest of the Lower City, driving the rebels before them and burning it as they went. The surviving rebels, abandoning their cause, scattered and ran.

John and Gioras, finding themselves deserted, had only one hope left – the city's sewers. They believed that if they hid in them, they would be safe, the idea being to make a complete escape when the Romans left the city. Before disappearing into this subterranean refuge, they sowed more discord and confusion and misery by running through the streets lighting fires at random. When the terrified owners attempted to leave their burning houses, they were murdered and robbed.

Turned loose, the Romans raced across the city sword in hand, cutting down without mercy all they met. Most of the houses they burst into in search of valuables were filled with the stinking dead bodies of the families who had died of starvation; the stench driving them out empty handed.

With the rampaging legions adding to the body count as they scythed across the city, the streets were soon impassable, as new corpses piled up on the older rotting dead. At night the legions rested and the city continued to burn. When the sun rose, it was on a city in flames. Only three massive towers remained untouched in this sea of fire. Phasael, Hippicus and Mariamme.

Eventually the soldiers tired of killing. With starving survivors appearing in large numbers, Titus gave the order to spare anybody not carrying a weapon.

Men in their prime were herded into the remains of the court of women, and held captive. To guard and manage these prisoners, Titus appointed Fronto, the *Tribune* commanding the two legions from Alexandria. As Fronto sorted through the captives, he identified a few who had taken part in the uprising. He persuaded them, with the aid of a red hot iron, to inform on the rest. He then executed the lot before sorting through the remainder. Picking out the tallest and most athletic looking, he ordered that they be fed. Eventually these would be exhibited in Vespasian's and Titus' double triumph in Rome. From his next pickings, a very substantial number were set aside for Titus' future needs, which meant they would die very soon in the arena, killed either in combat or torn to pieces by wild animals. During the week or so it took Fronto to sort out his prisoners, eleven thousand died of starvation. Some of them died because food came too late, and others refused to eat it.

The number of prisoners that eventually passed through Fronto's hands totalled a hundred thousand. Another three hundred thousand had already been captured during the seven years of war and sent to the slave markets. The total number of the Jewish dead in the war was over a million. Of these the great majority were Jews by race but were not citizens of

Jerusalem, the population of Jerusalem having been swelled by mercenaries, refugees and pilgrims who had come to the city for the feast of Passover and been caught up in the war.

Later, when the Romans came to realise that people had taken refuge in the sewers, they organised what they unfeelingly referred to as rat hunts, though participating in this grim task was a duty the troops despised. For every living person they flushed out, they came across ten dead. Over ten thousand Jews died below ground, either from starvation or suicide. Time and again, the foul stench of decay drove the Romans back. Not even the chance of finding gold would persuade them to continue.

Eventually, starvation forced John to give himself up and beg for mercy. Gioras, however, who had anticipated having to take refuge in the sewers, was better prepared. While the Romans were sacking the city, he sneaked underground with a carefully chosen group of his most trusted officers, including a number of miners he had recruited. Together they went down into a hidden, little known sewer, taking with them supplies of food and tools for tunnelling. After walking to the head of the tunnel they attempted to cut through its end wall, hoping to extend it and eventually emerge into open countryside.

After days of hard work, progress was halted by a wall of solid rock that proved impenetrable. With food and water running out Gioras, like John, was forced to surrender.

Both men were held in chains and closely guarded, to await Titus' pleasure.

The Romans now began to plan the levelling of the city. Their first task was to dismantle the walls. Their ultimate objective was to raze the city to the ground. Eventually, they would leave no stone standing on another. First though, they would hold a double celebration to mark the taking of the city and the beginning of Vespasian's second year as Emperor.

34

Jewish resistance had been stubborn to the point of madness. Unwilling to take a backward step they had fought to the death, street by street. Eventually, the drains contained so much coagulated blood they stopped flowing.

In the end the weary Romans had leant, panting, on their blood stained shields. There was no one left to kill, so their fury had ebbed away and sanity returned, leaving the greatest city on earth waiting like a dying bull for the coup de grace.

Josephus sat in his tent, head in his hands, weeping. He was to write later "To understand the suffering of the Jews, brought about by the loss of the Temple and Jerusalem, is to understand that suffering is not just a matter of what has been lost. It is measured by what is taken away from us".

As the new master of the city contemplated the smoking ruin that was his prize, he felt no sense of victory, only bitterness. He was at a loss as to what to do next. It was Mucianus who reminded him that his original orders still stood. So Titus commanded that the city be razed to the ground; a task that would take years to achieve. That meant he would need accommodation for the troops left behind to carry out this task, so he ordered that the greatest of Jerusalem's towers should be preserved to serve as protection for the garrison, and for future generations to wonder at; a monument to Rome's irresistible military power.

Having been given their orders, the engineers cleared the debris surrounding the designated fortresses - Phasael, Hippicus and Mariamme. At the same time, they repaired a stretch of the west wall to provide additional defences. After consulting with his senior generals, Titus ordered the Tenth Legion, supported with *auxiliary* units of horse and foot, to take the first tour of duty in policing the city.

Knowing that in the aftermath of so long a struggle the exhilaration of victory would give way to nervous exhaustion, Titus decided the army would celebrate. The spoils of victory were theirs to be enjoyed. They would, he decided, receive them from his own hand. A dais was erected on the parade ground outside the city walls. Surrounded by his generals, the young Caesar took his place centre stage.

He thanked the whole army for their loyalty, not just to Rome, but to him personally. He was, he said, proud to be one of them. Rome knew of their exploits, their bravery, their acts of personal courage and sacrifice, because he had ensured they had been recorded in his despatches to the senate. The citizens of Rome, who slept safe in their beds, did so because of men like them. They knew that their victory had been over a stubborn and brave enemy, who had asked no quarter and given none.

"You have", he said, "shown the world that no matter who or what Rome's legions face, they will never back down. No matter the wealth and power and the size of their enemy's armies, the strength and daring of their warriors, the legions of Rome will always be victorious. Your campaign in Judaea has been a legendary feat of arms; one that has tested Roman endurance to its limit. It was a campaign fought so brilliantly that the people of Rome turned to its legions in Judaea for a new leader, a proven man to be their Emperor. The victorious army in Judaea sent them their commander, Vespasian, declaring him Imperator on the field of battle".

As he finished speaking the entire army cheered him to a man, the thunder of their swords beating against their shields reverberating around the parade ground. Titus then ordered his officers to proclaim the name of every man, living or dead, who in the course of the war had performed an outstanding feat of bravery. Then, as those heroes who had survived came forward, he saluted them and awarded them military decorations made from gold and silver.

Men came forward to be promoted to a higher rank. Then every *century* received its share of the spoils of war, a vast treasure of gold and jewels to be divided so that every man received his fair share. With his men rewarded, Titus offered prayers for the whole army and sacrificed a white bull. More bullocks were brought forward and herded around the altars. He ordered that these were to be sacrificed and their meat divided among the troops for a victory feast. As he dismissed the legions to their quarters, it was to the rolling thunder of spears and swords beating on their shields.

Back in his own quarters, Titus had one more task to perform. He visited Josephus who, since his elevation by Vespasian, now had his own tent and a secretary to assist him as he wrote the history of the Jewish war. Titus recognised the strain the Jew was under. It was plain to see in a face grown gaunt and a premature silvering of his hair and beard. When the Temple had fallen, Titus had invited him to take whatever he wished from the Temple treasury, but had been politely refused. He had, however, pleaded for the lives of those members of his own family who had survived – his mother, father, younger brother, plus a dozen cousins and other relatives. He was also able to secure the freedom of five hundred people whom he had known and his family counted as friends. For days Josephus had stayed alone in his tent, refusing to see anybody, banishing his camp servants and his secretary. He was mourning the death of the Holy City. He, more than anybody, knew the extent of that loss, of the terrible price his people would pay for what had happened.

When Titus entered Josephus' tent, he was accompanied by several of his men. He brought with him the only thing that he knew Josephus would accept; the sacred scrolls Titus had rescued from the burning Temple. With trembling hands Josephus took them, tears coursing down his cheeks, prostrating himself at the feet of the man who had conquered his people.

Titus then took three days to celebrate with his officers before reassigning the majority of his army to new postings. The Tenth

Legion would remain to garrison Jerusalem. Remembering that the rebuilt Twelfth Legion had been defeated while under the command of Cestius Gallus, he sent it to Melitene on the Euphrates. Two legions, the Fifth and the Fifteenth, he would keep to make the planned journey to Egypt. He then ordered the entire army to march to Caesarea on the coast, where he stored the vast treasure looted from Jerusalem. With the summer over a voyage to Italy was impossible, which meant that he would have to make arrangements for the custody of his prisoners in Judaea. Those that lived would eventually be displayed in Rome.

From Caesarea, Titus travelled to Caesarea Philippi, accompanied by King Agrippa and Berenice. With Titus' obvious interest in his sister, the King, with his eye on further advancement, encouraged this liaison and sought comfort in the arms of Amal, his sister's handmaiden and confidante.

He then diplomatically announced that he needed to visit his northern cities, having been absent too long. This sudden need to travel signalled to Berenice that, as far as he was concerned, she was free to indulge in a liaison with the obviously infatuated Titus. In any event, Agrippa had reasoned he couldn't lose. If the affair fizzled out she would return to his bed. If it was to be more than a brief love affair, his standing with the man who would one day be Emperor could only rise. Perhaps, he mused, like Herod the Great he would be appointed titular King of the Jews. Certainly his blood line was more 'royal' than the Idumaen could ever have hoped to claim. Meanwhile, he would console himself with the considerable charms of Amal.

A besotted Titus, entirely captivated by the Jewish Queen, was agonising over how he could take advantage of the King's absence without making a fool of himself, when he received an invitation to dinner. After spending an extraordinary amount of time over his toilet he advised his senior officers that he was calling on the Queen at her request, muttering something about official state business which nobody believed for a second, but nodded in grave agreement.

As the sun slipped down the bald slopes of the blue-grey Judaean mountains, Titus made his way somewhat breathlessly to the Royal enclosure. Here he was received by Nathan, captain of Berenice's bodyguard, who led him personally to the Royal Pavilion, the entrance to which was protected by six warriors, magnificent in their dress uniforms. As they saluted, Titus noted with quiet satisfaction that there was nothing ceremonial about the weapons they carried.

Berenice's private quarters consisted of a series of silk lined pavilions. Joined together they became a tented palace whose opulence included a walled garden complete with a pool and several fountains. Shown into the Queen's inner sanctum, Titus was stunned by the magical interior which was decorated with silk carpets whose antiquity and beauty were beyond price. Myrrh and incense in silver braziers scented the air. From outside the sound of a harp drifted through the night. Jewelled lamps hung from the silk lined ceiling, filling the space with a soft warm light. Cushions were mounded invitingly on either side of a table inlaid with precious stones and decorated with mythical beasts.

A black slave, dressed in a white shift, held a silver bowl of water. Her companion proffered a cotton towel. A third came forward, head bowed, to offer wine in the rarest of drinking vessels – a goblet fashioned from flawless rock crystal, something Titus had never seen before.

Along one side of the pavilion, Numidian girls dressed in Egyptian costumes stood like statues ready to serve the waiting banquet; antique pieces of silver engraved with bunches of grapes, the emblem of Israel, decorated the snow white tablecloth. Silver lamps suspended above were wreathed in desert orchids.

The only male slave in the room, a eunuch, was dressed in gold livery that would have been the envy of a nobleman. He was responsible for the amphora of a fifty year old Corcubian wine, swaddled in damp cloths, resting in a hip bath cut from a single block of green veined marble.

Berenice, in an ivory silk robe, her only jewellery a string of black pearls, advanced to meet him with a dazzling smile and the deepest of curtsies which afforded him a glimpse of her magnificent breasts. The perfume she wore was opobalsam, which was procured in miniscule quantities from the Arabian interior. None was ever offered for sale; the entire production – a single casket – was offered every year to Berenice as a gift.

As Titus extended a hand to assist her in rising, words failed him, so he simply offered her the gift he had brought, presenting it with a single word "Majesty". It was an emerald and diamond tiara, the stones set in a filigree of gold and silver. Reputed to have been owned by Cleopatra, the merchant who had sold him this breathtaking piece swore by the gods that the jewel's provenance was unimpeachable. Titus, uncaring of the fortune in gold it had cost him, without speaking a word placed it gently on the brow of the woman who, from the first moment he had seen her, had captured his heart.

Standing inches apart he was only aware of two things – the wild beating of his heart and the golden eyes gazing into his. As she leaned forward to brush his cheek with her lips she whispered huskily, "My Lord, you honour me beyond measure".

With his heart singing with joy, Titus embraced her. Hungrily they clung together, indifferent to the slaves who turned their eyes down and with heads bowed drifted away.

Breathing heavily, his head swimming, Titus finally released her saying shakily, "I have waited for you without knowing, all my life".

Berenice caressed his face and released the clasp holding his cloak. As she regarded him with smoky eyes, she felt her loins melt. Casually she unclipped the brooch holding her dress at the shoulder and kicked it away with an insouciant gesture. She was completely naked.

Without taking his eyes off her, Titus loosened his toga. In the soft glow of the lamps his hard muscled body was like sculpted marble. They stood apart, holding hands like the first man and the first woman, eyes locked, savouring the moment.

From that night Titus was determined that they would never be separated.

To ensure her company, he stayed in Caesarea Philippi for months, during which time she never left his side. Together they dreamed of Empire with her as his Queen.

To celebrate his victory, Titus staged shows of every kind. From their President's box in the arena they dined on delicacies imported from Rome – dishes that were more to Titus' taste than Berenice's. As the prisoners Titus had brought with him died in the arena, he feasted on pork womb and slices of elder, a delicacy made from a cow's udder, and potted dormice served with a prune salad and washed down with a ten year old Falernian wine.

During the triumphant Roman's stay in Philippi, Gioras, led by a ring through his nose, was brought before him. Titus ordered that the greatest of care should be taken of his prisoner. He wanted him in good health for the triumphal procession he was planning for Rome.

35

With the capture of Gioras, Titus left Philippi for Beirut in high spirits. With Berenice at his side, he was looking forward to performing a very pleasant duty. He planned to celebrate his father's birthday with a spectacular series of games. The couple's welcome was fulsome. Beirut, a city in Phoenicia, was a Roman colony settled by veterans and expanded by Greeks and Syrians into a magnificent cosmopolitan provincial capital. It was also a city where Jews had always lived in large numbers. The biggest Jewish colony, however, was at Antioch, which was their next visit. It was while staying in Antioch, that Titus learned that his father had made a royal progress round Italy, and been received rapturously wherever he went.

Titus' games at Antioch in honour of his father, were to be remembered as the most spectacular ever staged in the city. Vast numbers of Jewish prisoners died, with an equally large number of exotic wild animals. The captives perished participating in lavish and spectacular shows, dressed in a variety of costumes and playing numerous roles. The spectators, enjoying this largesse, were also treated to free food and drink as they marvelled at the entertainment. From Antioch, Titus and Berenice made an unhurried progress through the principal towns of Syria whose citizens, coming out to meet them, lined the roads throwing flowers in their path and calling down every blessing on Titus' head.

He then set out for Egypt, looking forward to showing Berenice the wonders and beauty of the Nile. Before leaving

Syria he enlarged Agrippa's kingdom with the district of Acra and announced his appointment as titular King of the Jews – which Agrippa received with a feeling of quiet satisfaction and fierce pride.

On the way to Egypt he visited Jerusalem to check on the progress with the levelling of the city. As the work had progressed, huge quantities of treasure were being dug up in the ruins. Even more was located as former slaves informed on their old masters. This wealth had been buried by its owners as the only hope of keeping it safe during the turmoil of war. Leaving Jerusalem behind, Titus and Berenice crossed the desert in a leisurely fashion, camping under the desert stars, enjoying nights of love neither would ever forget. They slept in each other's arms, safe in the knowledge that the Fifth and Fifteenth legions had thrown a discreet ring of steel round the pavilions of their campsite.

Titus had laughed uproariously when, before setting out, Berenice informed him that she never travelled light. She was a Queen after all. His jaw had dropped when they had made their first night's stop at an oasis. Already in place was a central pavilion lined with silk and strewn with Persian carpets. Furnished with low tables and cushions, it was lit by hanging silver lamps. The six other pavilions linked to it were, Berenice informed him, for their servants, particularly the cooks and musicians. There was also, she told him, accommodation for her maids and Titus' aid-de-camp. Further accommodation housed private toilet facilities. The piece de resistance of this entourage was the leather bath and its frame, housed in its own tent. Where the hundred gallons of water required each day for its operation came from in the desert, he didn't bother to ask.

After twenty two idyllic days, they arrived reluctantly in Alexandria. Having been given a civic welcome, Titus received a deputation representing the Greek majority who lived in the city. They requested that the few remaining Jews in the city be stripped of their civil rights and banished. He refused this, reminding them that as authorised residents they had the right in law to domicile. Providing they obeyed the law, the law would protect them as citizens of the Roman Empire. He now intended to sail for Italy, so he thanked the two legions who had accompanied him and Berenice and sent them back to their old stations.

Before leaving Antioch he had ordered that Simon and John, with ten thousand picked male Jews, be sent to Italy to await his arrival.

After an uneventful voyage, Titus and Berenice arrived in Italy to a rapturous welcome – at least, it was for him. For Berenice there was studied politeness. Roman society was wary of foreign Queens. The disastrous liaison between Anthony and Cleopatra was still fresh in the memory.

But all this was swept aside, when Vespasian himself, and Titus' brother Domition, turned up at the quayside to welcome them. Berenice, always gracious and unflinchingly smiling, was introduced to Roman society. Even in the face of veiled disapproval, she remained regal and charming, her poise never deserting her, her beauty wowing the men and causing the mother of every unmarried daughter to grind her teeth.

After allowing the couple a week of receptions and banquets, Vespasian claimed Titus to join him in planning a joint celebratory triumph, though the senate had authorised each to have a separate Triumph. But father and son were unanimous. There would be one Triumph, shared equally between them. The date was set for six months' time. The senate agreed and criers proclaimed it throughout the city and the Empire.

Came the day and every man, woman and child stopped what they were doing to find a place in the packed streets.

Josephus had also got up very early. He had been dreading the day ahead and would have given anything to have stayed at home, But Titus had invited him to attend and his absence from the stand, with its reservation for special guests, would not just be notice, it would be deemed an insult. Setting his teeth against the bile that rose in his throat, he had bathed and dressed, before being carried in a litter to the Palatine from where the procession would be watched. Much to his discomfort, he found himself sitting next to King Agrippa and Berenice who returned his greetings with a cold politeness.

Berenice was wary of her cousin Josephus, unable to acknowledge the jealousy she had for Titus' friendship with him. Agrippa was equally uncomfortable because Josephus reminded him of the many compromises and accommodations he had made in support of the Romans, in order to gain their favour.

The night before the big day, the legions in their centuries had formed up on the field of Mars, the *Campus Martius*, the old parade ground by the Tiber. At daybreak, Vespasian and Titus arrived from the Temple of Isis, where they had spent the night. Now clad in the traditional crimson robes and wearing wreaths of bay, they walked with measured tread to the Portico of Octavia to join the members of the senate, knights and senior magistrates, who were awaiting their arrival.

A dais had been built in front of the colonnades and furnished with ivory thrones. As Vespasian and Titus mounted the dais, there was a spontaneous cheer from the serried ranks of legionaries. Vespasian gave them a moment before acknowledging them and signalling for silence. In absolute quiet, Vespasian strode centre stage and offered the customary prayers. Titus followed suit. Vespasian then made a short speech and sent the soldiers to breakfast, while he and Titus repaired to the Porta Triumphalis for the same purpose and to change into their robes of office, for they were to sacrifice to the gods that stood on either side of the gate.

Then, to the sound of trumpets, they crossed to the field of Mars to be presented to the vast crowd gathered there. From here the Triumph got underway, a spectacle of dazzling, awe-inspiring magnificence. Only those persons fortunate enough to be in Rome on such particular and infrequent days would ever witness such a sight.

Over three miles long, the column of tableaux, chariots, marching legionaries, military bands, wagons filled with booty, and exhibits of every kind including animals and people, would take six hours to complete a single circuit of its planned route.

A stunned population gazed in wonder at structures sometimes four stories high. These theatrical sets included costumed players who re-enacted the famous battles that Vespasian and Titus had fought during the Jewish war. Placed on each stage was the leader of a captured town, dressed as he would have been when captured. Later he would die in the arena or face summary execution as a sacrifice to the gods.

Cages mounted on flat bed carts and filled with exotic beasts from Africa and India, were hauled along by captured Jews who would later face these monsters in the arena. Then came the treasures; the wealth of Israel.

Hauled by oxen, one thousand carts overflowing with silver coins were followed by an endless convoy of wagons brimming with priceless works of art and precious objects. Garlanded maidens skipped along the sides of these wagons with baskets of silver coins into which they dipped and flung into the air a sparkling shower of wealth; Vespasian's beneficence to the people who had come to adore him.

Next came the Jewish captives, chained to wagons draped in purple and loaded with the priceless treasures of the Temple. Displayed on its own, made of solid gold, was the sacred table on which the shewbread had been displayed daily. The next wagon also carried a single priceless item - the Menorah – the lamp of God; a seven branched candelabra made of solid gold standing nine feet tall. This symbol of Israel since ancient time was used to celebrate Hanukkah, the festival of lights, an eight day Jewish holiday commemorating the rededication of the Holy Temple. Next, displayed on frame, was a huge tapestry. This was the "Veil" that had separated an inner room from the rest of the Holy Temple. The Jews believed it was God's special dwelling place in the midst of his chosen people. It was the Holy of Holies. The tapestry, made of fine linen, was richly embroidered. Figures representing the angels who served God were depicted in great detail.

Next came gangs of Jewish captives carrying biers on their shoulders displaying life-size images of the Roman Gods, made from ivory and inlayed with gold. The first of these was *Jupiter* representing victory. Behind them, in two magnificent chariots enamelled with lapis lazuli and malachite, decorated with precious stones, and drawn by matching white horses, came Vespasian and Titus. Domition, mounted on his black stallion, rode respectfully at their side.

To honour ancient customs the procession eventually came to its conclusion at the temple of *Jupiter* on Capitoline Hill. Here they would wait until Gioras the Commander in Chief of the enemy was dead. John escaped execution but was sentenced to life imprisonment – a living death in the Empire's mines.

Gioras, who had acted like a king, was treated like one. At a signal from Vespasian, he was dragged to the spot in the *forum* declared by Roman law as the place of execution for those condemned to death. But first Gioras was stripped and flogged. Then, barely conscious, he was tied to a post and, to loud applause, garrotted. With him dead, the priests led the sacrificial animals to the altar and cut their throats, according to ritual. Then the *haruspices* split a beast down the middle and pulled out its entrails. These, with the liver and heart, were examined for any abnormalities. With the omens pronounced favourable, the crowd cheered wildly.

Agrippa, his face expressionless, his emotions carefully hidden, gave no indication of his thoughts or feelings. Berenice, a shadow creeping across her heart, gripped his arm. Unable to contain herself she said "What have we done?" The King, astounded by this outburst, was literally rendered speechless. Josephus, ashen faced, bowed his head in anguish. Berenice had given voice to that which he had always failed to acknowledge. That in the future all three of them would be judged as traitors.

Vespasian and his sons, unaware of the sudden tension, joined their principal guests. Accompanied by the city's *consuls* and senators, judges and priests, they returned to the palace for the celebration banquet.

As they left the dais, Berenice murmured to Josephus saying, "Did we make a mistake?"

Unable to speak, struggling with his tears, he stumbled down the steps. What Agrippa, Vespasian, Berenice, or for that matter any one of his fellow Jews thought, was irrelevant. Neither the state nor its laws, emperors, priests and their theologies, took precedence over conscience.

With an enormous effort of will, Josephus straightened his shoulders and held his head high. He genuinely believed he had acted according to his conscience. God would judge him.

As he left the stand Josephus murmured to himself the *Shema*, the great prayer of the Jewish people; the proclamation of their faith in God.

Hear, O Israel, the Lord is our God, the Lord is one.

And you shall love the Lord your God, with all your heart, with all your soul, and with all your might.

And these words which I command you this day, shall be upon your heart.

Appendix I
Jewish Priesthood And Sects

The High Priest of all Israel – The most senior person in the priesthood. After finishing his term of office (one year) his title changed to High Priest.

The Sadducees – An elite group who followed the laws of the Hebrew Bible (the Torah) but rejected newer traditions. They rejected the teachings of the Pharisees and did not believe in life after death.

Pharisees – Influential Jews who advocated and adhered to strict observance of the Sabbath, purity laws, tithing and food restrictions, based on the Hebrew scriptures. They believed in resurrection of the dead. Paul of Tarsus (St Paul) was a Pharisee.

Tribe of Levi – Priests had to be men from the tribe of Levi (Levites). Any Jews from the eleven other tribes could *not* be priests.

Levites – Those who were not priests assisted as Temple servants in the practical operations of running the Temple (20,000 of them) – butchers, Temple police and administrators. It was *Priests* who offered the blood sacrifices from sunup to sunset every day. They also took care of ritual matters.

Scribes – Priests specially trained in writing. They were important as interpreters, teachers of the law and acting as agents of the rulers. Important in the administration of the Temple.

Elders – Worked closely with the priests. They were the 'older men' of the community. Who formed the ruling elite. Were often members of various councils.

Essenes – A small sect that lived a communal life. Principal centre was Qumran from the second century BC to the first century AD. They regarded the Jerusalem priests as illegitimate, since they were not Zadokites (from the family of the High Priest, Zadok). They rejected the validity of Temple worship. They expected God to send a great prophet and *two* different Messiahs – one Kingly, one Priestly.

Appendix II
Glossary Of Roman Words

AEDILE – One of four Roman magistrates who were responsible for the city of Rome.

ATRIUM – The main reception room of a Roman house.

AUXILIARY – A legion incorporated into a Roman army without its troops having the status of Roman citizens.

BRUNDISIUM – The most important port in southern Italy.

CAMPUS MARTIUS – Situated north of the Servian Walls, used by the army as a temporary camp site during military exercises and military training.

CENTURY – The centuries of the legions contained up to one hundred men.

CIRCUS MAXIMUS – The old circus built by King Tarquinus Priscus before the Republic began. Held between 100,000 and 150,000 people.

CLIENT – The term denotes a man of free or of freed status, who pledged himself to a man he called his patron.

CLIENT KING – A foreign monarch who pledged himself as a client, in the service of Rome as his patron. The title 'Friend and Ally of the Roman People' was a statement of clientship.

CAEMENTICIUM – Literally, concrete. The Romans mixed an aggregate of sruched rock, lime and volcanic dust with water to make concrete. So strong it would set under water, it was used extensively to construct harbours and breakwaters.

CONSUL – Senior Roman magistrate having Imperium.

COHORT - The tactical unit of the Roman legion, comprising six centuries of troops. Usually a legion had ten *cohorts*, e.g. 6,000 men.

CONSULAR - Title given to a man who had been a consul.

DENARIUS/DENARII (pl) - Except for the rare issue of gold coins, the denarius was the largest denomination of Roman Republican coinage. Of pure silver, it was 3.5 grams of the metal.

DIGNITAS - Marked a man's ethical worth, his reputation and entitlement to respect.

DOMINUS /DOMINA - Lord/lady

ETHNARCH - The Greek term for a city magistrate.

FORUM - An open air public meeting place for many levels of business, both public and private.

FORUM CASTRUM - The meeting space inside a Roman military camp. Positioned next to the general's command tent.

FREEDMAN - A manumitted slave who remained in the patronage of his former master. If his former master was a citizen of Rome, he too became a Roman citizen.

FREEMAN - A man born free and never sold into slavery.

GARUM - A popular (particularly with the army) fish sauce. Very concentrated and eye-wateringly pungent.

GODS (ROMAN) - The Roman attributed their position as a world power as a result of maintaining good relations with the gods. Religion was seen as a source of social order and was part of daily life. Every home, rich or poor, had a household shrine that housed the family's ancestral deities, to which prayers and libations were offered daily. Imported religions, some offering salvation in the after-life, were permitted but they came second to Roman gods. Religions that were *thought* might pose a threat to Roman gods were ruthlessly put down. Ironically, Rome's gods were borrowed from the Greeks, though they did change their names, e.g. Zeus, god of the sky and the king of Olympus, the home of the 12 gods and goddesses who ruled the universe, was renamed Jupiter. From the second century BC, Rome's emperors were attributed at death to not dying but becoming gods and joining Jupiter and the Olympian gods on Mount Olympus. In his final years Nero demanded to be addressed as 'Divinity' or Apollo, the god of music and healing.

HELLENIC - The term used to describe Greek culture.

IMPERIUM - Was the degree of authority invested in a magistrate. Having *Imperium* meant a man had the authority of his office and could not be gainsaid. It also applied to military commanders appointed as governors and procurators appointed to Roman provinces.

KNIGHTS - The *equities*, the members of the *Ordo Equestor*. To qualify as a knight a man had to have property or income in excess of 400,000 *sesterces*.

LEGATE/LEGATUS - The most senior members of the Roman general's staff were his legates. In order to be classified as a legatus, a man had to be of senatorial status. Often was consular in rank. Legates answered only to the commanding general and were senior to all types of military *tribune*s.

LEGION - The smallest Roman military unit capable of fighting a war on its own. It was self-sufficient in man-power and equipment. C6,000 men.

LEGIONARY - The correct word for a soldier in a Roman legion' though I have used legionnaire because of its familiarity in today's usage.

LICTOR - A public servant in the employ of the People of Rome through the Senate. They provided escorts for all holders of Imperium at home and abroad.

MAGISTRATES - The elected executives of the Senate of People of Rome. They represented the executive arm of government.

OSTIA - Rome's closest seaport, situated at the mouth of the river Tiber. It had its own granaries to receive the daily arrivals of grain ships from Egypt.

OPTIO - A legion's second in command. Had to be literate and numerate. Responsible for the legion's administration.

He was quartermaster, responsible for all records, down to every single soldier. He held this job prior to being promoted to Centurion.

PATRICIANS - The original Roman aristocracy – old money.

PORT OF ROME – Portus - On the Tiber, a collection of wharves to service the heavy traffic of barges and small merchantmen that came up from Ostia.

PRAETOR - Next to the most senior Roman magistrates.

PRAETORIAN - A former Praetor. A member of the Emperor's bodyguard.

PREFECTUS - A general term used for different army ranks.

PRINCEPS SENATUS - Chosen, as a patrician senator of unimpeachable integrity, to lead the senate.

PRO-CONSUL - One serving as a consul. This imperium was usually given to a man who had just finished serving as a consul, who went on to govern a province or command an army in the name of the Senate and the People of Rome. He could also be assigned a specific task by the Senate.

QUASTOR - A quastor's principal duties were fiscal.

REPUBLIC - Founded by the Romans as an alternative to monarchy.

SESTERTIUS/SESTERCES(pl) - The commonest Roman coin. A small silver coin it was worth one quarter of a denarius.

SUFFECT CONSUL - A temporary un-elected stand-in when an elected consul died in office.

TOGA - Could only be worn by a full citizen of Rome. Made of finely spun wool.

TRIBUNE - One of six assistants to a legion commander, the *Primus Pilus*. Usually a young senator learning the basics of his career.

TUNIC - This was the basic item of clothing worn by the ancient Mediterranean peoples. A simple shift with or without sleeves, pulled over the head like a night-shirt. Could be belted.

VILLA - A country house, completely self-contained, with farmland, farm buildings and stables.

VESTAL VIRGINS - Chosen by lot at the age of seven from a group of specially selected, physically perfect, girls, to serve the goddess Vesta. Took vows of chastity. Their chastity was Rome's luck. If deemed unchaste, she was tried. If found guilty, she was burned alive.

Appendix III
Other Sources & Evidence That Jesus Had Siblings

Encyclopaedia Britannica, under James: One of the Lord's brethren.

The Bible: In Matthew XII: 47 and Mark VI: 3 we read of James who, together with Joses, Judas and Simon was a 'brother' of the Lord. The Epithanian view is that Jesus' brothers and sisters were born after the birth of Jesus.

The **Helvidian theory** as propounded by Helvidius and apparently accepted by Tertullian, makes James a brother of the Lord, as truly as Mary was his mother. This seems to be more in keeping with the Gospels (see W. Patrick *James the Brother of the Lord* 1906, page 5).

James the brother of Jesus who became leader of the Church in Jerusalem. The Lion Handbook of the Bible, page 666, James 1:3 (Lion Publishing). He was traditionally the author of the Epistle of the New Testament which bears his name (see Epistle of James).

According to **Hegesippus** (see Eus H.E. 11 23) he was a Nazarite and because of his eminent righteousness was called 'Just' and 'Oblias'. So great was his influence with the people that he was appealed to by the scribes and Pharisees for a true (as they hoped) unfavourable judgement about the Messiahship of Christ. But from a pinnacle of the temple he made public confession of his faith and was seized by the temple priests, hurled to the ground and murdered.

A detailed account of this event is covered on pages 99 to 100 under the heading The Martyrdom of James ' the Lord's Brother' in **Eusabius'** *The History of the Church*, published by Penguin Classics in 1965, translation by G. A. Williamson. This was immediately before the Roman Siege. Deuteronomy 20.16.18 Passage refers to alleged order from the God of the Jews to commit genocide against the Canaanites.

Josephus (Antiq. xx 911) tells that it was by the order of Ananus the high priest that James was put to death. Josephus' narrative gives the idea of some sort of judicial examination, for he says that James and some others were brought before an assembly of judges, by whom they were condemned and delivered to be stoned to death.

Josephus is also cited by **Eusabius** (H.E. ii 23) to the effect that the miseries of the siege of Jerusalem which was led by Vespasian, were due to divine vengeance for the murder of James. According to Eusabius (H.E. vii 19), his Episcopal chair was still shown at Jerusalem.

St. Paul also corroborates the existence of James as the brother of Christ in Galatians 1:20 on making a trip to Jerusalem. "I saw only James, the brother of the Lord".

A Dictionary of Christian Biography and Literature edited by Henry Wace, DD, Dean of Canterbury and William C Piercy, MA, Dean and Chaplain of Whitelands College SW, published by John Murray 1911. See page 436 an account by Hegesippus of James the brother of Jesus being brought before Ananus the high priest and the assembled judges of the Sanhedrin, accused of blasphemy and stoned to death.

Penguin Classics *Eusabius, History of the Church.* Introduction page 9, James, the Lord's brother was the Bishop of Jerusalem.

Encyclopaedia of the Occult by Fred Gittings, Century Hutchinson.

The Later Herods by Stewart Perowne, MA, FSA, Hodder and Stoughton 1958.

The First Century. Emperors, Gods and Everyman, by William Klingaman, BA, PhD, Gould Publishing 1990.

The complete works of Flavius Josephus by William Whiston, M.A., Cambridge, England. T. Nelson and Sons, London, Edinburgh and New York.

280

Flavius Josephus by Rev. A. R. Shilleto. M.A., Trinity College, Cambridge, England. Whiston's translation revised. George Bell and Sons, London 1890.

Josephus The Jewish War by G. A. Williamson. Penguin 1959.

Myth, Magic and Morals by Fred Cornwallis Conybeare, M.A., Oxford. Watts & Co., London 1910.

The Satanic Cult by Gerhard Zacharias. George Allan and Unwin 1980.

The Book of Ceremonial Magic by Arthur Edward Waite. Rider 1911.

The Heirarchy of Hell by Lauran Paine. Robert Hale, London 1972.

Myth and Ritual in Christianity by Alan Watts. Thames & Hudson 1954.

The Encyclopaedia of Witchcraft and Demonology by Russell Hope Robbins. Spring Books, London 1959; Crown Publishers, New York 1959.

Quo Vadis by Henryk Sienkiewicz, J.M. Dent, London 1898.

www.ingramcontent.com/pod-product-compliance
Lightning Source LLC
Jackson TN
JSHW020016141224
75386JS00025B/546